Also by
KELLY RIMMER

THE GERMAN WIFE

THE WARSAW ORPHAN

TRUTHS I NEVER TOLD YOU

THE THINGS WE CANNOT SAY

BEFORE I LET YOU GO

KELLY RIMMER

THE
GERMAN
WIFE

GRAYDON
HOUSE

GRAYDON
HOUSE®

Recycling programs
for this product may
not exist in your area.

ISBN-13: 978-1-525-81143-2

The German Wife

Graydon House
22 Adelaide St. West, 41st Floor
Toronto, Ontario M5H 4E3, Canada
www.GraydonHouseBooks.com
www.BookClubbish.com

Printed in U.S.A.

For Amy Tannenbaum Gottlieb

THE
GERMAN
WIFE

1

Sofie

Huntsville, Alabama
1950

"WAKE UP, GISELA," I MURMURED, GENTLY SHAK-ing my daughter awake. "It's time to see Papa."

After the better part of a day on a stuffy, hot bus, I was so tired my eyes were burning, my skin gritty with dried sweat from head to toe. I had one sleeping child on my lap and the other leaning into me as she sprawled across the seat. After three long weeks of boats and trains and buses, my long journey from Berlin to Alabama was finally at an end.

My youngest daughter had always been smaller than her peers, her body round and soft, with a head of auburn hair like mine, and my husband's bright blue eyes. Over the last few months, a sudden growth spurt transformed her. She was now taller than me. The childhood softness had stretched right out of her, leaving her rail thin and lanky.

Gisela stirred, then slowly pushed herself to a sitting position. Her eyes scanned along the aisle of the bus as if she were reorienting herself. Finally, cautiously, she turned to look out the window.

"Mama. It really doesn't look like much…"

We were driving down a wide main street lined with small stores and restaurants. So far, Huntsville looked about as I'd expected it would—neat, tidy…segregated.

Minnie's Salon. Whites Only.

Seamstress for Colored.

Ada's Café. The Best Pancakes in Town. Whites ONLY!

When I decided to make the journey to join my husband in America, segregation was one of a million worries I consciously put off for later. Now, faced with the stark reality of it, I dreaded the discussions I'd be having with my children once we had enough rest for productive conversation. They needed to understand exactly why those signs sent ice through my veins.

"Papa did tell us that this is a small town, remember?" I said gently. "There are only fifteen thousand people in Huntsville and it will be very different from Berlin, but we can build a good life here. And most importantly, we'll be together again."

"Not all of us," Gisela muttered.

"No, not all of us," I conceded quietly. Loss was like a shadow to me. Every now and again, I'd get distracted and I'd forget it was there. Then I'd turn around and feel the shock of it all over again. It was the same for my children, especially for Gisela. Every year of her life had been impacted by the horrors of war, or by grief and change.

I couldn't dwell on that—not now. I was about to see my husband for the first time in almost five years and I was every bit as anxious as I was excited. I had second-guessed my decision to join him in the United States a million or more times since I shepherded the children onto that first bus in Berlin, bound for the port in Hamburg where we boarded the cross-Atlantic steamship.

I looked down at my son. Felix woke when I shook his sister, but was still sitting on my lap, pale and silent. He had a head of sandy curls and his father's curious mind. Until now, they'd never been on the same continent.

The first thing I noticed was that Jürgen looked different. It was almost summer and warm out, but he was wearing a light blue suit with a white shirt and a dark blue bow tie. Back home, he never wore a suit that color and he *never* would have opted for a bow tie. And instead of his customary silver-framed glasses, he was wearing a pair with thick black plastic frames. They were modern and suited him. Of course he had new glasses—five years had passed. Why was I so bothered by those frames?

I couldn't blame him if he reinvented himself, but what if this new version of Jürgen didn't love me, or was someone I couldn't continue to love?

He took a step forward as we shuffled off the bus but didn't even manage a second before Gisela ran to him and threw her arms around his neck.

"Treasure," he said, voice thick with emotion. "You've grown up so much."

There was a faint but noticeable American twang in his German words, which was as jarring as the new glasses.

Jürgen's gaze settled on Felix, who was holding my hand with a grip so tight my fingers throbbed. I felt anxious for both children but I was scared for Felix. We'd moved halfway across the world to a country I feared would be wary of us at best, maybe even hostile toward us. For Gisela and me, a reunion with Jürgen was enough reason to take that risk. But

Felix was nervous around strangers at the best of times, and he knew his father only through anecdotes and photographs.

"Felix," Jürgen said, keeping one arm around Gisela as he started to walk toward us. I could see that he was trying to remain composed, but his eyes shone. "Son…"

Felix gave a whimper of alarm and hid behind my legs.

"Give him time," I said quietly, reaching behind myself to touch Felix's hair. "He's tired and this is a lot to take in."

"He looks just like—" Jürgen's voice broke. I knew the struggle well. It hurt to name our grief, but it was important to do so anyway. Our son Georg should have been twenty years old, living out the best days of his life. Instead, he was another casualty of a war that the world would never make sense of. But I came to realize that Georg would always be a part of our family, and every time I found the strength to speak his name, he was brought to life, at least in my memories.

"I know," I said. "Felix looks just like Georg." It was fitting that I'd chosen Georg for Felix's middle name, a nod to the brother he'd never know.

Jürgen raised his gaze to mine and I saw the depth of my grief reflected in his. No one would ever understand my loss like he did.

I realized that our years apart meant unfathomable changes in the world and in each of us, but my connection with Jürgen would never change. It already survived the impossible. At this thought, I rushed to close the distance between us.

Gisela was gently shuffled to the side and Jürgen's arms were finally around me again. I thought I'd be dignified and cautious when we reunited, but the minute we touched, my eyes filled with tears as relief and joy washed over me in cascading waves.

I was on the wrong side of the world in a country I did

not trust, but I was also back in Jürgen's arms, and I was instantly at home.

"My God," Jürgen whispered roughly, his body trembling against mine. "You are a sight for sore eyes, Sofie von Meyer Rhodes."

"Promise me you'll never let me go again."

Jürgen was a scientist—endlessly literal, at least under normal circumstances. Once upon a time, he'd have pointed out all the reasons why such a promise could not be made in good faith—but now his arms contracted around me and he whispered into my hair, "It would kill me to do so, Sofie. If there's one thing I want for the rest of my life, it's to spend every day of it with you."

"Many of our neighbors are Germans—most have just arrived in Huntsville in the last few weeks or months, so you will all be settling in together. There's a party for us tomorrow at the base where I work, so you'll meet most of them then," Jürgen told me as he drove us through the town in his sleek black 1949 Ford. He glanced at the children in the rearview mirror, his expression one of wonder, as if he couldn't believe his eyes. "You'll like it here, I promise."

We'd be living in a leafy, quiet suburb called Maple Hill, on a small block the Americans nicknamed "Sauerkraut Hill" because it was now home to a cluster of German families. I translated the street signs for the children and they chuckled at the unfamiliar style. Our new street, Beetle Avenue, amused Gisela the most.

"Is there an insect plague we should worry about?" she chuckled.

"I really hope so," Felix whispered, so quietly I had to strain to hear him. "I like beetles."

As Jürgen pulled the car into the driveway, I couldn't help

but compare the simple house to the palatial homes I'd grown up in. This was a single-story dwelling, with a small porch leading to the front door, one window on either side. The house was clad in horizontal paneling, its white paint peeling. There were garden beds in front of the house, but they were overgrown with weeds. There was no lawn to speak of, only patchy grass in places, and the concrete path from the road to the porch was cracked and uneven.

I felt Jürgen's eyes on my face as I stared out through the windshield, taking it all in.

"It needs a little work," he conceded, suddenly uncertain. "It's been so busy since I moved here, I haven't had time to make it nice for you the way I hoped."

"It's perfect," I said. I could easily picture the house with a fresh coat of paint, gardens bursting to life, Gisela and Felix running around, happy and safe and free as they made friends with the neighborhood children.

Just then, a woman emerged from the house to the left of ours, wearing a dress not unlike mine, her long hair in a thick braid, just like mine.

"Welcome, neighbors!" she called in German, beaming.

"This is Claudia Schmidt," Jürgen said quietly as he reached to open his car door. "She's married to Klaus, a chemical engineer. Klaus has been at Fort Bliss with me for a few years, but Claudia arrived from Frankfurt a few days ago."

Sudden, sickening anxiety washed over me.

"Did you know him—"

"No," Jürgen interrupted me, reading my distress. "He worked in a plant at Frankfurt and our paths never crossed. We will talk later, I promise," he said, dropping his voice as he nodded toward the children. I reluctantly nodded, as my heart continued to race.

There was so much Jürgen and I needed to discuss, including just how he came to be a free man in America. Phone calls from Europe to America were not available to the general public, so Jürgen and I planned the move via letters—a slow-motion, careful conversation that took almost two years to finalize. We assumed everything we wrote down would be read by a government official, so I hadn't asked and he hadn't offered an explanation about how this unlikely arrangement in America came to be.

I couldn't get answers yet, not with the children in earshot, so it would have to be enough reassurance for me to know our neighbors were probably not privy to the worst aspects of our past.

Jürgen left the car and walked over to greet Claudia, and I climbed out my side. As I walked around the car to follow him, I noticed a man walking along the opposite side of the street, watching us. He was tall and broad, and dressed in a nondescript, light brown uniform that was at least a size or two too small. I offered him a wave, assuming him to be a German neighbor, but he scoffed and shook his head in disgust and looked away.

I'd been prepared for some hostility, but the man's reaction stung more than I'd expected it to. I took a breath, calming myself. One unfriendly pedestrian was not going to ruin my first day in our new home—my first day reunited with Jürgen—so I forced a bright smile and rounded the car to meet Claudia.

"I'm Sofie."

She nodded enthusiastically. "Since we arrived last week, you are all I've heard about from your husband! He has been so excited for you to come."

"I sure have." Jürgen grinned.

"Are you and the children coming to the party tomorrow?" Claudia asked.

"We are," I said, and she beamed again. I liked her immediately. It was a relief to think I might have a friend to help me navigate our new life.

"Us too," Claudia said, but then her face fell a little and she pressed her palms against her abdomen, as if soothing a tender stomach. "I am so nervous. I know two English words—*hello* and *soda*."

"That's a start," I offered, laughing softly.

"I've only met a few of the other wives, but they're all in the same boat. How on earth is this party going to work? Will we have to stay by our husbands' sides so they can translate for us?"

"I speak English," I told her. I was fluent as a child, taking lessons with British nannies, then honing my skills on business trips with my parents. Into my adulthood, I grew rusty from lack of speaking it, but the influx of American soldiers in Berlin after the war gave me endless opportunities for practice. Claudia's expression lifted again and now she clapped her hands in front of her chest.

"You can help us learn."

"Do you have children? I want Gisela and Felix to learn as quickly as they can. Perhaps we could do some lessons all together."

"Three," she told me. "They are inside watching television."

"You have a *television*?" I said, eyebrows lifting.

"We have a television too," Jürgen told us. "I bought it as a housewarming gift for you all." Gisela gasped, and he laughed and extended his hand to her. I wasn't surprised when she immediately tugged him toward the front door. She'd long dreamed of owning a television set, but such a luxury was out of reach for us in Berlin.

I waved goodbye to Claudia and followed my family, but I was distracted, thinking about the look of disgust in the eyes of that passing man.

2

Lizzie

Dallam County, Texas
1930

I SPENT THE WHOLE DAY PLOWING, AND EVEN ten minutes after I climbed down from the tractor, phantom vibrations ran through my hands as if I were still holding the steering wheel.

"It'll rain now. Sure as anything," Dad said. He and my brother, Henry, had been plowing another field with the horses earlier in the day, but horses tire quicker than tractors, so they'd taken them to rest in the barn and come to survey my work. "When you cultivate the soil, it exposes the moisture in the deep dirt to the sky. That's what attracts the clouds. Rain follows the plow, sure as sunset follows the sunrise. You remember that, kids. It's science you can trust."

This was not the first time he'd dropped that kernel of wisdom, and me and my brother had been farming with our daddy since we first learned to walk, so we knew the theory as well as he did. We always plowed twice after harvest—first to pulverize the topsoil, to break the upper crust into small sods. After that, we'd go over the land with the disc harrows, a process that broke the little sods up completely—leaving the soil fine and silky, which Dad said gave the seeds room to grow. We bought the tractor brand-new after the bumper crop in 1929 and it made the whole process so much easier.

But that day, as I watched a dust haze settle back over the field, I felt a pang of anxiety. It usually rained in the autumn shortly after we plowed, just as Dad said. But it was supposed to rain during the spring and summer too, and that year, the clouds seemed to have forgotten how to work.

"I hope you're right about the rain, Daddy," I said cautiously. "It's been awful dry lately."

"Dry comes and goes." Dad shrugged. "You'll see that in life. Good, bad...exciting, boring. Life is all about the ebb and flow between those extremes, and sometimes, you just have to patiently ride it out."

It was all well and good for Daddy to talk like that. His entire life was riding out the waves of his moods. Even when things were easier, before that dry year, Dad had good days and bad days, and it was me, Henry, and Mother who picked up the slack when he was down. I adored my dad, but he was so passive sometimes, he just about drove me crazy. Me and Henry exchanged a glance, and I knew my brother was thinking the same.

"Let's head back to the house," Dad said. "We have just enough time to go past the pond before sunset."

I sighed as we all climbed up onto the tractor. This time, Dad was driving, and Henry and me sat on the little platform at the back, traveling backward.

"There's going to be cows in the mud," I said, leaning close to whisper in my brother's ear. We farmed grain mostly, but we also kept a small herd of cows for meat and, when we could borrow a bull to breed them, calves to sell and milk to drink.

The cows lived in a narrow rectangle field adjacent to our yard, with a large pond at the edge. The water was almost gone from the pond after the dry year, leaving a wide band of stagnant mud around the edges. Even that was rapidly drying, but while it was still wet enough for a cow to sink into, it was dangerous as all hell.

At any other time we might have moved those cows to another field, but we needed to plow to prepare for sowing, which meant churning up what might have been feed. And there was no easy way to keep them out of that mud. Every day for over a week, we'd had to drag at least one cow free of it.

"There's clean water right there," Henry complained. We'd set up a brand-new trough for them against the fence, just a few dozen feet away. "Why the heck do those stupid cows keep getting stuck?"

"They've been drinking from that pond since they were born, that's why," I told him. "We need to face facts and sell them. We'll run out of feed in that field sooner or later anyway."

Not one but two cows were in the mud now—one in mud halfway up her legs, the other buried up past her shoulders and left weak from struggling all day.

Working together, me, Dad and Henry managed to push the first cow out of the shallow mud by hand. The other cow's rescue operation was more complicated because she was too tired to help herself. Daddy looped some rope around her neck and tied it to the tractor, and I drove it slowly away from the pond's edge, pulling her, while Henry and Dad stood in the mud and pushed her from behind.

We were all exhausted, filthy, and deflated by the time we

finished—coated in a thick layer of mud that smelled so bad, it would stick to our skin for days.

"We should sell the cows," I said.

Dad sighed impatiently. "It'll rain any day and soon enough that pond will be full again. And anyway, the cows will eventually realize there's an easy way to drink without risking their neck."

"Well, the way things are going in this county, the price per head is sure to drop," I said.

"Leave the business decisions up to me," Dad said abruptly. "We're not selling the damned cows."

With that, he stomped back to the tractor and started off toward the barn without us. That was fine by me and Henry—the house was only a few hundred feet away.

"So in the meantime we just keep pulling the cows out of the mud every damned day?" I complained.

"They'll have to learn to use the trough when the last of the water dries up." Henry shrugged. Then his tone softened. "You need to stop assuming the worst all the time."

I groaned and started walking toward the house.

"You're as stubborn as the cows, Lizzie," Henry called after me, chuckling. I ignored him, stomping all the way up to the house. I washed up as well as I could with cold water from the hand pump. As I was finishing, Mother brought me a towel.

"What's got your father in such a low mood?" she asked quietly.

"Cows in the mud at the pond again," I muttered, taking the towel gratefully. "I told him we should sell them."

"He's convinced the rain is coming," she sighed, then shrugged easily in that gentle, patient way of hers. "Daddy is doing his best. We all are."

I couldn't sleep that night. There was so little I could control. I couldn't make it rain; I couldn't make Dad face reality; I couldn't move the cows away from the mud.

My family accepted it was a problem that could not be solved. But in the depth of that night, I considered the same situation and decided it didn't have to be a problem at all.

The next morning, I pulled a wide leather hat over my orange-red hair and popped the collar up on one of Henry's old shirts to protect my neck from the sun. Then I took a shovel and I walked back to the pond.

"What in God's name are you doing?" Henry asked. It was lunchtime but I was still working, so Mother sent him down with a lunch pail and some water. If I'd been a little dirty the previous day, I was utterly filthy now that I'd been shoveling sloppy mud for hours.

"Exactly what you told me to. I stopped assuming the worst and started expecting rain."

I stuck the shovel into the firmer mud so that it stood upright, then dropped onto my haunches beside the pond. Henry watched with obvious amusement as I tried to clean off my hands so I could eat the sandwiches. After just a moment or two, I realized that was a futile exercise and I was famished, so I picked up the sandwiches anyway.

"So what's the plan?" Henry asked, squatting beside me.

"I'm going to scrape every bit of wet soil from the pond to expand its capacity."

Henry looked from me to the pond, then back to me incredulously.

"That will take you days."

"Yep." I narrowed my eyes at him. "Unless someone helps me."

He threw back his head and laughed.

"You're crazy, sis."

Henry went back to plowing with Dad that afternoon.

Mother came down and helped me for a while, but she had her own jobs to do, so didn't stay long.

And for three long days, mostly on my own, I scooped and dug and smoothed mud all over the dried field in a thin layer, so it was no longer a danger to the cattle. With no alternative, the cows finally figured out they needed to use the trough.

We sold the cows a few months later anyway, when their ribs started to show through their skin. The price of fodder had gone up so fast we couldn't justify the cost to keep them. By then, the market was flooded with skinny cows just like them, so we sold those girls for a pittance.

The pond was soon a huge, dried crater in the field—twice the depth it was once, ready to store a heap more water than it ever had before.

I was a realist who loved my land and my life enough that when a moment called for it, I thought nothing of working until my hands were red-raw if it meant turning a problem into an opportunity.

That was the kind of girl I was, once upon a time.

3

Sofie

Huntsville, Alabama
1950

RIGHT UP UNTIL THEY TUMBLED INTO BED JUST after sunset, Gisela was clingy with Jürgen and Felix was terrified of him. It was going to take time for us to reconnect as a family. As I took a shower to freshen up, I reminded myself that, surreal as it was, we were in America to stay, and one thing we had plenty of was time.

Freshly bathed and in clean nightclothes, I joined Jürgen at the dining room table. The house contained only essential furniture, plus a lonely bunch of flowers on the dining room table that Jürgen purchased to "warm the place up" for me.

He opened a bottle of wine and was reading some paperwork as he waited. Had he noticed the strands of silver at my hairline, just as I noticed that his hair was thinning a little at the crown? Jürgen closed the folder and pushed the documents away as I sat beside him, then poured two glasses of the wine.

"Right up until today, when I saw you on the bus, I was terrified you'd change your mind."

"I did have second thoughts. Constantly," I admitted, accepting a glass. "Berlin is a mess, but it's home."

"Why did you decide to join me?"

"You, mostly," I admitted. Jürgen set down his glass and took my hand. He'd been touching me all afternoon—brushing my hair back from my face, cupping my cheek, hugging me. After five of the loneliest years of my life, I was basking in the attention. "Germany is still in ruins, and the wreckage of the national psyche and the culture is even worse. But I'd have stayed there, lamenting everything that happened, feeling broken about it all, probably for the rest of my life."

A sudden shame sprang to Jürgen's gaze. I knew he was thinking about the millions of souls injured or killed in our name...on our watch. I did that too, constantly cycling through memories and facts, as if *this* time when I played them through my mind, I could change the outcome. "I spent the first few years after the war focused on surviving and it was hard enough to get through each day. It was like I'd been sleepwalking, and when your letter arrived and I learned you'd survived, I suddenly woke up. Despite everything that has happened, the crisis is over and now there *has* to be an after. I don't know how we move on from the war, but I do know that Gisela and Felix and I have the best chance of finding happiness with you. That's why I'm here—to be with you, to build a future with you, to do good here with you."

"But..." Jürgen said carefully. "No Laura?"

I already had plans to write to tell our eldest daughter about Huntsville and to send her a photograph of us with Jürgen in case that softened her heart. On some level, I knew that such efforts would be pointless. I just had no idea how to let her go.

"A few months after the war ended, I had an especially

miserable day. It was hard to find food, the electric was still out…and I was heavily pregnant with Felix," I admitted sadly. "I wondered aloud if we'd ever know what happened to you. Laura told me that if you wrote and she found your letter, she would burn it. I knew she meant it, too—she'd been collecting the mail every day and I thought it was a good sign that she was trying to be helpful. To this day, she is more loyal to the Nazis than she is to her family. When I tried to convince her to come with us to be with you, she ran away…to be with *him* instead. I haven't seen her since."

"I find it so hard to imagine Germany after the Nazis, finding its soul again and rebuilding in a kinder, healthier way," he said, shaking his head. "I'm less surprised to hear children like our Laura are struggling to move on. She was force-fed that poison through the most impressionable years of her life."

"I know there was a point along the way where the outcomes could have been different, but I can't figure out where that was."

"I still ask myself that question constantly too," Jürgen said, his gaze steady on mine.

"Is it safe to talk here?" I asked, instantly unnerved at the thought of the conversation veering near contentious subjects. He gave me a sympathetic look.

"Yes, my love."

"There are no listening devices in this house? You're sure?"

"I'm certain."

"It's just…we thought that the last time." I knew how small those devices could be—how cleverly they could be hidden.

"We are safe here. I remember how difficult it was for me to get used to that, but I promise it's true." His expression suddenly softened. "You must have so many questions. Let me try to answer them before you even have to ask."

A few days after Berlin fell to the Soviets, Jürgen and I

were lying in our bed, holding one another as we planned his surrender. A knock came at the door just after dawn, and he opened it anxiously, expecting to find Soviet soldiers to take him in. But these men were Americans—miles ahead of the rest of the US forces, on a covert mission to retrieve my husband. He went willingly. I watched him walk down the path, and then for over three years, I had no idea what became of him. I gave birth to Felix and celebrated three birthdays with him before I could even tell Jürgen we'd conceived a fourth child.

Life grew more and more difficult in Berlin over those years. Jürgen and I lived in a large villa in the suburb of Lichterfelde West, and we'd inherited the building next door, including the small, now-vacant apartment that had once been Jürgen's aunt Adele's home. We had existing tenants in her building, but they were all out of work, and that meant no one was paying their rent. I couldn't evict them—not only would Adele have come back to haunt me if I tried, but any new tenants would have the same problem anyway.

Desperate to support myself and the children, I rented out our main house to the American Army, and Laura, Gisela, Felix, and I crammed into Adele's one-bedroom apartment.

The constant stream of American soldiers through the neighborhood was uncomfortable at first, but I made friends with as many of them as I could. Just as I'd hoped, from time to time one would take pity on me and try to find out what happened to my husband, but they always came back with the same news. His fate was top secret. They couldn't tell me if he was alive or dead.

"They kept me in Berlin for a few weeks," Jürgen told me quietly. "After that, I was imprisoned at Fort Bliss in Texas. The American rocket program was in its infancy, but I felt lucky to teach them. In return, they taught me English, and fortunately, I picked it up quickly." He'd spoken only basic English before, but I wasn't surprised that Jürgen was now fluent. He'd always been a quick study with languages.

"But you weren't allowed to contact us?"

"I was very much a prisoner and the whole project was top secret. I kept requesting permission to write you, and they kept refusing. But after a year or so, I sought out Christopher Newsome, who's one of the officials from the Office of the Secretary of the Army. I knew he was involved in the plan to bring us here, so I asked him when I'd be sent home to face trial. He told me that there was no plan to return me to Germany, and I wouldn't face trial at all because my record had been 'taken care of.'"

In his early letters, Jürgen simply told me that he was working with the American government. Later, he told me we'd been approved to join him in Huntsville and that he'd purchased us a house, so I assumed he was enjoying some version of freedom. I'd been desperately curious about how that came about—but it hadn't occurred to me that his situation was as tenuous as this seemed to be.

"But there are other Germans here. Some of them must surely know the truth."

"Yes," Jürgen conceded. "But those who know have secrets of their own. I do understand your concerns, Sofie. I was also anxious about this arrangement, so I asked Christopher what would happen if the skeletons in my closet ever were exposed."

"What did he say?"

"He said that the skeletons have not just been buried—they have been erased," Jürgen said quietly. "My official files paint a picture of a man who survived the Nazi years unscathed without a single moral compromise. Only a handful of senior officials know that is not the full story."

"No one survived the Nazi years without moral compromise," I whispered.

"Maybe the American officials know that too. Maybe that's why they've done this. Christopher said that even Calvin Miller, my boss here at Redstone Arsenal, has no idea my official file is fictional. There's even talk about citizenship in a few more years."

"Citizenship..." I repeated. "How do you feel about that?"

Jürgen hesitated.

"I'll always be German. I just don't know what that means anymore. America has become home to me, and that will be the case even more now that you and the children are here. I'm grateful. I'm relieved. But..." He shook his head, shadows in his gaze. "I don't deserve this second chance, but it's been offered to me. That's some astounding grace, isn't it? How else could I respond to that but to work tirelessly to build a life here I can be proud of? It won't erase what happened at home—nothing can do that. The most I can hope for is to one day again be proud of the man who stares back at me in the mirror."

"You only ever wanted your work to benefit mankind. To extend our reach and understanding."

"Exactly." He smiled sadly. "I have a chance to do that now, and I intend to grab hold of it with both hands."

"Then that is what I will do too."

Later that night, I unpacked the last of my clothes into the dresser in our bedroom, and I took a tattered, multicolored blanket from my suitcase and spread it on the end of the bed. That blanket and the little collection of photos I brought from Germany were my most prized possessions.

One was a photo of my first three children. Georg and Laura sat cross-legged on the ground, beaming, with newborn Gisela lying on a rug in front of them. It felt like a moment from someone else's life, but I adored it anyway. That was how I needed to remember Georg and Laura—innocent, happy, untarnished.

The next photo was of me and Jürgen on our wedding day, young and blissfully in love and so carefree, as if the world had only peace and happiness to offer us. Then there was a photo of Jürgen's great-aunt Adele, sitting in her courtyard—smiling serenely as she looked past the camera, to the sanctuary she'd built herself over many years.

The final photo was of me with my best friend, Mayim. We were standing arm in arm in the lobby of my family's mansion in Potsdam, suitcases at our feet, grinning like loons as we stood at the threshold to adulthood—the Star of David on a chain around her neck, stark against her pale skin. My last-ever nanny took that photo when Mayim and I were hours away from embarking on the journey to finishing school in Lausanne.

I knew I'd have nightmares that night—I did most nights since the war, and I expected that Jürgen would too. I kissed each of those photos gently, and then set them on the bedside table to watch over me and Jürgen while we slept. Maybe their presence would bring us peace, because while that pile of photos represented so much loss, they also carried so much love. The sum total of those moments was the woman I had become.

4

Sofie

Berlin, Germany
October 1930

I'VE ALWAYS LOVED EARLY AUTUMN. THE TREE-lined streets around my home in Lichterfelde quickly shifted from a canopy of summer foliage to a ceiling of reds and golds and deep, rich brown. It was still warm enough in October that we didn't need our coats, but not so warm that it was uncomfortable. I married Jürgen in early autumn 1929. And twelve months later, early in the autumn of 1930, I discovered I was pregnant with my first child.

I told Jürgen and Mayim right away, but weeks later, I was finally ready to share the news with our wider circle of friends—starting with Lydia zu Schiller.

When I arranged lunch with Lydia, I planned to tell her my news as soon as Mayim and I sat down. But everything changed in the interim. Now it seemed that all of Germany was trying to process the results of our most recent election.

"I still can't quite believe it," Mayim said, as she stared blankly at a menu. I was so worried for her. I had the impression she was in a state of shock, as if she'd witnessed an accident or injured herself. "Even in these wild times, I didn't expect this."

"A hundred and seven seats! They are the second-biggest party in the Reichstag now," Lydia said. Then she glanced at me. She was referring to the *Nationalsozialistische Deutsche Arbeiterpartei*—the National Socialist German Workers' Party, known as the Nazi party. "I know you're not one for politics, Sofie, but they only held twelve seats last term, and before that, they were a fringe party. No one took them seriously."

Lydia was right that I wasn't a political expert. Even so, I bristled at her condescending tone. I wasn't fascinated with politics the way Jürgen was, or so determined to climb the social rungs in Berlin that I had to keep abreast of the most popular figures and fashions like Lydia and her husband, Karl. That didn't mean I was ignorant. My best friend was Jewish—of course I noticed when a party founded on a platform of anti-Semitism had a sudden and shocking rise to prominence.

"It is terrible," I said, squeezing Mayim's hand. "But we must keep our spirits up. This is not a representation of who we are as a nation. People are scared about political instability, and the rising unemployment isn't helping." Mayim raised her gaze to mine, and I squeezed her hand again. "Even wealthy families are struggling."

Not mine, thankfully. My family estate was flourishing—in fact, at that moment my father was in New York, taking advantage of the aftermath of the Wall Street crash to expand his business. Lydia's family was fine too. Her father possessed extraordinary wealth, and Karl was a descendant of Prussian kings and German emperors. As the eldest child in his family, he inherited an incredible fortune when his parents passed.

But Mayim's father, Levi, had taken out extensive loans to shore up his business through the hyperinflation crisis after the Great War. For years, he worked himself ragged to meet his repayments and keep his company afloat. Then came the Wall Street crash in 1929, and as the banks began to struggle, they called in the balance of Levi's loans, years ahead of schedule.

Just one year earlier, Mayim's family enjoyed a lifestyle of comfort to rival the wealthiest families in Germany. Over the space of just a few shocking months, they lost everything they owned.

Lydia shifted awkwardly in her chair, then flicked Mayim a hesitant glance.

"How *is* your father?"

"He's found work," Mayim said, forcing a smile. "So that's something."

"But…his business?"

"Gone. And the house."

"He must have retained something. His cash, surely? Some artwork or a property or two?" Lydia pressed, as if the alternative were impossible. Mayim shrugged noncommittally, and we fell into a slightly strained moment of silence. Comprehension finally dawned on Lydia's face and she gave me the horrified, panicked look of a wealthy woman who had never considered that someone of *her* social class could ever be penniless.

"I have news, Lydia," I blurted. She still looked frazzled, but she raised her thin eyebrows in question, and I smiled. "I'm expecting. The doctor says I'll deliver the baby in January."

Thankfully, the conversation moved quickly on from that moment of awkwardness, as Lydia predictably squealed. I then carefully managed to tie together two new threads of conversation—baby chat and matchmaking chat, as I discussed the "wealthy, handsome, preferably Jewish" young men Lydia or I could possibly set Mayim up with. I felt so terrible for her and I wished we *could* set her up with a suitable young man. She desperately wanted a family of her own, but potential suitors in our social circles dried up when her family's wealth did.

Lydia knew for months that Mayim was living in one of my guest rooms. Maybe now that she knew the truth about Levi's circumstances, she'd deduce that Mayim wasn't really staying with me to keep me company while Jürgen went to the university to work on his thesis each day. There were only two bedrooms in her family's new apartment. Jürgen and I insisted Mayim live in one of our spare rooms when we learned she was sharing a bedroom with her brother, Moshe. We tried to invite the rest of her family too, but they refused.

After we ate, Mayim excused herself to use the restroom, and Lydia leaned forward and whispered with audible shock, "Is it true? They have *nothing*? How can this be?"

"Levi felt so guilty that his staff was losing their jobs that he was determined to pay out as much of their entitlements as he could. He sold everything they owned, right down to the silverware. He's working as a clerk for the City of Berlin and they're living in a *Mietskaserne* in Mitte." A tenement building, and in this case, one of the worst in Berlin. "Their situation is very bad, Lydia. Please try to be sensitive."

"I will. My God, I can't even imagine what that would be like, and especially for them. How on earth are they coping?"

"Better than you or I would, I suspect," I admitted.

"I just mean it must be especially hard for them." She was laboring a point and I didn't understand why.

"I don't know what you mean?"

"Sofie, my God. You know how the Jews are. They just *love* their money."

The waitress came to clear our plates, so we fell silent, and by the time she finished, Mayim returned. She and Lydia easily slipped back into the conversation about my pregnancy, but I sat in uneasy silence.

Later, we parted at the roadside in front of the café. Lydia kissed my cheek, then Mayim's, and waved to us as she slipped into the back seat of her car. Mayim and I climbed into mine, and my driver pulled out into the traffic.

"You're awfully quiet," she murmured. "Are you feeling unwell?"

"I'm fine," I told her, forcing a smile. "Just tired."

Why was I so unsettled by Lydia's comment? It was a throwaway line, a silly, reductive stereotype that people joked about all the time. I tried to reassure myself that Lydia didn't mean a thing by it. She wasn't anti-Semitic. How could she be? She was one of Mayim's best friends.

Besides, Mayim didn't even hear what Lydia said, so no harm was done. Not really.

5

Lizzie
Huntsville, Alabama
1950

"I'M ALREADY LATE, HENRY," I SAID, SHIFTING from one foot to the other as I peered under the hood of my car. "Cal's going to think I'm not coming. Can you just—"

"Lizzie, I'm working as fast as I can. Would you just—" My brother pressed the heel of his palm into his forehead and took a long, slow breath. "You harping at me isn't going to make me work any faster."

"Sorry," I said weakly. "We fought, that's all. I really don't want to go to this thing."

Henry pursed his lips as he tightened a bolt on my engine with a spanner.

"I still can't believe he's a part of this," my brother muttered, shaking his head.

I knew the feeling well. I was running late to a party intended to welcome a group of German families to their new home in Huntsville—celebrating their arrival as if they were special dignitaries. I hadn't even left my driveway and my skin was already crawling.

Throughout our marriage, my husband and I rarely disagreed. But in the year since Calvin was transferred from El Paso to Huntsville, we'd rarely gone more than a day without arguing about the men he was now referring to as "our Germans." He said everyone on base called them that, but whenever I heard those words, I wanted to scream.

My brother stepped out from beneath the hood, then slammed it closed. It seemed that whether he found work processing insurance claims in Chicago or laboring on the railway in Tennessee or selling tickets at a fair in Nashville, things inevitably went sour and Henry ended up back with me and Calvin. We never minded when Henry came to us—we'd even added a small studio apartment over the garage so he'd have a private place of his own. When Henry told me he was coming back this time, I called around until I found him some work at a lumberyard just a few miles away. A few weeks in, he seemed to be doing well.

Even so, if we'd had any other surviving family anywhere other than Huntsville, I'd have suggested he go to them instead. Henry spent less than a year in Europe in the dying days of the war and he never spoke about his time there, but he had come back a broken man. And now my brother did not need to be living in a town lousy with Germans.

Henry had changed even since I saw him at Christmas. Sometimes he would get a glazed, confused look about him—as if he were drunk. It was even more perplexing that he'd gained maybe fifty or sixty pounds in just four months and his once-muscular frame seemed bloated. I was worried that he'd been unwell, but Henry said he'd been eating too much fried food at that traveling fair. I couldn't shake the feeling that wasn't the whole truth. How much fried food could one man eat?

He wiped his hands on his thighs and gave me a dark look. "There. New spark plugs. Have fun with your Nazi friends." He was joking, but his tone was so bitter, I felt a pang of guilt. He suddenly paused, then added softly, "Lizzie, please be careful."

"Cal says they aren't a threat..." I said, but I trailed off. That *was* what Calvin said. The problem was, in the beginning, Calvin fought tooth and nail against those men being allowed into the community, and for good reason too.

"Men like that are a threat as long as they're breathing," Henry said abruptly.

"I don't even want to go," I insisted. Attending the lunch felt like a betrayal of my brother. I could stay home, but that option felt like a betrayal of my husband. "Calvin says it's important that I show my support."

Henry shrugged and turned back toward the house.

Every now and again, I remembered the jubilation I felt the day he came home after the war. It once seemed a miracle that he'd returned physically unscathed. But after five years of ups and downs, it was clear that while Henry's body was intact, his mind wasn't. I also knew exactly who was to blame. And I was about to go drink champagne and nibble on sandwiches with a group of them, on a lawn at the Redstone Arsenal facility.

6

Lizzie

Dallam County, Texas
1933

MY FATHER AND I STOOD SIDE BY SIDE, STARING
out at a wide, flat field. Every now and again, he wheezed or
released a cough that sounded as dry as the earth. A haze of
dust lingered across the field and all around us, but there was
nothing subtle about it this time—a brown fog had blown in.
It would take time for that dust to fall back to earth and longer to clear from our lungs.

"It'll rain now," Dad said, nodding with satisfaction toward
the field we'd just plowed. "Sure as anything. Rain follows
the plow, sure as sunset follows the sunrise."

This was one of Dad's good days, so I didn't point out that
his theory had well and truly been disproved. We'd plowed
straight after the harvest in '30, '31, and '32, but we hadn't
had decent rain in years. I nodded as if I believed him, but I
didn't know what to believe anymore.

"Are you two going to stand around all day admiring your handiwork, or will you bring the tractor back to the barn so I can take a look at that dicky disc?" Henry called.

Dad and I turned toward the sound of my brother's voice and found him strutting toward us.

"Why does that boy always look like he just invented ice cream?" Dad muttered. I nodded in bewildered agreement. Much as I adored my brother, I rarely understood him. Henry was born with a uniquely sunny disposition and a charm that meant he could talk his way out of any scrape. That was fortunate, because he also found his way into more scrapes than most.

"Well, aren't you two peas in a pod," Henry laughed when he neared.

"Plowing is dusty work, Henry," I reminded him. "You wouldn't know because you've never done any."

He threw back his head and laughed, then waved a hand vaguely toward my dusty body.

"I didn't mean because you both look like someone buried you alive. I meant because you're both standing there with your hands on your hips. You're even wearing that scowl you both love so much." I glared at him, and Henry laughed again. "Are you done with the tractor? I have a date with Betsy tonight, so if you want to plow again tomorrow, I need to get started now."

I liked Betsy and I wasn't jealous that Henry had someone special. Despite our dire financial situation, he still went out several nights a week to see her, but I didn't begrudge the gas he used driving the Model T into Oakden. They'd been dating for over a year and Henry had wanted to propose for almost as long.

I'd been on enough dates these past few years to have quietly decided that romance wasn't for me. I liked simpler things—

the feel of sandy dirt on my skin after I plowed a field, the joy of a new foal's birth, the sight of those first green shoots breaking through the soil as the wheat seeds germinated. There was nothing I enjoyed more at night than to sit out under the stars, taking cautious sips from the bathtub gin Henry secretly brewed in the barn, enjoying the silence of the high plains with my brother by my side. But admittedly, on nights Henry was out with Betsy, I felt awfully lonely. I had no idea what I was going to do when he finally had the money to marry her.

"You can't take the car tonight," Dad said abruptly, turning toward the tractor.

"What?" My brother's trademark smile slipped into a frown. "But, Daddy, me and Betsy were—"

"We need to save the gas."

Before Henry could say another word, Dad climbed up and started the tractor. The engine roared to life, and without delay, he drove it past us. I coughed as the tractor sent a fresh wave of dust over me, and it was Henry's turn to scowl.

"I can't even call her to tell her I'm not coming," he grumbled, shaking his head. Dad said we couldn't justify the monthly service fee to have the telephone connected. "What's gotten into him? Today didn't seem like a bad day."

"Maybe he's just tired from being on the tractor for five hours."

We started walking back toward the house in silence, until Henry muttered, "It might be the wheat, you know. Judge Nagle told me last night that even the best crops were only fetching sixty cents per bushel."

"What would he know? He doesn't know a single thing about farming, as far as I can tell."

Judge Nagle was Betsy's dad, and the wealthiest person we knew. As the little northwest Texas town of Oakden had grown over those past few decades, he'd purchased and rented out most of the town's new commercial properties. The Nagle family attended the Oakden Methodist Church, the same as we did, and I'd known him long enough to notice he was prone to condescension when it came to those of us who grew the food he ate.

Henry pursed his lips but didn't say anything, so I pressed on. "Dad said it didn't matter that we didn't even harvest a thousand bushels because the price would be higher."

"I remember what Dad said. It made no damned sense at the time, but I trusted him because he seemed so sure about it. The papers say that people in the cities don't have any money now with this Depression. They don't even have money for food. The price of wheat changes based on demand."

"What happens if we really did only get sixty cents a bushel?"

Henry shrugged, then aimlessly kicked a rock in the soft dirt beneath our feet as he walked.

"I don't know. I guess we try to sell the tractor."

I stopped dead in my tracks.

"No," I said flatly. Henry gave me a pained look.

"Lizzie, there's not much else to sell." Betsy's family lived in a two-story house just behind the courthouse in Oakden, and her home had multiple living areas and indoor plumbing. We didn't even have electric lights and I considered myself lucky that the outhouse was closest to my bedroom so my midnight runs to the bathroom were short. Every step counted on those bitter winter nights. I knew we were humble folk, but I'd never thought of us as poor.

"Don't panic yet," Henry reassured me. "I'm just guessing. You said today was a good day, right?"

"You know as well as I do that good days have nothing to do with money or with harvests or anything else," I muttered. Dad's bad moods weren't the usual kind of bad mood. They didn't only come on when things were bad, and they didn't always go when things became easier.

Henry shrugged.

"Let's ask him later. At dinner, maybe."

"But what if he says we need to sell the tractor?"

"Then we sell the tractor and we make do with the horses for a year or two until we get a better crop. It has to rain sometime, and when it does, the yield will go back up and the price won't even matter as much."

Just as I'd been doing for my entire life, I took comfort in my brother's confidence. I was soon too busy feeding the animals to worry, anyway. Henry fixed the wobbly disc on the plow, and Mother made navy bean soup for dinner. But as she was clearing the table after we ate, Henry cleared his throat.

"How much did the wheat fetch, Daddy? Judge said even top condition grain was only fetching sixty cents a bushel."

Mother froze, her hand still extended toward my plate. She flicked a panicked look from Henry to Dad. Then she forced a smile and said, "Let's not talk about that now—"

"Yes. It's true," Dad said. "Top grain got sixty cents. We got forty-two."

The words fell like a bomb into the middle of the room. Henry and I sucked in air, and Mother sank back into her seat, resting the plates on the table in front of her chest.

"Will we sell the tractor?" Henry asked quietly.

"Can't," Dad said abruptly.

I was immediately pleased that a tractor sale was out of the question, but still, I clarified, "Can't? Won't, you mean."

"No, Lizzie. We can't," Mother said quietly. "I mean, we could, but it won't do us any good. We owe much more on the finance than it's worth now."

"But…we bought it in 1929. Shouldn't we have paid it off by now?" Henry said.

Dad huffed an impatient breath and rolled his eyes toward the ceiling. "Jesus Lord, give me strength. Henry, how am I ever going to send you out on your own if you don't have the good sense to know it takes years to repay a tractor?"

"And how would I know, Dad, if you don't tell me these things?" Henry said stiffly.

"Well, since we're clearing the air now," Mother began gently, "there's a few other things you should know. We're a little behind with the tractor repayments, and more than a little behind with the property taxes." I gasped, and she flicked a sad smile my way. "You knew these last few years have been tough and there was a lot riding on this year's harvest. We didn't want to worry you with the details, but you two are adults now. Goodness, Lizzie—you're seventeen now. Dad and I were courting when I was your age. We need to stop sheltering you."

"You kids don't need to worry because I'm going to see the bank manager tomorrow," Dad said, pushing his chair back. "He'll sort us out with a line of credit to catch up on everything and see us through to next year's harvest. And it'll rain soon. Probably any day, now that we've plowed. You'll see, things will go right back to normal next year."

It had been a blisteringly hot day, and with Dad out in Texline at the bank, Henry and I plowed the back field while Mother did some canning. Now the sun was low in the west, and I enjoyed the milder warmth of the sunset as I collected the eggs from the hen yard. I was sunburned, as I was most days over the summer and sometimes the winter too. Mother always said that my "pretty red hair" was a blessing. Since my favorite place in the world was out under that big Texas sky, I was constantly reminded that the ghostly white skin that came with it could also be a curse.

When I was little, I told Mother that I wanted to be a farmer when I grew up. She gave me that soft look that parents often wear when children ask for something impossible—part amusement, part pity, part fondness.

"Girls don't become farmers, honey. Girls become farmers' *wives*. That's what you'll be."

Even as a little girl, that struck me as absurd. My mother was as much a farmer as my father was. If he was in the field working, she was often right alongside him, or back at the house tending that vegetable garden that was almost a farm in itself. When Dad wanted to buy the tractor, my mother sat in on every call and every meeting, and they made the decision between two models together. Mother's temperament was made of cast iron. Nothing scared her. Nothing fazed her. And *nothing* was too hard for her.

Girls *could* be farmers. I'd seen it with my own two eyes in Mother.

I heard the roar of an engine as I set the last of the day's eggs into my basket. Being so far back from the main road, we didn't really get any drive-by traffic, so I knew it was Dad, and the violent acceleration and grinding gears were a dead giveaway—the meeting had not gone well.

When I went inside, I found Mother sitting at the table, a bowl of half-shelled peas in front of her. She forced a smile, but I could see the strain around her mouth. Dad was in his room with the door closed. If it was daytime and that door was closed, then Dad was in bed, and he wasn't coming out anytime soon.

"They can't give us the loan," she said in a low voice. "Since the banking crisis, the manager can't lend money as easily as he used to. We didn't understand the new rules." The banks had all been closed for a time earlier in the year. With the Depression worsening, there had been a panic rush of people trying to withdraw their money, and that led to a bunch of banks collapsing. The government closed them all, made sure they were viable, then reopened most of them with new rules to keep people's money safe. "Dad thought the farm would be good for collateral, but the bank said the price of land is dropping so fast they can't risk it. We don't have anything else to offer as security, so..."

The truck started just then, and I ran back to the door, just in time to see Henry spin the wheels as he took it right back out the drive.

"Those boys of ours, Lizzie..." Mother sighed, shaking her head sadly. "Neither one of them has the good sense to drive properly when they're upset."

"Where is Henry going?"

"I expect he'll be going off to see Betsy," she said, reaching for the peas.

"What are we going to do?"

She thought about that for a long time—long enough that I'd taken the seat opposite her and started helping with the peas before she answered.

"You know, I really do not have any clue how we'll do it, but I *am* sure we'll figure it out," she said at last. "This isn't the only crisis your dad and I have navigated together, honey. When we got married, Dad wanted to expand the farm to a thousand acres and he used to say we'd need a whole lot of children to help us run it. But that first year..." She sighed and turned back to the stove, where the peas were now over heat, bubbling away beside a pan of potatoes, sizzling in bacon fat. "You know it took us a few years to get pregnant after we were married. Then we had that tiny baby girl who was born way too early, and I got so sick after she was born."

Mother never spoke her name aloud, but I knew about Elsie, the baby who didn't ever get the chance to breathe. On Sundays, Mother always dressed for church early. An hour or even more before we had to leave for service, she'd walk a hundred feet or so to the lonely tree on our property. In the summer of 1909, when Mother and Dad took possession of the first two hundred acres of land around that spot, she had shipped in five little Texas live oak saplings—intending to grow them all together in a row to create a shady spot for future children to play in. One by one and despite her best efforts, the first four trees died. Mother had been a typist in Chicago before she married Dad. She didn't know a thing about growing plants until she learned the hard way on the land.

After the baby died, Dad built a little bench seat beside that last surviving tree, and he inscribed the name *Elsie* on the back of it. That was Mother's remembering place. When I learned to read, I asked about that scripted lettering etched into the back of that chair. In haunting, uneven tones, Mother told me about the tiny baby girl who didn't survive.

"The doctor came to check on me a few months after she was born. I asked him about having another baby and he looked down his nose at me and he said, 'Mrs. Davis, some people just are not meant to be parents,'" Mother said softly. "But I knew in my heart I was meant to be a mother."

I didn't know how to tell her that I knew something in my heart too. I had known my whole life that I *wasn't* meant to be a mother. Maybe I'd been traumatized by the way she spoke of that poor lost baby. Maybe I'd been too afraid of that heartbreaking seat beneath the oak tree when I was little, or maybe I'd indulged my fascination with farming too much, like Mother sometimes said when she was nagging at me to be nicer to the boys at church. She so desperately wanted me to find a boy to date. But even at the age of seventeen, I was certain.

The problem was, I still couldn't quite figure out how to

avoid being a mother. Henry would inherit the farm, so it seemed the only way to get my own farm was to get married. Marriage meant children, and children would mean less time for farming. More time for diapers and feeding, more time for keeping the house. Less of what I knew I loved.

"Two years later, Henry was born, and eventually you joined us too," Mother said, her gaze softening. She waved a hand vaguely as she added, "For that first year after we lost that baby, everything felt hopeless. We were all alone in this tiny little house with that great big sadness." She smiled, then nodded, as if she'd convinced herself too. "This moment feels just like that one. I don't know *how* things will work out, but in my heart, I am certain that everything will be okay. All you and I have to do is to have faith and keep our chins up."

7

Sofie
Huntsville, Alabama
1950

A CROWD WAS ASSEMBLED BENEATH THE SHADE
of a cluster of oak trees that day. I was heartened to see that
after just a few minutes, the American and German children
were all mingling freely. Language didn't make much difference when it came to climbing trees and playing tag.

The formalities began when a man clapped his hands and
called us all to order, then took a microphone and stepped up
onto a box. He introduced himself as Christopher Newsome,
and a young man beside him translated his words into perfect
German. Newsome pointed to a tall, bearded gentleman with
thick glasses that magnified his eyes.

"I'm sure you all know Calvin Miller—he's the general
manager of this program." More translation, and then a smat-
tering of applause. "First of all to our new German friends,
welcome to America!" Translation. Applause. "Now, to all of

you American ladies—I want you to listen carefully. These women have come all the way round the world to start a new life here, and we need to support them. Make a new friend today. Make plans to meet up for coffee or for dinner or to get the children together to play, okay?" Translation. *Much* weaker applause. The popping of champagne bottles.

The Germans had been working alongside the American scientists at Fort Bliss for some time before they all transferred to Huntsville, and their rapport was obvious. Jürgen was soon surrounded by men listening intently to his every word. At least one thing hadn't changed in my husband—that obsessively focused look in his eyes when he talked about rockets was as familiar as the back of my own hand.

I took a glass of champagne and walked lazily around, observing the crowd. The women quickly formed two distinct groups. The American women were the louder group—their voices and laughter rang across the lawn. On the other side of the table, the German women were standing clumped together as if they were all trying to hide, their voices low and their eyes downcast. I helped myself to a plate of food and then approached the German side.

Claudia's eyes lit up. "Everyone, meet my new neighbor, Sofie," she said.

"Hello," I said, waving vaguely. I recognized several faces as women I'd met once or twice over the years in Germany. "Oh, hello there, Greta. Margarethe, how are you? It's been so long. Elsa, nice to see you too." And to the rest of them, I waved and smiled. "It's nice to meet you all."

"Sofie is Jürgen Rhodes' wife," Claudia added cheerfully.

Was I imagining the tension? It was as though the smiles on those women's faces intensified just a little when I approached, shifting from genuine to forced. I looked back to Claudia, who seemed bewildered.

I was not bewildered. This was exactly why I'd hoped none of Jürgen's former workers had come to America.

"I really need some more of that chicken," Greta said.

"I'll go with you," Margarethe added.

"Oh, I need to find a restroom," one of the other women said.

"I know where it is," Elsa interjected. "I'll show you."

The group dispersed quickly.

"That was strange," Claudia said slowly. "It's probably just that some of those women have been here in the United States for a few months already, and maybe a little clique has formed..."

"*Gu-ten tag,*" an American voice said, and we turned to see a short blonde woman had joined us. She spoke very slowly but butchered the pronunciation badly.

"Hello. I speak English," I said, then motioned toward Claudia. "But my friend here doesn't."

"Oh!" the American woman said, surprised but visibly relieved. "I'm trying to be friendly, but it's awfully hard when we're speaking different languages."

"They'll all learn in time," I told her. "I'm Sofie, and this is Claudia."

"Hello," Claudia said awkwardly. The woman beamed at us.

"I'm Avril Walters."

Claudia excused herself, wandering just a few steps to join a little cluster of German women. One by one, their eyes all flicked to me, then quickly away.

"Which one is your husband?" Avril asked. I pointed to Jürgen, and her eyes widened. "Jürgen Rhodes is your husband? Well, isn't that something? My husband says he's a genius."

"Which is yours?" I asked. She pointed to two men who were standing side by side at the table. I recognized one as

Calvin Miller, so knew her husband must have been the man beside him.

I glanced back to the German women and saw Claudia was whispering with one of them, her brows drawn. She shook her head fiercely, then looked back at me, but now when our eyes met, she looked away. My heart sank. The German men had been brought to America as prisoners, and even those who knew Jürgen's history had no choice but to work with him, especially in the beginning. It was different for the wives. We had arrived as free women and could socialize, or *refuse* to socialize, as we saw fit.

"I'm just so excited to meet you," Avril gushed, startling me with the volume of her voice and her enthusiasm. "I've never even met someone from Germany before. How did you learn to speak English so well?"

"I had British nannies when I was young, and sometimes we traveled with my parents," I said absentmindedly, watching Claudia studiously avoid my gaze.

"You know what, Sofie?" Avril said, flashing me that warm smile. "We should have coffee next week."

8

Lizzie

Dallam County, Texas
1933

DAD DIDN'T COME OUT OF HIS ROOM THAT NIGHT, and Mother retired to join him just as soon as she finished her meal.

I decided that Henry wouldn't mind me raiding his stash of gin, so I let myself into his bedroom and retrieved the bottle from under his bed. When I heard the sound of the Model T returning, I met him on the porch.

"Hey, sis," he greeted me. He took the bottle of gin out of my hand, opening it and downing a few generous gulps without preamble. He never did seem to notice the burn the way I did.

When he finished, he motioned toward our usual spot. We liked to sit a little ways from the house—just far enough from Mother and Dad's bedroom that we could drink gin and stay up as late as we wanted. Once upon a time, our spot was covered in grass.

We perched ourselves on the low wooden chairs Henry made us one quiet winter. Just a slip of the moon was visible, which meant I could see more stars. I looked hopefully toward the barest wisp of cloud on the horizon and said a quick prayer that it might build to something. Beside me, Henry was drinking much more than he usually would.

"You went to see Betsy?"

"Nope," he said abruptly. "Went to see Judge Nagle. I asked him if he'd lend us some money." I felt a sharp pang at the thought of Henry begging his girl's father to bail us out. "What choice do we have?" he argued. "We don't know anyone else rich enough to help us, and we have to do something. Besides, he's bought up half of Main Street in the last ten years. The man has more money than God. He may as well share some."

"How would we even pay him back?" I said uncertainly.

"The same way we were going to pay the bank back—we sow a crop," Henry said, shrugging.

"The bank would take the farm if we defaulted, right?" My brother nodded, and I said impatiently, "Well, Judge Nagle would do even worse! Do you really think he'd let you see Betsy if you let him down with a loan? Let alone *marry* her?"

"He was never going to let me marry Betsy, Lizzie," Henry said softly, heartache beneath the words. "He told me as much tonight. Said he likes me and that's why he's let me hang around, but he really should have put a stop to things a while back."

"I'm so sorry," I whispered, stricken.

"The judge was never going to let his daughter marry a man who can't even afford a telephone to call her."

"So if you break up with Betsy, he'll give you the money?"

I said hesitantly. "That sounds like he's bribing or blackmailing you."

"It wasn't like that at all—we just had an honest and, frankly, overdue conversation and came to an agreement. And he's not *giving* me the money—he's lending it to me. We'll be able to repay it next year when the harvest comes in."

"But what if—" I started to ask.

But he cut me off, suddenly urgent and animated as he said, "Never in the history of the world has there been a drought that did not end. I looked it up at the library in Oakden a few weeks ago. Droughts come and go, yes. But they *always* end within a few years. We got a little rain a few weeks ago, remember?"

"It was less than a quarter of an inch!" I exclaimed.

"But that's how it starts!" Henry said, bending forward to rest his elbows on his knees. "Don't you see, Lizzie? The weather pattern changes slowly—a quarter inch here and there becomes half an inch becomes more and then *enough*. Normal rain will be here before the winter is over."

"And if you're wrong?"

Henry took another gulping swill of the drink, then exhaled slowly.

"That's why I asked for two years to pay it back. There's *no* chance the drought would last more than another year. Besides, if I am wrong, we were going to lose the farm anyway, so it makes no difference." At my gasp, he shot me an impatient look. "What do you think happens when people don't pay their property taxes, Lizzie?"

My stomach churned. I set my mug down in the dust and took a few deep breaths until it passed.

"How much did you borrow?"

"I know how much they'd have got for a harvest on a good year. That's how much I borrowed."

"But the farm has got to be worth much more than that."

"This land is barely worth the paper the deed is written on just now—that's why the bank wouldn't help us. But…yeah, in the longer term, it's probably worth more than I borrowed." He shifted awkwardly, then dropped his voice as he admitted, "It's just that Judge Nagle wasn't keen at first. He likes me, but he's shrewd, you know? I had to show him that I was serious about this. But he wouldn't really take the farm. He's a good man, and besides which, it's not like he's short of cash. What would he want with this place?"

"Daddy is not going to be happy about this."

Henry shrugged, all calm and confident again.

"He doesn't really have much choice. The judge drew up a contract and I signed it right away. Betsy is going to go to the bank when it opens tomorrow and she'll deposit the check into Daddy's account."

My parents' bedroom door was closed when I got out of bed the next morning, and I had a feeling Dad might not make it out of bed that day. I went out to use the washroom, but while I was there, I heard Dad and Henry shouting. I ran back to the house just as the bedroom door slammed again, and a defiant Henry stomped down the hall, joining Mother in the kitchen.

"What did you do, Henry?" Mother whispered, visibly upset. He raised his chin stubbornly.

"You'll see," he told us both. "Everything will turn around next season. That money is going to save us."

Maybe Daddy was worn down by the dry and the hopelessness, or maybe he knew Henry had ultimately done the right thing, because as much as he grumbled, Daddy didn't even try to give that money back to the judge.

9

Lizzie

Huntsville, Alabama
1950

AS I'D DRIVEN TO THE PARTY, MY INTENTION was to seek Calvin out and apologize. I had a perfectly good excuse for my tardiness. This wasn't the first time my car had needed some cajoling.

But as I approached Cal, I heard snippets of the conversation around him. These men were speaking English, but much of it was heavily accented. Henry's taunt about my new "Nazi friends" rang in my ear, and I felt a shock of outrage.

No.

It just was not right for these people to be mingling with the rest of us, enjoying the sunshine on their faces, sipping champagne, and laughing so freely.

I spun on my heel and made a beeline toward more familiar faces. My friends Becca, Juanita, and Gail were there with a handful of other women. Avril Walters was there too, talking quietly with a woman I didn't know—a woman with auburn hair and a milky, clear complexion I couldn't help but be jealous of. Was this new woman German? I looked between the groups and quickly decided she must be the wife of one of the new American scientists. Calvin's team had expanded so quickly, it was hard to keep up.

"You look like you need a drink," Becca said, and she picked up a champagne flute from the table and handed it to me.

"Thanks," I muttered. I downed the glass, then glanced toward the German women. I dropped my voice. "I just cannot believe this. We're supposed to just mingle with them like we don't know where they're from?"

"No need to whisper, honey," Becca laughed gently. "It seems none of those women speak a word of English. But Mr. Newsome still wants us all to invite them for coffee to help them settle in."

I looked at her in disbelief.

"Are you going to?"

"Well, it's hard when they don't even speak the same language, but yes, I was going to try. For the program, you know, but…" She winced. "It doesn't feel right, does it?"

"These people should probably be on trial at Nuremberg, not sipping champagne in Huntsville. They'll infect this town like a disease." I took a second glass of champagne and looked around the crowd. Elijah Klein was with the men, but his wife, Leah, was standing behind Becca, flicking decidedly uncomfortable glances at the Germans. "It's bad enough that these monsters aren't in prison, but to put them to work, side by side, with American Jews?"

"It's not right," Leah said flatly. "I didn't want to come today, but Eli insisted. I just *hate* that he's working with these men."

"How does he stand it?" Becca asked, her voice hushed. Leah sighed impatiently.

"He says the end justifies the means. Honestly, does it even matter if we put a rocket into space? Who *cares*?"

"Kevin says that if we don't work with these men, the Soviets will beat us to it," Becca muttered, shaking her head. We all paused. No one wanted the Soviets to beat us at anything.

"The problem isn't that we're working with them," I muttered. "The problem is that they're here as free men."

"The Germans murdered millions of people! Millions of Jews," Leah said, her voice trembling. "We should not be welcoming them to this country."

A small crowd was gathering around us as we talked, the American women ending their private conversations and listening in to mine.

"Are you going to invite these women for coffee, help them settle in and all that?" one woman asked. "I was going to, but it didn't sit right with me…"

"Don't," I said abruptly. "Especially if it makes you feel uncomfortable."

"How could anyone be comfortable with this situation?" another woman remarked. "I'm so happy you're speaking out, Lizzie."

"We don't *have* to welcome them," I said flatly, meeting the gaze of each of the women as my confidence grew. "We can take a stand. I mean, for God's sakes, someone has to."

"Excuse me," a voice said. I glanced toward the voice and saw that the woman Avril was speaking with had joined us. "Yes, many Germans made terrible mistakes in a time of immense pressure, but it would be unfair of you to paint all of us with that same brush. There are plenty of bad Americans, just as there are bad Germans. You should not assume we are

Nazis, and you should not assume we are guilty. Some of us didn't even know what was happening."

She spoke in clear, fluid English—but her accent was unmistakable, as was the look of defensiveness in her eyes. A burst of adrenaline shot through my body.

"Do you really expect us to believe you Germans had no idea what was happening in your own country?" I asked in disbelief, then glanced around the crowd of women listening to us. Some nodded to encourage me as I scoffed, "If the American government decided to commit genocide, I would *do* something."

"And tell me, madam, what do you do when you go to a restaurant and there is a sign in the window that says Whites Only?" the woman demanded, jabbing her finger toward me aggressively. "Do you 'do something'? Perhaps you should look into your own backyard before you make sweeping judgments about things you do not understand." Her tone was dismissive and haughty, and all of the American rocket program wives were staring at us. My embarrassment and temper flared.

"I hate that Huntsville is segregated, but you'll never convince me it's the same as what you people did. I've heard the news and I've read the papers. I know the kinds of things the Nuremberg trials have uncovered." Her lips thinned, but that she had no immediate retort only reassured me I was right to take a stand. "Can you honestly tell me you had no idea about the camps? No idea about the terrible things being done in the name of your country—things being done in *your* name?"

I expected her to deny it. Instead, her eyebrows knit, and her gaze dipped as the silence began to stretch. I felt no triumph at the raspberry flush that stole up her cheeks, only a horrified sense of disgust.

"You did know," I whispered, stunned. "Well, isn't that something? Lady, if you knew and did nothing, you're as guilty as the men who pushed those innocent people into gas chambers. How do you even look at yourself in the mirror—"

"That's enough!" Calvin hissed. I startled and looked past her to see my husband striding toward us, his eyes wide with disbelief and disappointment.

Only then did I realize that the entire gathering had fallen silent. Dozens of people were staring at me and the German woman. The only partygoers who hadn't stopped to watch the spectacle were the children, who were still laughing and playing together.

Every now and again, I had a moment where I felt as though I stepped out of my life and looked at it from the outside. Whenever that happened, I was left with one stunning question I could never quite figure out the answer to: *How did I get here?*

As Calvin offered soothing smiles to the women, and gently took my arm to lead me away from the garden party, I had a moment like that—a stark, shocking instant where I had the distinct impression that I had somehow got myself trapped living someone else's life.

10

Sofie
Berlin, Germany
1933

I WAS HOME THAT NIGHT LATER THAN I'D EX-
pected, and as I let myself inside, I hoped Jürgen would be in
bed asleep. I wasn't ready to face his questions about why my
dinner with Lydia lasted six hours.

I knew Mayim would be awake, listening for the children
from the sitting room. Georg was almost three, and Laura was
eight months old. They both slept poorly, but Mayim often
read until the small hours anyway and helped with the children overnight. This was one of the magic aspects to having
my best friend living under my roof. Mayim was more than
just a houseguest to my children—more even than a quasi
aunt. She was almost like a third parent to them, a vital and
much-loved part of our family structure.

I found her curled up in one of the armchairs in the formal
sitting room, reading by the glow of a lamp. The blanket over

her lap was her own creation, a jumble of colors knit from yarn left over from her many other projects. As she often did, she had the fire roaring. I kicked off my pumps as I entered the room and breathed a sigh of relief as my tired feet hit the cool floorboards. The sole of my left shoe was badly worn, and a blister was forming.

I could scarcely believe that I couldn't even afford to repair a shoe. My whole life changed in a single afternoon three years ago, a few months after my father died of a stroke during a business trip to New York. My brother Heinrich was twenty-six years older, and little more than a stranger. But as the eldest, Heinrich inherited the von Meyer estate, and it fell to him to break the news that my generous monthly stipend would be no more. Father mortgaged every family property to the hilt, including the city villa—the home he'd gifted Jürgen and me for our wedding. Heinrich agreed that we could keep our house—but only on the condition that we assumed the mortgage for it too.

I'd never wanted for any material things, and I assumed that would always be the case. It turned out our father was much better at presenting a facade of extreme wealth than he was at managing the modest wealth he did possess, once upon a time.

"How was it?" Mayim asked, as she closed her book and looked up at me. I dropped into the chair opposite her and struggled to put the right words together.

It had been a shocking few months in Berlin. First came the destruction of our parliament building, the Reichstag—then a series of communist attacks across the nation were only narrowly averted. I'd pored over the details of the planned terror campaign in the newspaper: bombs hidden under bridges and in train stations, women and children used as human shields, the execution of swaths of public officials, poison in the Berlin water supply.

Even through all of that, I had never once been as terrified as I was at the rally I just attended with Lydia.

"There was a lot of passionate analysis of the problems we face as a nation, a lot of hints about who's to really blame."

"Who might that be?" Mayim said lightly, but I could hear the tightness in her words.

"They managed to be hateful toward the Jews for hours on end without saying the word *Jew* even once."

"They adjust their rhetoric depending on where the rally is being held. In the country, they can say what they really mean. But we're in the cosmopolitan city, so I suppose here they know to hide their hate beneath a veneer of respectability."

By the end of the rally, I'd felt physically ill, and that sensation surged all over again as I sat in my living room and thought about what I'd heard.

"A *Volksgemeinschaft* is possible!" one speaker thundered, as he painted the image of a German *people's community*, which sounded almost Utopian until he followed it up with references to the racial purity it would be built upon. Another looked to the past and found a villain he didn't need to name. "The Treaty of Versailles was designed only to cripple us! We were stabbed in the back by those who agreed to it." We all knew this was a clear reference to the long-standing conspiracy theory that Germany had not really lost the Great War, but that our brave soldiers were betrayed by those at home, mostly Jews, who fomented unrest and undermined the war effort.

Another man spoke in generalities—rattling off a long list of the challenges we faced as a nation, from economic woes to the ever-increasing political instability—and then he simply shrugged and said, "Germany should be for Germans. We shall bear our national misfortune no longer." That use of the word *misfortune* struck an uncomfortable chord. I'd seen it on the Nazi posters around the city, usually beneath a crude, offensive caricature of a Jew.

"People seemed enthralled, Mayim. Like they were under a spell," I said uneasily. "It was a flashy affair—almost like a concert, with an orchestra and a choir and boundless enthusiasm and passion. I just don't understand how a bit of music and some theatrical speeches could turn a crowd like that into a bunch of raging anti-Semites."

A flicker of uncertainty crossed Mayim's face. We had been best friends since before we even started at elementary school—our families once residing in side-by-side, twin mansions in Potsdam. I knew her well enough to know she had something to say.

"Speak your mind," I prompted. Mayim sighed impatiently.

"You have no idea how anti-Semitic this country really is, Sofie. You can't understand it the way my family does."

"Your family is my family," I said. I was a late-in-life surprise for my mother, who gave birth to me when she was forty-eight years old. Anna von Meyer had no interest in starting all over again nine years after her fifth son, so she generally left my care to my nannies. My family was cold and formal, so I much preferred spending time at Mayim's house, with her lovely warm mother and her jovial, kind father. Even Mayim's little brother, Moshe, had always annoyed and amused me.

"You're my best friend in the whole world—a sister if not by blood, then by choice. But you can't know what it's really like to live your whole life under the shadow of hate. To wake up every morning knowing that there's a large portion of your own countrymen who would sooner see you gone. You've seen the big, openly aggressive moments—but you don't notice the way people look at me when I'm on the trolley car. You might notice the No Jews sign in the windows of some stores, but don't hear the undertone in the grocer's tone when he counts my change, or the casual way people joke about me and my family, sometimes right in front of our faces. You said it was like the crowd tonight had been turned into raging anti-Semites by the rally, yes?" I nodded slowly and she shrugged. "All Hitler and his ilk are doing is connecting with something that has always been there."

I knew that in other countries, even Poland, where Mayim's mother was born, many Jews lived in Jewish Quarters or Districts. It was different in Germany. In my country, especially in Berlin, Jews lived and studied and worked alongside everyone else, so much so that I often had no idea if a person was or wasn't Jewish unless their surname gave it away. For the first time, it occurred to me that perhaps our integrated society also gave cover to subtle incidents of bigotry. Even Lydia sometimes made those silly, casual remarks about the Jews.

"What about people like Lydia and Karl?" I asked hesitantly. "You and Lydia are friends."

"Lydia and I *were* friends," Mayim said quietly. "I hardly see her these days. I highly doubt she or Karl have been spending much time socializing with anyone with a surname like *Nussbaum* since they joined the Party."

That was the other great shock, and one I still couldn't make sense of: Lydia and Karl had joined the Nazi party.

"But why?" I'd blurted when they told me, too surprised to temper my reaction.

"Perhaps there were some less-than-savory aspects to their politics historically," Lydia admitted. "But the other parties only offer the same tired rhetoric, with no plan to stabilize the nation. We decided to throw our money and our time behind a party we feel sure can win."

"When the Nazis come to power, they will end all of the madness and things will go back to normal," Karl added pleasantly.

"But at what cost?" Jürgen asked. He looked as shell-shocked as I felt.

"The Party know they need to clean up those rogue elements to win the election, I can assure you of that," Karl said, and then came the first of countless invitations. "Why don't you come to a rally with us one day?"

It was true that Lydia's coolness toward Mayim had been more pronounced that year, but it was also true that distance had been growing between them for much longer than that. I shifted uncomfortably, and Mayim sighed.

"You think it's about my family's financial circumstances, not because we are Jews. Perhaps that is a factor."

"I *know* it is a factor!" I said, throwing my hands up in the air in frustration. "If I ever had any doubt about how shallow our social circles are, I've had the truth of it well and truly rammed home for me in the last few years." It wasn't just Lydia who withdrew from Mayim. One by one, most of her friends had drifted away. Jürgen and I hadn't purposefully hidden our own circumstances from our friends—but having witnessed Mayim's increasing isolation, we'd hardly advertised our struggle.

"It would be different if they knew about *your* situation," Mayim said, correctly reading my thoughts.

"No, it wouldn't," I said, laughing miserably.

"This is exactly what I mean, my friend," Mayim said gently. "You don't even see it. The people who no longer invite me to their parties were always looking for an excuse to exclude me. It's never been socially acceptable to admit you don't want to invite the Jewish girl to the party, but it's fine to leave the poor girl out."

I felt a pinch in my chest. I stared at her for a moment, thinking about the injustice of it all.

"Are you hurt that I went tonight?" I asked her suddenly. Mayim's gaze softened.

"I know exactly why you went. Did Karl say anything more about the job?"

Like most employers in Germany, Jürgen's university was struggling with an ever-shrinking budget, and they'd cut staff salaries by more than half. His income no longer covered our living expenses, even though we'd laid off all of our household staff and sold our cars. We were selling my family heirlooms now, but it was a short-term solution. Some rooms were already devoid of all but the most essential furniture.

That was why it seemed like such a miracle when Karl called to ask Jürgen if he was interested in a new job. Karl wouldn't say much, just that it was an exciting and lucrative new opportunity and he'd be in touch soon. But days turned into weeks, and every time I tried to organize a casual catch-up with the zu Schillers, they were busy campaigning for the Nazis. I caught Lydia on the phone a few times, but she couldn't or wouldn't tell me anything.

"Karl will tell you more when he sees you both," she kept saying.

Every time a significant Nazi event was held in Berlin, Lydia had her staff drop off free rally tickets. I usually threw them into the trash, but when the latest tickets arrived, my impatience got the best of me and I decided to go.

It was a clumsy, flawed plan. Karl was already at the rally when Lydia's town car arrived to collect me, and although he sat with us during the proceedings, he was busy on official business before and after, and I didn't have a chance to speak to him.

"Something has to give," I whispered to Mayim, my throat tight. "We can't afford this place anymore, but even if we sell it, we won't clear the mortgage. Where would we even go?"

Mayim rose and came to take the seat beside me, resting her hand over mine on the armrest.

"Go to bed, Sofie," she said softly. "Things will look better in the morning."

She had a way of soothing me, without saying much at all.

"What would I do without you?" Mayim flashed me a soft smile.

"I really have no idea. Lucky for you, I'm not going anywhere."

I crawled into bed soon after, so drained I could barely keep my eyes open, but the minute my head hit the pillow, my anxiety resurged. Even the very real threat of losing my home suddenly paled in comparison to the fear that the men I'd heard speak at that rally might soon be in power. I thought about Mayim and shivered with fear.

"You weren't at dinner with Lydia tonight, were you?" Jürgen said, startling me. I turned toward him guiltily. He was lying on his back, wide-awake and staring up at the ceiling.

"I did have dinner with her…" I admitted. "Then I went with her to the rally."

"Sofie, what on earth were you thinking?"

He was annoyed, but when tears filled my eyes, he sighed heavily and reached for me. I relaxed immediately, sinking into the comfort of his arms.

"I thought you felt the same way I do about the Nazis," he said.

"I do. I was just hoping that if I engineered a chance to see Karl, he would tell me more about this job."

"Well, did he?"

"I never got the chance to speak to him."

"I've tried to call him a few times."

"You did?" He hadn't mentioned this, but I knew Jürgen

felt guilty that he couldn't support us, so I hated to force him to talk about it.

"Young people are looking for work to try to support their families—no one has the capacity to study these days. What happens if there's no work for me in the new academic year?"

"I can't even let myself think about that," I said. Jürgen had been working toward his doctorate when my brother broke the news that we needed to generate our own income, and although he'd been forced to abandon his studies, he was quickly employed to teach. Just a few years later, though, things were different. Six million Germans were out of work in a severely depressed economy. If Jürgen lost that job, he'd be unlikely to find another.

"Karl has been so busy that I haven't managed to catch him on the phone, and he no longer has time to attend our meetings," Jürgen admitted. Karl and Jürgen were both founding members of the *Verein für Raumschiffahrt*, the Society for Space Travel, and they spent their Saturday mornings tinkering with homemade rockets at an abandoned dump outside of Berlin. Their dream was to design a rocket that would take man to the moon, a prospect so absurd I struggled to understand why Jürgen even entertained it. "That's what concerns me, Sofie. Karl is consumed by his work with the Party these days. I can't imagine any position he knows of would be one I'd be interested in."

"You think the job is with the Nazis?" I said, heart sinking.

"I fear it is, yes."

"The fervor tonight shocked me. I don't know what happens to this country if those men find their way to power."

"There are some who believe the Nazis set that fire in the Reichstag, you know."

"Wasn't it the Dutchman?"

"A mentally unwell Dutchman, with a loose association to

an independent communist party in his home country, was somehow able to single-handedly destroy Germany's parliament building?" Jürgen asked wryly.

"To think that the only thing standing between those dreadful terror attacks planned against this city was the SA." The *Sturmabteilung* was one of the Nazi party's paramilitary wings. They were also known as Brownshirts, named for their uniform, and they'd been instrumental in uncovering a mass terrorist threat the previous week. It terrified me to think we were days away from catastrophe and the only thing that saved us was one of the Nazi paramilitary organizations.

"The Nazis have yet to release a single shred of evidence about those terror attacks, even though they promised they would immediately. I think we have to at least consider the possibility that the terror plot wasn't real."

"But the papers say—"

"This is my point, my love," Jürgen interrupted me. "The papers say what the Nazis want them to say, now that the Reichstag Fire decree enables them to control what's published. Doesn't it strike you as odd that some unstable man supposedly commits an act of terrorism and by sunset the next day the government has discovered some fantastic plot to upend life as we know it, arrested most of their opponents, and passed a decree overriding our constitutional protections? If they really do have this overwhelming evidence, why would they need a right to arrest and detain their opposition indefinitely, without so much as a trial? And why would they need to end the free press or end our right to personal privacy? In the context of some of the things those men have said in the past, this Nazi power grab leaves me feeling anxious."

"Surely even the Nazis wouldn't lie about such serious, world-changing events," I said uncertainly. "If those reports were fiction, how could we trust anything politicians say ever again? We couldn't."

"I don't know what to tell you, Sofie. What worries me most is that in fraught economic times like these, with men starving to death on the streets, people cast their votes impulsively, out of desperation instead of reason and compassion. The Nazis know this, and they purposefully present a powerful front—that's why they love to hold military parades. That's what I fear the announcements about the terror plots were designed to do—to stir up more uncertainty and then to paint themselves as the only solution."

I'd been feeling anxious about the future for a long while, but that was the first night my worries kept me awake until dawn. And I was right to worry. A few weeks later, when the election results were announced, we learned that 44 percent of Germans had voted for the Nazi party. Joining forces with the Workers' Party, they easily formed a majority in the parliament.

The Nazis were no longer a fringe party, no longer hovering on the edge of the German political system. Now they were at the very center of it, and from there, they could shape it as they pleased.

11

Lizzie
Dallam County, Texas
1935

"IS MOTHER READY?" HENRY CALLED. "LET'S GO!"
He only saw Betsy at church now, and he didn't want to waste
a minute of his only chance to be with her.

"She's over at the tree," I muttered as I peered at myself in
the hall mirror, turning this way and that to see myself from
all angles. I'd lost some weight that year and my dresses hung
on me like sacks, so Mother took in one of her old dresses for
me to wear for my Sunday outfit. It was an older style, stiff
cotton with little black buttons down the front of the bodice,
leading to a heavy flared skirt.

"Go get her, sis," Henry said, pleading. "You know I hate
going over there."

"So do I," I said pointedly. There was something unnerving about the way Mother held herself on Sunday mornings
when she visited that bench. She often sat slumped and mel-

ancholy, as if her grief were still fresh but she had to condense it down into a single hour each week. Elsie had been lost for more than twenty-five years. That Mother was still so sad after all that time never failed to confuse Henry and me.

Henry glanced down at his watch and then sighed impatiently and left the house. I heard movement from Mother and Daddy's bedroom, so I walked quickly down the hall, knocked, and pushed the door open, holding my breath while I waited to see how Dad was that day. Ever since Henry borrowed that money, the pattern of his good days and bad days reversed. It was as if he'd suffered a terrible injury that left him with a permanent disability—only the injury wasn't to his body, but to his pride.

Dad wasn't dressed for church but there were some positive signs. He'd opened the drapes and was sitting up in bed, reading the newspaper we'd brought back from Oakden the previous Sunday. On very bad days, Dad barely seemed to realize I was there. Mother said it wasn't his fault.

"It's tiring trying to make sense of things that make no damned sense at all," she told me. "Your daddy is a farmer to his very bones. When farming isn't working as it should, he's just a husk of his real self."

The drought changed a lot of things and none of it made sense to me either. I still got out of bed and I still did my share. Mother, Henry, and I didn't have a choice—we had to get used to a new way of operating because running the farm was a four-man operation. The price per bushel for wheat in the 1934 harvest was higher, and that might have been a relief had it not been our worst season ever, both in terms of the condition of the grain and the yield. We sold only six hundred bushels, each one fetching a miserable thirty-three cents.

We didn't square the debt with Judge Nagle that year. We didn't even manage to make regular repayments. Henry told me to "keep my chin up," but I knew it was already too late. Even if we had buckets of rain, there would be no crop this year. I had no idea what we were going to do, other than to throw ourselves on the good graces of Judge Nagle and ask for more time.

"You look pretty as a picture," Dad said, and if the shock on his face was any indication, he was as surprised by his remark as I was. I did a mock curtsy and mumbled something about it being Mother's old dress. "Oh, I remember it well. She used to wear it back when we were courting. It suits you just as well as it suited her then." He set the paper down on his lap and frowned at me. "Lizzie, you're almost nineteen. When are you going to get yourself a boyfriend?"

"I don't want a boyfriend," I said, raising my chin.

"Your mother and I were married by the time she was your age."

"Daddy."

"What? You know it's true."

"Maybe I'm not cut out for all that," I muttered, embarrassed.

"Nonsense. Don't you want a farm of your own? Children?"

"I…" I didn't want to waste a rare good day by telling him no. "Of course," I lied, convincing myself that it was okay to lie on Sunday if it was only half a lie. After all, I *did* want a farm of my own. That I would likely need a husband to go with it was an inconvenient reality I was still trying to make peace with.

"Then maybe make eye contact with some of the boys at church," Dad suggested, picking his paper up again. "That would be a good start."

I stopped at the linen cupboard on my way to the Model T, fetching a small towel to protect the dress, then stopped again to pat the horse and to check on her harness. Jesse and

Joker were all we had left by way of livestock other than the chickens, and although the chickens still gave us plenty, the horses were the most valuable asset we owned now.

A man from the bank arrived without warning one day to load the tractor up onto the bed of a truck. The only sign we'd ever even owned it was the mound of debt it left behind. Around the same time, we could no longer justify the cost of running the Model T. We tried to sell it, but with so many cars for sale, no one wanted to pay a fair price. Henry and I removed the engine and then took out every bit of glass and superfluous metal from its body, making it as light as possible. When we finished, we rigged up a mechanism to fix the horses to it—turning the car into an elaborate cart. Plenty of others had the same idea. We called them Hoover wagons, after the president we loved to blame for our miserable circumstances.

"Come on, Lizzie," Henry called impatiently, as I petted Jesse's nose. She was taking us to church that day, and Henry was already in the "driver's seat," holding the reins.

Mother beamed at me from the front passenger's seat, pleased with his enthusiasm, and I sighed and made my way to the back. The week's eggs were all packed carefully onto the seat beside me, ready to go to the grocer on the way to church. I wiped my side of the seat with the towel before I climbed in. As Henry steered the cart along the drive, dust billowed up around us, and I looked down at the white dress and felt a pang of despair.

"Dusty today," Mother said, but the ambient dust those wheels were stirring up was the least of our worries. Dust and sandstorms were blowing through with such regularity that we had a whole routine when we saw one on the horizon. Henry would lock the horses in the barn, Mother would hurry to take any clothes off the line, and I'd run from room to room checking that windows were closed. It was Dad's job to prepare his bedroom for us all to shelter in. By the time we all ran inside, he'd be ready to close the door behind us and put a wet towel down against the gap beneath it. He'd have food and water inside his closet, tucked under a blanket to shelter it from the dust. Dad would hang a damp sheet over the window to catch the dirt that threatened the gaps. On the bed, he'd have a pail waiting with wet dish towels for us to put over our mouths, and a little tub of Vaseline for us to smear into our nostrils. The dirt in the air during one summer storm had irritated the lining of our noses such that we all had nosebleeds for days.

All of this, and it wasn't nearly enough. Dirt or sand or dust would sneak in between the gaps in the floorboards or the walls, and by the time the bad storms passed, those wet tea towels would be black or red or yellow with the dirt they'd kept from our lungs, and there'd be mounds of dirt around the skirting boards. Every storm was different depending on whether the soil blew in from Oklahoma or Ohio or Kansas, or maybe the farm right next door. In the beginning, we'd peer at the dirt and discuss its potential origins—analyzing the color and texture and wind direction. By the time the storms were coming almost every week, the novelty of our dirt detective game had worn off. One storm lasted a full twenty-four hours. By then, we were so accustomed to them that we didn't even panic. We just sat in Mother and Dad's room and we listened to the wind howl for hours on end.

"How long are we going to be stuck in here?" I muttered at one point.

"That's the wrong way of looking at this, Lizzie," Mother gently chided me. "We have a roof over our heads. Somewhere to shelter. We have one another."

"We aren't *stuck* in here," Henry added. "We're safe in here."

But over time, even Mother had grown tired of the relent-less storms, and the dust that seemed to permeate every single crevice in our lives. Now when a storm came, we just sat in a miserable, heavy silence, listening to the wind as it bathed our house and fields and vegetable garden and barn in dust.

Even on a beautiful Sunday morning on our way to church, we barely saw the sun or the bright blue sky. All we saw was the dust.

"Good morning, Mrs. Davis," Judge Nagle greeted us, nod-ding politely as we mingled in the vestibule of the church be-fore service. "And you too, Miss Lizzie." His gaze landed on my brother and he added quietly, "Henry."

"Good morning, sir. Mrs. Nagle, you look lovely today," Henry said, but he rushed through the words. It was obvi-ous he only had eyes for Betsy, who was standing beside her parents. She looked beautiful as she always did. That day she was wearing a yellow dress with a soft skirt that skimmed her calves. She'd probably made it herself, because Betsy sewed for fun even though she could afford to buy clothes ready-made.

"I love your dress, Lizzie," she said sincerely. "Those cute little buttons! It suits you so much."

I flushed, embarrassed at the attention, but remembered my manners enough to thank her before I shuffled away to take my seat. Any other girl might have been mocking me with a compliment for such an old dress, but Betsy was nice. The judge and Mrs. Nagle were good people too, of course, even if I'd become increasingly nervous about Judge Nagle's demeanor.

Henry said that I was imagining things, but with every passing Sunday, Judge Nagle seemed a little cooler toward us—toward Henry in particular. That made perfect sense to me. Henry borrowed all of that money two years earlier, and he'd promised to repay it by the coming harvest. The judge would know as well as anyone that we had almost no chance of doing that now.

I swallowed the lump in my throat as the service began. Pastor Williams was in good form, bringing yet another variation on the theme of the times. *Keep faith. God is in control.* Every Sunday it was a similar angle, because what else was there to say to people who were suffering so immensely? Our whole economy ran off produce, and after so many failed crops, farmers had long since run out of savings and were down to their last ounce of faith. The main street of Oakden was one long row of boarded-up windows because all but the most essential stores had already gone bust. I saw how empty the collection plate was each week, and yet every Sunday, Pastor Williams took to that pulpit to thunder about resilience and hope and faith.

"Bow your heads and pray with me," he said, at the end of the sermon. But as I bowed my head, I glanced across the aisle and felt a chill run down my spine. Everyone else was praying, but Judge Nagle was staring at Henry.

The judge wasn't angry. He was heartbroken. Somehow, that was worse.

I tried to talk to Henry as we made our way out to lunch, but my brother was busy chatting up the older ladies in church. When I caught his arm, he waved me off impatiently. Being the most handsome and popular boy in town, Henry got a little vacation at church from the stress and isolation on the farm. Most weeks I was content to just find a quiet corner to wait for him to finish charming his way through conversations.

"Miss Davis. You look so lovely today," a deep voice said. I glanced impatiently toward the source of the voice and found Chad Glass—a boy a few years older than me. He was handsome enough and polite enough, but he was also a mechanic. The last person on earth I'd want to date was someone who didn't even have a farm to offer me.

"Thank you, Chad. Please excuse me," I said, stepping around him to chase after Henry.

But my footsteps slowed when I saw that he was with Judge Nagle. The two exchanged some quiet words in the vestibule. Then Henry sucked in a breath as he followed Judge Nagle out the door. I walked briskly after them—reaching the door just in time to see them crossing the street and disappearing together into the courthouse across the road.

I hesitated for a split second before I slipped from the church, jogging unsteadily in Mother's old shoes until I stood beneath the windows of Judge Nagle's office. At first I couldn't hear anything, but a sudden sliding sound fixed that—the judge was muttering about the heat and had opened the window. That allowed me to hear the low murmur of voices.

"...son, I understand. But I know you've seen Main Street. More than half of the businesses gone bust are in buildings I hold mortgages on. I still have to pay the bank, but no one is paying me rent. I can't even sell those stores because this town is dying. I need you to repay me that money. All of it. Some of it. Whatever you can come up with."

"I'm really sorry, sir," Henry said. I could imagine my brother maintaining eye contact, looking cool and calm, as he started to panic inside. Part of Henry's magic charm was his ability to appear neutral even when he was guilty as hell. "As I'm sure you know, the harvest isn't looking so good this year for us either."

"Surely you have an asset you can sell."

"Sir, we don't even have a tractor anymore. And I tried to sell the car, but no one was buying."

"Then we find ourselves at an impasse," the judge said

heavily. There was a pause. Then his voice was barely above a whisper as he said, "Henry. I don't think you appreciate how desperate I am. It's been almost two years, son. In all of that time you've done no more than throw a few pennies my way—you owe me hundreds of dollars."

"I know, Judge," Henry said urgently. "I'll think of something. I really will."

There was a terse pause. I pressed my hand to my mouth.

"Do you know what would happen if I tried to sue you, Henry?"

"No, sir."

"The case would go before the court in Dalhart. And do you know who the judge is there?"

"No, sir."

"Judge Nolan Wickingham. I'm not saying he'd rule in my favor, Henry, but I am saying I went to law school with him and I was best man at his wedding."

"Sir, I promise you. I'll do everything in my power to pay you back as soon as I can. But I have nothing for you to take even if you did decide to sue me."

"You have land."

"My *father* has land—" Henry corrected him. I could hear the panic in his voice, and I felt it in my chest.

"I'm not so sure Judge Wickingham would see it that way, Henry. That asset will be yours soon enough. Maybe the courts would see fit to pass the land on to me a little early so that I can sell it to recoup my losses."

"Sir," Henry croaked. "I mean no disrespect, but who's buying farmland right now?"

"No one is buying stores in a dying town in the middle of nowhere—but I know I could find someone to take a five-hundred-acre farm off my hands for the right price."

"Sir—*please.*"

"I don't want to do this, Henry. Do you hear me? I need you to find some money somehow or I'll have no choice." I heard sudden movement inside, and, worried that the judge was moving toward the window, I panicked and ran back to the church. I stepped inside just as Mother put her hand on the door, apparently about to come looking for us. She had a plate of food in her other hand.

"Where on earth have you been?" she asked, peering at me in confusion. "You're missing the luncheon. Go quickly before all the good food goes." When I remained frozen in place, catching my breath, she dropped her voice and added, "You know as well as I do this is the best meal you'll have all week. This is not the time to go wandering away!"

I saw Henry and the judge walk into the vestibule a little while later. Henry had Mother's coloring—warm brown hair and skin that tanned instead of burned—but that day, he was as pale as I'd ever seen him. I waved at him and pointed to the chair beside me, where the plate of food I'd fixed for him was waiting. Beads of sweat covered his brow as he moved the plate to sit down.

"Everything okay?" I asked him.

"Everything's just fine," he lied, forcing an unconvincing smile as he began to pick at the food.

The next day, Henry and I went to check on the crop in one of the fields farthest from the house. We rode the horses side by side, their hooves sinking into the thin dust with each step. My cheeks were windburned, and nothing I did seemed to help. I tried smearing them with Vaseline to protect them, but by the time I walked from the house to the barn, the Vaseline was coated in dust. The best I could do was wear a kerchief over the lower part of my face for as much of the day as I could stand. The wind had become relentless, blowing for weeks; the only difference each day was whether it was a gale or a breeze. That day it was somewhere in the middle.

I'd wanted to talk to Henry the previous night, but as determined as I was, he seemed equally determined to avoid me. He'd gone to bed at the same time as Mother and Daddy. Now was my chance.

"I followed you and the judge to the courthouse and listened through the window," I told Henry, deciding it was best to just blurt it out. The only sign he gave that he'd even heard what I said was the way his mouth tightened. "Do you think he's right? Could he really take the farm?"

"This is their game—I don't even know the rules I'm playing by. Maybe Judge Nagle just said he'd take the farm to scare me. He seems as desperate as we are, so I guess that's possible. I just don't even know who to talk to. We can't afford a lawyer of our own. I don't even have a copy of the contract."

"So what do we do?" I asked, feeling queasy. Henry brought his horse to a stop and swung down to the ground. He fetched a small spade from the tool kit he kept on his saddle, and in silence, he started to dig—sending dust flying all over the withered plants in the field. Less than half the seeds had germinated that year, and most of the plants that did died before they even formed seed heads. Our fields contained row after row of patchy and deformed brown stalks. Even the weeds were unusually sparse that year—all the soil seemed able to produce was the occasional patch of Russian thistle or bull nettle. The dead thistles rolled all over the fields in the dust storms, getting stuck on the wire and providing a framework for the dust to settle on, until every fence had disappeared beneath a mound of dirt.

"What are you doing?" I asked Henry, but he kept on digging. He dug until his brow was covered in grime from dust and sweat, until his face was red with exertion. I knew that there was no resistance in the soil. And that didn't change even as Henry dug down twelve inches…two feet…and farther and farther he went, until he was standing in a hole.

After a while, I swung off my horse and stepped closer, touching his shoulder gently to get his attention. Henry looked at me, his eyes wild with panic and rimmed red with sweat and irritation from the dust, and maybe some tears. This wasn't like Henry—he was usually calm as a cucumber, even when he'd messed up.

"Look at this," he said, his voice breaking. "Just look at it, Lizzie. They say that there was damp soil all over these high plains, down at the three-feet mark. It didn't matter how dry the season was—the moisture was always there. But look at this. Just *look at it*."

I looked down at the dusty hole he was standing in.

"No wonder the crops aren't growing," he whispered miserably. "We're trying to grow them in a goddamned desert."

With Henry standing in that hole, for the first time in our lives, I was taller than he was. I clapped my hands onto his shoulders and gently shook him.

"Sorry," he said. He cleared his throat and lifted his chin. "I'm sorry, Lizzie. Don't fret—I promise it's going to be fine. I'll fix this. Maybe I can get a job on an oil field. Or I read in the paper that there were jobs in El Paso on one of those New Deal projects. I'll move away…get a wage. Then we can keep the farm *and* pay him back."

"Henry." Mother and Dad seriously considered letting him go off in search of work after the bad harvest in '31. Dad talked him out of it because he expected things would turn around quickly, and in a good year, or even a reasonable year, it would have been tough to run the farm without Henry. But it was way too late for that. The papers were full of stories of rural folk like us who left their farms, hoping to find better conditions in the cities, only to find things there were a different kind of awful.

"What are we going to do?" I whispered unevenly.

Henry climbed out of the hole. He dusted himself off and he swung himself back up onto the horse.

"The best we can do is go down to the far field and see if there's any good news down there. Then we go back to the house and we'll collect the eggs. We'll feed and water the horses." He nodded, as if he was talking to himself more than me. "Yep, that's it. One foot in front of the other. We'll think only about whatever the next step is and we'll do that over and over for as long as we have to until things get better."

After that day in the field, Henry just stopped talking. He was still working as hard as he always did—always fixing something or building something, making the most of every minute of sunlight. But as soon as the sun went down, he went to bed, and most mornings, I had to wake him up because for the first time in his life, he was sleeping in. He didn't even want to go to church.

One Saturday night, after he'd gone to bed early again, I sat out under the stars on my own, looking up through the lingering dust haze to the stars. I was trying to figure out what to do. I didn't want to alert Mother and Dad to the situation with the judge because I didn't want to betray Henry's confidence, but I couldn't shake the feeling that my brother needed help.

When I heard the door open, I assumed Henry changed his mind about going to bed, but it was Mother who sank into his chair opposite me. I started and almost dropped my mug of Henry's bathtub gin in my haste to hide it.

"Give me some of that," she said.

"It's—uh— Mother—"

"I know about Henry's grain alcohol, Lizzie," she said, making a grabbing motion for the mug. Shocked, I passed it to her, only to be even more shocked when she knocked the whole lot back. She shuddered, then exhaled and rested her head against the back of his chair.

"You think you're like your daddy, don't you?" she said, eyes still closed.

"I am like Daddy," I replied. Everyone always said so. Dad and I were famously quick with a scowl or to point out the negative in a situation, unlike Mother and Henry, who were the sunshine to our rain.

"Honey, you're me all over. You have your dad's hair and his pragmatic nature, but that's about it. You're strong as an ox in body and spirit. Those boys of ours aren't like us."

"I don't know what you mean," I said.

"You and me are survivors, Lizzie. We keep moving forward. We find a way, and if there isn't a way to be found, we make one. Those boys are more inclined to crumble and break than you and I are to even consider giving up."

"Henry isn't like that," I argued. "Henry is like *you*."

"Don't kid yourself, honey. I don't know what's going on with Henry at the moment, but that boy is every bit as tormented as your father is on his worst days."

"Judge Nagle wants the loan settled," I blurted. Mother sucked in a sharp breath. "He's pressuring Henry for money. The judge is having trouble of his own because so many of his tenants have gone bust. He says he might sue Henry to get the farm even though the deed is in Daddy's name. It can't be true, can it?"

"Honey," Mother said gently. "If Dad had been able to get that loan from the bank two years ago, we'd have already lost the farm."

I was startled to realize she was right. Whether the money came from Judge Nagle or from the bank, we still had no way to repay it. I looked out over the moonlit fields and felt a pang of presumptive grief for a loss I hadn't even realized was inevitable. "Mother, I love this place."

"I know, Lizzie. I do too. But you know what I love more?" I looked at her, and in the darkness, I saw the gentle smile she offered me. She reached across and squeezed my hand. "This *family*, honey. Family is everything. I thought I'd already taught you that."

"You did," I said. We weren't the kind of family to say *I love you* or to express our feelings aloud, but she'd taught me in other ways. Even those hours she spent on the bench near the Texas live oak reinforced to me that what mattered in life was to love so deeply that sometimes you were truly tormented by it.

"The weather let us down, not the judge. At least he gave us a chance and he bought us two more years here. We should be grateful to him, not scared of him or angry with him. Knowing the judge as I do, I know he wouldn't be demanding money from us unless he really needed it. I bet he's as distressed about this as we are."

There was strength and dignity in that statement that astounded me. I stared at Mother in the moonlight—all calm and compassionate, even though she'd just acknowledged she was on the verge of losing everything.

"How are you so strong?" I asked.

"That's what I'm trying to tell you, Lizzie. You are just like me. I know they say women are the weaker sex, but there's nothing weak about the women in this family. The strength of generations runs through our veins. It doesn't matter what life throws at us—we find a way to keep going. And it seems to me that those of us who are strong have an obligation to care for others when they aren't." Mother suddenly pushed herself to a standing position. "You aren't going to solve this sitting out here on your own tonight. Let's skip church tomorrow. We can drag Daddy and Henry out for a drive if the weather is good. Maybe they can get some perspective if we get them off the farm."

12

Lizzie

Huntsville, Alabama
1950

I'D HEARD CALVIN USE A SHARP TONE A HAND-ful of times over all of the years of our marriage, but never before had it been directed at me. I didn't quite know how to deal with it.

"What the hell were you thinking?"

"I was thinking that *this* is insanity!" I blurted, pointing to his office window and the civilized party beyond it, still taking place on the lawn just a few hundred feet away. "They just bring a bunch of Nazi families here and let them roam free and think everything is going to be fine?"

"Not every German was a Nazi, Lizzie," he sighed.

"But some of those men *were*," I said quietly. Cal inhaled sharply. "I'm willing to play the game in public, but when it's just you and me, I shouldn't have to pretend I don't know that."

"You call *that* playing the game?" Cal said, waving vaguely toward the window overlooking the party. "This new program is a golden opportunity for Huntsville and it's a golden opportunity for me. I need your support in this." I scoffed impatiently, and Calvin threw his head back in frustration. "Do you even know who you were shouting at down there?"

"Does it matter?" I exclaimed.

"It was Sofie Rhodes, Lizzie. Jürgen Rhodes' wife." *Oh hell.* Out of all the German scientists, there were only a handful that Calvin seemed particularly awed by—and Jürgen Rhodes was right at the top of that list. "He's waited five years for her to join him here, and before I even had the chance to introduce myself, you started an argument with her."

"She started the argument with *me*," I muttered.

"It doesn't matter!" he shouted, and I startled in surprise. Calvin squeezed his eyes closed and drew in a shaky breath. "Lizzie, you're my wife. Even if you can't support me, I need you to pretend you're behind me all the way."

"I am behind you," I snapped. "But you were outraged at all of this too a few years ago. These men didn't change—you did."

I spun on my heel and left his office, slamming the door behind me. My temper ran hot even as I walked from the office building, across the lawn, and back to the party. As I returned, I was pleased to see the Rhodes family walking across the lawn toward the cars. It felt a little like Sofie Rhodes was running from our argument, and that was infinitely satisfying.

But Brianna was crying, sitting awkwardly on Becca's lap, her face pressed into her mother's neck. My heart contracted at the sight of her. Over the years, I had grown so fond of Brianna, and her sister Ava too.

"What's all this?" I asked her, taking the seat beside Becca. Brianna pointed to a nasty scrape on her knee.

"That German girl pushed me over."

Just as my anger started to fade, it burst back. Becca was shaking her head in disgust.

"I didn't see it but Avril did. She said some Kraut kid came barreling around the tree and just pushed Bri over. She didn't even apologize."

"Typical," I muttered, shaking my head. I brushed a lock of Brianna's hair back from her face and said quietly, "Don't you worry about it, honey. You just stay away from those kids, okay? They'll be at your school this week, but you don't have to play with them. It's not right that they're here. You're a nice girl, so I know you want people to like you, but you don't have to go along with something when you know it's not right."

The sun was low in the sky as I parked in the driveway, but the lights were out in Henry's apartment above our garage. Calvin would soon follow me in his own car once he finished saying goodbye to the guests. He was still angry with me and I hated that, but I wasn't sure what to do about it.

I found Henry in my kitchen. A pot of potatoes was bubbling furiously on the back burner, and on the front, he was frying chicken.

"Mmm," I said, surprised. "That smells good."

"I was bored, so I thought I'd cook us some dinner," he said, looking down at the pan. "How were the Nazis?"

"Terrible," I muttered, throwing my keys and handbag onto the table. "One of their kids pushed little Brianna clean over and then refused to say sorry, and one of the women actually picked a fight with me."

Henry looked up at me in alarm.

"Who picked a fight with you?"

"You know how Cal keeps talking about Jürgen Rhodes? The man who designed those V-2 rockets that did so much damage to London?" Henry nodded. "Well, I was talking to Becca, and then his wife started yelling at me about—" I broke off. It was all a bit fuzzy, my memory blurred by the champagne and the anger I'd felt. "Something about how segregation is the same as the extermination camps." I paused. That wasn't quite it, but it was close enough.

Henry stared at me, his jaw open but his eyes a little glazed, like he wasn't quite following the conversation.

"Segregation *is* terrible," he said.

"I know," I sighed. Having lived in El Paso for years, I was no stranger to bigotry. Half of that city was Mexican or of Mexican descent, and white folk often acted like that was a bad thing. Huntsville was like two separate towns that happened to be colocated, and it seemed that having poorly treated Black staff members within a household was just the normal order of business for some. I hated it. Not that I was about to admit that to Sofie Rhodes.

"My division liberated a camp in Germany," Henry said suddenly, turning his attention back to the chicken.

It was my turn to feel dazed. Henry spoke so rarely about his deployment that I'd given up asking about it a long time ago.

"You did?" I said, stunned.

"It was April, like now," he murmured, almost to himself. "There were wildflowers growing on the side of the road as we advanced and that morning I was thinking about Betsy. A few years after I enlisted, I wrote her and asked how she was. She wrote me back and told me she'd married a man and was expecting a baby. I bet that baby is real cute but I was glad she didn't send me a photograph."

"You never told me any of that."

"I wanted her to know I'd found my feet, you know? That I thought of her fondly and always would. And ever since that first letter, she's written to me every few months. If I'd found a way to marry her, I'd have picked those wildflowers in Germany and preserved them to bring them home to her."

"And…the camp?" I prompted gently. He reached for the tongs, then lifted a piece of chicken out of the pan to rest on a plate. "Henry?" I prompted.

The front door slammed and Henry startled. He dropped the tongs and accidentally touched the hot plate when he tried to pick them up, then cried out with pain and panic as he looked to the kitchen door as an unsuspecting Calvin appeared.

Since Henry's troubles began, I'd come to suspect he had what they called combat fatigue, although I'd never been able to get him to see a doctor. One day, I went to the library in El Paso to find some information. One of the books the librarian gave me said that when a man had combat fatigue, the trauma of war didn't return to him as memories, but as reactions. In moments like that one at the stove, it really did seem that Henry's brain had been switched off and every move he made was pure, unfiltered instinct.

"Henry?" I said softly, but he was still looking around the room like he wasn't sure where he was. I spoke louder, stepping closer to him again, trying to get his attention. "Henry! Are you okay? Honey, I'm right here with you."

"What's going on?" Calvin asked, concerned. Henry pushed past me and Cal—stomping down the hall and out the back door toward his apartment, slamming the screen door behind him. Calvin looked at me, scanning for injuries. "Did he hurt you?"

"Of course he didn't hurt me!" I snapped.

Five long years had passed since the war ended. Most of the time I thought I'd come to accept that Henry would never again be like he was, but every now and again, I discovered I had to grieve all over again. I pointed after my brother as I glared at Calvin and said, "This is what those bastards did to him. And Christopher seriously thinks I'm going to invite them over here for coffee?"

"You know I don't mind helping Henry—however and whenever we can. But if having the Germans in town is too much for him, we should try to find him somewhere else to stay, because these people are not going anywhere."

We stared at one another—the space between us thick with tension—and then Calvin sighed miserably and left the kitchen, as if he couldn't bear to keep arguing with me. I understood. I hated arguing with Calvin too.

I already felt enough guilt at the unusual nature of our marriage. I hated to add to it by finding myself on the other side of a disagreement with no easy solution.

But this was too important. The injustice of the situation was just too great for me to ignore, not even to please my husband.

When I went to check on Henry in his room an hour later, he was lying on the bed, staring at the wall.

"Are you all right?" I asked him tentatively.

"Yeah," he said. His voice was still hoarse. "Sorry for all that."

"You've seemed so much better lately," I said quietly. Henry had been flat and irritable at Christmas, but since returning a few weeks ago, even Cal remarked how much calmer he seemed. Henry sighed, shrugging noncommittally. "Is your hand okay?"

He rolled toward me and lifted his fist. The skin on his knuckles was busted and there was a purple bruise forming. I was confused at first. I'd been asking about the burn from the stove, but this was something else.

"How did you do that?"

"Sorry," he whispered, pointing to the wall beside the door.

I turned and saw the four jagged holes he'd punched in the drywall. I swallowed a gasp. "I'll fix it up when I get my next paycheck."

"Don't you even worry about it," I said, but my voice was strained. For all of Henry's troubles over the years, that kind of destructive violence was new, and I wasn't quite sure what to make of it.

I patted him gently on the shoulder and rose to leave the room, but as I took my first steps, he said, "Lizzie?"

"Yeah?"

"It's not right," he said. "Those people coming here after what they did. I sometimes walk past Sauerkraut Hill and there are some real nice houses there. It really worries me that the families in those blocks around them might not realize who their new neighbors really are. And besides, why have those men been given such cushy jobs working with the very Army that lost so many good men defeating them?"

"I know, Henry," I sighed.

"Why did they come here, anyway?"

"The men didn't have a choice in the beginning," I reminded him. "They were brought to America as prisoners. But they do have it pretty good here now. Why would they leave?"

He sighed too and rolled away from me, staring at the wall again.

"It's just not right," he murmured. "It's just not right."

I agreed, but as I left his apartment, I was only grateful that Henry didn't know the half of it.

13

Sofie
Berlin, Germany
1933

A FEW DAYS AFTER THE ELECTION RESULTS WERE announced, I took the children to visit Jürgen's great-aunt Adele. As I opened the gate between our courtyards, Laura was on my hip, chewing on her fist and drooling all over my shoulder. Georg ran ahead, stopping to inspect some chamomile blossoming along the edge of a garden bed. He bent to pick a bunch, then, clutching the stems tightly in his chubby fist, toddled along in front of me, making a beeline for the entrance to Adele's apartment. When we found her setting up morning tea at the eat-in table in her kitchen, Georg ran toward her to show her the flowers.

"Oma!" he greeted her. Georg had seen Adele most every day of his life—but every time we stepped into her house, he seemed surprised to find her there. "Flower. Blue flower."

"These are *white* flowers, Georg," she said. Adele made

a great show of taking the makeshift posy and inhaling the scent as if it were a rose. She rested the bouquet on the table, then scooped my daughter from my hip and promptly pressed a hard ginger cookie into her hand. "Chew on that. It'll help with those sore gums."

I had no idea how old Adele was. She said it was impolite to ask, and if anyone tried to, she refused to answer. She was Jürgen's late grandmother's eldest sister, and he guessed that she was in her late seventies or maybe early eighties. Adele religiously wore a hat outside even in the winter, and her face was surprisingly smooth. Her long white hair was invariably wound into a bun or, for special occasions, elaborate braids.

Like Mayim, she was a part of the circle of our little family. Adele adored Mayim and Jürgen, and she all but worshipped my children. Her feelings for me were obviously more complicated.

"Why Sofie?" I overheard her ask Jürgen when he and I first started dating. "She's spoiled. Shallow."

"She's wonderful," Jürgen said simply, and although that warmed me, the knowledge that Adele did not approve of our relationship hung over our courtship in the early years.

Jürgen was seven when his family home in Freiburg was bombed in the dying days of the Great War. His parents and infant sister, Ilsa, perished. Adele was in Berlin, on the other side of Germany, grieving the loss of her own family—both of her sons and her beloved husband, Alfred, were all killed at the front. "Three miserable telegrams over three miserable months, and then I was alone," she told me.

But then a fourth telegram arrived. This one was from a friend of Jürgen's parents, and it informed Adele that Jürgen had been orphaned and she was the only family they could find who might care for him. Adele's sister, Jürgen's grandmother, passed years before, and until that telegram arrived,

Adele didn't realize her nephew had married and had a family of his own.

Still, she had her driver take her to collect Jürgen the next day—ten long hours in a car, traversing the country. She had cared for him ever since. Even now that he was an adult with a family of his own, she still sometimes babied him.

Over the years, I'd made some kind of peace with Adele's reluctance to embrace me. I'd also made peace with the reality that I had an obligation to care for her anyway. She had been a godsend to my husband, and that meant I was going to do my best to be a godsend to her, whether she liked it or not.

"How are you?" I asked her, and she rolled her eyes at me, as if the very question were absurd.

"Just fine," she said, quickly turning her attention to Laura. She tickled Laura's cheek, and my daughter gave a grin, opening her mouth so wide that the inflamed buds of her new teeth were visible on her lower gum. "Where's our Mayim today?"

"She seemed anxious. I suggested she go visit with her parents."

"Ah, that is good," Adele said, nodding in satisfaction but also surprise, as if it were a great miracle that I'd done something that pleased her. "She needs them, and they need her as we wait to see what the great buffoon is going to do to this country."

I walked around the table to fill her kettle with water. Once I'd set it on the stove, I turned back to try to reassure her with words I didn't quite believe myself.

"We'll probably be back at the polls before we know it and common sense will prevail. We just have to be calm and patient."

"Don't you dare come into my house and speak to me like I'm a senile old fool, Sofie von Meyer Rhodes." Adele gently rested Laura on a rug on the floor beside Georg, then dropped herself heavily into a chair at the kitchen table as she shot me a sharp look. "Even if there were another election tomorrow, those Nazis wouldn't honor the results. They started as thugs in 1920 and they have done nothing but stir up instability ever since. I am old enough to know that history is not an archive—it is a crystal ball. People don't change, and political parties change even less than that. From the Party's very inception, its intent has been clear. They plan to segregate Jews from Aryan society and to strip them of their rights."

"We just have to stay calm and keep level heads," I repeated. I had plenty of practice ignoring Adele's rants and her tendency toward hasty judgment. "There isn't anything we can do about it now anyway."

Adele sighed wearily, then turned her attention back to the children, seated on the rug beside her.

"I only care for the sake of you young people, you know. Hopefully God will take me soon and I can be with Alfred and our boys, but you and these babies have a lot of living left to do, and so does Mayim and her family. I just can't see how a man like Hitler can bring anything but chaos, especially for the Jews."

"We could talk about this all day and we still won't solve it. Let's talk about something more pleasant."

"Actually, there are some other unpleasant matters that you and I must discuss," Adele said. Then she tilted her head at me. "I've been waiting for an opportunity to talk alone. Don't think I haven't noticed your artwork and furniture vaporizing over the last six months. I know things are tough for you and Jürgen. He tells me that you are determined to hold on to your family home, and I understand that better than most."

Like me, Adele had grown up in a family of considerable wealth, and Alfred made a comfortable living for them both.

But Adele unexpectedly found herself with a young child to care for right when the hyperinflation crisis began.

She laid off her personal staff, and when that wasn't enough to stabilize her financial situation, she remodeled, converting her family's expansive ancestral home into apartments. She kept the smallest of these for herself and Jürgen and rented out the rest. Her apartment now comprised only the back part of the ground floor of her building. Her front living room was a studio apartment occupied by an elderly Bavarian couple, and her entryway and stairwell were common space for all of her tenants.

Adele was left with her original kitchen, a bathroom, and her bedroom—and most importantly, private access to her courtyard. She converted that space into something of a miniature farm, keeping chickens and rabbits, and a small collection of fruit trees, berries and vegetables growing in boxes and tubs. Adele had a network of widowed friends all across the city, and in the worst times, I'd watched a seemingly endless stream of silver-haired women visiting each day, leaving with a basket of produce. I once saw Adele's best friend, Martha Breuer, holding a box as she waited for the trolley. As I approached her, one slender gray ear appeared from the top.

"Is that a rabbit?" I said blankly.

"Two," she chuckled.

"Where on earth are you taking those?" I asked her, and Martha shrugged.

"There's a poor family on my block with a new baby on the way. Adele insisted I take this breeding pair of rabbits for them. They'll have fresh meat for the babe next summer."

Adele was savvy, hardworking, stubborn, and compassionate. It stung sometimes that she seemed capable of boundless love for strangers, but she still seemed to have little affection for me.

"Sofie, you and I also know that my nephew is a man of great intelligence…but he is not without his limitations." Adele sighed heavily. "We both know he's unlikely to ever find work outside of academia, and even when the economy stabilizes, your family income will be modest. What is your plan for the future?"

"We're getting by," I said stiffly. But she wasn't wrong about Jürgen's employment prospects. His undergraduate focus was engineering and physics, but he'd focused his postgraduate studies narrowly around rockets—a technology that remained in its infancy. The last time I went to a space society launch, I'd watched the little prototype fly as high as forty or fifty feet, then tilt alarmingly to fall right back down toward the group of men who'd designed it, sending them all scattering in a panic. No one was going to pay him to play with dangerous toys.

"Why don't you take whatever money you have left and remodel, as I did? You could sell or rent the top floors as apartments."

"No one is buying apartments now, Aunt Adele," I pointed out.

"A house is always worth something, Sofie, even in a bad market," she said patronizingly. "Now, if you were *really* smart, you could sell the whole lot and move in here."

"Are some of your tenants leaving?"

"No one is leaving," she said abruptly. "I meant you could move into this apartment with me. It would be a little cramped—"

"A little cramped?" I repeated incredulously. When Jürgen was a child, she gave him the sole bedroom while she slept on the sofa in her kitchen. Did she think I could put my children in her bathtub to sleep each night? "Aunt Adele, that's a very generous offer, but it's just not practical. We wouldn't fit here. And where would Mayim go?"

"She'd have to go home, of course, but the rest of you could live here for free. You could live off the profit from the sale of your home for a long time if you were careful with it, regardless of what happens with Jürgen's job—"

"Father borrowed against the villa when the market was high," I interrupted her, flushing. "If we sell it now, we lose my family home and we still walk away with a debt. All we can do is hold on and hope things turn around."

"Wishful thinking is not a plan—"

"But wishful thinking is all I have left," I snapped. I spun back to the kettle and moved it off the heat too fast, splashing drops of scalding water onto my skin. I cursed and dropped the kettle into the sink, then ran cold water over my hand. Small, angry spots appeared on my skin, but it wasn't a bad burn—my pride hurt more than my hand. Adele rose, approached me slowly, and peered over my shoulder at my hand.

"You know it is my intention to die in this house, just as I was born here. But, Sofie, attachment to our family homes doesn't mean we can't adapt. You simply must find a better way forward."

I didn't stay for tea. I packed the children up and left to nurse my aching wrist and my bruised pride at home.

When Karl invited us to meet him and Lydia for a picnic on Saturday morning, Jürgen and I were of two minds about accepting their invitation.

"He might have news about this job, and it would be good to know one way or another," Jürgen said heavily. "Besides, I want to ask them what their thoughts are on these new laws." The Nazi government utilized the Enabling Act and passed the Law for Rectification of the Distress of Nation and Reich. It allowed the chancellor and his cabinet to create legislation and to enshrine it in law without the support of the parliament.

Hitler argued that this was necessary to bring stability, but to me it seemed increasingly apparent that whatever instability we were suffering from was by his design and at his pleasure.

"What if we don't like their answers?" I said hesitantly.

"Then at least we'll know the friendship is over," Jürgen sighed.

That was how we found ourselves spread out on a rug beneath an ancient red oak tree in the park between our homes, eating rye bread thick with cultured butter and salami with soft cheese. Karl and Lydia left their young twins, Horst and Ernst, at home with their nanny, but Georg and their four-year-old son, Hans, were running circles around the rug. I invited Mayim, but she opted to stay home with Laura.

We spent a few minutes catching up—discussing the children's antics and swapping pleasantries. Lydia and Karl were both profusely apologetic for their unavailability over the past few months.

"This country has been adrift for far too long. We knew we needed to do our part to ensure our national future," Lydia offered by way of explanation.

"How do you feel about...?" I began. Then I broke off. It felt so awkward to raise the subject of the new government's tolerance for violence against the Jews, and I wasn't quite sure why that was, given I'd always thought of Karl and Lydia as reasonable people, and I was still hopeful they were as quietly as horrified by it all as Jürgen and I were. I tried again. "I was wondering what your thoughts are on..."

"You're concerned about the new laws, especially in the context of the Nazi racial policies, aren't you?" Karl said, flashing me a gentle smile. I nodded, and he added, "Aligning oneself with a political party always requires a degree of compromise."

"You aren't concerned that Hitler now rules a dictatorship?" Jürgen asked skeptically. Karl shook his head.

"The parliament is so hostile to this new government— how else could the Party bring stability but to bypass them?"

"He promised to restore law and order," Lydia reminded us. "That's a difficult thing to achieve without a few hard decisions along the way."

"And these reports of the SA barricading Jewish businesses? Of harassment of Jews on the streets? The book burnings?" Jürgen frowned. "What do you make of these things?"

"Some incidents were real—but the rest of what you speak of is mostly rumors." Karl shrugged. "You know how whispers spread, especially in certain communities."

"Which communities do you mean, Karl?" I asked, frowning.

"Would you look at that," Lydia said suddenly, and we all followed her gaze to where Hans and Georg were seated side by side on the ground, a little collection of stones between them. "Sofie, we must get Hans and Georg together more. They'll grow up to be dear friends, just as the four of us are." Karl turned to look at them too, and he smiled softly at the sight. But Jürgen and I exchanged a glance. The conversation was clearly over, but I didn't feel reassured at all.

"What were you and Karl talking about today when you walked away from us? Did he mention the job?" I asked Jürgen later that night, once we were in bed. He had been unusually quiet through dinner. When Georg made silly faces and Mayim and I gave him the laughs he so clearly expected, Jürgen barely managed a smile.

But we'd been married long enough for me to know that Jürgen needed the cover of darkness to open up about his worries. And the minute my head hit the pillow, my curiosity got the better of me.

"Do you remember a few weeks before the election, when the space society held our last launch?" Jürgen asked.

"I do."

"Karl brought an audience without warning us. It turns out the men were senior officials in the Nazi party."

That startled me. I sat up and flicked on my bedside lamp, then turned to frown down at him. Jürgen also sat up and retrieved his glasses from the table on his side of the bed. We stared at one another.

"Did you know who they were at the time?"

"No, I didn't—but I was humiliated, and frankly, irritated with Karl for bringing anyone at all. Besides, it didn't seem to matter much at the time." Jürgen drew in a deep breath. "Only it turns out the Nazis want to establish their own rocket program. Karl told me today that the position he's been hinting at would be with a new division within Army Ordnance."

"A job? In *rockets*?" I was so startled by this, I couldn't hide my shock.

"You've never taken my work seriously," Jürgen said abruptly. He was right—I had not. But for good reason.

"Your rockets explode without warning at least half the time! Including this exact launch we're discussing, if I remember correctly. Isn't that what happened?" He didn't reply, so I pushed again. "It floated—"

"It *flew*, Sofie. Rockets don't *float*. They are propelled with force—"

"—for fifteen seconds. Then it exploded. Didn't you say that a chunk of debris hit one of the other space society members and burned a hole in his coat?" At this, Jürgen fell silent. I sighed impatiently. "I'm allowed to be a little skeptical. You're talking about flying to the moon with something that can't get more than a few feet off the ground."

"Do you really think I'd have invested these years into

rocketry if it wasn't a viable technology? At present, our prototypes aren't reliable, but inevitably they will be perfected.
Every failed launch is an experiment we can learn from."

"Have they offered jobs to everyone in the rocket group?"

"Karl and I to start with, although I suspect others will be
approached soon. As keen as Karl is on rockets, he's no scientist. He will handle the business aspects of the program, and
they want me to lead the technical side."

"And the ultimate goal is to send a man into space?" I clarified, because this still seemed so unlikely I could barely believe my ears. The rockets Jürgen's group experimented with
weren't just unreliable—they were toy sized.

"There's a possibility that they have an ulterior motive."

"What else could they possibly want them for?"

"Sofie. Think about the launches you've been to. Half the
time, the rockets explode, don't they?" I stared at him blankly,
and he prompted, "They *explode*...just like a bomb. That's an
unfortunate side effect of the fuel's volatility. But just imagine what they could do if we were to intentionally use them
as explosive devices."

To me they always seemed like dangerous toys, foolish toys.
But in an instant, I understood that in the wrong hands, those
"toys" could have a distinctly dark purpose. Jürgen's friends
were very careful when handling the rockets, but even so, from
time to time someone suffered an injury. The best launch they
had ever achieved stayed in the air for a full five minutes before it exploded, but it exploded nonetheless.

"You think they want to...*weaponize* them?"

"An attempt at reaching space makes some sense in terms
of rebuilding our international reputation. Simply getting a
device to the edge of the atmosphere would attract world-
wide praise."

"It would be incredible," I whispered. "But is that possible?"

"With the right team and the right budget, I'm confident we could produce rockets capable of traveling many miles."

"How many miles?"

I could almost see the cogs turning in his mind as he considered this. After a moment, he said, "The moon is 200,000 miles away, and although I still believe it can be done, I'm not convinced I'll see it in my lifetime. The edge of space is around sixty miles… With enough money and a few decades of development, that's likely possible. The problem is that even in designing a rocket that can travel sixty miles vertically, we'd have inadvertently designed an explosive device that could land far from its launch point." At my blank look, he explained patiently, "Gravity is an immensely powerful force. They'd only need to develop ways to manage the angle of the fall so they could target the impact point. It's a hideous thought, but a well-designed rocket could bomb countries some distance away, without requiring a pilot."

"But we are prohibited from rearmament. Under the terms of the Treaty of Versailles. And exploding rockets…*bombs*…"

"Ah, you see—that's the trick, isn't it? The Treaty doesn't mention rockets," Jürgen sighed. "Only a handful of people in the world had even heard of the concept in 1919, when the Treaty was written."

"Oh."

"If representatives of any other chancellor of our lifetime made me this job offer, I'd have accepted that a space mission was the goal, probably without thinking twice."

"For as long as I've known you, you've always imagined that one day someone would pay you to work on these prototypes."

"My income from the university is unpredictable at best now. I'm not a great teacher, but I could be great at this. And we're at real risk of losing this house. But despite all of that…"

"It's too risky," I finished quietly. "If you took the job and the

Nazis told you to turn them into bombs, it would be too late to protest." Jürgen nodded. He seemed relieved that I quickly realized this too. The door closed the minute it opened, but I was apparently keen to torture myself, because I asked, "Did Karl mention the salary?"

"The budget is virtually limitless. The salary is commensurate with the importance of my unique set of interests and skills. They are setting up at Kummersdorf, but they'd give me a car for the commute. They'd even pay for me to complete my doctoral dissertation while I worked. But if this technology works the way I imagine, it could be co-opted into the most destructive weapon man has ever seen. I'd be placing that power into the hands of a regime that already terrifies me."

We fell into silence. After a while, Jürgen asked me to turn the light out. We shuffled into a new position, side by side, hands entwined. I lay staring at the ceiling for a long time. As the alarm clock beside our bed clicked over to 1:00 a.m., Jürgen cleared his throat.

"I'm sorry. I want to give you everything—to provide the kind of life you and Georg and Laura deserve," he whispered. "But the risks are just too great." After a moment, his hand tightened on mine. "You understand that, don't you?"

"Of course I do," I whispered sadly.

"The Nazis are dangerous, my love."

"I told you right away. I know you can't take the job…" He shook his head and I trailed off, frowning. "Well, what do you mean?"

"I just want to make sure we're on the same page about this in case they try to assert some pressure to force our hand," Jürgen said gently.

"What makes you think they would do that?" I said, alarmed.

"There are few people in Germany who *could* do this job.

It's even more reason for me to say no, but we need to understand that they may not like it if I do."

"Whatever happens," I promised, "I support your decision."

It was an easy promise to make in the dark of night, when we had no idea that the decision had already been made for us.

14

Lizzie

Huntsville, Alabama
1950

CAL WAS A CIVILIAN AERONAUTICAL ENGINEER with the Fort Bliss experimental aviation division through the war. After it ended, he was quietly promoted to a classified project so secretive that, at first, he wouldn't tell me a single thing about it.

I was too easily deterred from pushing him for the details, distracted as I was by Henry's behavior after the war. The rest of the world was celebrating, but my brother was sleeping at all hours of the day and night, and irritable whenever I tried to encourage him to get out of the house. Then came the drinking, and after that, he started disappearing for days, returning broke or beaten up, or sometimes just beaten down.

After a year, Henry told me he needed to stand on his own two feet, and announced that he was leaving El Paso. I tried to convince him to stay, and Cal tried too, but Henry was determined that he knew what was best for him. We were worried, but he was an adult. We had to let him go.

Only after Henry left did Calvin finally tell me the truth about his new job. He was supervising a handful of highly trained, specialized scientists captured in Germany after the war ended, brought to America under the Operation Paperclip program.

I knew right away that something was rotten about that arrangement. Even if my common sense didn't tell me that inviting a bunch of German scientists to America was a bad idea, Calvin's tense, uneasy tone did.

"There's a dossier on each of them," he said heavily. "I've read them all, and they suggest that these men were geniuses and spent the entire war making scientific discoveries. Apparently their hands are clean."

"But you don't believe that's true."

Cal pushed his glasses up and rubbed his eyes.

"No one can know what I'm about to tell you, Lizzie. It has to stay between you and me."

"Of course."

"It's just too convenient. I asked Newsome when he was in town last week. At first he insisted the dossiers were completely accurate. Only when I really pushed him did he admit the truth. It seems some...maybe *most*...of the German scientists we're working with *were* active in the Nazi party. He's even seen evidence that some of the senior scientists were officers in the SS."

My mouth went dry. I followed the news about the Nuremberg trials so closely it was borderline unhealthy. I knew all too well what kinds of evil the SS had been responsible for.

"Those Germans must have lied to our officials! Our government would never knowingly allow anyone like that to come here," I whispered sickly.

"Truman only allowed Operation Paperclip to proceed on the condition that no Nazi party members were included. But the skill these men have to offer us is so valuable. Even the junior Germans I'm working with are skilled far beyond any of the Americans on my team. One senior German scientist was deemed to be so important, a team of US soldiers was sent into Berlin to capture him before the dust settled on the German capitulation. American lives were put at risk to secure that man's knowledge. I can easily imagine officials at the Office of the Army Secretary looking at someone like him and deciding to whitewash his history."

"Christopher Newsome can't be comfortable with this," I said uneasily.

"He said he's come around to see the logic in it. He believes that those who were mixed up in the Party were probably forced to join."

"Forced," I scoffed. "There's no circumstance on earth that would have convinced you or me to join the Nazi party."

Calvin gave me a helpless look.

"That's exactly what I said."

"Don't you have a right to know who you are working with? These men could be murderers, Calvin," I pressed.

"I'm frustrated and concerned, sure. But I guess I have to remind myself that these Germans are locked up on base and no threat to anyone at Fort Bliss. We can learn from them now, then ship them home to face trial later, if that's what the situation calls for."

But over the years, more and more German scientists were brought across the Atlantic. And as the size of the team expanded, their privileges expanded too, until the Germans lived and worked on base but were free to do as they pleased. Calvin protested this fiercely—but his pleas fell on deaf ears.

"So…will these men still face trial once they finish sharing their knowledge with you?" I asked Calvin one day.

"I thought that was the plan, but…it's looking like they'll be offered permanent jobs. Maybe even citizenship."

"But you said…you said some were probably party members. Some might even have been SS officers!" I exclaimed furiously. "We can't just let them become Americans. What happened to justice for their victims?"

"I'm not thrilled about it either, Lizzie. But these men really can change the world. Their skills and knowledge can be the foundation of a space program. Space! One of the senior scientists is convinced we can get a man to the moon, and you know what? I'm starting to believe him."

"The moon?" I repeated, staring at him in disbelief.

"Working with these men? Yes. This is the opportunity of a lifetime," he said passionately. "I've done nothing remarkable with my life, Lizzie. We don't even have children. But if we can learn to accept the moral compromise of working with these Germans, I could go down in history as the man who took this country to space. This could be my legacy. Tell me you understand."

Ours was a complicated relationship, but I adored my husband and I wanted to please him. I could see that he wanted my approval, but I couldn't give that to him—and it turned out, he didn't really need it.

I begged him to look for another job, but he stayed with the program anyway. And for the first time in over eleven years of marriage, we found ourselves on the opposite sides of a moral divide, with no common ground to be found.

15

Sofie
Berlin, Germany
1933

WE WERE EATING DINNER WHEN A KNOCK CAME at the front door. The children had been fussing, and Mayim and Jürgen had taken turns tending to them, but I'd just finished my meal, so I motioned toward my plate as I rose.

"I'll get it."

"Are we expecting anyone?" Jürgen asked. I shook my head and pulled the front door open. I was startled to find Karl on the doorstep, carrying a small model rocket mounted on a stand. A few days had passed since Jürgen told Karl he would not take the job. We'd both been surprised at how easily Karl accepted the refusal—but my heart sank now, realizing he hadn't accepted it at all. Karl flashed me a charming smile.

"Mrs. von Meyer Rhodes," he said playfully. "How are you this evening?"

It had been reasonably easy to keep Lydia and Karl out of

our house since we'd laid off the staff. The park between our homes was usually a better option anyway, given our house had only the small courtyard, and Hans and Georg both loved to run. When that approach failed, I always suggested their house. It was easily twice the size of ours, set on acres of gardens, and Lydia was always happy to host.

I knew that Karl and Lydia would find out about our financial problems sooner or later, but I was determined to put it off as long as possible. With Karl arriving unannounced for the first time ever, I feared the moment had finally come.

"Karl, we weren't expecting you," I said. His charming smile did not shift one bit.

"I know. And I am sorry to just drop in unannounced like this. I was hoping you and Jürgen might give me a few moments of your time."

"The house is a bit of a mess, Karl..."

That much, at least, was true.

"Sofie, please understand that I'm here as a friend first and foremost, even though I am also here on official business. I wasn't permitted to offer Jürgen the job until he was thoroughly investigated. I was as surprised as anyone to learn of your financial problems." At my look of alarm, he raised a hand as if to pacify me, and his gaze softened. "I'm here to help, my friend. We both know you cannot afford for him to refuse this position."

"Why don't you go wait in Jürgen's study?" I said heavily, motioning toward the doorway off the hall.

"Hello, Karl," Jürgen said as he appeared behind me.

"I'll go make some tea—" I started to say, but Karl stopped me.

"Actually, Sofie, I was hoping you'd join us."

I frowned, glancing between him and Jürgen, who gave me a bewildered shrug.

"I'll just ask Mayim to watch the children."

By the time I returned to the study, Karl and Jürgen were seated opposite one another by the window. That little model rocket was now sitting atop Jürgen's bookshelf. I glanced at it as I pushed the door closed.

Karl followed my gaze. "This was one of our earliest prototypes at the space society," he said. "It misfired, remember?" Jürgen nodded slowly. "I kept it, thinking that once we perfected the technology, you and I could look back at that model and marvel at how far we'd come. When you called me a few days ago, it occurred to me it might make a nice gift, so I had it mounted." His gaze shifted to Jürgen. "I wanted to remind you of the dream we've shared for all of these years."

I forced a smile, but Jürgen still looked somber. I took the seat beside him and he immediately reached for my hand.

"I told you on the phone," Jürgen said quietly. "This job isn't for me. I'm happy at the university. We are getting by—"

"That's simply not true and we all know it, so can we just drop the pretense?" Karl said impatiently. "Let's focus on the bigger picture—bigger than your finances. Can you imagine the way the world would react if we were to achieve the first space flight? If you won't take this job to solve your family's financial woes, then do it for your country. Jürgen, you could be instrumental in restoring our reputation on the international stage."

"Could you guarantee that any potential rockets this program created would never be weaponized?" Jürgen asked bluntly. I held my breath as I turned my gaze to Karl, who answered calmly.

"We are prohibited from rearming by the Treaty of Versailles."

"I'm not a fool, Karl."

It was rare for my mild-mannered husband to raise his voice, and I jumped. Karl stared back at him impassively.

"I'm saying it as plainly as I can. The goal is *space*," he said flatly. "This isn't a job developing rockets for the Nazis— certainly not a job developing weapons for Hitler. It's just like taking a job as a town planner for the City of Berlin, or as secretary for the Department of Health—you'll be working for the people of Germany, not whomever the current government happens to be." I could see Jürgen was unconvinced—his lips remained pursed, his shoulders stiffly locked. We sat in silence for a long, tense moment—then Karl's tone abruptly softened as he pleaded with us. "Jürgen—Sofie. Just promise me you'll think it over, okay? This is the chance of a lifetime. As your friend, I can't bear to watch you let it pass you by, especially now that I know how badly you two need the money."

Jürgen caught my eye, and I gave a subtle shake of my head. That Karl was pushing this hard only reinforced my feeling that this job was not a smart move for Jürgen. I saw the relief in my husband's eyes.

"I'm sorry, Karl," Jürgen said. "This job is not for me."

Karl seemed frustrated, but he stood and Jürgen and I followed him to the front door. There, he paused.

"I am your friend, and I understand your decision. I just hope you both realize there may be others who do not."

Less than an hour after he left for work the next day, Jürgen returned home, calling out to me as he came through the front door. I found him in his study standing at his desk, staring down into a large box, a distant expression on his face.

"What on earth are you doing home so early?"

"Professor Koch said it came from above his head. Above the dean's head, even. He said they had no choice but to let me go."

"Who gave them no choice?" I said tightly. Jürgen reached

into the box and withdrew a folder, placing it down into his drawer. "Jürgen, *who*? Was it Karl?"

He was silent as he reached into the box again and withdrew a book, silent as he walked across the room to place it on a shelf. When he turned back to me, I was startled by how pale he was.

"It doesn't really matter who did this because we do know why they did it."

That night, Jürgen and I sat around the dining room table with Adele and Mayim, trying to find an alternative to the Army Ordnance position.

"Cut your losses. Sell the house," Adele announced. "Move in with me."

"I'll move home," Mayim said quietly. "It won't be so bad."

"Aunt Adele, there simply isn't enough room unless you evict a tenant, and we all know you could never bring yourself to do that," Jürgen said gently. "Besides, even if we did move in with you, you can't support us forever. I'd still need to find another job."

"Maybe I could look for a job?" I said. Everyone stared at me. I scowled. "What?"

"You're no more qualified for a job than I am," Mayim pointed out. "And I've never even come close to finding work."

"Even if I do find another job, who's to say this won't happen again?" Jürgen said, frustrated. "Whoever insisted I be fired today must have immense power, and they must desperately want me in that program."

"We are still discussing this as if you have some choice here," Adele sighed. "The men who had you fired are likely the same men who are running the country. Today they are playing with your career—what will they try next if that fails?"

After a sleepless night, we woke to find a letter from the

bank waiting for us on the floor of the front hall, having been pushed through the mail chute while we slept. I watched anxiously as Jürgen tore it open.

"What does it say?" I asked, although I already had an inkling.

He raised his gaze from the paper to mine, frustration and shame in his eyes.

"They've been alerted to a change in my employment circumstances, and if I can't prove we have a source of income to cover the mortgage, they'll have to call in the loan."

"We'll figure something out, my love," I whispered through numb lips. He gave me a frustrated look and went into his study, closing the door firmly behind him.

Mayim and I took the children next door to visit Adele after that. I was trying very hard to remain calm, but as I sat down over my steaming cup of tea, all I could think about was Jürgen alone in his study.

"They say this program is all about space," I blurted. Mayim and Adele just looked at me. "It was always Jürgen's dream to work with rockets like this. If he must take this job, it might not be so awful for him."

Adele sighed and shook her head, shooting me a frustrated look.

"Mark my words, child. If Hitler wants to develop a rocket program, you can bet your last Reichsmark that at some point in the future, it will be used to hurt someone."

But in just two days, the Nazis had taken away our only source of income and threatened our home. We knew the pressure would only increase if we continued to resist, but we had so little left...only the most important things in our world. Our family and our lives. Once we realized that, saying no was no longer an option. By the end of the following week, Jürgen had started his new, highly paid civilian position at the Army facility at Kummersdorf.

16

Sofie

Huntsville, Alabama
1950

JÜRGEN AND I AGREED THAT WE SHOULD TRY
to get into a routine as quickly as possible. A whole group of
German children were starting school the Monday after the
party, and Gisela was starting with them.

I helped her don her favorite dress and styled her hair into
two long braids, then showed her the lunch I'd prepared for
her—dark rye bread with liverwurst, and nutty *Elisenlebkuchen*
cookies for snacks. She barely managed a smile.

"Are you ready to go?" Jürgen asked as he joined us in the
kitchen, dressed for work. He had purchased a second car for
me but it wouldn't arrive until later in the week, and I needed
time to learn the road rules anyway. So for the time being he
would drop Gisela at school, and Felix and I would walk to
pick her up afterward.

"Mama," Gisela whispered. "I'm so nervous."

"Just stay with the other German students. You'll all be in the same boat, but the very best way to learn a new language is immersion. Isn't that right, Papa?"

"It absolutely is," Jürgen said in English, and Gisela gave me one last terrified look, then followed him out the door. As soon as they were gone, I crouched to meet Felix's gaze. He had been hiding beneath the dining room table.

"Are you ready to come out yet, little man?"

"Is he gone?" Felix asked, glancing anxiously about the room.

"He's your papa," I scolded him gently. "You're going to have to get used to him sooner or later."

"Later," Felix decided, and he climbed out and hooked his arm around my thigh, resting his head against me. I reached down to touch his soft curls. "Breakfast, Mama?"

Once Felix ate and was dressed for the day, I packaged one of the extra batches of *Elisenlebkuchen* into a brown paper bag, and we walked hand in hand toward Claudia's house. I knocked on her door, and when she opened it, I offered her the bag.

"I brought you a little gift." I smiled. "I thought maybe we could have a cup of coffee? Get to know one another?"

She reached tentatively for the bag but didn't move out of the doorway. Instead, she tilted her head at me.

"I haven't forgotten how awful it was back then," she said, dropping her voice as she glanced at Felix. "Sometimes you had to pay a price just to keep your family alive. I do understand that. But is it true?"

"I don't know what you mean," I replied. Her eyes narrowed.

"I think you do. Can you honestly tell me that Jürgen wasn't involved in what happened at Mittelwerk?"

How could one word have so much power? As Claudia said *Mittelwerk*, my stomach dropped, and a wave of shame and guilt rushed over me, so powerful I swayed with the force of it. Felix was oblivious to all of that. He tugged at my hand, impatient to go inside to play with Claudia's son Luis. Eventually, I wanted to tell my children everything, but he wasn't even five years old. It wasn't time yet for him to overhear a conversation like the one Claudia was trying to prompt.

My voice was thick with emotion as I managed, "As you say, Claudia, things were very difficult during the war."

"Some of my friends joined the Party or turned a blind eye to the harassment of Jews on the street," she said stiffly. "These things I can forgive. But I absolutely draw the line at running a—" she looked from me to Felix and then mouthed dramatically "—*forced labor camp.*"

"He didn't run a *camp!*" I exclaimed fiercely, but then I sighed, knowing I'd already lost this battle. "Maybe we can sit down, and the children can play while I tell you the whole story? We didn't have any choice about what happened."

I felt sure if Claudia heard me out, she'd understand the impossible position Jürgen and I had found ourselves in. But she had already made up her mind. She stepped back inside and gave me a grim look.

"There's always a choice, Sofie. *Always.*"

She moved to shut the door, but I couldn't let the conversation end like that, so I stuck my foot out to hold the door open.

"As I understand, you and Klaus were living a long way from Berlin during the war," I said firmly. "And you're younger than us—I'm assuming Klaus was very junior at his workplace back then. You don't know *what* you'd have done if you were in our position."

Claudia raised her chin. "Actually, we refused to join the Party, and that meant Klaus was passed over for every promotion and pay rise. At times, those people made our life very uncomfortable. But more importantly, we held on to our self-respect." She flicked a glance down to Felix and added, "I understand that Klaus and Jürgen will work together—that is unavoidable. But I have come a long way to remove my children from the influence of Nazi ideology. I am sure you understand why I do not want them mingling with the family of a man who enforced it."

"But—"

"Please excuse me. I need to do some housekeeping."

She pushed the door and I had no choice but to remove my foot. As the latch clicked into place, I looked down at Felix, who was staring up at me with big, sad eyes.

"Am I going to play with Luis today, Mama?"

"Not today," I said heavily, turning back toward home.

Misery threatened to envelop me, but I shook myself. I had to keep perspective. Things in America were more complicated than I'd expected, but still not as bad as everything we'd already endured.

17

Sofie

Berlin, Germany

1935

ONCE WHEN I WAS YOUNG, I TAGGED ALONG ON my parents' resort vacation to Étretat, in France. I was fascinated by L'Aiguille, the famous needle rock formation, as well as the archways of rock that looped out over the ocean. But my favorite feature was a little cave, tucked at the other end of the beach opposite the resort. I'd been exploring its nooks and crannies all week. On the last morning I sat with my nanny, side by side at the cave's mouth, watching the waves roll toward our ankles.

"How did this happen?" I asked her. I stared up at the rock ceiling and enjoyed a shiver of adrenaline as I thought about the weight of the coast's famous alabaster chalk above us.

"It takes a very long time to carve out a cave like this," she said. "Millions of years. Every wave washes away just a tiny bit of the rock. Even this week, it's grown. It's just happened too slowly for us to see it."

I thought about that a lot after the Nazis came to power and the trickle of anti-Jewish decrees began. The new laws were so narrow at first that they attracted little outcry. First came the Law for the Restoration of the Professional Civil Service, which mandated that civil servants provide proof of Aryan heritage. Most were easily able to do this. Those who had Jewish heritage, like Mayim's father, Levi, were quietly dismissed.

Then came limits on the number of Jewish students at certain schools and colleges. Few beyond those directly affected even understood the impact of this. And when restrictions came for Jewish doctors, their licenses weren't revoked—not at first. They could still practice, only now they could not claim reimbursement from public health insurance funds. Who would protest a minor administrative change? Not the Aryan doctors, that was for sure—they benefited because their Jewish competition soon went out of business. And by then, the rest of us were awash in propaganda that painted Jews as money obsessed and greedy. Few paid any attention when Jewish doctors tried to protest.

Hundreds of these decrees were passed, one by one. This is how polite society gives way to chaos. The collapse that comes at the end of the process is a consequence of the slow erosion over time.

The shift was happening with Lydia and Karl too, long before I recognized it. That polite distance between the zu Schillers and Mayim was once easy to explain away. But ever so slowly, the pattern of inviting Jürgen and me to this outing or that, leaving Mayim out of the equation altogether, became entrenched.

"Maybe Mayim could tag along?" I suggested one day, when Lydia invited us to the opera.

"Oh, I only have four tickets," she told me. And then a few weeks later, when I wanted to bring Mayim to dinner: "Karl and Jürgen need to talk about rocket business, and you know how secretive all that is."

After that, Lydia called to plan a trip to the Berlin Zoo for Horst and Ernst's birthday. I twisted the telephone cord around my hand, feeling strangely nervous as I suggested, "Mayim can join us. She loves the zoo, and she'll be such a great help with the children."

"Oh, no nannies this time. Better if it's just us, I think," Lydia said lightly.

"You know very well that Mayim is *not* our nanny, Lydia," I snapped. "Do you have a problem with her?"

"Of course not," Lydia said, laughing easily, as if I were foolish to ask. "I'd prefer we keep it a small group, that's all."

Karl and Jürgen now worked closely together and there seemed no easy way to extract myself from my friendship with Lydia, even after a dinner party that removed any doubt.

I'd been anxious about the dinner for weeks. Lydia assured me we needed new dresses for the occasion, and while I was grateful to be able to visit the dressmaker without worrying about the cost, her insistence only reminded me what a milestone this event would be. The rocket program was almost two years old and the tiny team that once comprised only Jürgen and Karl had grown to dozens of men. This would be the first social gathering of the most senior of the staff with their wives—and most importantly, Jürgen and Karl's boss, Otto Werner.

"Well, aren't you a vision?" Jürgen said, when I joined him in the foyer. He had been paid a huge bonus when the rocket program successfully launched a small prototype the previous summer, and he'd given me every cent. I saved some in the safe in Jürgen's office and gave the rest to Mayim, and she convinced her parents to take it. After Levi lost his civil service job, he found work in a quarry—but within a few months, he badly injured his back. Now he couldn't work at all—some days, the injury left him bedbound. The family had been surviving on Moshe's scant wages from his part-time bakery job before school, as well as help from the Reichsvertretung, the Jewish self-help charity. Jürgen and I agreed that we would give them every Reichsmark we could spare.

I admired the fit of Jürgen's double-breasted silver-gray suit, and the tight knot of his navy-and-white polka-dot tie. He scooped a gray hat from the rack, then extended his elbow toward me.

"Shall we?"

But then the children appeared on the landing, dutifully coming downstairs to say goodbye. Georg was five and looking forward to entering the *Grundschule* elementary school program in the summer. Laura, at three, had a striking combination of my auburn hair and Jürgen's thick waves, his bright blue eyes and my petite nose.

"Mama, you look so pretty," Georg told me, eyes wide. The morning of the party, I'd been to the salon and had my hair set, and I'd purchased a new lipstick. I was touched that my little boy noticed the extra effort.

"Thank you, treasure."

"Laura has some lipstick too?" Laura asked hopefully. Mayim, who joined us in the foyer, hid a smile as she extended a hand. Laura ran unsteadily down the last set of stairs to take it.

"Maybe you can try some of mine on after we have dinner," Mayim told her. Laura gasped in delight as they waved us off.

I was nervous about meeting Otto. He wasn't just Jürgen

and Karl's boss and a manager with the program—he was also a senior member of the Nazi party. Otto's wife, Helene, would be in attendance too, as well as the other senior staff from the Kummersdorf program…and our neighbors Dietger and Anne Schneider, who lived across the road from us.

Dietger had recently been appointed the official Nazi *Blockleiter*—our neighborhood block warden. He was the perfect choice. He had always been the neighborhood gossip, and the authority that came with the role only amplified his keen observation skills. I had no idea how he kept abreast of the business of the entire neighborhood, but if a window was smashed, he knew how it happened, seemingly before the owner did. If a husband and wife had an argument, he knew who was at fault and who had been wronged. It was because of Dietger that Jürgen, Mayim, and I realized we had no choice but to adopt the now-standard greeting—the Hitler salute. Another neighbor from around the corner, Leopold Braunbeck, refused to give Dietger the salute. By the next morning, Leopold was imprisoned in one of the horrid concentration camps the Nazis had set up to punish their political enemies. It was months before Leopold was released, and when he came home, he was a quiet, compliant shadow of his former self.

Maybe once upon a time, we'd have said a variation on *hello* or *good day* a handful of times each day, but now we were absurd parrots, greeting every person we encountered with a *Heil Hitler.*

Dietger's remarkable ability to keep track of the neighborhood's business was deeply unnerving. In the beginning, I dared to mention this to some of the neighbors, and we all agreed we were feeling more than a little paranoid. But over time, as none of us could figure out how he knew so much about our private lives, we realized it wasn't even safe to speculate. A call from a *Blockleiter* to the Gestapo guaranteed trouble, usually starting with a knock at your front door in the middle of the night.

Our second-story bedroom window opened to the street, and I'd heard some of those overnight visits. First came the roar of an engine, then the sound of hard-soled boots on the pavement and men scurrying like rats. Even if I didn't hear the thumping on the door and the cries of protest as people were dragged from their homes, I often heard the car speeding away. Dietger was always there, seemingly delighted at the cascading fallout from his phone calls.

"What should I expect tonight?" I asked Jürgen, as he drove us to the party in his new Daimler 15. I pressed my hands over my stomach, trying to quell the nervous butterflies. Jürgen's entire life had changed with that new job—he now worked from sunup to sunset, six or even seven days a week, out at Kummersdorf, a forty-minute drive from Berlin. But while I'd been a firsthand witness to the changes in wider Berlin society, I felt so removed from Jürgen's work life.

"The staff are all scientists—just ask them about their work and you can let your mind wander while they ramble on. You're good at that after all of these years with me."

"Very funny." I swallowed a lump in my throat and prompted hesitantly, "And Otto and Helene?"

"I've never met Helene. Otto takes some getting used to."

"In what way?"

"He reminds me of your brother, actually." Jürgen paused, then clarified, "Which one is the pastor? Is it Alwin?"

"Alwin married that peasant girl," I corrected him. I didn't blame him for confusing my brothers—they all looked similar, and he'd only met them three times: at our wedding, and then at each of my parents' funerals. "Edwald is the pastor. So Otto is very religious?"

"He's a zealot, but not for the Christian faith," Jürgen said heavily. "He's a Party man—very much all about his ideology. It's hard, Sofie—I won't lie to you. You'll hear things you don't like. But for God's sake, don't argue with him—it would do me no favors at Kummersdorf, and from time to time I get the impression he only tolerates me because he needs me."

"I hoped that the program was so focused on the rockets, you weren't dealing with any of *that*."

Jürgen parked the car, then turned the ignition off. He sat for a moment, pondering this. Then he turned toward me.

"My work—my team's work—*is* about the rockets, that's true. But there's no escaping 'that,' not even at Kummersdorf. I bite my tongue every day. Every hour, on the worst days."

"You never talk about that side of it."

"Of course I don't," he said. "I'm your husband. It's my job to shelter you, not burden you."

"But...I want to support you. To help."

His expression softened, and Jürgen reached for my hand.

"My love," he said quietly. "As you'll see tonight, there's really not anything you can do to help with this. We just have to keep our heads down and not draw attention to ourselves."

I nodded silently, but there was a rock in the pit of my stomach. Whenever I asked Jürgen about work, he always spoke only about the science—and never in much detail, because the program was becoming increasingly secretive.

We mingled in Lydia's sitting room—a space so expansive it may as well have been a banquet hall. Every new scientist I met said some variation on the same thing. *Jürgen is a genius. Jürgen is my hero. Jürgen is a visionary.* As he often did at parties, Jürgen followed me around like a lost puppy. He waved away these compliments and occasionally blushed in a way I found so endearing.

But while I found the scientists exactly as I expected, Lydia surprised me. We'd gone to such lengths to plan our new outfits and I'd expected Lydia to dazzle in her new plum frock—inspired by the height of the season's fashion. Instead, she was dressed in *Trachtenkleidung*—a traditional folk outfit. She wore a long, full brown skirt with a thick black band encircling the hem, paired with a white blouse with gathered sleeves and a crocheted collar, and over the top, a black bodice.

I'd known Lydia since my first day at finishing school, and I'd never seen her dress in such an old-fashioned way. I tried to ask her about it, but when she wasn't busy with guests, she was busy with her staff. After a while, I decided I would talk to her when things were a little quieter. While I waited, Jürgen and I made obligatory small talk with Dietger and Anne.

"And how are things at the Rhodes household?" Dietger asked. I smiled politely and rested my head against Jürgen's arm, stifling my irritation. He knew how things were in our household. He spent a good portion of his life staring out his front windows, watching us.

"I hear you are doing great work for the Reich these days, Jürgen," Anne said quietly.

"I am fortunate to have the opportunity to work with such exciting science," Jürgen said carefully. Just then, Otto and Helene approached, exchanging warm and familiar greetings with the Schneiders.

"And you must be Sofie," Otto said, finally glancing my way. "It's a pleasure to meet you." His tone conveyed a different feeling. His brow furrowed as his gaze roamed over my face and then quickly down my body, before he pursed his lips. I flushed self-consciously, then glanced at Helene. Otto was older than I'd imagined he would be—at least in his fifties, maybe older. He was a portly man with thinning silver hair.

Helene was decades younger than Otto and she was pregnant, her small belly jutting out.

Like Lydia, Helene was dressed in *Trachtenkleidung*. Unlike Lydia, Helene did not wear a scrap of makeup, and her light hair was clumsily braided. Was my modern style the reason for Otto's displeasure?

"Do you have children?" she asked me quietly.

"Two," I told her, smiling. "Georg has just turned five, and Laura is three."

"Your husband is a gifted man, Sofie," Otto said. "I hope you realize how lucky you are to bear his children for the Führer. The Reich needs Aryan families to be productive."

I lifted my wine to my mouth to take a sip, only to choke as I swallowed. Jürgen gently tapped me on the back—the gesture both comfort and warning. We did hope to have more children—but we were also unconcerned that I hadn't got pregnant again. I was only twenty-four, after all. There was plenty of time left for us to expand our family.

Just then, Lydia sailed past me on her way to the kitchen. I excused myself, insisting she required my help. I caught up with her in her kitchen, where she was delivering sharp chastisements to her staff about a delay with the starters. When she was done, she turned to me. My gaze dropped to her clothes automatically and she grimaced.

"Yes, I know. I look like I've just come in from the fields on some godforsaken farm," Lydia whispered. "But it's the newest style, apparently. I picked it up from the *Deutsches Modeamt* today."

The *Deutsches Modeamt* was a fashion department backed by the Nazi government, advocating for German designers and German fabrics. I'd heard they made beautiful clothing, but as I took in Lydia's outfit, I struggled to hide my confusion.

"I think this was the style some time ago. Didn't we move on to more modern clothing?"

"And did you notice Helene isn't wearing makeup?" Lydia murmured, as we walked back toward the party. "I bought a traditional outfit when Karl asked me to, but if he tells me to stop wearing my eyeliner, I'll throw myself off a cliff."

"I doubt Karl even knows what eyeliner is."

She laughed. "Otto says it's *unfeminine* for women to wear modern clothes or makeup. But the worst…" She groaned and touched a careful hand to her blond bob. "He says German women should never dye their hair. I can't go back to mousy brown, Sofie. I just can't." Lydia visited the salon so often, I never noticed a shadow at her root line.

"You really needn't concern yourself with what Otto thinks," I said quietly. "He's not your husband."

"Sofie," she scolded. "Don't you realize how important Otto is? Our husbands have the ear of a man who has the ear of the Führer."

It quickly became clear that what Otto thought about any particular subject was of great concern to the rest of the dinner party, and he monopolized the conversation that night. It didn't matter who was speaking or what the discussion was about—Otto found a way to interject, often to disagree.

I always loved Lydia and Karl's dinner parties, in that beautiful dining hall with its high ceilings and elaborate chandeliers. That night had all the makings of a fun evening—dressing up, socializing with clever and important people, beautiful surroundings, excellent food. Jürgen was seated to my right, beside Otto, and on my left was Aldo Radtke, a recent university graduate and the youngest scientist present. As the scent of roasting pork knuckle wafted from the kitchen, I sipped on my wine and turned to Aldo, trying desperately to ignore Otto's booming voice.

"I've only been working at Kummersdorf for about six months, Mrs. von Meyer Rhodes—"

"Please, call me Sofie."

"Sofie," the young scientist said, his cheeks turning pink. "I'm an electrical engineer. You see, there are many ways to control—"

But once again, Otto was delivering a sermon. My ears pricked up, and I turned ever so slightly toward him.

"...when a man is sick, you cannot just treat the symptoms. You have to rid him of the underlying cause of the sickness—the germs. It is like this with the Jews, you see. While the Reich is riddled with Jews, society cannot function as it should. That's why the Party's highest priority is addressing the scourge."

I turned fully toward Otto, but I was looking beyond him at the reactions of those at the table. Whenever I'd encountered such hateful comments in the past, I'd noticed a split-second pause after the words—as if the audience held their breath to see how others would respond. Even if no one spoke out, that pause reminded everyone that a line had been crossed.

But there was no pause when Otto spoke. Every single guest seemed enthralled. A chill ran down my spine when my gaze landed on Lydia. She was seated beside Karl. Her cheeks were rosy red, from the fire or the wine or the excitement of the evening, her eyes bright. I wanted so much for her to look at me, even for a second. What would I see in her eyes? We once had a good friendship—a solid friendship—but my respect for Lydia was disappearing by the minute.

"They look human, I know," Otto continued, louder now, pleased to have the attention of the entire gathering. "It can be confusing to those who do not yet understand, but the science is clear—Jews are truly subhuman creatures. They lack the intellect and the moral purity the Aryans possess. It is such a problem that they have weaseled their way into secret positions of authority, pulling the strings of so many inferior nations. Even our nation in the past."

"Which is it?" I whispered under my breath to Jürgen. "The Jews are intellectually inferior, or they are smart enough to secretly run the world? Surely both things can't be true."

"Sofie?" Karl called on me suddenly. "Did you have something to add?"

All eyes turned to me. I imagined two paths forward—the first, where I repeated my question again, louder. This was surely the moral thing to do. How could I sit idly by?

But how would the room react? Otto would be embarrassed and furious. Even if he didn't report me to the Gestapo for disloyalty, Dietger surely would.

Who would support me if that happened? Karl was the man who put me on the spot. Lydia looked confused, her gaze flicking between me and Otto. Jürgen turned to face me too. I saw a mix of panic and pleading in the depths of his blue eyes.

My face flamed as I realized I had no choice but to choose the other path—the lesser path. The Nazis had not just made comments like Otto's acceptable—they'd made them fashionable. That was why there was no pause, no silent acknowledgment of the line that had been crossed. The line had been moved. How on earth had the Nazis flipped things around so quickly?

"I'm embarrassed to admit it," I said, forcing a weak laugh. "I was just wondering how far away that pork knuckle is. Doesn't it smell delicious?"

The brittle tinkle of laughter echoed around the table. Jürgen almost slumped with relief, and he fished for my hand under the table, then squeezed it. Hard.

But Otto's eyes stayed on me a moment too long, as did

Dietger's. Before the main course was served, I was counting down the seconds until we could leave.

Guests were excusing themselves by eleven o'clock. Dietger and Anne were the first to go, rubbing their full bellies and thanking Lydia and Karl as they left. When Aldo rose to leave, he stumbled as he tried to push back his chair. The wine and beer had flowed thick and fast all evening, and many of the men looked disheveled.

There was a flurry of conversation about how everyone would make their way home. Jürgen offered to take Aldo. We'd be traveling well out of our way, but I didn't mind—the young man was clearly in no state to drive. Others decided to drive despite their evening of indulgence. To my surprise, Otto asked for assistance.

"Do you think you could see to it to have your driver help Helene and me get home?" he asked Karl. He'd had plenty to drink, but it was over many hours, and he seemed relatively sober compared to some of the others.

"I'll fetch Gerhard," Lydia said, offering Otto a reassuring smile before she turned toward the staff wing. Jürgen was still deep in conversation with another colleague, so I fell into step beside her, frowning.

"Gerhard?"

It struck me suddenly that it had been some time since I'd seen Karl's driver, Fischel. That wasn't unusual—the zu Schiller staff generally remained invisible unless there was a need for them.

"Yes," she said lightly. "Our lovely new driver."

"What happened to Fischel?"

"It was time, Sofie," she said, dropping her voice.

"You *fired* him?" My stomach dropped. Fischel worked for

Karl for years—since even before he married Lydia. I thought the two men were friends.

"He moved on," she simply said. "And thank God he did, because I'm fairly sure Otto is only asking to use our driver to double-check that we let the Jew go. It really was for the best."

If I'd been a braver woman, I'd have asked: The best for who?

But that lonely moment at the table was so fresh in my mind, and I hadn't even had the chance to sort through my thoughts on it.

I fell behind as Lydia powered toward the staff quarters, but a sudden wave of sadness hit me, and instead of waiting for her, I turned and walked back to Jürgen and Aldo.

"You just can't do things like that," Jürgen said. We were still at the curb out front of Aldo's parents' home, watching as the young man walked unsteadily up the path toward the front door. Jürgen pinched the bridge of his nose, knocking his glasses askew. "I told you in the car on the way to the party. You have to ignore the comments you don't like. It's the only way."

"Did you know Karl and Lydia fired Fischel?"

Jürgen sighed and tilted his head back, as if looking to the heavens for help.

"What?" I said impatiently.

"Of *course* they fired Fischel."

"But—"

"Unlike me or most of those men you met tonight, Karl is replaceable. He doesn't have a science background to bring to the program, so instead, he plays politics to advance his career," Jürgen said. "It's working for him so far. Otto is fond of him."

"But Fischel has been on Karl's staff as long as we've known him. I cannot believe that Karl would fire him just to climb the ladder."

"Maybe Karl's decision is just like when you and I realized we simply have to give the salute."

"So...you don't think Lydia and Karl really buy into all of that nonsense about the Jews?" I asked Jürgen uncertainly.

"If they are acting, they are doing a very convincing job of it."

"We could ask them."

He pulled away from the curb, sighing heavily.

"It's my intention to do everything I can to focus on my work. If we force a confrontation with the zu Schillers, there's a good chance we're going to be disappointed with how they respond, and by asking the question, we've revealed our discomfort. It's like listening to Otto when he rants about the Jews or the disabled or the homosexuals. I could argue back—I mean, for God's sakes, what 'science' is this? But does that really help? Does it change Otto's mind? No. All it does is force him to confront the reality that he and I disagree. It's best to stay focused on what we still have in common. In the case of Karl and Otto and me, that's the rocket program. For you and Lydia, it's our children and our friendship."

In those first few early years of Nazi rule, each day mostly felt like the one before—warm family dinners, lunches at the park with Lydia while our children ran wild around us, frustrating and wonderful moments with my children, Mayim and I chuckling over some private joke, sharing glances at Adele each morning as I somehow, yet again, managed to offend Jürgen's aunt with a single word or phrase.

But when I was forced to look back at how life changed in such a short period of time, I could barely believe I was in the same city. Outside of our family and outside of our home, the nation had morphed, and every interaction was now fraught.

As Jürgen parked the car on the street outside our house, I looked across the road to the Schneider house just in time to see an upstairs curtain swing back into place.

"Dietger keeping watch on us?" Jürgen asked. When I sighed to confirm his suspicions, Jürgen waggled his eyebrows at me and leaned in as if he was going to kiss me. "Should we give him a show?"

I laughed and moved to push him away playfully, but he caught my hands in his and his expression suddenly sobered.

"I'm important to the program in a way that Karl is not. I have no interest in joining the Nazi party, let alone climbing its ranks. I hope we'll be okay, but you do need to understand…" He cleared his throat, then jerked his chin toward our house. "I hope to God it doesn't happen, but the day may come when it's a problem for a man like me to have a Jewish friend, especially one who lives under his own roof." I opened my mouth to protest, but he said gently, "You've seen how quickly things have changed. You know in your heart that what I'm saying is true."

My heart sank. I looked back toward the house, chest tight as I whispered, "And if that day comes?"

"Let's cross that bridge when we come to it," he said. I turned back to scowl at him, and Jürgen's gaze softened. "I just wanted to make sure you were thinking about it, because the day may come when our relationship with Mayim becomes a problem."

Early at the start of the new school year, Mayim's brother, Moshe, learned that his school's quota of Jewish students had been reduced. He was sixteen and had already decided to train as a baker, so he dropped out to free up a space for another student.

Levi and Sidonie decided that Moshe should go to Krakow to live with his grandfather because "it's only a matter of time before it becomes illegal for a Jew to even bake bread in this country." Like Sidonie and Mayim, Moshe was a Polish citizen. This was not an uncommon scenario—there were tens of thousands of people born in Germany to Polish parents who were automatically granted Polish citizenship.

A boy like Moshe had become a walking target on the streets of Berlin by then. He'd been harassed by Hitler youth thugs a number of times and lucky to escape with only minor scrapes and bruises.

Mayim asked me to go with her to say goodbye to Moshe, so we left the children with Adele and took the trolley car across to Mitte. By the time we arrived at the tenement building, she was weeping. We paused at the bottom of the stairs so she could compose herself.

"I don't want to upset my parents any more than they already are." Mayim sniffed as she wiped her eyes with a handkerchief.

"Moshe is a strong boy. And he's resourceful. Remember that summer at Potsdam when he had been sick, so your mama wouldn't let him tag along when we played in the creek? And he set that dishcloth on fire in the kitchen sink to distract her so he could run off after us?"

She laughed through her tears, but the grief and the fear returned to her eyes almost immediately.

"He's just sixteen. He shouldn't be sent away like this. We barely know my grandfather."

"Your grandfather also raised your mother, and she's one of the finest people I know."

I felt like an intruder as they prepared to say goodbye—a feeling reinforced by the fact that there wasn't enough room in the kitchen for a fifth chair. Sidonie insisted I take hers, but that simply meant she hovered behind me, wringing her hands and sobbing. Levi was beside me, his face blanched with pain as he sat twisted on the hard wooden chair. He was determined the family should farewell Moshe together, and the original plan was for us to meet at the train station—but his back was so bad that day, the kitchen was as far as he could manage.

"We mustn't take long or Moshe will miss his train," he said stiffly, and after that, Moshe went to fetch his suitcase from his bedroom. When he returned, Mayim embraced him, weeping into his chest.

"I love you. I'll miss you," she choked out. I couldn't remember when he grew taller than us, but at sixteen, Moshe towered over Mayim and me. He seemed mature beyond his years—calm and reserved. When the time came for Moshe to hug me goodbye, he spoke quietly in my ear.

"Look after her, won't you?"

I'd been dry-eyed as Mayim's moral support, but the concern in his voice made my eyes sting. I cleared my throat as we separated and tried to keep my voice light as I said, "Isn't it you we should be worried about, venturing off into the big wide world on your own?"

Moshe shook his head.

"I'll only be in Krakow," he said quietly. He glanced toward his family, then dropped his voice as he added, "I wish they could all come with me." The rest of the family were Polish citizens, but Levi was not, and Poland was issuing few entry visas to German Jews. "Papa says Germany is our home, but is a place really 'home' if you're not welcome there anymore? I'll be safe in Poland. I wish I could say the same for those I'm leaving behind."

18

Lizzie

Dallam County, Texas
1935

MOTHER WAS BAKING BREAD. I SMELLED IT IN the air before my eyes opened at dawn, the delicious scent overpowering the ambient scent of dust.

Today was going to be a good day. We had fresh bread and Mother knew about Judge Nagle and she thought I was strong like her.

"I talked to Dad last night," Mother murmured as I came into the kitchen. My jaw dropped, and she smiled sadly. "We don't keep secrets from one another and he needed to know."

"Was he…?"

"He took it about as well as you'd expect. Makes it even more important that we have some time together today. That's why I'm making us a picnic," she told me firmly.

"That bread I smell?" Dad called gruffly from the bedroom.

"Yes, Hank. Get yourself up and dressed. We're going out."

"I don't feel—"

"Hank."

I couldn't even see Dad's face, but I could sense the change in mood. There was a stretch of silence and then a heavy sigh before I heard him moving about in the bedroom. Mother and I shared a smile.

"One down," she said under her breath. "One to go."

There was no resisting Mother in that mood—Henry wouldn't even try. I threw my arms around her, feeling a rush of affection.

"I love you, Mother," I said. The words felt stiff and awkward on my tongue, and for the briefest moment, I wasn't sure how she'd react. She loved me—of course she loved me—but did she want to hear me say it? Mother's arms wrapped around me and she squeezed me back, hard.

"I love you too, honey. Now, boil me up some eggs. We're having egg sandwiches."

It was the perfect day for a picnic. After weeks of that constant wind that left us so tired, the day was completely still. The dust haze cleared and the heat felt promising instead of menacing, like the spring days of old.

A basket full of egg sandwiches and some bread and butter pickles didn't fix a single thing, but it did give us an excuse to take the Hoover wagon into Dalhart, where we sat in the park beneath some trees. It had been some months since Daddy even made an attempt to leave the farm, and I couldn't actually remember the last time we'd all been out together for fun. We sat on a rug as Mother poured sweet tea from a thermos into little metal mugs.

"No sadness today," she announced. "I don't want anyone talking about the drought or the wheat or the farm or what's going to happen. Today, we're just together." She made eye contact with each of us, then added pointedly, "Got it?"

We all nodded obediently, and for the next few hours, it was like we didn't have a care in the world.

Later that afternoon, Dad and Mother left me and Henry to do the Sunday chores while they went into Oakden to drop the eggs off at the grocer. As the cart rolled out the gate, I glanced up at them and saw that Dad had his arm around Mother, and she was resting her head on his shoulder as he drove.

The picnic had gone a long way to soothing the ache in my soul, and something about that brief glimpse of the affection between my parents settled the last of it.

"What are you cooking for dinner?" Henry asked.

"Who says I'm cooking? Mother just said *we* have to do it."

"Lizzie, please. You know I can't cook." He held up his hands, always stained with dirt and rough from work, his fingernails black and chipped. "These hands were made for man's work."

I held up my hands too. They looked exactly like Henry's, only smaller. He grimaced, then said wryly, "Geez, no wonder you can't find a boyfriend."

"Shut up, Henry," I exclaimed, but I was laughing as I said it, because he seemed so much better that afternoon. The day off the farm seemed to have lightened his mood. "I think I'll make us hot water corn bread and heat up canned rabbit to go with it."

Henry had a love-hate relationship with that canned rabbit meat. Jackrabbit had been breeding like crazy through the drought, and the population was now dangerously out of control, so the community had to reduce numbers. We would line up in a giant square, across acres of land, spaced out at first but gradually coming closer together, pushing the rabbits into a fenced area in the middle. There, the animals would be clubbed to death, and the carcasses distributed for food. Jack-rabbit drives were unpleasant—brutal, even—but we knew they were necessary. Henry knew those animals would de-stroy our crops and breed until they took over every square inch of our land, but he could not stand to see them suffer, and as hungry as we were, he struggled to eat them.

"Is there anything else?" he asked.

"Not that I know how to cook." I shrugged. He sighed, nodding in resignation. "We have to wash some clothes too." I was dreading that task even more than the cooking. We were washing the clothes in handmade soap, formed with tallow and lye. It was hell on my hands.

"Well, since you're doing the washing and the cooking, the least I can do is to fetch you the water," Henry announced.

"So gentlemanly of you," I muttered. "And then what are you going to do?"

"I might take a nap." My jaw dropped, and he threw his head back and laughed. "I'm kidding! Mother asked me to shovel some of the dirt away from the barn in case we get an-other storm." The dirt was halfway up the side of the barn now. We'd only been shoveling it away from the door, doing the bare minimum to get the animals in and out.

"Henry, we are idiots," I said suddenly. "We should have offered to take the eggs in for them."

Henry and I looked at one another, and then we both started laughing.

I was drying my hands on my apron as I walked onto the porch just after five o'clock. The fine strands of hair that had come loose from my bun suddenly rose until they were stand-ing high above my head, as the hairs on my arms and the back of my neck rose too. The eerie sensation left me shuddering, and I knew exactly what it meant.

A duster was coming—and given how strong that static electricity was, this was going to be a big one. I took two more steps, looking toward the horizon, but then stopped.

There was no wind to warn us what was coming that day, just a silent wall of black, so high and wide that I wondered if I was seeing things. That couldn't be a dust storm—not with such clear edges. Dust storms weren't so self-contained that you could see bright blue sky right above them. They came on slowly, always preceded by a noisy high wind. This one wasn't following the rules.

"I just got shocked off that metal near the barn, so bad it knocked me down. The wire on the fence is glowing blue too. Feels like a big duster is co—" Henry said behind me, but then he too stopped dead in his tracks. "What in God's name is that?"

We stood there staring for a beat longer than we should have, because whether we could comprehend it or not, that monstrous black wall was moving toward us, swallowing the flat fields of half-dead wheat.

"Get inside, Lizzie," Henry said. I ignored him, spinning toward the gate to see if Mother and Dad were, by some miracle, back already. All I saw were the hens running for shelter, and the long, empty drive beside them. "Lizzie!" Henry shouted. "Get inside and get some cloth ready!"

The panic in his voice startled me. I spun back into the house, trembling as I ran to the linen cupboard. I scooped a whole stack of whatever cloth I could find into my arms and threw some sheets on top, and I ran to the pail beside the stove. I'd washed corn bread batter off my hands in that water two minutes earlier, but there was no time to fetch a fresh bucket.

I threw the cloth into the bucket and took it into Mother

and Dad's room. I closed the window, then hung a dripping sheet from the frame, and set the sopping towel near the door, ready to block the gap beneath it. I fumbled in Mother's dresser for the Vaseline for our noses, then ran through the house. Every window was open, so I closed and latched them all before I went back to the porch.

The wind was picking up—a gentle breeze now rustled my static-ravaged hair. The storm was moving so fast—already at the far reaches of our farm. The duster would swallow the house in minutes.

"Henry!" I shouted, my voice breaking. "Henry, hurry!"

He sprinted up the stairs onto the porch, grabbing my elbow to tug me inside. I stopped to close the door, then tore the drapes down from a nearby window to stuff them under the door—one more gap plugged, although I knew it would make little difference.

Henry had the presence of mind to take the tub of batter I'd made and drop it over the fire, instantly smothering the flames with a sizzle and a burst of oddly delicious, corn-scented smoke. Next he scooped a lantern off the kitchen table, and I followed him back to Mother and Dad's room. While I pushed the wet towel beneath the door, he lit the lantern.

"We can sit on the bed today," Henry reminded me when, out of habit, I moved to sit on the floor. I felt a pang of distress.

"They're out in this," I whispered.

"I know."

"There isn't even any glass in that car."

"I know, Lizzie. They'll stop at someone's house. They'll find shelter. They know what to do."

We could see the road when we moved the sheet over Mother and Dad's window. In that direction, it might have been an ordinary afternoon. The wind was picking up, stirring the dust around the house, but the sun was still shining.

As I spread gobs of Vaseline under my nose, I stared at the road, hoping to see the Hoover cart.

The golden afternoon light was tinged with brown and gray, and then the whole world took on a red-brown sheen, as if the glass became colored. Then, so quickly I could scarcely believe it, the light faded away until I couldn't even see the empty driveway, not three feet from that bedroom window. We had been swallowed into the belly of the beast.

"Henry," I croaked, as swirling dust began to creep in through the cracks in the roof, the walls, the floor—carried by startlingly icy air. Henry already had his wet cloth over his mouth and nose, and he motioned for me to do the same. It had been so still all day, but now the wind began to thunder against the house, until the whole structure was shaking, and so were Henry and I. We sat side by side in a terrible, terrified silence, listening helplessly as the barn of the chicken coop collapsed, and as a window in another room of the house shattered.

"Do you think this is the end of the world?" I asked Henry after a while, my voice small.

"Don't be silly, sis," he said. "It's just another storm. It's a bad one, sure, but it's just a storm."

By then, there was so much dust in the air in Mother and Dad's bedroom that my eyes were watering. I closed them because there was no point keeping them open—I could only just make out the flame in the lantern two feet away from me. In the rush of the wind outside, I imagined I heard sounds of suffering—a horse neighing, chickens clucking their distress, coughing and crying and someone hollering for help.

"Do you hear that?" Henry said suddenly.

There it came again.

Help. Come help. Please. Oh God. Please.

We both shot off the bed but Henry reached out to stop me.

"You stay—"

"Like *hell* I will."

For only a split second, he hesitated. Then he fumbled for my hand and squeezed it fiercely.

"Do not let go of me," he hissed. "If we lose each other, we're gone. Do you hear that?"

"Stop babying me and just go!"

I followed Henry by feel, not by sight. He had the lantern in his hand, but I could tell from the cautious steps he took that it wasn't helping much.

Henry stumbled near the door, and I felt the crunch of corrugated iron beneath our feet—a piece of the barn roofing had come through the window. He struggled but managed to pull the door open, only to find that walking outside in that wind thick with dirt was like swimming through cement. We were making such slow progress that I was starting to fear we'd be dead from suffocation before we even figured out who was calling out for us.

"Help…" The voice came again, and this time I knew it was Daddy. Henry sped up, just a little, stumbling forward down the stairs of the porch. I lost him for a brief second, so threw myself forward and went weak with relief when my hand landed on his shoulder.

"Call again, Daddy!" Henry shouted.

"Henry. I'm over here!" Dad called back.

"Keep calling so we can follow your voice!"

Slowly we inched toward the sound of Dad's voice, but it was only when I kicked the wheel of the car by mistake that I realized we'd overshot our mark.

I tugged on Henry's shoulder to pull him in the right direction and we felt our way along the car. Finally, my hand connected with hair, covered in a layer of soft dirt.

"Mother!" I cried. I pulled the car door open and bent

down to shelter behind it. Mother was curled in a ball between the back and front seats.

"Oh, honey," she wheezed, and then she gave a spluttering
fit of coughs. "Clever girl. You...found us."

She sounded hoarse and weak and defeated. I took the wet
cloth off my mouth and pressed it over Mother's, ignoring the
way she fumbled at me to protest. I tried to stifle the immediate urge to cough, but every breath I took now filled my
lungs with unfiltered dirt. Soon, I was coughing and wheez-
ing just like Mother.

"How far are we from the house?" Dad shouted.

"Close," Henry shouted back. "Maybe twelve feet?"

"I tried to find my way but I was too scared I'd get lost and
wouldn't get back to Mother in the car."

We figured it out quickly from there. I'd follow Dad, holding on to the back of his shirt. Dad would carry Mother,
throwing her over his shoulder so one hand was free to hold
on to Henry's hand, and Henry would lead the way.

Henry said it was only twelve feet or so from the car to the
house, but every single step into that swirling black dust felt
like a marathon. I was dizzy from lack of air, like every panting breath I sucked in only brought me closer to suffocation.
By the time we made it back to the bedroom, and Henry
closed the door and propped the towel beneath it, I couldn't
take another step. I sank to the floor in a heap by the door.
The wet cloths we'd taken outside were now dripping with
mud—a whole other kind of suffocation. There was no way
to filter the air other than to pull our dry shirts up over our
mouths—a measure so ineffective we wouldn't have bothered, except that we were desperate for any measure of relief.

For an hour, we sat and waited. Finally, the wind began to
slow and then the darkness lifted, and then after all of that,
the thickness of the dust in the air started to ease.

I was too exhausted to be relieved. Crumpled in that weary heap by the door, I was gradually becoming aware that I was hurt—that the sand-filled wind outside had burned my exposed skin, especially my cheeks.

Henry was the first to rise. He came to my side, gently swept the dust from my head and the uninjured skin of my face with his fingertips.

"You're bleeding here," he said gently, motioning toward my face.

"I figured," I whispered back, both of our voices raw and thick. He helped me up and dust poured down from my clothes, running down my body like waterfalls after rain. I blinked over and over again, trying to clear my blurry vision, only to realize that my eyes were as burned as my skin was. I wouldn't see clearly again until they healed.

"Mother? Dad?" I croaked, fumbling toward the bed. I could hear the rattling of Mother's breathing even from the door, even over the sound of the fading wind. But it was only when I came closer that I realized how bad she was. Dad had her in his arms, and he was touching the skin of her face gently, whispering in her ear. He was wearing a strange, panicked smile on his face, as if he were trying to stay calm. One side of his face was bruised, the skin around his eye black and purple and swollen.

I sat gently beside Mother and took her hand. It was icy cold, so I rubbed it to warm it between my fingers.

"What happened?" Henry asked, coming to the side of the bed beside me.

"Tried to beat the duster but it came on so fast," Dad said hoarsely. "Never seen anything like it. I completely lost my bearings once it got dark—kept getting in and out of the car trying to figure out where we were. Couldn't find any landmarks I recognized, and the barn wasn't where I expected it to be, so I thought we'd come in the wrong gate. Jesse was flailing, knocking the cart around as she reared up, so I got out to let her off her harness, but she knocked me to the ground. That's the last thing I remember for a while."

"Why is Mother in such bad shape?" I asked Dad, and he looked stricken.

"She must have unhitched Jesse and then she somehow hauled me back into the car, because by the time I came to, I was in the back seat and she was curled over my face, trying to keep the dust off me. I don't know how long she was exposed like that. Too long. The dirt was filling up around us in the car. I thought we'd drown in it."

We all looked to Mother then. Her lips were tinged with blue, and the skin on her face had a gray hue.

"We need a doctor," Henry said.

"How?" Dad said brokenly, looking toward the window. It was light out again, but the sun would set soon, and all I could see was dust. The barn was completely buried—I could tell from the height of the mound that it had collapsed under the weight of dust. Poor Joker was gone, and whether she ran out into the storm or suffocated, Jesse was as good as gone too.

Our nearest neighbor was three miles away, and just like us, the Hutchinson family had neither a phone nor a car. There was a chance if one or more of us tried to walk there, even through the dark and the tail end of the storm, we'd find they were not in any position to help us. And then we'd have a three-mile walk home in the dark to contend with.

"I'll go," Henry said.

"You can't," Dad said flatly, shaking his head. Henry opened his mouth to protest and Dad exclaimed, "Goddammit, Henry! Would you think something through for once in your god-damned life? What if the storm rears up again? The only reason Mother and I didn't suffocate right away was that we had the car to shelter in. It's not worth the risk."

"But—she looks—" Henry started to say. Then he broke off.

"Dad," I whispered, a different kind of tear filling my eyes now. "I don't know if Mother can wait until tomorrow."

"Well, she has to," Dad snapped, but then his expression crumbled, and he looked between me and Henry, remorse in his gaze. "She'd kill me if I let you go out there again. We just have to wait." He turned his attention back to Mother, and he kissed her forehead and whispered gently, "You have to hold on, Ida, you hear me? Just until the sun comes up. Then we'll get you help."

Henry went outside to bring us fresh water and to survey the damage, but he refused to give us details of what he'd seen. Dad stayed in the bedroom with Mother, but I got a broom and started to clean. I swept so much dirt out of that house that there were piles of it, two and three feet high, all along the edge of the porch.

Within an hour, it was dark again—this time as it was supposed to be, because the sun had finally set.

I don't know when I realized Mother wasn't going to make it. Maybe I should have known from when I first saw how bad she was, or maybe it was better that I didn't realize, since there was nothing I could do anyway. Slowly, though, over the hours of that long night, I started to wonder and then I started to suspect and then a heavy dread settled over me.

Dad was crying on and off, sometimes silent tears rolling from his eyes that might have been from the dust anyway. Other times his whole body shook with sobs. Henry sat on the floor in the corner of the room, arms wrapped around himself as he stared off into space. I took a clean damp cloth and wiped the dust from Mother's face and hands. I wet her lips and tried to trickle water into her mouth. Her breaths grew shallower as the night wore on, and the hint of gray and blue in her skin became more obvious, even in the dim light of the kerosene lamp.

"I'll go anyway. I'll walk all the way to Oakden if I have to—" Henry blurted, stumbling to his feet, but Dad shut that right down.

"It's still windy outside and we have no idea if the whole storm has passed. I am not losing two of you in one night!"

Henry slumped again, and the next time I tried to get Mother to drink some water, it ran from her lips onto the pillow. She was limp and heavy against the bedding.

"Please wake up, Mother," I choked out. There was still grit in my eyes and in my hair and even between my damned teeth. We were all still covered in the very thing that was taking her from us, and there was no way to fix that. We just had to sit in it. "Mother, I love you. Please wake up."

Not long after that, she exhaled one last gentle breath and she never took another. By then, we were all too exhausted to cry. We sat around her body on the bed, me and Dad holding her hand, Henry slumped by her thighs. The horrible events of those past twelve hours started to feel warped, like I was caught in a surreal dream. Henry eventually climbed up onto the bed beside Mother's body, as if he were too tired to hold himself up. I stretched out too, still holding her hand.

I didn't mean to doze, but the highs and the lows of that day drained every bit of strength from my body and sleep simply overtook me. Sometime later I was startled awake by a loud sound. I sat up, confused and bleary-eyed, then cast my gaze around the room.

Mother's body was on the bed beside me. Henry bolted upright too, his eyes as red-raw as the skin on his face.

But Dad was nowhere to be seen. I went to slip off the bed

to look for him and to investigate the sound, but Henry put his hand out to stop me.

"No," he whispered. "No."

"But where is—"

"Stay *here*," he hissed, and something about his tone scared me so badly, I did. I watched him run from the room, my heart starting to race with a fresh wave of confused dread. Then I finally looked at Mother.

The sun was rising outside and she was bathed in the delicate light of a new day—casting a pinkish glow over her skin. I touched her cheek, telling myself we got it wrong and she was still there—but her skin was cold and she was really gone. How on earth would we go on without her?

Not all of us would.

Some of us wouldn't even try.

And then I knew what the sound had been. I scrambled from the bed after Henry, running through the house and over the dusty porch, stumbling through the mounds of soft earth that had been dumped all over our home and yard.

I came to a screaming halt when I rounded the corner of the house closest to the bench seat and that Texas live oak. The sun was rising behind the tree, casting vibrant shades of pink and red and gold over the new morning.

In silhouette, I saw the outline of that battered tree and I saw the bench beneath it, and then I saw my brother on his knees in the dirt, cradling my father's body in his arms.

19

Sofie
Huntsville, Alabama
1950

"HOW WAS HER DAY?" JÜRGEN ASKED AS HE walked into the house that afternoon. I was sitting on the couch, Felix on one side of me watching the television, Gisela on the other, crying miserably into my shoulder. I looked at him pointedly, and his face fell. "What happened?"

"Kids here don't eat real bread!" She wept.

"Uh…" Jürgen gave me a confused look. "Americans eat a lot of bread, Gisela. Maybe you're confused—"

"*Their* bread isn't brown. It's white. It's different and they were all laughing at me because I had the wrong bread. I didn't know any of the words my teacher said and Mrs. Schmidt's children said they weren't allowed to play with me and then none of the other German children wanted to play with me either and the American children already hate me so I *sat by myself* and I hate it here!"

Later, once she'd calmed down a little, we retreated into his bedroom and closed the door.

"I spoke to Claudia today," I told him. "She told me she doesn't want her children mingling with ours. She said it's one thing for Klaus to work with you, but that she has come too far to protect her children from Nazi ideology to allow them to 'mingle' with the likes of us."

Jürgen rubbed his face wearily.

"Should I talk to her? Or to Klaus?"

I thought about the anger in Claudia's eyes and I shook my head.

"No. Not yet, anyway. But if the German children won't play with Gisela and the American children won't play with her, she's going to be miserable."

"Let's just give it a little time. We can start with her lunch—if eating our food is really such a big deal, we'll go to the grocery store right now and buy some American food."

"I don't even know what American children eat." I winced.

"Then maybe we need to find you an American friend," he said pointedly.

And all of a sudden, I remembered Avril Walters.

"Mama!" I heard Gisela cry from the front yard the next morning.

"Sofie, can you come here, please?" Jürgen called. I was in the bathroom doing my hair and I sighed, frustrated with the interruption. What were they doing back already? They'd only walked out the front door a few minutes earlier. Avril Walters was due in an hour and I needed to wash the dishes before she arrived.

"What is it?" I called, as I walked to the front door. I glanced in at Felix, who was sitting just a foot away from the television—eyes wide as he stared at the screen. He seemed determined to sit in front of it every waking moment. I wasn't thrilled about that but reassured myself that at least he was hearing *some* English.

I found Gisela sitting on the doorstep, resting her forehead in her palm. She gave me a miserable look.

"What is it?"

"Look," she muttered. "It's not just the kids at school who hate us. It's *everyone*."

Jürgen was at the side of the road, standing with Claudia and Klaus. Several other neighbors had come out of their houses too to see what the commotion was about. It was a beautiful day—blue skies and bright sunshine.

But no one was looking up at the sky because everyone was staring at the road. I left Gisela on the doorstep and went to see what the fuss was, but my heart sank as I came closer.

In crude red letters almost as high as the narrow road, someone had painted the word *NAZIS*. The graffiti had been carefully positioned right at the mouth of the street—centered right in front of our house.

"I can sort this out—you head into that safety protocol workshop," Jürgen told Karl as I approached. "But, Claudia, since Sofie isn't quite up to speed with American road rules, would you mind driving Gisela to school with Mila?"

Jürgen gave her a hopeful look. Claudia muttered something under her breath about it being the first and last time, but the next thing we knew, she was backing out of her driveway with Gisela in the back seat.

I called Avril to postpone our coffee to the next morning. She was horrified when I told her about the graffiti, and her reaction reassured me. *Some* Americans were kind—even supportive. After I hung up, Jürgen called the police. I sat in the living room with Felix and listened to his side of the conversation.

"...right out the front of my house—that's at 1401 Beetle Avenue, sir...Yes, it says 'Nazi'...I'm not sure what you mean... Well, no, sir...Actually, yes, I did think you would come to—I see. Is defacing public property not a crime in this country?... No, no. I understand. Yes, okay. Thank you. Fine."

He came to the door of the living room, his expression grim.

"What are they going to do?" I asked.

"Officer Johnson said if it was bothering me, I could paint over it," he said, shaking his head in disbelief.

"Aren't they coming to investigate?"

Jürgen unwound his bow tie as he shook his head.

"But...why not? This is harassment!"

"The police officer said it's to be expected, given the circumstances," Jürgen muttered bitterly. "He suggested I might want to buy the paint in bulk so I've got some ready for next time."

20

Lizzie

El Paso, Texas
1935

HENRY AND I SOLD EVERYTHING WE COULD AT a yard sale and bought bus tickets to El Paso. We arrived on a blustery spring day in 1935, just a week after we buried our parents, and checked into a rooming house, with every little thing we had left in the world neatly packed into two suitcases.

I'd never been to a city before. I'd seen photos in the newspaper, so I thought I knew what it would be like, but I wasn't prepared for the sensory overload. Cars and trucks roared past us, people hurried by, store signs and street signs and clothing were all so *bright*. Even the air smelled wrong, like a tractor had just backfired right near me.

There was no time to say goodbye to the land we loved or to begin to mourn our parents, but as I found myself completely out of place, the immensity of the loss and the abruptness of the change all hit me at once. I hadn't cried much other than the day Mother and Daddy left us. I didn't even cry when Pastor Williams picked us up from the farm to take us to the bus stop. But it wasn't car exhaust causing my eyes to sting as I looked around the tiny room Henry and I would be sharing. He set his suitcase on the bed and I set mine on the little sofa, staring down at it so Henry didn't see the tears in my eyes.

"Lizzie," he said gently, and when I composed myself and turned back to face him, he grinned and pointed to a string hanging from the roof. Back home, electric lights were only for the rich—but it was obvious that the rooming house wasn't a place for rich people. I found the contradiction to be perplexing. I walked briskly across the room to tug the string. The light flickered on, so I pulled the string again, to turn it off, then repeated the process, momentarily distracted by the novelty.

"And indoor plumbing too," Henry said, as he stretched out on the bed and crossed his arms beneath his head. "See? This is fine. And once I start working for the CCC, you'll have this room all to yourself."

Henry was convinced he'd find work in the city, all because of an article he'd read in the newspaper about Roosevelt's Civilian Conservation Corps—the CCC. He was only a few months away from twenty-five, and as far as we could tell, the program was only for young men *up* to twenty-five. But Henry "had a good feeling" they'd take him anyway.

"What kind of a job do you think I'm going to get, Henry?" I shifted the pile of linen to the side of the sofa and sat. It was springy and lumpy and it smelled suspiciously like someone else's sweat.

"Well, sis, you just have to ask yourself what you want to do. I like working with my hands—fixing things, building things. What do you like?"

"Farming," I said flatly. Henry winced.

"We're in the city now."

"That's my point, Henry. All I know how to do is drive a tractor. Collect eggs. Help a horse if she's stuck in foal. I can sew a button on but I can't sew a dress. I don't have any skills."

"Tomorrow you get out there and go talk to some businesses."

"And if the CCC hires you, you'll live there?" I asked. My voice wobbled but I lifted my chin. I told myself that things had changed, and I just needed time to get used to it, but I was terrified of being separated from Henry. All that had got me through that awful week was the hope that he'd make sure that we were both okay.

"You aren't afraid, are you? You've never been afraid of anything."

If only he knew. There wasn't much in life that scared me, but the thought of being all alone in that city was enough to make my stomach cramp.

"Don't be ridiculous," I said abruptly, and I started to make up the sofa. "I'm just wondering when I get the good bed."

But just two weeks later, Henry and I found ourselves standing on the street with our suitcases by our feet. As cheap as it was, the rooming house fees had cleaned us out, and the CCC did not offer Henry a job. Even if they had hired him, his employment would only have lasted till his twenty-fifth birthday— just two short months away. Not even Henry's charm could circumvent the eligibility criteria for an in-demand government program. We learned that when the CCC advertised vacancies in the past, the line of applicants stretched around several city blocks. For every potential job in El Paso, there was a hundred or more desperate candidates.

"It will be okay," Henry said firmly. "Maybe we sleep outside tonight, but something good will come up tomorrow."

I was already growing a little tired of Henry's insistence that things were going to turn around, but it would do me no good to discourage him. I scooped up my suitcase and pointed to the west.

"I saw a camp of homeless folk that way," I said wearily. "Let's see if we can find somewhere to sleep down there."

Days began to blend into weeks, but I was too tired to keep track of how long we'd been in the city. We found ourselves a cast-off square of canvas and Henry fashioned it into a kind of tent, strung across rope between a tree and the side of a bridge, in a camp full of other makeshift tents. We slept on piles of old newspapers I collected from trash cans while Henry lined up at a church, waiting to be given someone's old blankets.

Henry and I traversed the city knocking on every door asking for work until we knew its dead ends the same way we'd once known every field on the farm. At the end of the day, we would meet up at a soup kitchen for dinner.

At night, as we lay top-to-toe beneath that tent, I'd think about Mother. I knew what she'd say if she was still with us. She'd remind me that I was strong. A survivor, she'd say. She'd tell me to have faith. She'd tell me to keep going, even when it felt hopeless.

But while I waited and I prayed and I tried to be patient as I persevered, I came across an emotion I'd never felt before— I started to feel lost.

I knew downtown El Paso back to front after a few months, but I still couldn't figure out who I was in that place, or who I was meant to be.

I'd been knocking on doors in the industrial district one day, and I was running a little early to meet Henry at the soup kitchen for dinner. I didn't want to stand in the line on my own, so I was dawdling when I found myself standing opposite the new Hilton hotel—the tallest building in down-town El Paso. I scanned the opulent front entrance, then cast my gaze up over twenty-one astounding stories to the roof-top balconies.

Just then, a woman emerged from the laneway beside the building. I recognized the exhaustion on her face—I'd seen it in the mirror a hundred times. That was the look of some-one who had worked an honest day's living, who had made it to the end of the day tired, dignity intact.

I *knew* that feeling. I wanted to feel that kind of tired again so bad, I could taste it.

That exhausted maid emerging from the hotel represented the first glimmer of familiarity I'd experienced in months. She might have laughed if she knew how inspired I was by the bags under her eyes and her slumped shoulders, her feet that dragged through sheer weariness.

But when I saw her, I also saw a way forward. I'd spent months trying to find work, finding every door I knocked on remained closed. Something had to change.

I was going to master city life, just as I'd mastered every skill I'd ever needed on the farm. I still didn't know how I was going to do it, but I had just decided where.

21

Lizzie
Huntsville, Alabama
1950

AS I PUSHED OPEN THE DOOR TO THE RESTAU-
rant, I studiously avoided looking at the Whites Only sign
hanging in the window. Ever since Sofie Rhodes mentioned
those signs, I was keenly aware of them everywhere I went.

I was late again that day. I'd noticed that one of Henry's
shirts on the clothesline had stains on it, so I took it back inside to treat it with turpentine. Henry did his own laundry—
one blessed habit he'd picked up in the Army—but advanced
stains like paint were beyond his skill set. He didn't like me to
baby him, so even once I got the paint out, I had to quickly
rewash the turpentine smell out of his shirt and hang it on the
line so he didn't notice I'd interfered.

It had been hard to motivate myself to shower, fix my hair,
and put my makeup on after that. Some part of me always
wanted to skip those lunches, but forcing myself to go had

become an ingrained habit. Now my heels echoed against the tiles in the restaurant as I walked briskly to the table where the Fort Bliss women sat.

"We almost started without you!" Becca said lightly. I reached to smooth my hair and forced a smile.

"Sorry," I said. "Busy day."

I paused to hug her and Juanita, then Gail and even Avril. When it came to Avril, I was polite all of the time, warm when it suited me, and never trusting. I had learned that lesson the hard way, once upon a time.

The five of us swapped notes on the move—who was still unpacking, whose kids were enjoying the new school, who had the worst neighbors. And then Becca sighed happily.

"I'm so glad we all wound up here together after all," she murmured, lowering her voice. "It feels like we moved from an emerging city to a dying small town."

"My new neighbors are so excited that we're here," Gail said, smiling to herself. "One of them says Huntsville will one day be known as 'rocket city.' Maybe we're arriving right at the start of something amazing."

"And what does your new neighbor think about these Nazis?" Becca asked pointedly. Gail shrugged.

"She doesn't seem too troubled that some of us are German. Besides, Trevor said that they aren't actually *Nazis*. He said they just had ordinary government jobs in Germany. It's not their fault the government happened to be run by the devil himself."

"I just find that so hard to believe," Becca said helplessly. She glanced at me. "Right from the beginning you said there was something rotten about the whole arrangement, didn't you, Lizzie?" I'd never hidden my concern or displeasure at the program Calvin was working on, but as he'd requested, I never told anyone why. I tried to shrug noncommittally.

"You know what Bob told me once?" Juanita said suddenly. Everyone turned to look at her, and she leaned forward and whispered, "He said he heard rumors at Fort Bliss that some of those scientists really were in the Nazi party. He even heard that a few were in the SS."

"There's no way they'd have been brought to this country if that was true," Gail said abruptly.

"I didn't make that up, Gail," Juanita said defensively. "One of the translators told an engineer and that engineer told Bob. He said that someone in our government falsified some of the German records so more men could come here."

"You shouldn't say things like that," Gail snapped. "It's just not fair. If those men had anything to do with what happened back there, they'd be rotting in a jail or executed at Nuremberg, not free on our streets."

I dropped my gaze to the menu, wishing I could hide under the table. When a long moment passed and no one spoke, I looked up reluctantly, only to find the whole table staring at me.

"You know who'd know for sure?" Juanita said, watching me closely.

"Calvin," Avril said.

"He wasn't thrilled when they were first allowed to move freely around El Paso, was he?" Becca said, then helpfully reminded me, "It's just I do recall you telling me he'd been arguing with Christopher Newsome when they were first let off base."

I glanced quickly at Avril, reluctant to confirm *any* of this. Cal would not be pleased if his name were attached to these rumors, especially since there was potentially truth behind them. But I couldn't figure out how to extract myself from the discussion without lying. Instead, I tried to redirect it.

"It almost doesn't matter if they were truly Nazis or if they had regular government jobs. Because even if they just had regular jobs, they *stayed* in those jobs. Gail, you know as well as I do that if Truman suddenly turned into a monster like Hitler, your sweet Trevor would be the first to resign. That these men didn't do that tells me they *were* supportive of what the Nazis were doing."

"I know you're not pleased they're here, Lizzie, but you really think the Germans are dangerous?" Becca asked, her voice a hushed whisper.

"My brother says men like that are always dangerous. And you all know he served in Europe, so he would know."

"I understand that these German men know an awful lot about rockets," she said with frustration. "What I do not understand is why most of the American scientists on the team have been so quick to assume they are worthy of a comfortable life here. They're Nazis at worst, or Nazi sympathizers at best."

"I'm not sure it is sunshine and rainbows for all of them," Avril said, in a tone that foreshadowed some exceedingly delicious gossip. I hated Avril's gossip and had been the victim of it myself. She seemed to delight in causing drama. "Sofie Rhodes called me a few days ago and begged me to come around for a coffee because her little girl is having some problems at school. I asked Patty, and she said that even the German kids won't play with Gisela Rhodes. It made sense that the American kids would be a bit wary of these new students, but the Germans ostracizing one of their own?" She gave us a triumphant look. "And I suppose you all heard about what happened at Sauerkraut Hill yesterday." When we shook our heads, Avril leaned forward and murmured, "Just before I was due to go meet her for coffee, Sofie called to cancel. Overnight, someone painted the word *Nazis* right on their street."

"Is it true, Lizzie?" Gail said. I wasn't sure what she was referring to.

"About the street? This is the first I've heard—"

"About records being falsified. About some of these men being members of the Nazi party, or even the SS." She paused, her eyes narrowing. "If anyone would know for sure, it's your husband, and you changed the subject when Becca asked you."

I cleared my throat. I never was good at lying.

"I shouldn't say," I said stiffly, but there was a collective gasp around the table. I flicked a glance at Avril Walters. She seemed equal parts scandalized and delighted. My heart sank.

"Do you know which of the Germans were Nazis? Who was in the SS?" Becca whispered in shock. I shook my head hastily, mind racing as I tried to figure out how to undo the mess I was making. Cal was going to kill me if he found out.

"If this is true, I bet they'd only have done it for the scientists they were really desperate to work with," Gail said slowly. The rest of us fell silent as we all thought about the superstar scientist on the team. "And—" Gail nodded toward Avril. "You said the German kids were ostracizing that Rhodes kid. It might just be that an SS officer for a father is just too much stigma even for them. The other Germans would know the truth."

"Ask Cal tonight," Becca pleaded.

"He won't tell me anything. He's still mad about the party and I know he's sick of talking about this." I glanced at Avril and suddenly frowned. "Did you say you're having coffee with Sofie Rhodes? I thought we weren't doing that."

"Oh, she's *so* lonely," Avril said sadly. "I just couldn't help myself. You know what a bleeding heart I am."

22

Sofie
Berlin, Germany
1935

GEORG'S FIRST DAY AT *GRUNDSCHULE* HAD AR-
rived. Mayim stayed home with Laura so we could walk him
to school on our own. At the front door, she bent to kiss his
cheek.

"Have a great first day, Georg," she said. He beamed at her,
revealing his two missing front teeth—a gap that caused certain sounds to escape with a lisp. He threw his arms around
Mayim's neck.

"I'll tell you everything tonight, Mayim. I promise."

"I know you will, little buddy," she laughed, squeezing
him tightly. Laura came running down the stairs, almost trip-
ping on her feet, then launched herself at Georg in a forceful embrace.

"Have a good day," she said, squeezing her eyes closed as
she hugged him. Georg hugged her back, and they stood like

that just for a second. Mayim and I exchanged quiet smiles. When Laura released her brother, she took Mayim's hand. Then, almost overcome with emotion, she shifted to stand behind Mayim's leg. Her gaze fell to the floor as she mumbled, "Goodbye, Georg."

Georg raised his chin and drew in a deep breath as if bracing himself, then said bravely, "Goodbye, Laura."

I reached for Georg's hand as we stepped onto the sidewalk outside our house, but he either didn't notice, or was reluctant to hold hands with his mother now that he was a "big kid." That stung. It seemed like one minute I was shaking with nerves while holding my newborn for the first time, the next we were walking to school.

"Are you scared?" I asked.

"No, Mama," he said. "Hans and me are going to have so much fun." Hans was a year older than Georg and already at school, but the boys were the best of friends.

Lydia was waiting at the school gate with Hans. The boys ran toward one another, meeting with a duet of excited chatter and cheering, then ran through the gate into the playground without even saying goodbye.

Shocked tears sprang to my eyes. Lydia laughed gently as she patted me on the shoulder.

"The first day is the hardest, Sofie, but there's no need to fret. These teachers will take your baby boy and transform him! He will leave this place well on his way to becoming a strong German man—the kind of man who will do this nation proud."

I looked into the schoolyard, hoping to catch one last glimpse of Georg. An icy chill ran down my spine as my gaze landed on the flag of the Reich, blowing gently in the breeze above the playground.

★ ★ ★

We soon found a new rhythm to our days, our routine now based around Georg's school hours.

"I wish I could take him," Mayim said suddenly one morning as I was pulling on my shoes at the front door, trying to make up some lost time because we were running late. I forced a smile.

"He'll be able to walk on his own soon anyway."

Berlin offered only hostility to a woman like Mayim, and that meant it was not safe for my children to be out with her. Besides, Georg was a fledgling part of the school community, and we were all anxious about what the other children and parents would say if they knew about Mayim. I could picture the crowd of parents at the gate hearing her Hebrew name and recoiling in shock. It was awkward and awful, but Mayim and I both knew that it was best she stay home.

Over the summer, Mayim, Adele, and I liked to sit in the courtyard after the children were in bed. We'd share a glass of wine, willing to endure the buzz of mosquitoes for the company and the chance of a cool evening breeze. On one of these evenings, Adele brought over strawberries from her garden, cut into thick slices and macerated with fine sugar. It was still warm that night, but to my great amusement, Mayim wrapped herself in her knit blanket anyway.

"Laura would be jealous if she knew," she said, helping herself to a strawberry.

"Laura need not be jealous," Adele said dismissively. "I saved my best strawberries for the children as I always do."

Mayim and I shared a smile. I stretched out my legs and rested my head against the wall behind me, casting my gaze over the silhouettes of the trees and the buildings behind us as the golden sun dipped behind them.

"No Jürgen again tonight?" Adele said. I could hear the disapproval in her voice. "So he's working the weekend, then. You need to help him find some balance."

"And how do you propose I do that, Aunt Adele?" I asked, swallowing a sigh. She wasn't wrong. Jürgen was sleeping on the couch at his office more and more.

"Did you hear about Mrs. Haas?" Adele asked us grimly, referring to one of her widowed friends. "Gestapo. They took her a few nights ago. She was no more engaged in activities disloyal to the Reich than I am a pumpkin. She was fighting with Walter Berner. He lives upstairs from her, remember? He just didn't like the way her dog barked at night. It seems clear that he called in a tip to the Gestapo out of spite, and now that poor, fragile old woman is in a concentration camp somewhere."

Mayim and I exchanged a glance over Adele's assessment of Mrs. Haas as *fragile* and *old*, given the woman was probably at least ten years younger than Adele. Even so, the thought of the Gestapo dragging her from her home left me ill.

"Aunt Adele…" I dropped my voice. "You shouldn't speculate like that. You never know when someone is listening." The courtyard was relatively safe, surrounded by other courtyards, and I couldn't hear any movement, so I assumed they were empty. But beyond the courtyards were windows, and who knew who might be behind them?

"I'll speculate all I want, Sofie," Adele said, looking down her nose at me. "What are they going to do—arrest me for pointing out the blindingly obvious?"

"You really do need to keep your voice down," Mayim whispered, her tone slightly panicked. Adele sighed, then nodded.

"Yes, okay. Thank you, Mayim."

"Every night before I go to bed, I review every interaction

from that day and ask myself—did I do anything that might be perceived as disloyal?" Mayim said softly, startling me. "Some nights I can't sleep because I worry that I might have accidentally said something to draw attention to myself—to cause trouble for us all."

"I hate that you have to live like that," I whispered, throat tight.

"The calculus is different for you, Mayim," Adele said gently. "And you have your whole life ahead of you. This is no way to live. Have you thought about that? What your future will look like?"

"I think about it every day."

Adele took a deep sip of her wine. "I don't say this lightly, but you need to leave Germany. I think of you as I think of our Sofie, as the granddaughter God forgot to give me—albeit a rather less aggravating version."

"Thanks, Aunt Adele," I said wryly. She winked to let me know she was joking, but quickly sobered, as did I. "But... where would the Nussbaums even go?"

Adele looked at Mayim, her gaze intense.

"Can you and your parents not simply go to Krakow with Moshe?"

"It is not simple, Miss Adele," Mayim replied. "My passport says I'm Polish, but I have never lived anywhere but here. Besides, my father can't just go to Poland. Even if he could secure a visa, he couldn't handle the train ride with his back. Things in Berlin are uncomfortable, but I am fortunate that I have you and Jürgen and Sofie and the children."

"And you," Adele said, turning her attention to me. "Have you thought about what will happen if they insist that you ask Mayim to leave?"

"It is not illegal to have a Jewish best friend," I said stiffly.

"Sofie." She sighed impatiently. "The time may come when it is indeed illegal."

"I hate that we're even discussing this," I whispered.

"Not discussing it would be worse," Adele said abruptly. "We need to face the facts." She turned to Mayim. "You know I am not wealthy, but between all of us, we could find the money for your father's visa."

"Truly, thank you," Mayim said miserably. "But that's really not the problem at all."

"Please, Mayim," Adele urged. "Please try to think of a way. It feels like the danger comes closer to this house every single sunrise. I can barely sleep at night worrying for you all."

Later, Adele excused herself to retire, and after she'd closed the little gate in the fence between our courtyards, Mayim asked me, "Is she right?"

"I don't know," I admitted. After a pause, I blurted, "Mayim, I'm so scared for you. And your parents. Germany doesn't feel safe anymore."

Mayim looked away from me, toward the fading red-gold sunlight that framed the apartment building behind us. I heard the sniffles she tried to hide, and I reached to squeeze her forearm. She turned back to me, her cheeks wet with tears.

"How much worse is this going to get before it gets better?"

"I don't know," I admitted. "I just don't know."

After a few months at school, Georg was proud to bring home his first satchel of readers to practice at home.

"Shall I read them with you?" I offered, as I finished dressing Laura after her bath. Georg gasped in horror.

"These are *special* home readers. Only for me and Mayim."

I kissed him good-night and watched as he walked to his bedroom, holding Mayim's hand. I tucked Laura into her bed, and then went downstairs to make tea for me and Mayim.

When she joined me in the sitting room a few minutes later, the color was gone from her face. She sat opposite me and rested Georg's satchel on the coffee table between us.

"Open it," she said. Her voice was hoarse.

I opened the satchel and withdrew the books. On the cover of the first was an image of a street parade. Most of the adults and children were giving the salute, and no less than eight swastika banners and flags were displayed in the scene. I made a sound of surprise, and Mayim reached forward, her movements jerky as she withdrew the rest of the books to spread them side by side.

I reached to pick the next one up, *Children, What Do You Know about the Führer?* I leafed through the pages, watching a fiction unfold about a benevolent Hitler who was restoring the Fatherland to glory. The second book was called *The Crossbreed*, and while the cover was of a cute puppy, I only had to skim the first few pages to realize it was a simplistic parable discouraging relationships between Aryans and Jews.

By the time I picked up the third picture book, my hands were shaking.

It was called *Never Trust a Fox on the Green Heath and Never Trust a Jew by His Oath*. On the first page, a handsome Aryan man was depicted beside a rotund, coarse man ostensibly representing the Jews.

When I looked up, Mayim was weeping.

"Please tell me you didn't read these to him, Mayim," I whispered sickly.

"He wanted that one," she choked out, pointing to the last book. "He liked the cover best. I managed to convince him we should read one of his own books and he was easily distracted, but that won't last forever. Sooner or later, he's going to realize that the Jews he's learning about are the same as the Jew in his house."

"I'll talk to him—" I started to say, but her eyes widened in alarm.

"And tell him *what*?" she said. Then she dropped her voice to a whisper. "Tell him that the Führer is wrong? That Jews aren't the enemy? You can't say those things to him. If he repeats them at school, you'll have a visit from the Gestapo."

"But I can't just let him think that this is okay," I whispered back.

Mayim choked on a sob. "He must have spoken about me in class. His teacher told him to make sure I read them with him. She was trying to make a point."

I was only grateful that Jürgen was coming home that night. He'd warned me he would be late, but I waited up for him.

"What is it?" he asked, taking one look at my face.

"We need to talk," I said grimly.

"Can we talk as I take a bath?" he asked tiredly. He waved a hand down over his rumpled suit, and then scrubbed his palm over the bristly growth on his cheeks. "It's hot as hell out there and it's been days since I washed. It's been a long week."

I followed him into the bathroom and explained what had happened.

"We can't say anything," Jürgen said abruptly.

I stopped pacing and frowned at him, surprised by his tone.

"But—maybe we just need to look at other schools? Maybe—"

"Almost every schoolteacher is now a member of the National Socialist Teachers League. The newspaper said it's over 95 percent."

"The papers *lie*!" I hissed. I knew that better than anyone. The press was an arm of the Department of Propaganda—controlled down to the font the newspapers were printed in.

"Maybe the papers lie about some things, but not about this. The curriculum has been standardized across public and private schools. We could move Georg to any school in the country but this isn't going away."

"So we're supposed to accept that he'll be brainwashed by this nonsense?"

Jürgen sighed as he stepped into the bath. He scooped water up to wash his face, then rested his head against the tiled wall behind him.

"All right-minded German parents are trapped, just as we are," Jürgen said tiredly. "I don't even think we have a right to complain. The cage we're trapped in is at least a gilded one."

"Sooner or later, he's going to realize that Mayim is Jewish. His teacher is going to make sure of it."

We stared at one another in the harsh light of the bathroom. Jürgen closed his eyes again.

"I know," he whispered, shaking his head. "I just don't know what to do about it."

Later, I stretched out on my luxurious mattress in the beautiful house I'd been so desperate to keep, but I had never felt less comfortable.

Just a few weeks later, Georg seemed to sink into a funk, and he wouldn't tell me what was wrong. After several days of trying to cheer him up, I called Lydia to see if she or Hans could shed any light.

"It's to be expected," she said sadly.

"I don't know what you mean."

"Hans said the boys have been teasing him about..." She paused, and then her tone sharpened. "Sofie. You *know*."

"Mayim?" I whispered.

"You can't harbor a Jew in your house and not expect the other children to notice."

"We aren't *harboring* anyone. It's perfectly legal for her to be here."

"Children are more perceptive than we realize sometimes," she said. "Look, why don't you come around tomorrow morning for tea and we can discuss it? I hate that your boy is unhappy, and it's been so long since we caught up. I'm sure we can figure this out."

It *had* been a while since I saw Lydia. All of our old friends were increasingly engaged in Nazi party activities, and I'd found myself withdrawing more and more. I was desperate to help Georg, though, so we agreed that I'd meet Lydia at her home the following day.

But as soon as I hung up the phone, a burst of frustration and anger overtook me. I picked up the handset and dialed Jürgen's direct line.

"I need you to come home tonight."

"I can't," he said automatically. His team were preparing for yet another test launch and there seemed to be no time in his schedule for anything else. "There's this panel giving us some trouble—"

"I think Georg is being bullied at school and I'm so sick of dealing with every little thing in this family on my own. I need you to come home tonight."

"Okay," Jürgen sighed. "Okay."

"Good," I snapped, but by the time Jürgen walked through the front door, my impatience with him had burned out. I pulled him close and kissed his cheek.

"I'm sorry," I said.

"Me too," he said. "I know you're carrying the load of the family. I don't thank you enough for that."

"I'm worried about Georg. Lydia said some of the boys may have been teasing him about Mayim."

"Ah," Jürgen said, wincing. Then he sighed heavily. "I'll put him to bed tonight and talk to him, man-to-man."

For the first time in a long time, the six of us were home

for a meal. We sat at the end of the long dining table in the formal dining room, Laura happily tucked between Adele and Mayim, Georg beside me opposite them, and Jürgen at the head of the table.

I was struck by the warmth that burned in my chest at the simple pleasure of us all being together around a table spread with good food. Adele served juicy slices of roast chicken, while Mayim and I began to dish out the vegetables. But when she tried to ladle carrots onto Georg's plate, he pushed the spoon away aggressively. His expression was sullen, and he refused to look at her.

"What's wrong, little buddy?" she asked him gently. "Aren't you feeling well?"

"Georg," I said, surprised. "You love carrots."

He looked up, then around the table, his eyes filling with tears as he flicked his gaze between me and Jürgen and Adele. I noticed then that he was going to some lengths to avoid looking at Mayim, dropping his eyes to the table every time they might pass her.

"I don't want carrots either," Laura said, as if she sensed a chance to avoid her vegetables.

"Everyone is having carrots," Jürgen said firmly, but then Georg burst into noisy sobs, pushed his chair back, and ran from the room. Mayim and I exchanged startled glances, as Jürgen also pushed his chair away from the table. "Let me talk to him."

I left Laura with Adele and Mayim and followed Jürgen and Georg down the hallway, but lurked outside Georg's bedroom, out of sight.

"What is it, Georg?" Jürgen asked softly.

"Papa," Georg said hoarsely. "Is it true? Is Mayim a dirty Jew?"

There was a long pause. I could hear my pulse in my ears as I waited for Jürgen to respond.

"Please don't use those words," Jürgen said carefully. "But yes, it is true that Mayim is Jewish. Why are you worried about that, Georg?"

"Mrs. Muller says that the Jews are the enemies of the Führer. Is she going to hurt us?"

"Of course she won't hurt us!" Jürgen said, flustered and frustrated.

"But the boys say that if she's in our house she will steal our money and make us sick." Georg gave a shuddering sob. "Papa, Hans won't play with me at school because he said I have dirty Jew germs. He said we might even die!"

"That's silly, Georg. You know that Mayim isn't dangerous."

"But Hans said—"

"I know what Hans said," Jürgen said abruptly. I could almost hear the cogs of my husband's mind turning. To defend Mayim was to invite trouble from the Gestapo. To not defend Mayim was to fracture our family. He paused, then called helplessly, "Sofie?"

I came around the corner and joined him in the room. Jürgen was seated at the end of Georg's bed. I sat beside Georg's pillow. He sat up and threw his arms around me, suddenly weeping anew.

"Mama," I heard him whimper. "I don't want Mayim to give me carrots anymore."

I wrapped my arm around him and looked over his head at Jürgen. My husband's shoulders slumped as he stared down at the carpet.

We gave Georg the option to return to the table to eat his carrots. He told us he just wanted to go to bed. Tears in my eyes, I kissed him good-night and let him have his way. By the time we emerged from Georg's room, Mayim was in her own room, and her door was closed.

"Let me put Laura to bed and then I'll see myself out," Adele said quietly. "It sounds like you two need to talk."

"Thank you, Aunt Adele," Jürgen said, and he bent to kiss her cheek.

We retreated into the study with a bottle of wine. I locked the door behind us, then wandered past his heaving bookshelves, over toward the armchairs in the corner. The study had grown dusty with Jürgen away so much. I hated to clean and we could have afforded a housekeeper, but I couldn't figure out how to bring someone into the sanctuary of our home without bringing Nazi ideology with them.

There was simply no escaping it.

I dropped myself into an armchair, stretching my neck to look at the ornate plastering on the ceiling.

"We could leave Germany," I blurted suddenly. Jürgen was uncorking the wine at his desk, but he paused and looked up at me in surprise.

"Where would we go?"

"Adele has been trying to convince Mayim to go to her grandfather and Moshe in Krakow. We could pack up and leave Berlin behind."

"We're going to uproot our entire family and move to Poland just because Mayim's grandfather lives there?" Jürgen said wryly, as he poured us each a glass of wine. I slumped. It was a terrible idea. "I don't love the idea of Poland. Neither one of us speaks Polish, for a start. But we could think about leaving Germany."

"Then where would we go?"

"England? My English is basic, but you know I'd pick it up quickly. You could help me."

"Or France," I suggested, since we both also spoke rudimentary French. We stared at one another, as if we were assessing just how possible this was. "How would we survive?"

"I'd find work at a university."

His salary would drop and we'd be back to trying to stretch our money as far as we could. Poverty seemed almost appealing if it came with the freedom to raise my children right. Only one thing gave me pause.

"Mayim's parents rely on the money we've been giving her," I said uneasily. We had been giving Mayim money every month ever since our own finances had stabilized, and I knew she passed almost all of it on to Levi and Sidonie.

Jürgen considered this for a moment. Then he sighed. "I suspect they would sooner see her safe abroad with us. They would find another way."

"And Adele?"

There was no hesitation this time before Jürgen said, "We'd try to convince her to join us too."

"She would never agree."

"I know." He rubbed his eyes. "She was born in that house—"

"—and she will die in that house," I finished on a sigh. "So you really want to leave the rocket program?"

"Truthfully, Sofie, it would be a relief," he admitted, staring down into his wine. His shoulders were stiff, his expression taut. In the time that passed since he took that "miracle" job, my husband had aged. There were fine lines around his eyes and bags beneath them.

"Has it not been going well?"

"Hitler is rebuilding the German military. It will be public knowledge soon." I gasped in shock. "Otto says that Hitler expects the world will sit idly by, and then the remilitarization will snowball. The rocket program has made incredible gains, but that only means that if they asked us to weaponize the technology, we could do so in just a few years. I've been trying to figure out how to extract myself for some time, but it's not going to be easy," he admitted, dropping his voice to a whisper. "They need me too much. They'll never let me walk away. We'd have to do this quickly and quietly. If you're serious about this—"

"I am," I blurted.

Our eyes locked over the wine. He nodded.

"Saturday. We'll pick a border, find the back roads, and pretend we're just going for a drive."

"*This* Saturday?"

"If we're doing this, we need to do it right away."

"Okay," I breathed, my heart rate accelerating.

"Talk to Mayim tomorrow. I'll talk to Adele. Other than that, we cannot breathe a word of it."

23

Lizzie

Huntsville, Alabama
1950

CALVIN WAS LEANING AGAINST THE KITCHEN door, looking up at the ceiling, as if he were praying for patience. This conversation was one I could not afford for my brother to overhear, so I waited until Henry was in bed before I confronted Calvin about Gail's suspicions.

"So? Is it true?" I asked. "Was Jürgen Rhodes in the SS?"

"Lizzie, sweetheart, you know I can't talk to you about this," Cal said, but he avoided my eyes as he spoke.

"My God," I whispered, my mouth going dry. "He lives on Sauerkraut Hill with the rest of them, doesn't he? There's an SS officer living two blocks away from us? Free in our community?"

"Even I don't know for sure," Calvin said flatly. "But yes, when Newsome admitted he'd seen evidence a senior scientist was in the SS, it was Jürgen he was referring to."

"This is an *outrage!*"

"Lizzie. Don't fly off the handle."

"Even you said in the beginning that it wasn't right—"

"I should never have said anything to you about any of this! It just never occurred to me that we'd end up living in the same community as these men," Calvin said.

"Because you knew it was dangerous!"

"I was nervous in the beginning, yes. But when it comes to Jürgen, I'm certain that the good he can do for this country far outweighs any risk he might have posed."

"Calvin, you have an SS officer working with American Jews!" I gasped. "Do you really think he's suddenly decided they are worthy of drawing breath after all?"

"Jürgen works closely with Eli Klein and I've never seen him speak to that man with anything but the utmost respect. Trust me when I say that man has no interest at all in anything outside of rocketry and his family."

"Men like that don't change, Calvin," I whispered. My voice thickened with emotion as confused tears sprang to my eyes. Calvin gently touched my upper arm, his gaze steady.

"War is brutal, Lizzie. Even if the rumors are true, there's possibly a whole background and context we can never understand."

"War is brutal *because* of men like that. This war didn't start itself—Nazis started it. Nazis perpetuated it. Nazis murdered millions of innocent people. There is no doubt at all who the villains are here."

We both heard movement in the hallway then. Cal and I stared at one another in alarm. Then he spun and pulled the door open. Henry was standing there, frowning.

"I thought you went to bed," I blurted. I could not have sounded guiltier if I tried.

"I just wanted a glass of milk," Henry said defensively. He

moved slowly, opening the refrigerator, pouring the milk, putting the bottle back into the fridge. As he was leaving the room, he shot me a pointed look.

"Good night," I said weakly.

"Night, Henry," Cal added.

"Hmm," Henry said, frowning. We watched until he disappeared out the back door, back to his apartment above the garage.

"Do you think he heard?" Cal said.

"No," I said, heart rate already settling. "He wouldn't have been so calm if he had."

"Henry can't know what we just talked about, Lizzie. Not just because no one is supposed to know. In Henry's case, it wouldn't be good for him to know."

"My first concern is always Henry's welfare," I snapped.

I woke that night to a thud and then a pained cry, and threw myself out of bed, rushing into the hallway. Calvin was there—standing in the doorway to his bedroom. We'd never shared a room, something that perplexed Henry the first time he stayed with us. I explained that Calvin snored terribly, and while my brother seemed unconvinced at first, the buzz saw–like sound that echoed down the hallway later that night when Cal went to bed seemed to reassure him.

Now I came to stand beside Calvin, and I rubbed my tired eyes as I mumbled, "Was that Henry?"

"I think so," Cal said.

"Lizzie!" I heard Henry cry. The sound was coming from the kitchen. Calvin ran ahead of me down the hall and pushed open the kitchen door, just as Henry shouted, "You leave her alone!"

His voice was strained, and he was flailing wildly. I reached for the cord to turn the light on, but Calvin caught my hand.

"He's sleepwalking," he whispered. "Just leave the light off and we'll gently reassure him first." Then he raised his voice a little and said firmly, "Henry, you're safe. No one is here."

"Henry," I called, keeping my tone soft. "Honey, wake up. You're okay!" Henry was throwing himself around the room as if he were tangling with an invisible assailant, and as his arms flailed, he knocked the fruit bowl to the floor. Apples rolled over the floorboards, and I sighed impatiently as I pulled the light cord. Cal looked at me, incredulous.

"One of us was going to break an ankle if I didn't," I muttered. Then Henry launched himself while Calvin was distracted.

"It's just me!" Cal groaned, as Henry knocked him violently into the refrigerator. Calvin's glasses fell off and clattered to the floor.

"Henry," I gasped, grabbing his upper arm and tugging at it. Henry shook me off and I stumbled backward into the door, releasing a cry of pain.

Just then, Henry backed away from Calvin, looking blankly around the room as if he had no idea where he was. He soon dropped to cower near the stove, panting as if he'd been sprinting, clutching his forehead in his hands. I pushed past Calvin to crouch beside my brother. Up close, I noted the sweat on his skin and the tears in his eyes.

"He was here," Henry said, still dazed. He looked around the room, then shook his head. "Where did he go?"

"It was just a dream," Cal said softly. "You were alone."

Henry blinked away the last of his tears, then scowled at Calvin.

"I know the difference between a dream and reality! He was *in this house*."

"This has happened before," I reminded him. "Remember? When you first came home to us in El Paso?" Henry's dreams were so vivid when he first returned from Europe and he often wandered around the house, sound asleep. After the night I found him standing at his car, keys in hand but deeply asleep, I began hiding his keys after he went to bed.

Those dreams seemed different from this episode, though. Back then, even when Henry acted out a dream, he was always fully alert as soon as I spoke to him—quickly aware he'd been dreaming. And he'd never hurt anyone before—but I shuddered to think what might have happened to Calvin if Henry hadn't snapped out of it right when he did.

"Someone was *here*, Lizzie. It must have been Rhodes," Henry insisted. Calvin bent, then felt around on the floor until he found his glasses. He sighed when he realized they were broken, and Henry looked at him, stricken. "What happened to your glasses, Cal? Did Rhodes do that?"

"You were in here alone," Calvin repeated. Henry frowned, shaking his head.

"He must have left before you came in." He paused, then nodded, as if he'd convinced himself. "That's it. He must have—" His gaze drifted to the window, and he frowned again. It was closed, the latch locked. His eyes flew to the door. "He must have gone out that way. Down the hallway. Out the back door."

"Why don't you sleep in the guest room tonight?" I suggested.

"We need to call the police," Henry said. He shot me a look of impatience—as if *I* were the irrational one.

"No one was here, Henry."

"You're not listening to me!" he exclaimed, raising his voice again. "I'm not crazy—I know what I saw."

"Why don't we call the police in the morning?" Calvin suggested. He caught my eye, and I gave a subtle nod.

"Good idea," I said gently. "If someone was here, they're

obviously gone now. Let's get some sleep and try to figure this out in the morning."

Once I got Henry settled in the guest room, I went to Cal's bedroom and closed the door behind me. Calvin was sitting on his bed, wearing his spare glasses. He was staring at the floorboards, his expression grave.

"He heard us for sure," I muttered.

"I know."

"What do we do?"

"He needs to see a doctor."

"A doctor?" I repeated. "For what? Nightmares?"

"I don't know what kind of episode that was, but it was more than a nightmare."

I shook my head. "He doesn't need some doctor telling him he's crazy, Calvin. He just had a bad night, and it's our fault anyway, since he heard us talking about—" I cleared my throat "—your *colleagues*."

"He knocked you into that door and he was ready to tear my head off. I'm worried about him, sweetheart."

"Me too. But he hates doctors."

"Do you want me to talk to him?" I shook my head. "Then you need to do it, Lizzie. Please, just check in with him. Maybe he just needs some sleeping pills?"

I slept on the sofa that night because it was in the room opposite the guest room. Every single time Henry stirred, I shot upright, ready to go to his aid.

Henry came into the kitchen and scooped up one of those bruised apples I'd put back in the fruit bowl at 2:00 a.m. He was dressed and ready for work but looked as exhausted as I felt as he took a bite out of the apple and sat opposite me.

"Did I hear you talking to someone a while ago?" I asked him cautiously. I took a quick shower as soon as I woke, hoping to be dressed by the time Henry woke up, but almost as soon as I stepped under the stream, I heard Henry speaking quietly in the hallway. By the time I was dressed, he had returned to his room.

"Yeah, I called Walt to let him know I'd be late," he said. He took another bite of his apple, and I noticed the *1401 BA SE* scrawled in ink on the back of his hand. What did that mean? Was it a lumber thing—a reminder to do something at his job? "Then I called the police. Someone is coming round shortly."

"What?" I said, as my heart sank. "Henry, no. I know last night felt real, but it was just one of those dreams you used to have. You've never even met Jürgen Rhodes. How would you know what he looks like?"

"How many other German men in this town have a beef with you, huh?" Henry said, frowning. "I know what I heard."

"When you woke us up, *you* were in the kitchen, thrashing around against no one," I said uneasily. "You know I'm not a fan of those Germans, but in this case, the intruder was in your imagination."

Henry's brows knit for a moment. Then he paused.

"Well, it won't hurt for the police to come and check the house."

Hell. How was I going to get through to him? I didn't even have time to think about it, because a quiet knock came from the door. I scurried after Henry when he rose quickly to answer it.

The police officer was middle-aged and sharp-eyed. He stood in my foyer and peered into the living room, notebook in hand. Henry introduced himself, then pointed to me.

"Officer Johnson, this is Lizzie Miller. Mrs. Calvin Miller. Cal was here last night, but he's at work at Redstone Arsenal now. He works on the rocket program there."

"I'm Detective Johnson, Mrs. Miller," the police officer said. "Pleased to meet you."

"And you too," I said weakly. Then I added, "My husband and I really didn't see a thing."

"Sounds like the intruder came in, realized he was outnumbered, and left," Johnson said grimly. He glanced at Henry and added, "Probably didn't expect to find two men here. You're sure the intruder was this Jürgen Rhodes?"

"Pretty sure," Henry said. Then he paused. "It was dark. But he had a German accent and Rhodes makes perfect sense. My sister had an argument with his wife last weekend."

The officer excused himself as he moved past me, glancing into each of the rooms. Henry followed him, and I followed Henry.

I tried to see the house through his eyes. My home was a picture of perfect order: expensive furniture and artwork, carefully selected and arranged, highly polished floorboards I mopped every single day, the drapes I kept free of dust, the windows I cleaned once a week.

Surely the police officer could see that this was not the site of a break-in and attempted assault. Not a single item was out of place. Even so, Henry spun the officer a story as he walked through the house.

I don't sleep well since the war. I was in bed, wide-awake. Heard a sound. Went to investigate. Saw Rhodes in the house. Chased him. A bit of a scuffle in the kitchen—pinned him against the fridge. Lizzie and Cal heard the noise and woke up just after Rhodes ran out. Probably out the back door. We never lock it.

This whole encounter was so absurd, I was starting to wonder if *I* was dreaming.

"I didn't..." I interrupted as Johnson looked closely at the latch on the back door. "Cal and I *really* didn't see or hear any of that. Not a thing." What was I supposed to do in this situation? I had to tell the officer that Henry was imagining things, but I didn't want to inflame him, and I certainly didn't want to embarrass him.

"You probably slept through it," Johnson said dismissively. He puffed out a breath of air, then looked between me and Henry.

"These Germans worry me," he told Henry.

"Me too," Henry said.

"You're a veteran?"

"Yes, sir."

"Pacific theater?"

"No, sir," Henry said. Then he drew in a breath and straightened his spine. "Europe."

"Thank you for your service, son. Must be troubling to have them walking around the streets of this country."

"It truly is, sir."

"Extra cautious from now on, all of you," Johnson announced, sliding his notebook back into his pocket. "Keep all the doors locked. And if you hear anything, you call us right away."

"Thank you, sir," Henry said grimly. We all walked back along the hall to the front door in silence. My heart was thumping wildly against my chest. I had to fix this—I just didn't have a clue how.

When the officer pushed my front door open, I panicked and blurted, "Are you going to arrest him?"

Detective Johnson turned back to offer me a gentle look.

"I'm sorry to tell you this, Mrs. Miller, but it would be very difficult for us to do that when none of you saw him clearly. I'll make some inquiries and we'll keep an extra close eye on your house with a night patrol for a few nights in case there's any more trouble."

Henry glanced down at the numbers on his hand and added helpfully,

"He's at 1401 Beetle Avenue, sir. In case you decide to interview him."

As the officer scrawled the address down, I looked at my brother in shock.

"How do you know that?"

"His address is in the public phone book, sis. Just looked it up to save this busy officer from hunting it down, that's all."

I looked from Henry to the detective, sucked in a breath, and tried one last time. "Sir, Cal and I really didn't hear *anything*—"

"Don't beat yourself up, Mrs. Miller," Detective Johnson interrupted me kindly. "You're lucky your brother here is a soldier. He'll keep an eye on you."

He tipped his hat and walked along my porch, then down to his car waiting in the drive.

"Henry," I whispered uneasily, "why would Rhodes come to his boss's house in the middle of the night to cause trouble? It makes no sense. He wasn't here last night. No one was."

"You were asleep," Henry said gently. "Just lock the house while I'm gone, okay? And if you're home alone, don't answer the door unless you're sure who it is."

My gaze dropped to that number on the back of Henry's hand and I blurted, "Just promise me you won't go to Rhodes' house."

Henry sighed impatiently.

"I'm not about to go looking for trouble. I was just trying to help, that's all."

With that, Henry pulled his cap on and left for work. I stood on the porch and watched my brother disappear down the street, sick with concern, but as soon as he was out of sight, I forced myself to go inside and call Calvin.

"Henry called the police, and a detective came by this

morning," I blurted, as soon as Calvin picked up my call on his office line.

"He *what*?"

"Maybe there *was* someone here?" I said hesitantly. "Henry seems so sure about it."

I heard Calvin breathing over the line, and I could easily imagine his pensive expression. "He was fighting thin air, sweetheart. You saw that as much as I did."

"I told them we didn't hear anything. I told the officer at least three times," I said heavily.

"Is there going to be any trouble from this, Lizzie? Should I warn Jürgen? Should I call the station and try to straighten it out?"

"I asked the officer if they'd arrest Rhodes and he said they couldn't because none of us had seen him clearly. He just said they'd keep an eye on the house, maybe make some inquiries."

"Lizzie," Cal said quietly. "Will you talk to Henry? Please? As a matter of urgency, sweetheart. He needs to speak to a doctor. This is serious now."

I agreed to speak to Henry that night, then spent the day wondering how I was supposed to do it without embarrassing him or setting him off.

Henry beat Cal home from work that day. He tousled my hair as he came past me in the kitchen, and I nudged him away impatiently with my shoulder because my hands were covered in ground beef.

"Is that meat loaf?" he said, peering hopefully at the bowl I was working on.

"Sure is," I said brightly. It was his favorite, and I was trying to butter him up. "How was your day?"

"Great," he said. "You? No trouble today?"

"Not a peep," I said lightly. I smoothed the last of the meat into the pan and washed my hands, then slipped the pan into the oven. Henry helped himself to a beer from the fridge and was sitting at the table reading the newspaper. "Henry, listen. I was thinking you might want to see a doctor."

He looked up at me blankly.

"A doctor? I'm not sick."

"Well, you said you don't sleep well now," I said carefully. "Maybe some sleeping pills—"

"I've tried them," Henry said abruptly. This was news to me.

"You have?"

Henry closed the newspaper and stood, taking the beer with him as he stepped away from the table.

"Those pills aren't for me, sis. Besides, it's *good* that I don't sleep well at the moment."

"How is that good?"

"I can keep you safe, Lizzie. I'll keep an eye on the house while you sleep."

He was walking away, beer in hand, already at the kitchen door—his swollen body straining the largest uniform the lumberyard had to offer, his shoulders slumped. My heart ached for Henry.

"No one was here last night, Henry," I said hesitantly.

"Sis," he said, glancing back at me to force a tight smile. "I know what I saw."

When Cal got home that evening, Henry was in the living room, chuckling at something on TV. Cal motioned for me to follow him into his study, then closed the door.

"Have you spoken to Henry about a doctor?"

"I tried," I said.

Calvin gave me a searching look. The compassion and sympathy in his eyes was so intense, it moved me to tears. Calvin Miller truly was the best man I knew.

"Can we just give Henry a few more days, Cal?" I whispered. "Please? Let's just let him settle in more before we make a big deal out of what was probably just a vivid nightmare."

"Okay, sweetheart," Cal said carefully, even though I could see he was unconvinced. "We can give him a bit more time to settle back in—but if there's any more trouble like last night, we'll have to force the issue."

"Thank you."

"I don't want to embarrass him—I truly don't. But it might just be that Henry's problems are finally bad enough that he needs to accept some help."

24

Sofie
Berlin, Germany
1935

JÜRGEN AND I TALKED UNTIL AFTER MIDNIGHT that night, trying to consider every possibility. Which border might we run for? How would we make sure we didn't arouse suspicion, especially with Dietger keeping such a close watch on us? What would Adele do? She would encourage us to flee without her—but we were anxious about leaving her behind. Would there be consequences for her?

There were too many questions we couldn't answer, and with Jürgen's eyes red from fatigue, we decided we'd sleep on it. I tossed and turned, asking myself a million variations of *are we really going to do this?* The last time I looked at the alarm clock, it was 2:33 a.m.

I was roused from sleep less than half an hour later by a thumping from the front door, the sound loud enough that the windows in our room rattled. Bleary-eyed and bewildered, I rolled toward Jürgen and shook him.

"What's going on?"

He groaned as he pushed himself upright, then slipped his glasses on, looked at the alarm clock, and turned back to me.

"A knock at the door at this hour can only mean one thing, my love."

We stared at one another in the dim light. My heart was pounding against my chest, static ringing in my ears.

"I haven't done anything wrong," he whispered. "I'm assuming you haven't either."

"Mayim," I choked out, closing my eyes.

"We need to answer the door before the children wake up."

I pulled on my housecoat and followed Jürgen down the stairs, my heart racing so fast I felt light-headed. When we reached the ground floor, he reached for the handle and I caught his elbow.

"We can't just let them take her!" I cried, belatedly panicking as I imagined Mayim being dragged out into the night. Jürgen hesitated, glancing between me and the door. The thumping returned.

"Open up!" someone shouted.

"I'm sorry, Sofie," Jürgen whispered, voice breaking. "We can't not answer."

Above us, a floorboard creaked. I looked up to find Mayim on the landing above us.

"What is it?" she whispered.

"Go into the closet in Laura's room!" I whispered fiercely. We could tell them Mayim wasn't home…tell them only our little girl was in that room… Maybe they'd believe us? Surely it was worth a shot. We had to do something. "Hide! Please!"

Mayim gasped, and a sudden terror crossed her face, but she didn't move.

"If I hide in there, Laura may wake up and see them take me!" she whispered back. She pursed her lips, then closed her eyes and whispered weakly, "I can't let that happen."

"Sofie…" Jürgen said. I looked at him, and his gaze was calm. "I'm sorry, my love. We can't hide her. We just can't."

I looked upstairs again to see Mayim walking away, but she returned just a second later, pulling on her coat, her chin high and her eyes clear.

"But she hasn't done anything wrong!" I cried as Jürgen threw open the door to reveal a group of men on the doorstep.

The Gestapo did not wear a uniform—they worked by stealth. These men could have just been a social group out for a late-night stroll but for the murder in their expressions. As my eyes adjusted to the darkness, I saw Dietger hovering on the sidewalk behind them.

"Jürgen Rhodes?" the man at the front said. Jürgen nodded silently. "You need to come with us."

My heart skipped a beat.

"But—wait. What?" I choked out, stepping forward. Jürgen looked at me in alarm. Then he shook his head and shot me a frantic look as I took a step closer. I pressed a hand to my mouth, suddenly terrified I was going to be sick.

"Can I change?" Jürgen asked the men, motioning down at his nightclothes.

"This isn't a social visit!" the man snapped. Jürgen didn't resist, not even as the men led him out the front door and into the night. I took a step forward into the empty doorway.

The streetlight glowed outside, bringing just enough light that I saw my husband pushed into the back seat of a black car. I watched until the car drove away, and the street was suddenly quiet again. I might have dreamed the whole thing, except that I was shaking from head to toe, and Dietger was still standing right outside the low stone wall between my front garden and the sidewalk.

Through my tears, I met his eyes. We had been neighbors for years, and we were at least friendly. He gave me a sad look, then slowly shook his head, as if he were personally disappointed in me.

"Where are they taking him?" I asked him hoarsely.

Instead of answering, he turned and walked slowly across the road, back to his house.

I paced in the foyer for a while, frantic and sobbing.

"I don't know what to do," I blurted, after a while.

"Could you call Lydia and Karl?" Mayim suggested. She was also crying, but lingering on the stairwell landing, as if the front door represented a threat to her physical safety.

I felt bad for waking Lydia and Karl, but to my surprise, there was no answer. I called again with the same result.

"Maybe they went away?" Mayim suggested, but I stared at her, then back to the phone, frowning.

"But I phoned Lydia after I picked Georg up from school yesterday, remember?" I slumped, shaking my head. "We were supposed to have morning tea at her house tomorrow—today. They must be home."

"What else can we do?"

"We have to wait," I choked out, and that was what we did. But every time I looked at the clock, I was surprised to find how little time had passed.

Eventually, Mayim and I shifted to the sitting room, and the sun began to breach the horizon, golden rays of light slowly filtering through the drapes. Mayim rose and made us some strong coffee in preparation for the children waking up. We sat together on the sofa and sipped the bitter brew.

"You thought they were here for me," she said after a while.

"It seemed the only obvious reason for their visit."

"You need Jürgen's job more than you need me," she said stiffly. "I'd rather stay at my parents' apartment than to watch Jürgen dragged from your house by the Gestapo on my account."

"Last night, Jürgen and I talked about leaving."

"Leaving…his job?" she said, eyebrows lifting.

"Leaving Germany. All of us. Him, me, you…maybe even Adele."

"Adele would never leave. She was born in that house—she wants to die in that house."

"I know," I laughed weakly, through my tears. Adele had trained us all so well—we each understood exactly what she wanted for the end of her life. "We were going to ask her anyway."

But then I paused, considering the sequence of these events. Jürgen was so convinced they'd never let him leave. That was exactly why we intended to go quickly and quietly.

"It was after you went to bed," I told Mayim, trying to join the pieces of the puzzle. "We were in the study. The door was locked. No one could have heard us."

"Maybe Dietger was sitting outside?" she said. "Near the window?"

"We were in the corner, in the armchairs. The window was closed."

I rose and walked back across the hall to the study. I had no idea what a listening device might look like—but if there was a microphone in his room, surely I'd be able to find it? Mayim came to help, but after we searched every nook and cranny, we found nothing.

"Isn't it starting to feel like they have eyes and ears everywhere?" Mayim whispered when we finally gave up and dropped our exhausted bodies back into chairs in the living room. "Nowhere is safe now. Not even our own home. And when we can't understand how they are surveilling us, we can't do a thing to avoid it."

We sat in silence for a long while after that. The sun rose all the way over the horizon. The coffee left in the pot had long gone cold.

"Mama," Georg said. I turned to find him standing in the doorway, eyeing Mayim warily. She and I shared a sad glance, and I rose from the sofa.

"I'll help you dress for school, Georg," I said, my throat tight. I hated to take him back to that place, but there was no alternative.

Not yet, and maybe not ever.

Lydia's nanny was at the school gate dropping off Hans.

"Has Mrs. zu Schiller been called away?" I asked her lightly. She shook her head.

"No, she's at home."

"There was a family emergency and I tried to call last night," I said hesitantly. The nanny looked at me uncertainly.

"There's a handset near my rooms. I'd have heard the phone if it rang."

"Would you mind asking her to call me when you get home?"

"Of course."

I sat by the phone in Jürgen's study, waiting for Lydia to ring. Mayim brought me more coffee, then took Laura outside to play in the courtyard. I stared at the window at the front of the room, trying to figure out how Dietger might have heard us.

"Mayim said they've taken Jürgen?" Adele cried, bursting into the study without warning. I startled, and she crouched in front of me, cupping my face in her rough palms. "Oh my

Lord, Sofie. I'm so sorry, treasure. I'm so sorry. Do you have any idea what this is about?"

"We…" I looked around the room, suddenly too scared to give voice to my suspicions, no longer even trusting the sanctuary of my home. "I don't know," I croaked.

Adele pulled me into an embrace, holding me hard up against her thin body with surprising strength. She released me, then rose.

"Is there anyone you can call? Those zu Schiller friends, perhaps?"

"I…I tried to call last night," I said. "They didn't answer. I asked Lydia's nanny to have them call me."

"Call her now," Adele said abruptly. It didn't occur to me to disobey her. I reached for the handset and dialed. This time, an answer came within a few rings.

"This is the zu Schiller residence," the housekeeper said.

"Hello, it's Sofie von Meyer Rhodes," I said. Then I cleared my throat and asked, "Is Lydia at home?"

There was an awkward pause before the housekeeper said stiffly, "Mrs. zu Schiller is unavailable."

"She's expecting me for tea this morning…" I said weakly.

"Mrs. zu Schiller is unavailable, Mrs. von Meyer Rhodes," she repeated firmly. "That includes for your morning tea, I'm afraid."

"I'll speak to Karl, then?"

"He is at Kummersdorf, of course."

"Did you have some phone trouble recently?" I whispered, closing my eyes.

At this, she paused. Then she said thoughtfully, "It's the strangest thing. Both of the phones had been unplugged. I only realized this morning when I was dusting. It must have been one of the children."

The children hadn't touched those phones. It had been Lydia or Karl, because they knew I'd be calling at an indecent hour.

There was a quiet knock at the front door just before noon.

Adele rushed to answer it, but Mayim and I followed at a safe distance. Jürgen was there, alone. One of his eyes was purple and swollen almost shut and he was visibly disheveled, but it seemed he'd suffered no other serious injuries. Adele embraced him, murmuring prayers of gratitude to God. Then she stepped aside, making room for me. I threw my arms around his neck and wept. He stood still and silent, his hands against my back, his breathing steady and calm.

But when I pulled away, I saw the miserable way he glanced between Mayim and me, and I knew this wasn't over yet. Aunt Adele turned away and was facing the hallway toward the kitchen as if she couldn't bear for us to see her cry, but her voice was thick with tears.

"I expect you'll need coffee."

"That would be wonderful. And we'll take it in the courtyard, thank you, Aunt Adele," Jürgen said quietly. Adele and Mayim whispered as they walked down the hallway, leaving me alone with my husband.

"The courtyard?" I said, protesting. "You need to rest."

"I am tired," he admitted, which seemed the understatement of the century. Even so, he forced a smile. "The sunlight on my face will help to wake me up."

We sat on the wrought iron chairs in the courtyard. Mayim brought a tray out and set it up in front of us, with rye bread and Adele's black currant jam, and coffee so strong I could smell it as she stepped out of the back door.

Once she was gone, Jürgen slipped his arm around my shoulders and drew in a deep breath, as if he were breathing me in.

"They knew we were talking about leaving. That's why they took me. My options are limited but simple. I'm alive and I work for the rocket program...or..." He broke off and I swallowed hard. "It's like I said last night. They need me too much to let me walk away."

Jürgen released me gently and poured himself a cup of coffee. He sipped it gingerly, then touched his swollen eye socket, wincing.

"They said it sends the wrong message to the public if a senior employee like me associates with Jews."

"Well," I said, trying to stay calm. "We can just—"

"Sofie, she has to go. We have to erase her from our lives. That's what they said." His voice sharpened with disgust. "*Erase her.* She's like your sister, and that means she's like my sister. She's a part of our family."

"We *can't*," I choked out, stricken.

"We'll be an example to the public one way or another. Do you understand what that means? It means if we aren't an example of how to shun a Jewish friend, we'll be an example of what happens to people who don't. I don't know how we survive if I lose this job, let alone if..."

"I wondered about the timing of this," I whispered. "Mayim thought maybe Dietger was outside the window."

"They repeated back to me what you and I said last night," Jürgen said. "There's no way Dietger would have heard us so clearly if he was outside. It was as though the Gestapo were in the room with us."

"I checked the study this morning," I said, shaking my head. "Surely if there was a microphone in there, we'd be able to see it?"

"Maybe not," Jürgen said hesitantly. He glanced at me. "There was talk at Kummersdorf about a weapons designer who went rogue. They say he was caught because of a passive listening device in his office. The Gestapo were supposedly sitting in the next building listening to every word he said. I never took the rumors seriously until last night. Secret listening devices? So small that a person wouldn't even notice them, so small that they can't even be found? The very idea seems so fanciful. I figured the rumor was just more propaganda. It would suit the Gestapo for people to think they could hear us even in the privacy of our offices or our homes too."

"But…there is no sign of a device in that room. Could they really have invented invisible microphones that don't even need electricity? There must be another explanation."

"If you told an electronics engineer that I have reasonably reliable rockets firing on a regular basis, he'd probably say that's absurd. For all we know, someone else working for Army Ordnance has designed passive microphones that really could be hidden in plain sight. We have to act as if it's true."

"We have to assume they can hear everything we say? Everywhere we go?"

"It's probably safe out here," he whispered. "Maybe there are ways we can cover the sound of our whispers inside, but we'll have to be careful. We'll never know which rooms they are listening in on…" He motioned toward Adele's building next door. "Or even which homes."

"Dietger was there when you were taken last night," I said, my throat tight. The existence of such a technology might explain his mystical ability to stick his nose in everyone's business. I felt physically ill. "I tried to call Lydia after the Gestapo took you. I didn't know what else to do. She didn't answer, and this morning their housekeeper told me they unplugged their phones last night."

Jürgen and I stared at one another, connecting the dots in the only way that made any sense.

"They knew you'd be calling," Jürgen said finally.

"You were friends with Karl and I was friends with Lydia long before you and I even started dating," I said. "If we can't trust them, who can we trust?"

The answer was in my husband's eyes. Moving forward, we would have to trust no one outside of our family.

"What do we do about Mayim?" he asked.

I could never bring myself to send Mayim away, but she couldn't stay. We couldn't allow our children to be brainwashed, but we had no choice other than to allow our children to be brainwashed.

I couldn't join my thoughts together in a way that made sense.

"My love," Jürgen said suddenly. I turned to him, and he gave me a gentle smile. The skin around his swollen eye crinkled. "Leave it with me, will you? Let me think on it."

He went inside to take a nap after that. Mayim retreated to Adele's house with Laura, and I went next door to join them. Adele made me sickly sweet, milky tea, and every time I finished a cup, she refilled it. In the end, we sat in near silence, but for the sound of Laura's chatter as she pottered around. I nursed that final cup of tea in my hands, too full to drink it but drawing comfort from the warmth.

When Jürgen woke he joined us, and he insisted I go home for a nap too. And when I roused again, I slipped out of the bedroom and into the living room, where I found Jürgen and Mayim sitting across from one another on the sofas. Mayim was crying, dabbing her eyes with a handkerchief.

"I had already decided to leave, Sofie," she said.

"But how will you survive?" I asked, stricken.

"I'm strong. My family is strong," she said, her voice breaking. "Besides, we don't have a choice. You know that's true, even if you wish it wasn't."

In the foyer less than an hour later, I stood opposite my best friend, staring into her eyes.

"I'm going to be okay," Mayim insisted. But she was pale, and I knew that she did not believe that any more than I did. I had been increasingly aware that she and her family were in danger. Until that moment in the foyer, I fooled myself that as long as she was in our house, she was safe.

But I had become someone who would sit at a dinner party and crack jokes about pork knuckle when a man spoke of Mayim and her family as vermin. I was someone who would let my child read anti-Semitic books.

I was someone who would let my best friend be sent away, even as our country turned its back on her.

She was in danger, and I was a part of the problem, not the solution. I just didn't know how to fix any part of that without risking Jürgen's life.

It was an impossible, unbearable position.

"I don't know how to get through the day without you," I blurted.

"Me either," she whispered unevenly. "That is something we are both going to have to figure out."

"I want my children to be like you," I said, hot tears rolling onto my cheeks. "I wanted you to help me shape them to be better people. I don't know how to be a good mother without your help."

"Nonsense." She pressed a hand to my chest, flattening it over my heart. "It's all here, Sofie. You're already a better mother than you know."

We were both sobbing now, each of us increasingly distressed. We'd been children together, and then we'd navigated adolescence, and those first brave steps into adulthood at finishing school, and then she'd been by my side when I married Jürgen and had my children.

Undeserving of her love though I knew myself to be, I was certain I was every bit as important to Mayim as she was to me. That was part of the wonder of her—that she loved me dearly, despite my flaws.

"Sofie," Jürgen said. He had taken her bags to the car and was waiting to drive her to her parents' apartment. He gave me a helpless look. "Mayim and I need to go."

I threw my arms around her one last time and I whispered fiercely in her ear, "Go to Moshe. Go to Poland." She stiffened, and I choked on a sob. I dropped my voice further, until I knew she had to strain to hear me. "Please. *Please*. Adele was right. Germany is not safe for you anymore. It hasn't been safe for a long time."

Adele came across that night and cooked dinner for us. I knew that the sausages and mashed potatoes would have been salty and buttery and delicious, but I pushed the food around my plate, too distraught to eat. Georg and Laura were unsettled too, each protesting at feigned outrages I was too depressed to acknowledge. When Laura threw a piece of sausage at Jürgen, seemingly without provocation, he pushed his chair back and said sternly, "Upstairs. Now. Both of you."

The children were visibly startled by their mild-mannered father, and they marched obediently upstairs with Jürgen close behind. The minute Adele and I were alone, I burst into tears. She came around the table to sit beside me and rested her hand over mine.

"You get tonight to sulk, Sofie von Meyer Rhodes. But tomorrow, you get up, you get out of bed, and you carry on. It's not always the strongest trees that survive the storm. Sometimes it's the trees that bend with the wind. And you, my treasure, find yourself right in a hurricane." She dropped her voice to the barest of whispers, so faint I had to strain to hear her even though her lips were against my ear as she added, "They insist you become a Nazi, so you pretend to be the best damned Nazi you can be. You will always know deep down inside what is true and what is right and they cannot touch your heart. But you have no choice now about the facade you present. Your husband and your children are counting on you to play the game." She pushed back her chair and said firmly, "You just need a strong cup of tea and some sugar. Everything is going to be just fine. You'll see."

It didn't feel like everything was going to be fine, not that night, and not the next morning, when Jürgen and I went through every room of the house, purging mementos of Mayim, erasing her from our lives as we had been instructed to do. I couldn't bring myself to dispose of the photos and the letters and the birthday cards, so Jürgen did it for me, burning them in the fireplace in the living room, right beside the spot where she liked to sit and read. I kept the knit blanket. It would be my comfort item now, to bring me a different kind of warmth when the world had turned so cold.

Georg said he was happy that Mayim was gone, but I could feel his grief, even if he didn't know how to make sense of it. He'd wake in the night calling for her, and I'd rush in to find him crying in his sleep. I promised myself that when all of it was over, I'd take him away to the country and I'd undo all of the damage those years were doing to his soul. In truth, I had no idea if that kind of healing was even possible. Isn't an adult just a child, shaped by experience? How *does* a person learn not to hate, when that hate has been imprinted upon them from such a young age?

Laura's grief was as uncompromising as mine at first. "I only want to eat Mayim's food," she told me stubbornly, and then it was "I only want Mayim to bathe me" and "I only want Mayim to dress me." Worst of all was "No, Mama! I only want Mayim's cuddles," after she'd scraped her knee one day. But she was five years old, and five-year-olds are, if nothing else, adaptable.

In time, Laura stopped asking for Mayim, and Georg stopped calling out for her at night, and as relieved as I was, it was like losing her all over again.

25

Sofie
Huntsville, Alabama
1950

JÜRGEN WAS SITTING IN THE LIVING ROOM, TRY-
ing to get Felix to accept a little wooden toy truck. Felix was
sitting behind the sofa, peeking out at the truck longingly,
but refusing to come out to get it.

There was a knock at the door, and Jürgen sighed and rose
to answer it, leaving the truck on the floor. I stayed in the
living room with Felix, hiding a laugh as he came out from
behind the sofa, scooped the truck up, and immediately took
it back into his hiding place.

"He's your papa," I said quietly.

"He's a stranger," Felix muttered, as he started rolling the
truck up and down the back of the sofa.

"Felix, go sit with Gisela, please," Jürgen murmured from
the door, as he returned with another man in tow. I quickly
shepherded my son down the hallway to Gisela's room, then

returned to find the guest was sitting opposite Jürgen, his expression solemn. He wasn't wearing a uniform, but something about his stiff posture spoke of authority—maybe even anger or aggression. I felt my heart rate kick up a notch as I carefully took a seat beside Jürgen.

"Can you tell me where you were last night at 2:00 a.m., Mr. Rhodes?" the man said. Jürgen and I shared a bewildered look. "I was here, of course," Jürgen said blankly. "Asleep."

"Does she speak English?" the man asked Jürgen, looking at me.

"I do," I said abruptly. I cleared my throat, then said, "I'm Sofie Rhodes. I didn't catch your name."

"Detective Johnson," he said. I recognized that name. This was the policeman Jürgen spoke to on the phone the day someone graffitied our street. "Can you confirm that your husband was asleep in your bed last night, Mrs. Rhodes?"

"Of course he was," I said. A strange, cold chill ran through my body, and a vivid image of a tiny, damp concrete cell flashed before my eyes. I tried to calm myself, reminding myself that American police were not the Gestapo, that Jürgen and I wouldn't wind up separated and locked up—not ever again. But even if my mind knew the truth, my body did not, and my stomach was churning violently. I could see the terror in Jürgen's eyes. I knew some part of him was back *there* too.

"Did you visit the Miller home last night?"

"*Calvin* Miller?" Jürgen said, confused. "No, sir. I've never been to his home, but I was just at work with him all day."

"Someone broke into their house last night, apparently looking for his wife. Are you telling me that wasn't you?"

"Of course it wasn't me!" Jürgen exclaimed. "Why would I break into my boss's house, then go to work the next day as if nothing happened? That's insanity."

"The intruder had a German accent, Mr. Rhodes. And

seemed to be looking for Mrs. Miller. I understand you—" his gaze moved to me "—and Mrs. Miller had an altercation last weekend."

"It wasn't an *altercation*," I said, my voice small as I stared at the carpet, unable to meet the detective's gaze. "It was a disagreement. I'm very sorry this has happened to them, but it had nothing to do with us."

The officer folded up his notebook and slipped it into his pocket. He stood, and Jürgen did the same. The two men stared at one another, both standing tall.

"I'm sure you know by now that this town didn't ask for you to come here."

"I appreciate that," Jürgen said calmly. "But your government did. We are committed to being good citizens and to contributing something to your nation. I want no trouble from you or from the Millers, Detective Johnson. You have my word on that."

"Frankly, Mr. Rhodes, the words of a Nazi don't mean much to me. That's what the graffiti in front of your street said, right?" He dropped his voice, his tone dark as he repeated the word. *"Nazi?"* Jürgen opened his mouth to protest, then thought better of it.

"I was not at the Miller household last night, sir," Jürgen repeated steadily. "I have no problem with Mrs. Miller, nor does my wife. I work very closely with Calvin Miller. His family has had no trouble from me, and they'll have no trouble from me."

"You should know, Mr. Rhodes—if there's one thing the boys at the station agree on, it's that if there's a chance to throw one of you in our cell, we're taking it."

After the detective left, Jürgen and I sat on the sofa, side by side.

"What on earth is going on?" I asked him uneasily.

"I don't know. And I don't know what to do." He pinched the bridge of his nose. "I saw Calvin in the lab early this morning. He seemed a bit weary, but he didn't say anything about this." Jürgen squeezed his eyes closed. "Things have been a little tense since the party."

"I'm sorry," I said weakly.

"No, no." Jürgen waved a vaguely dismissive hand in my direction. "I know you wouldn't have spoken without provocation. It's just…you know how men can be about their wives. He's protective of her, as he should be, and so knowing you two had that disagreement… I suppose things have been tender between us. I figured it was for the best that we just got on with work instead of trying to hash it out. But now—how am I going to talk to him about *this*?"

"I think this must be his wife's doing," I whispered. Jürgen frowned. "She made it pretty clear she doesn't want us here. Maybe she's just trying to cause trouble for us. Calvin might not even know."

"So…do I talk to him about it tomorrow?"

I shrugged.

"To what end? So he goes home and argues with his wife?" Jürgen nodded slowly.

"He has a lot of influence, Sofie," he murmured, closing his eyes briefly. "I really cannot afford to get on Calvin Miller's bad side. His recommendation will make or break my citizenship application one day."

We woke up the next morning to find graffiti had been painted on our street again. Bright red letters, over the black paint from last time, all across the entrance to the street. It was already dry by the time Klaus walked out his front door to go to work and noticed it. He came to let us know.

"Lucky I took Detective Johnson's advice and bought the paint in bulk," Jürgen sighed.

"This is ridiculous," Klaus muttered, glancing at the paint resentfully. Other families were coming to their doors now, but the women quickly shepherded their children back inside after they saw the paint. There was a brief meeting between the German men after that, most of them already dressed for work as Jürgen was.

I watched through the window as they stood on the street and stared at the paint. What were they thinking? The truth was, many of these men *were* members of the Nazi party. Did they feel shame at the reminder, or just frustration at the inconvenience? The answer was there in the slumped shoulders and downturned mouths.

After a few minutes, Jürgen returned to the house, already unbuttoning his shirt.

"What are we going to do?" I asked him. He shrugged sadly.

"There isn't much we can do if the police aren't interested in helping us. We thought about a roster of men to watch the street and try to catch the perpetrator, but there seems little point—what would we do with them once we did? The men are in agreement that the best strategy is to paint over it and hope the culprit gets bored of the game."

I stood on the porch and watched as Jürgen got to work, carefully rolling paint over the words on the street. The events of the previous night, and now this, left me unsettled and confused. I was trying to keep perspective, reminding myself I'd expected a transition period where things might be uncomfortable—but then a man rounded the corner into our street, on the sidewalk opposite our house. I'd seen him before, on that first day as we arrived from the bus station. Maybe he had to pass through our street as he walked to and from work.

The man stopped a dozen or so feet from where Jürgen was painting over the graffiti. Jürgen looked up at him and offered a nod in greeting, which the man did not return. He just stared at the road for a long moment, his face twisted into a smirk. Then the stranger continued casually on his way.

I waited until he was well out of earshot before I walked down the porch stairs and onto the front path. As I approached Jürgen, he turned back to me and shrugged.

"I thought being in a neighborhood with the other German families would be for the best, but it seems there are some downsides to everyone knowing which street we all live on."

"Yes, I'd say there are some downsides," I muttered. "I saw that man the first day we arrived and he was no less hostile then."

"It will get better. This is still new for everyone. The town will adjust to our presence here in time."

"I hope so," I said softly, extending my hand. Jürgen took it and squeezed it gently. "And this time, at least we're together through the struggle."

26

Lizzie

El Paso, Texas

1937

AFTER TWO LONG YEARS IN EL PASO, I HAD FI-
nally carved out a life for myself. Everything started to turn
around when I stopped waiting for a door to open for me and
started looking for ways to force one open.

I set my sights on a housekeeping job at the Hilton, and
because a sign in the front window assured me they weren't
hiring, I started lingering in the laneway near the staff entrance. From a distance, I noticed staff coming to that back
door with their arms loaded with trash, struggling to carry it
to the industrial bins a little way down the lane, then having
to rest the trash on the ground while they shifted the heavy
lids off the bins. A second set of hands made that whole process
so much easier, so I turned their problem into an opportunity
and appointed myself the Hilton's unofficial trash assistant.

I did this for weeks, right through the worst of a bleak win-

ter, wearing multiple layers so I didn't freeze. Henry thought
I'd lost my mind, until the day the housekeeping manager
came to the door and greeted me by name. She didn't offer
me a job right away. Instead, she let me clean the staff room
and work in the hotel laundry, places where I'd never see a
guest or their belongings.

"I can't pay you," she said bluntly. "But I can promise if
you're reliable and prove you're trustworthy, you'll be at the
front of the line when a position does come up."

And six weeks later, when one of the maids quit to get married,
my hard work paid off. We had one hundred and thirty guest
rooms to service and I was the first to raise my hand to complete
a task, even if it was onerous or particularly filthy. That ingra-
tiated me to the rest of the team. I wouldn't say I made friends
at work, but I certainly earned the respect of Mrs. Thompson
and the other maids—and more importantly, I learned to fit in.

The housekeeping job brought enough income for me
and Henry to move back into the rooming house, but better
accommodation wasn't the magic fix for Henry's mood I'd
hoped it would be. His charm had always defined him, but
it was impossible to charm his way to employment when he
always seemed to find himself at the back of a line of desperate men.

My brother had never lied to me before, so I took him at
his word when he said he'd been out looking for work during the day, but I wasn't surprised his job search was going
badly. Even now that he had access to laundry facilities and
a washroom, Henry wasn't cleaning himself up. It perplexed
me as much as it frustrated me.

"Maybe if you...you know, got up a little earlier?" I suggested. Then I drew in a deep breath. "Maybe you could shave
too. I could give you some money for new clothes—"

"Don't judge me, Lizzie," he snapped. Henry had never

been one to speak harshly to anyone, especially me. Something was changing in him. There was a dullness to his eyes.

The rooming house was vastly more comfortable than the homeless camp, but I figured that if I had a deposit for rent in advance on an apartment, we'd be well-placed to move once Henry found work. Within a few months, I had a little bundle of bills in that envelope. I was devastated the day I came home from work to find it gone.

"You shouldn't have left money in the room," Henry said when I told him we'd been robbed. I recoiled, stunned by his sharp tone.

"Where else would I leave it?" I needed a man to come to the bank to sign for me to open an account, which Henry offered to do, but I worked such long hours that we just hadn't found the time.

"I don't know, Lizzie!" he exclaimed. "This place isn't much better than the homeless camp. I'm so *sick* of the noise and the smell of cabbage from the damned kitchen and waiting to use the bathroom!"

"But…it's all we can afford," I said, stunned. He scrubbed a hand down his face, drew a few ragged breaths, then gave me a miserable look.

"I'm sorry. I never thought it would be like this."

"I know," I said uneasily. "Something will come up…"

"Maybe we should try to go somewhere else. I've heard there's more work in California—farmwork, even. We could take some of your wages and buy bus tickets. Try our luck there."

"Henry, no," I said, startled. Farmwork did sound much better than housekeeping, but I couldn't leave a real job for the chance of a theoretical one, especially after how hard I had worked to get it.

"Maybe I should just go, then," he said flatly. "I lined up

to ask about this new unemployment compensation program today. They'll give me five dollars a week for fourteen weeks. I could save it all. Use it for bus fare."

"Something will come up," I said, throat tight. "Please don't give up just yet."

I was already working six long days a week, but watching Henry's mood spiral downward, I grew desperate to change something—*anything*—that might help him. When I told the housekeeping manager I needed more money, she found me a night shift in the hotel restaurant, waiting tables. And finally, Henry and I moved into an apartment.

It was a fifth-floor walk-up, just three small rooms, but we had our own kitchen and bathroom. I experienced a new level of tired, working double shifts every day, but in addition to the bump in my wages, there were other unexpected benefits. In that little hour between my jobs, I could take the elevator all the way to the top of the Hilton.

The rooftop balcony had been converted into a beautiful outdoor area for the guests. From one side, I could see right over the Rio Grande into Mexico, and from the other, mountains and rocky outcrops and clear, open space. I'd walk to the edge and look out to the northeast, staring until my eyes watered, as though if I just looked hard enough, I'd see all the way up through New Mexico, back to my home in Dallam County.

The top of the Hilton El Paso wasn't quite as sacred or peaceful as Mother's moments on that little chair with Elsie, but the idea was just the same. I had to compress all my grief and my longing into those few minutes each day. It was the only time I ever stood still long enough to let myself acknowledge all that I'd lost, and just how lost I was in El Paso.

One night, I placed a steaming hot plate of food in front of one of our regular guests. His name was Calvin Miller, and he stayed at the hotel for a night or two each week, sometimes longer. He liked to stay in a room on the highest available floor, and rumor was he was a widower, consulting on new airplanes at Fort Bliss.

I wouldn't have noticed Calvin if I walked past him on the street. I guessed he was in his late thirties, probably close to fifteen years my senior. He was tall and wiry with a neat dark beard trimmed close to his face, and he wore thick glasses that magnified his hazel eyes. Having serviced his room, I knew he was fastidiously clean and he always traveled with piles of aeronautics textbooks. Overall, Calvin looked and carried himself like someone too clever for an ordinary existence.

"You're not your usual self this evening, Miss Lizzie," he said.

"Everything's fine, Mr. Miller," I said, as brightly as I could, but I struggled to fix a professional smile on my face. I'd been mugged walking home one night—the thief making off with my bag and apartment keys but no money, given I didn't even have any spare change that week. Even working as hard as I was, I was barely covering the expenses on the apartment.

"You have this worry line, Miss Lizzie. Right here." Calvin touched the spot between his eyebrows.

"Just tired, I guess," I said, flushing. "Can I get you anything else?"

"It's quiet tonight, huh?" he said. It was almost ten o'clock, and only a single table of businessmen remained in the restaurant, finishing their drinks. The restaurant would close soon, and then I'd start my cleaning. "Have you eaten?"

"I…uh…I usually eat when I finish my shift."

"Take a seat, Miss Lizzie," he said, motioning toward the chair opposite him, then toward his plate. He'd ordered his usual—steak, fries, and a side of vegetables. "Share this and chat with me."

"Oh no, I—"

"Come on," Calvin cajoled. "Haven't you heard I'm a lonely widower? Your boss won't mind if you sit a minute and keep me company. If you get in trouble, I'll tell them I insisted."

I took another glance around the room, just in time to see the table of businessmen I'd been serving drop their napkins onto their plates. One of them waved at me as he left, and since Calvin and I were alone in the restaurant anyway, I sank into the empty chair opposite him.

"Did you grow up here, Miss Lizzie?"

I shook my head.

"My family had a farm near Oakden."

"Oakden…? I don't know it."

"I'm not surprised. It's a tiny little town in Dallam County."

"What brings you to El Paso?"

"My brother and I came here looking for work. We lost the farm in the drought."

He grimaced. "Lots of families losing their farms these days. I'm sorry."

I nodded silently, and he twisted the plate so that the fries were closest to me. Just as I began to tell him I wasn't hungry, my stomach rumbled at the scent. I sighed and took one.

"Thank you. What do you do for work, Mr. Miller?"

"Call me Calvin, please," he said. "I'm an aeronautical engineer. I work for a specialist firm up in Albuquerque."

"Isn't Albuquerque a long way from here?"

"Not too far, four or five hours, depending on how busy the road is. This is just a temporary contract," he said.

"I'm worried about my brother," I suddenly admitted, not sure why I felt comfortable sharing this with a stranger. "He can't find work. I don't know how to help him."

"How old is he?"

"He's almost twenty-seven."

"Plenty old enough to help himself."

"It's not always that simple."

Calvin nodded. Then he offered me a quiet smile.

"It all depends on how big your heart is, I guess."

When I got home that night, Henry was in bed. I turned on the light in the little kitchen and sat beside him.

"Henry?" I whispered.

His eyes opened a crack, and he peered at me in the dull light coming through the kitchen door. His eyes were bloodshot, and he smelled like whiskey.

"I took the money from the pantry," he said miserably.

"You took the money for the electric bill?"

"It's not the first time I did it either. I took that money from your envelope back at the rooming house." His voice cracked as he confessed, "Lizzie, I don't know what I'm doing."

He looked so dejected, I couldn't even bring myself to be mad, but I was plenty hurt. I blinked quickly to clear the tears from my eyes before Henry could see them.

"It's okay," I lied uneasily. "Did you take all of it this time?"

"No. About half."

"Okay," I whispered.

"Lizzie, I don't know how much longer I can go on like this." The air in the room was thick with tension. My brother seemed genuinely exhausted and I had a sudden, terrifying understanding: he was tired from the effort it was taking him to keep breathing. When I blinked, I saw him cradling Dad's body beneath that tree on the farm, the sun rising behind them, our entire world changed with one split-second decision. "I'm letting you down, Lizzie. I'm a burden to you, and—"

"Don't you dare speak like that. You're the only family I've got now, and you'd never be a burden to me." He blinked hard; he couldn't quite clear the tears before I saw them. "We're a team, right? We always have been."

"It's not a team when one player is doing all of the work, sis," he whispered. Then he offered a weak smile. "Hey, listen—I'm tired, and you must be too. I need to get back to sleep."

He was right—I was exhausted. Even so, I was too scared to fall asleep, in case he wasn't there when I woke up.

"You have that worry line between your eyes again, Miss Lizzie," Calvin said, a few weeks later. We'd fallen into a habit of chatting the nights he was at the hotel, and I generally looked forward to his company, but I felt uncharacteristically fragile that night—like if he prodded me, I'd dissolve into a puddle of tears.

I'd worked three Sundays in a row so we could meet the electric bill, but I had to keep the cash in my locker at work. Henry was disappearing for days.

I set Calvin's steak and fries on the table, then forced a smile. "It's just been a long day, that's all."

Calvin lingered over his meal that night. I'd long cleared his plate and finished my cleaning, but he was still sitting there, making notes in the margins of a document. I glanced at the clock on the wall. It was just after eleven.

"I'm so sorry, Mr. Miller," I said, approaching his table. "The restaurant is closed now."

"I know," he said. He closed a folder over his document, then lifted his briefcase up onto the table and slipped it inside. "There's a diner just down the road where we can go for a milkshake, or we can have a chat while I walk you home. Up to you."

"Thank you, Calvin," I said quietly. "I appreciate it, but I'm okay. Really."

Only as soon as I said those words, a tear leaked onto my

cheek. Mortified, I swiped at it with the back of my hand, but Calvin's expression only softened.

"Lizzie…"

"I'm okay," I insisted weakly. "I'm fine. I'm just tired."

I was worn-out from worrying and utterly exhausted. Every single night, as I made that walk home, I wondered what I'd find when I opened the apartment door.

"Come on," Calvin said gently, rising to his full height. "Let me put this up in my room and I'll meet you in the lobby in a few minutes."

I was seated opposite Calvin in the diner down the block, a milkshake untouched in front of me. He'd devoured his, and now he was listening intently as I rambled about my brother.

"My father had these black periods his whole life—good days and bad days—but especially once the drought got bad. I mean, things *were* bad—don't get me wrong. But sometimes it seemed like things were worse for Dad than for anyone else." I struggled for words as I rubbed my forehead. "There's a darkness that runs in the men in my family. Henry isn't lazy or overreacting. I know that things really do feel hopeless to him, but he's not even trying to find work now. Not really. Do you know what I mean?"

"I do."

"Henry's pride is hurt because I'm supporting him, and now that's part of the problem. But what am I supposed to do? Quit my jobs, let us live in a homeless camp again?"

"Good grief, Lizzie. Of course you shouldn't do that."

"I think it was the same for our father and I bet Henry knows that. Dad was so reliant on Mother, and then when she died—he didn't even try, not for a single day. He—" I broke off, reluctant to even say the words aloud. Calvin winced, then leaned forward.

"Did your father take his life?"

I nodded, feeling myself becoming emotional. I had survived so much, but I had no idea how I'd go on if I lost Henry.

"Sometimes a mind can play tricks on a person," Calvin said, his eyes kind. "There is no shame in that for you or for Henry. For your brother, the best thing is probably the structure of a job. A reason to get out of bed each day and a paycheck, so he can feel proud again."

"I know," I said heavily. "I don't mean to say he hasn't tried. In the beginning, he really did try everything."

"Maybe I could make some inquiries for you."

"Would you?" I said in surprise. "You barely know me. You've never even met Henry."

"I can't make any promises." He shrugged. "But I can talk to some people. Let me see what I can do."

The next week when he was back in town, Calvin again suggested we go for a milkshake after I finished my shift. As we walked from the hotel toward the diner, he cut straight to the chase.

"I know this might not be what you had in mind, Lizzie, but has Henry considered enlisting?"

I stiffened.

"It's hard to enlist these days."

"It is. The military has turned away more men than they've taken over these past five or six years." The Depression had even hit the government hard and military budgets weren't what they once were. "I hoped I could find him some labor work on base, but there's just nothing there to find. Not for a civilian. But if Henry were willing to enlist, I could put in a good word for him. I spoke with an Army enrollment officer and he said that would mean something."

"Why would you do this for us?"

"I like you." Calvin shrugged. "It's lonely here sometimes. You keep me company. We're friends now, aren't we?"

"I guess we are," I said, but then I hesitated. "But he'd have to go live on base, wouldn't he?"

"Of course. And there's no guarantee he'd be stationed here."

"I just don't think…" I trailed off, unsure of how to express my thoughts without insulting my brother. Henry couldn't handle a jackrabbit drive. How would he handle a military career? I couldn't even imagine him in a uniform.

"It would mean three hot meals a day, a roof over his head, and more importantly—structure and a reason to get out of bed. I know this much for sure—every man needs a purpose."

When I opened the door that night, I was immediately hit by a wave of body odor. The apartment was still and silent, and the lights were off. On previous nights I'd turned the kitchen light on so as not to disturb Henry, but I offered him no such kindness that night. I turned the main light on, the one right above his bed. The blankets rustled, and then in a furious movement, he pulled them over his head.

"Don't start, sis," Henry mumbled, voice thick with sleep. I crossed the room in a few brisk steps, then threw the blankets back. Henry covered his face with his arms and made more sounds of irritation and complaint. He hadn't shaved or showered, and he was still wearing his trousers from the previous day.

"You should enlist," I blurted. Henry stilled, then gradually opened his eyes, squinting against the light of the bulb.

"I went to an enrollment tent when we first got here. I waited in line all day, didn't even get the chance to sit down for an interview. They were turning almost everyone away."

"But if they would accept you, you would *want* to enlist?" I asked, surprised.

Henry dragged himself into a sitting position, still rubbing his eyes.

"Dad once told me that there are some men who are cut out for that life, and some men who aren't. I don't know that I'm the right kind of man," Henry muttered, idly scratching the scruffy whiskers on his cheek.

I stared at my brother, absorbing the shadows under his eyes and the bleakness of his gaze. I knew exactly what Henry meant—he was soft and sensitive in the very best kind of way. Wouldn't those traits be liabilities for a man in the military?

But we were at peace, and anyway, Henry wouldn't have to remain in the Army forever. All we needed was to force structure into Henry's life—to prop him up for a few years until the economy recovered and he could find a civilian job.

"My friend at the hotel knows an enrollment officer and thinks he can get you accepted. You need to do it." I drew in a deep breath. "I am asking you to do it."

Henry blinked. Then he frowned.

"But, Lizzie—" he started to protest, but I reached to take his hand, squeezing it forcefully as I said, "We can't go on this way. We just can't, Henry."

I watched the emotions play out on my brother's face. First came shame and guilt and remorse, then frustration and irritation and embarrassment and anger. But all of this faded as quickly as it rose, and then Henry looked away as he nodded. By then, he simply looked resigned.

27

Lizzie

Huntsville, Alabama
1950

"HOW ARE YOU DOING, HENRY?" I ASKED ONE night a few weeks later. He was pushing his casserole around his plate, his expression distant until he looked up and gave me a tired smile. His mood seemed a little low, but it was hard to be sure since I'd barely seen him for more than a few minutes at a time in weeks. Henry had been going in early and coming home late, and he'd even taken some weekend shifts.

"Just not used to the long hours on my feet. I'll get used to it." He stifled a yawn, then pushed his chair back. "I might turn in. I've got an early start again tomorrow."

"Walt sure is working you hard," I remarked as he stood. Henry shrugged.

"I'm volunteering for every shift I can get. I'm thankful for the work."

He took his plate to the sink, and as he did, a scrap of paper fell from his pocket, fluttering to the floor and landing under the table right near me. I leaned and picked it up.

"Do you need this?" I asked. A large *S* was marked at the top of the page, and beneath it was some kind of schedule—the days listed down the left-hand side, followed by columns of scribbled times. The slip was in my hand for a second—long enough for me to register that Friday morning was underlined—before Henry plucked it from my fingers.

"Phew. Lucky I didn't lose that," he said with a strained laugh. "That's my work hours for the week so I can fill in my time sheet on Friday."

The explanation made perfect sense and should have been reassuring. But if he were telling the truth, why did Henry snatch the paper back from me?

Overall, my brother seemed settled. There had been no more midnight incidents, no more wild stories about intruders, no more unnecessary calls to the police. He had thrown himself into the job at the lumberyard, just as I'd hoped he would.

If he was a little withdrawn, it was probably because he was bone-tired from trying to make a good impression at work. This was a good thing. For years, I'd hoped and prayed for Henry to find a job that stuck, and despite the rough start, it seemed my prayers had finally been answered.

"Did you ever talk to Jürgen Rhodes about…about that detective? And Henry?" I asked Calvin one morning.

He sipped his coffee thoughtfully, then explained delicately, "You and Sofie Rhodes getting off on such an unfortunate foot makes things with me and Jürgen a little awkward."

"Oh."

"He lived and breathed to bring them here, Lizzie. For *years*. Whenever he speaks of his wife, his adoration of her is evident. I thought about warning him the day Henry called the police, but the opportunity never arose, and then I figured that if there had been any trouble, Jürgen would have mentioned it to me." Cal set the coffee cup down and seemed to brace himself before he asked gravely, "Has something else happened?"

"No, no," I hastened to assure him. "It's been a few weeks and, like I hoped, Henry seems to have settled right down. I was just curious."

But I kept thinking about that conversation with Cal over his coffee. It took me a few days to figure out why it left me feeling so uncomfortable.

I *needed* to think of those Germans as monsters—especially Rhodes, given what Calvin suspected about his past. It was unsettling to think of the same man as an ordinary person, with a family he loved and a wife he adored.

When Becca called to invite me to another lunch with the Fort Bliss wives at what she was already calling "our usual restaurant," an image of that Whites Only sign in the window flashed through my mind, and I shivered.

"Do come," Becca pleaded. "I need all the moral support I can get. Avril's on a one-woman seduction campaign, determined to make Sofie Rhodes her new best friend. You know how she gets. And the upside is, I'm sure she'll have some delicious gossip from it."

Discomfort sat like a stone in my gut. I always hated those lunches and I knew how that particular one would go. Avril would be all sweetness and light, batting her eyelashes innocently, but there'd be real venom in her words. I didn't want to feel sympathy for Sofie Rhodes, but by the same token, I knew that Avril would be coming along to that lunch with the sole purpose of betraying her new "friend."

I thought about my garden. I thought about the bliss and

ease I felt being out there, dirt beneath my nails and clean air in my lungs.

"I'm just so busy at the moment," I told her lightly. "I'll have to miss it this week."

28

Sofie
Berlin, Germany
1936

LAURA STARTED SCHOOL IN THE SUMMER OF 1936. On her first day, I walked her to the gate, then went back alone to Adele's house for morning tea.

I still visited Adele every day, but I no longer told myself that I made those visits for her sake. Now that I felt so alone, I finally realized that Adele was not. She had a network of friends all over the city—strong, independent women like her best friend, Martha, who had also outlived her husband, and her children. Adele was busy with those friends and her garden and her tenants. I'd always somewhat resented having to care for her. Only once Mayim left did I finally realize Adele never needed me at all.

"How did Laura do?" she asked as I let myself in through the back door.

"Not a tear. Not from her, anyway," I said, setting my hat

down on the kitchen table. I'd shed a few myself on the walk home. I couldn't believe my baby was at school. "She had a terrible night's sleep, but that was from excitement, not anxiety."

"That's our girl," Adele chuckled, as she poured steaming hot water into a teapot. She turned back to the counter and retrieved a tray. "I made you some bee-sting cake. I thought you might need the treat."

"Thank you," I said, surprised. She smiled and cut a piece, flipping it onto a plate for me with the side of the knife. I cut into the cake with a fork and sighed happily as it all but melted onto my tongue. Cake, honey-glazed almond slivers, and pastry cream tasted like pure joy.

"Listen, I'm having a little problem and I was hoping you could help me," Adele said. I frowned at her unexpectedly somber tone.

"What is it?"

"One of my tenants is struggling financially," she told me. "And that means I am having a little trouble making ends meet."

"Oh?" I said, startled. "Which tenant? Do you want me to speak to them—"

"No, no." She shook her head slowly. "I've spoken to them about it, and they are going to try to make amends. It's just that while they catch up, I wondered if you could maybe lend me a little money?"

"Of course," I said, without hesitation. "Just tell me what you need and when."

I'd mention it to Jürgen when he next called, but I knew he wouldn't mind.

Knowing that the house was wired with some kind of audio surveillance, Jürgen and I were performing all the time. Even when we were alone, we said and did all the things good Nazi parents were expected to do.

But Jürgen and I had systems to try to claw back at least a little privacy. We had to connect on a genuine level sometimes or we'd lose our minds.

Sometimes when he was home we drove out of Berlin and took long hikes, the children running up ahead in front of us through the forest or climbing to the tops of trees as Jürgen and I whispered to one another. Other times we'd hide in the bathroom, running all of the taps to cover the sounds of our voices. And I moved the wireless into our bedroom, and I'd turn it on every night whether Jürgen was home or not. We had scripted conversations about how I was becoming an insomniac and needed the background noise to sleep.

In reality, though, this was a cover—a way to protect us from prying ears when we pulled the blankets over our faces to whisper.

"Hi," he'd whisper, even though we might have been together for hours by then. I always felt I was removing a suffocating mask as we pulled those blankets over our heads, even though there was so little air, and every now and again, we'd have to pull the covers down, gulp in a breath, then dive back in.

We talked about Lydia. She'd transformed herself into the perfect Nazi wife, no longer dyeing her hair or wearing makeup, and pregnant—again. I felt such complicated emotions about her—a mix of nostalgia for our once-genuine friendship and swirling shades of distrust, resentment, and hurt. I had never confronted her about the way she let me down the night Jürgen was taken. There was no way to hold her responsible without drawing attention to our disloyalty to the Reich. I saw Lydia now only when I had to, and even then, I was polite but distant.

Jürgen told me about his work. He had just overseen a test launch of a new prototype, the first-ever test launch at Kummersdorf before an audience.

"There's been so much skepticism about the technology. Karl and Otto want to expand the program, but they first need to prove to officials that the concept is viable."

"So will you get the funding?"

"Yes. The general approved the request after he saw the launch."

"And what does that mean?"

"A huge bonus, for a start," Jürgen said. I didn't even feel the slightest flutter of excitement, only regret. Once upon a time, I'd have given that money to Mayim, but now I had no idea where she was or how they were. Every time the Nussbaums came to mind, I felt a deep, uncompromising grief. "We can give it to Aunt Adele," Jürgen said, and that did ease the ache in my chest a little. As I'd expected, he wasn't at all troubled by her request for financial assistance. Adele was independent enough that we knew she'd only ask for the help if she really needed it. "That's the good news. The bad news is they are talking about moving the entire program to a new development site."

"Where?"

"Peenemünde." I didn't react, so he clarified, "On the Baltic Sea."

"Four hours' drive?"

"Closer to five."

"I'm guessing you're not inviting me and the children to move with you."

"No. They are going to build us accommodation. It won't be family friendly."

"You're never home as it is."

"I know."

"So that's about to get worse?"

"Probably."

I digested this, grateful for the pitch darkness beneath the covers, so that he couldn't see the tears in my eyes.

"Sometimes, it feels like living this life is like listening to a piece of music played by a beginner. Most of the song is fine, isn't it? Most of the time I am engrossed in my work. That prototype we fired this week is like a baby version of the device that might take us to the moon one day—and it *works*, Sofie. I helped make that happen and there is pride in that. We have this beautiful house. Perfect children. We're healthy. We don't have to worry about money anymore. But...there are dissonant notes...sometimes even discordant phrases. And we have to keep smiling regardless. In fact, we have to smile even harder when we hear those sounds, just to cover up how jarring they are."

"Sometimes I don't know if I can bear it."

"Sofie, believe me, it helps to focus on the parts that you can bear."

"And for you, that's the rockets."

"That's right. And for you, it's this house, isn't it? This lifestyle?" I didn't have the heart to tell him those things had long since lost their shine, but he correctly read my silence. "There has to be something. The children? The new baby?"

I had just discovered I was pregnant again, but my feelings even about that were muddled. With my first two pregnancies, I told Jürgen and then Mayim before anyone else—even Adele. I was reluctant to break the tradition, even though I knew it was inevitable that I'd have to.

I even felt conflicted about bringing another child into this world. Every day, Georg and Laura were slipping a little further from me, even though we were all still under one roof.

The same would happen with this baby, unless something drastic changed before he or she was old enough to start school.

But Jürgen was right—there had to be something positive to focus on so that I could get through each day.

"The children," I whispered back. "And you. And Aunt Adele."

"I remember when you two didn't get along."

"These days," I confessed, "I don't know what I'd do without her."

Georg's birthday loomed, and all he wanted to do was to have a party with Hans. I gently tried to suggest other children, but Georg and Hans had the kind of friendship I'd shared with Mayim, so I couldn't bring myself to refuse the request.

We invited Adele to the picnic, but when she heard that the zu Schiller family would be there, her hip was suddenly too sore. Instead, she came to have breakfast with us beforehand. We had fat ham steaks and eggs, and she brought a photo of Jürgen from his first birthday in her house.

"He looked just like you do now," she told Georg, showing him the faded black-and-white image. "See?"

"We could be twins, Papa," Georg said, holding the photo beside his face. There was a strong likeness there, even if Georg had inherited a darker shade of blue eyes from me. Jürgen and Georg grinned at one another, then dissolved into mirroring one another's silly faces. Laura sighed impatiently at their antics.

"She's becoming such a serious child. Just as I recall you were," Adele said wryly, glancing at me.

"I was terrified of you. I remember talking to May—" I stopped myself just in time, drew in a breath to collect myself, then continued as smoothly as I could. "—to my friends about cranky Mrs. Rheinberg, who lived next door to our city house."

When I was a child, Adele and Jürgen were the slightly odd pair in the house next door to my family's city house. Then one day I visited our Lichterfelde West house, and that lanky, bespectacled boy next door suddenly seemed irresistible. Later, he admitted he'd been trying to connect with me for years, and he found himself struck mute every time we made eye contact.

"Cranky Mrs. Rheinberg," Adele chuckled. Then she struggled to her feet. It was easy for me to forget Adele's advanced age sometimes because she was generally free of health problems, but recently, I'd noticed her occasionally wince in pain, and some days she'd look especially pale. If I asked, she'd mutter something vague about her heart not being what it used to.

"Come to the garden," she said. "I want to show you a special flower."

She had let the chickens out for a scratch, and now she shooed them away as she led me into the far corner of her courtyard. There, she gestured for me to lean close.

"Mayim and her parents have moved in with Levi's brother. It's a little cramped, but they are getting by and no longer have to worry about rent. She knows you're well and expecting again."

I pulled away in shock.

"But…how do you know I'm pregnant…?"

"You've been turning green when I offer you coffee. The same thing happened with your first two babies. I know you're under a lot of stress, Sofie, but you do need to look after yourself. You're not showing yet, although I daresay that's because you've lost so much weight these months since Jürgen's… accident."

"How did you see Mayim?"

"I didn't. I won't. I'm too close to you, and we don't know if they are watching me. But...the one advantage to being a little old lady is that no one expects you to cause trouble, so some of my friends have been taking advantage."

"The Nussbaums wouldn't go to Poland?"

"It's going to be very expensive to get Levi an exit visa now," Adele said gravely. The Reich Citizenship Law and the Law for the Protection of German Blood and German Honor had been enacted. The first stripped Jews of their German citizenship, leaving them subjects of the Reich rather than citizens. Levi was stateless.

Suddenly, Adele's eyes twinkled, and she leaned even closer and whispered, "It's going to be expensive, Sofie, but we're trying to find a way."

"The money you've borrowed!" I whispered in shock. She winked at me, then touched a finger to her lips.

"Every single Reichsmark filters through to the Nussbaums via my friends."

I threw my arms around her and whispered in her ear, "Aunt Adele, I don't know how to thank you."

"Look after yourself and your family," she whispered back. "*That* is how you thank me."

At the park, we were joined by Lydia and Karl and their little tribe—Hans, Horst and Ernst, their toddler Werner and new baby Gertrude, with Petra, their terrifyingly stern nanny. While Petra pushed the stroller to soothe Gertrude to sleep, Karl and I sat with Jürgen and Lydia at a picnic table. The older children chased one another, giggling and shouting.

"Goodness, they'll be wondering in Düsseldorf where all that noise is coming from," Karl chuckled, as Georg and Hans ran past him, shouting at the top of their lungs. Just then,

Laura and Horst and Ernst flew by from the other direction, squealing with laughter.

"Our boys are growing up so fast," Lydia remarked, watching fondly while Hans and Georg roughhoused. "It pleases me so much to think that children like ours are the future of this country."

"Me too," I said, and for once I was being honest, because I believed that deep beneath the ugliness he'd absorbed, Georg was still a good person.

Jürgen and Karl exchanged a look, and then they rose simultaneously and wandered a little way away from us, talking quietly in a huddle.

"Rocket business," Lydia sighed, shaking her head. "It never ends, does it?"

Jürgen's expression of rapt concentration told me she was right, and I bit back a sigh. The children did another lap—this time, all five of them in a line. Hans was in front, and Georg was chasing him, waving a small stick in front of himself.

Hans suddenly, theatrically, fell to the ground, moaning and writhing as if he were dying. Georg approached, pointed the stick, and cried, "Boom!" I gasped and opened my mouth to protest the proximity of the stick to Hans's face when Georg added in a triumphant voice, "Die, Jew, die!"

Hans gave his final groan and went still. Georg, Laura, and the twins all cheered, throwing their hands in the air to celebrate.

"Your children are developing as they should at last, and it's all because you removed the negative influences from your family," Lydia said, waving toward the children. I was too stunned to reply. She sighed happily. "This is what gives me so much hope for the Reich. If children so young can already see that the Jews need to be dealt with, can you imagine what they are going to be like as adults?"

That very thought sent a wave of nausea and panic crashing over me. I could barely breathe with the desperation to ask, *When did your mind change about the Jews? How did your heart change? Does any part of you doubt these things you're saying?*

"I'm sorry," I blurted, and on shaky legs, I made a beeline for a nearby garden bed, where I lost every bite of food I'd eaten. By the time I finished retching, Jürgen was at my side, rubbing my back.

"Can I do anything?" he asked, dropping his voice. I knew he assumed this was just sickness from the pregnancy. I shook my head, indicating I couldn't yet speak. The nausea was gone, but panic was now clawing at me. I tried to suck in air, but my chest felt tight.

My children were playing "shoot the Jew" and I was not allowed to discipline them.

"Water," I croaked, and he moved hastily, fetching me a glass of water from the table. I was trapped. The children were trapped. Standing in a public park on a magnificent day for my son's birthday party, the claustrophobia was overwhelming.

Ignore the dissonant notes. Focus on the music.

I closed my eyes and tried to breathe my way through the panic. I had to think of something—anything—positive to cling to, but every idea that came to mind represented more misery. *Jürgen is never home. Mayim is gone. The children have been brainwashed. My country is broken.*

An idea finally struck me and I gasped, the tightness in my chest easing as I sucked in fresh air.

The baby. The baby. I must stay calm for the baby.

I sipped at the water slowly, ever so slowly, as my heart rate began to settle. Jürgen gave me a searching look, but I forced a smile to let him know that I was fine. I walked back to the table, offered the same smile to Lydia, and announced, "We're expecting."

My voice was a little hoarse, but that was not unusual,

given I'd just been so ill. Lydia didn't miss a beat—she gave me a delighted grin and exclaimed, "What marvelous news!"

Karl had taken the seat opposite her, and she leaned toward him and said, "Karl, we owe these two congratulations. They are finally pregnant again!"

"Congratulations!" Karl boomed, helping himself to some sweets.

"We're hoping for another baby right away too," Lydia said happily, touching a hand to her belly. "These new little ones can be the best of friends, just like the older children."

"You know the Führer has asked all Reich men to sire four children. Lydia and I are hoping to more than double that," Karl announced. Then he thumped Jürgen on the back. "I'm so thrilled for you that you're doing your part too."

Over his shoulder, I saw that Laura now held the stick, and she was chasing the other children around, laughing and squealing. This time, it was Georg's turn to fall dramatically to the ground, writhing as he "died."

Ignore the dissonant notes. Ignore the dissonant notes.

"Maybe it's time for cake," I said brightly. "Come on, children. Gather round."

Focus on the music.

"Are you still comfortable enough to travel?" Jürgen asked when he called in late November. I looked down at my swollen belly. It had taken me much longer to show with my third pregnancy, but I'd more than made up for lost time, and with ten weeks to go, I was already bursting out of my maternity smocks.

"Travel *where*?" I asked him warily.

"Otto has decided we need to hold a launch in a few weeks here at Peenemünde. Some of the top brass will be in attendance. He suggested you and Lydia might want to come too."

My back ached. My ankles were swollen. I was so cranky and uncomfortable, I dreaded the thought of a car ride across the city, let alone a five-hour drive across the country. I closed my eyes and imagined how good it would be to see him—to hold him. I'd only seen him a handful of times over the course of the whole pregnancy.

"I'll be there," I promised him.

I left the children with Adele and arranged for Lydia and her driver to pick me up. We were on the road before dawn to make the trip to Rügen. From there, we would travel to the island by boat.

"They've canceled the pomp and circumstance," Lydia said with a sigh as we traveled. "I'm so disappointed. I was looking forward to some flair."

The weather had been dreadful, so the observation towers remained unfinished, and worse, no less than three test launches had failed unexpectedly. This forth test launch would go ahead, but there would be no audience for it beyond me and Lydia.

"I think Otto is only allowing us to visit because morale has been low. And Karl tells me Otto and his superiors have been very pleased with—" she cleared her throat delicately "—well, with Jürgen's improved attitude in recent times. They wanted to reward him, I think. That's why they've booked us hotel rooms on Rügen for the night, so we don't have to stay in the dormitory on the island." She gave me a hopeful smile. "I hope you know, my friend, the future is so bright for you two if you keep on this path."

When I blinked, I was back in the courtyard with my exhausted husband, staring at his blackened eye. *Keep on the path?* Taking even a step off meant death.

"Jürgen is devoted to the program," I said hollowly. "We're both committed."

★ ★ ★

Karl met us at the jetty on the island, and after greeting Lydia with a kiss, he helped me disembark and then led me to a waiting Army vehicle. As a young soldier drove us to the other end of the island, Karl poured us hot tea from a thermos and offered treats procured from a café in Rügen. The car came to a stop on a hill, and Karl opened the door for us. There was little shelter—just a small, three-sided wooden shack.

Farther down the hill a larger building had been erected, along with two half-constructed towers and some half-built stands, clearly intended for a future audience.

"Where is Jürgen?" I asked Karl, as he helped me to a seat in the shack.

"All going well, you'll see him after the launch," he assured me. Then he pointed ahead. Some distance from the other buildings, a white rocket was visible beside scaffolding. It was difficult for me to judge its size at first—until, with a start, I realized that the swarm of dark objects moving around the base was people.

"How big is it?" I asked Karl uneasily.

"This is the Aggregate 3. She's twenty-two feet long and two and a half feet wide. She weighs over 1,600 pounds." He tilted his head at me, brows knitting. "Are you not feeling well, Sofie? You're awfully pale."

"I was just picturing something more like the rockets you two used to fire from that dump in Berlin," I admitted. "Maybe a *little* larger but…" This rocket was many times larger than I was anticipating. They'd done all this in *four years*?

Karl gave a generous belly laugh and patted my shoulder as if I were an amusing child.

"Did you hear that, Lydia? Sofie thought that we were firing those tiny toys we played with in Berlin."

"Oh God, no, Sofie." She laughed too. "They were—what? Four feet high?"

"Five at best," Karl chuckled. "And so narrow too." He gave me a gentle smile as he explained, "I'm surprised Jürgen hasn't kept you abreast of his brilliant work."

"He respects the secrecy of the program," I said weakly.

"These rockets run on liquid fuel and require a *lot* of that to achieve the height and the distance that we are aiming for."

"Will these rockets go to the moon?" I asked.

"Oh sure," Karl said, waving his hands dismissively. "I mean, in theory these kinds of rockets could do many things. And it is still the intention of the program that we will one day launch a space mission. Sure, of course. One day."

The men around the base retreated, and a sudden flare of light fired from the base of the rocket. The supporting structure fell away and the device smoothly and effortlessly rose into the sky. I held my breath, terrified by the might of the thing, and then I gave a squeak of panic when after just a few seconds, it wobbled.

I heard Karl curse beside me, and I turned to him in alarm, fearing we were in danger. But he didn't seem scared—just frustrated. He snatched his hat from his head and threw it furiously onto the ground, then stormed off, cursing under his breath. The rocket was still wobbling as it traveled up and out over the ocean. It disappeared from view, and then in the distance, flames rose over the water.

"Karl mentioned that there's been problems with the guidance system," Lydia said as she helped me to my feet, and we began to make our way slowly back toward the car.

"Mr. zu Schiller has asked me to take you to the office to wait until they have debriefed. You can have some food there and freshen up," the driver said.

"Thank you," Lydia said politely. She insisted I take the

front seat and I was grateful for the extra space to stretch my legs. As we pulled away from the viewing site, I noticed an immense crater in the earth just a few dozen feet away from where we'd been sitting. It was dozens of feet across, and even deeper than it was wide. It could have swallowed maybe half of a city block.

"What's that?" I asked the driver.

"That's the impact from the failed launch from last week," he said. Then he whistled. "Didn't get off the ground properly before it detonated. It almost knocked me off my feet even over the other side of the island. That is why we aim them into the ocean."

I failed to hide my distress, and he misread it, giving me a gentle smile.

"Oh, don't worry, Mrs. von Meyer Rhodes. That one was launched from the other platform. You weren't in any danger today."

Nothing went the way we planned. Yet another launch had failed, and instead of taking the afternoon off with us, Karl and Jürgen were both called into meetings. The afternoon dragged by, and as the sun began to set, Lydia and I were told we'd be shepherded back to the hotel in Rügen.

"Do you think I'll get to see Jürgen at all?" I asked Lydia miserably.

"Maybe later," she said gently. "You know the work must come first."

At the hotel lobby, she dealt with the staff, checking us into our rooms, arranging for our bags to be ferried inside.

"I've organized for a meal to be brought to you. Why don't you take a hot bath and get into bed? I know you're keen to see Jürgen, but you really need to rest. I'm just a few doors down if you need me."

I considered the bath, knowing the hot water would be blissful against my bones, but when I stared at the little tub, I realized I'd be unlikely to get back out on my own even if I did manage to fit inside.

Instead, I nibbled at the food Lydia arranged and then sat on the bed and waited for Jürgen. I thought about the launch and the crater and the millions of questions I wanted to ask him— but we'd have to assume someone was listening in on the hotel room. Once again, we'd be whispering under blankets.

At this realization, tears filled my eyes. I flicked the wireless on to mask the sound, then lay on the bed to weep. What would it be like to be in some far-flung city when a rocket like that came out of nowhere? The technology couldn't have advanced enough that the rocket would know which building to land on. What if one landed on a school?

It was all too terrible to be real, and too ugly to be the brainchild of my beautiful, sensitive husband. I curled myself around my belly and cried until I fell asleep.

I woke to the sound of a key in the lock, and Jürgen was inside by the time I pushed myself into a seated position. I stared at him with bleary eyes, noticing that he looked every bit as tired as I felt. I tried to get off the bed to run to him, but my belly got in the way.

"My, haven't you grown?" Jürgen said, laughing softly as he set a little overnight bag down on the floor, then rushed to my side. He dropped to his knees beside the bed and placed his hands tenderly on my belly. But then he paused, and he lifted his eyes to mine.

"You are so beautiful, Sofie."

I started to cry again—tears of exhaustion and relief and fear.

"I'm a mess," I choked out.

"Even a mess, my love. You are beautiful. I've missed you so much," he whispered.

"I miss you too," I whispered back.

There was no need to whisper. We were only saying what a husband and wife would be expected to say after two months apart. But there was every need to whisper, because this was a moment just between him and me. It was far too precious to be shared with anyone else.

Later, lying under the covers, I resisted the pull of sleep, determined to make the most of every second with Jürgen. I pulled the blankets over our heads and snuggled as close to Jürgen as my belly would allow.

"The rockets really are huge flying bombs now, aren't they?" I whispered.

"They have no intention of a space mission," he admitted.

"When did you realize that?"

"Around the same time we tried to run away."

"Oh."

"A space mission would be the work of visionaries. It is well evident by now that these men are not that."

"What went wrong today?" I whispered.

"Are you really interested?"

"I am," I said, throat tight. "I'm sorry. I've underestimated your work so badly, Jürgen. I underestimated *you*."

I started to cry, and his arm contracted around me.

"Sofie, it's okay. Truly," he whispered, his breath hot on my ear. "My love, even Otto underestimates this technology sometimes. We've made decades' worth of progress in just a few short years. It's okay that you're not up-to-date with every detail. There is so much secrecy, Sofie. I wouldn't always tell you even if you asked."

"I feel like we're living completely different lives."

"It can't be helped."

"What went wrong today?"

"Technical problems too complex to explain to you when we are both this tired."

"Can you fix the problems?"

"Yes. It is only a matter of time."

A sudden vision of that immense crater on the island flashed before my eyes.

"*Should* you fix them?"

"We've spent a fortune on the program but still don't have a model that can be mass-produced. This series of launches was supposed to show the top brass that we'd turned that around. The pressure is growing."

"Why would they even want to mass-produce bombs right now?"

"My love, you are smart enough to know the answer to that."

I found myself suffocating, so I pulled the blankets off our faces and drew in some deep breaths. Jürgen did the same. When my lungs no longer felt as though they were bursting, we returned to the blankets and I whispered, "They want to go to war?"

"A man like Hitler always wants war. He wants power and land, and no one is going to give those things to him. At some point, he'll try to take them."

29

Sofie
Huntsville, Alabama
1950

THREE WEEKS HAD PASSED SINCE WE ARRIVED in America. They were weeks of pure, unexpected bliss, of snuggling on the couch with Jürgen every night, of sleeping in his arms, and of watching him work like crazy to connect with Felix and to support Gisela as she settled in.

Weeks familiarizing myself with a town that seemed wary at best, hostile at worst—of trying to encourage my daughter to be brave, of giving her permission to take her novels to school so she could at least read at recess because none of the German children would speak to her, and none of the American children could.

Weeks of waking up some mornings to find graffiti on our street, sometimes just a day after we painted over the last lot. That black patch of paint on the road was growing so thick, soon we'd feel the bump as we drove over it.

In those weeks, the man in the brown uniform walked past my house several times every day. Since I was checking the mailbox constantly, hoping for mail from Laura, I found myself in the front of the house when he passed sometimes, and I felt the hostility coming off him in waves. Sometimes, he sat under the tree just around the corner from my house and stared into my street, as if he were waiting for something to happen.

And over those weeks, some of the stores added No Germans signs to their front windows, right alongside the Whites Only signs.

It felt a little like the town was trying to beat down my spirit, but I refused to allow it. I was determined to build bridges in Huntsville. Whenever I met any of the locals who seemed even a little receptive to friendly conversation, I went out of my way to connect.

"My daughter is learning English, but it's going to take some time," I told the bookstore owner. I'd gone in to see if he could source us some more German-language novels as a treat for Gisela for persisting with school despite the challenges. "She's a voracious reader."

"Well, we can't have a young lady at a loss for reading material," the man said, his eyes twinkling. "I'll make some calls."

"Thank you so much."

"It's my pleasure," he told me brightly. He scribbled down my name and number on a notepad, then asked, "How are you finding things here?"

"It's challenging at times," I admitted. "But we're very honored to be here."

"I've watched this town wither over the last thirty years, Mrs. Rhodes. All of the jobs dried up, so the young people get to a certain age and move away. The way I see it is that if a bunch of clever scientists happen to come to town to set up a world-class rocket program, jobs are sure to follow. Besides, imagine if it's a rocket designed at Huntsville that gets man into space? To the moon? We'll be famous the world over. Seems to me that so long as we don't run you out of town before you can work your magic, *your* people might just be the salvation of this town. In time, I reckon everyone else will see that too."

"Thank you," I said, overcome with emotion. "I truly hope we can do good things for your town. For your country."

"It's plain as day that you must all be normal Germans who had no idea what was really going on over there. Our government would never let Nazis into this country. You're all about as safe as houses, and I'm telling everyone who asks that they can be sure of that too."

I smiled quietly and left the store, heart heavy as I went. The bookstore owner had been so kind—and he was right. People like Jürgen and I meant no threat to his town or his country.

But how could I possibly explain how complex our situation back home had been? The deception was necessary. That didn't mean it was comfortable.

Another bright spark in those first difficult weeks was Avril Walters. She came round for coffee one day and promised she'd get her daughter Patty to look out for Gisela in the playground. Then she came back the next day with a bag of groceries to help me pack a more American-style lunch for Gisela. White bread and peanut butter featured much more heavily than I anticipated. She returned again later in the week with a bag of Patty's old clothes for Gisela and helped me cut some of the length from Gisela's hair so she could wear it down at school like the American girls.

Gisela and Patty hadn't really clicked, but that wasn't for lack of trying. Patty liked sports and dancing; Gisela preferred reading and drawing. The language barrier was just the final straw. I had a feeling that, but for Avril's encouragement, Patty would have given up on Gisela right away, and I was grateful that she hadn't. She seemed Gisela's best chance for a friend, now that Claudia was still refusing to let Mila play with my daughter.

Avril insisted on taking me for driving lessons to help me learn the differences in road rules. She loaned me her camera, so that I could take some photos of Felix, Gisela, and Jürgen, then drove me to the store so I could get the film developed. When the photos were ready, I wrote a note to Laura, and Avril drove me to the post office. She came around for coffee or cake or lunch several times a week, and even once it became apparent the children had different interests, she still organized playdates with us. She was a godsend—my guide to all things American.

Avril and I were walking through the grocery store together one morning when I noticed Claudia Schmidt at the counter. She looked close to tears, frustrated as she tried to communicate with the clerk, who was visibly annoyed.

"Like I already told you," the store clerk said, speaking slowly as if that would translate his words. "We won't have any until next week."

Claudia drew in a deep breath and held up a card. She pointed to it, nodding hopefully.

"Ma'am," the clerk said again, drawing the word out even more. "We. Do. Not. Have—"

"Please excuse me a moment," I said to Avril. Then I walked over and tapped Claudia on the shoulder. She scowled at me, then looked back to the clerk and pointed to the cardboard again.

"Let me help, Claudia," I said, switching to German. She hesitated, then nodded reluctantly.

"I have no idea what the problem is," she admitted. "I just want to pick up some confectioners' sugar."

"He's saying that they've run out and won't have any in until next week."

"Oh," she said, her expression clearing. "Oh good. I thought he was telling me which aisle to look in." She smiled at the clerk and nodded as she said in heavily accented English, "Please."

"Thank you," I corrected her. Claudia sighed miserably.

"I'm never going to learn this language."

"You'll get there," I told her gently. "You just need time and practice."

She turned as if she was going to leave but paused at the last minute and looked at me hesitantly. "Could you ask him which day I should come back?"

"I have some at home," I said. "I'll bring it over this afternoon."

"You don't have to do that."

"Please," I said. "I want to."

After she was gone, I went back to Avril, and we continued walking through the aisles, Todd and Felix walking ahead of us. At least the little boys didn't mind too much that they couldn't converse. They found other ways to amuse themselves, like giggling together and running ahead when Todd dropped an apple and it rolled down the aisle.

"Forgive me for speaking out of turn," Avril said quietly, "but I get the distinct impression those other German women are not especially kind to you. And Patty says that the German kids all play together, the girls all in their braids and those dresses and the boys wearing those odd little shorts—"

"Lederhosen," I said. I wasn't the only German mother struggling to figure out how to help her children adjust to American school.

"I understand that the local kids are a bit wary, but the German kids all seem to be looking after each other...except poor Gisela. Patty says she sits by herself to read her books. Do you know why that is?"

"I have my suspicions," I muttered, picking up a box of flour and adding it to my cart. Avril cleared her throat, and I looked back to find her gaze troubled.

"I've told everyone it couldn't *possibly* be true," she blurted. "But people are talking about you and Jürgen. Lizzie Miller said that you and Jürgen were members of the Nazi party. I only hope that the German women haven't heard such vicious lies, but being married to Calvin, her words do carry some extra weight." I was so shocked, I found myself momentarily lost for words. "There was more, but it's too terrible to say."

"Please tell me," I said weakly. "I'd rather just know."

"She said that Jürgen may have been in the SS—that he even ran some kind of terrible camp."

My breath hitched in my throat. I forced myself to keep walking, but my every instinct was to leave the store and run. Not from Avril, but from my past. Avril was watching me closely, and I realized I had to say something. I drew in a breath.

"Early in the Nazi years, Jürgen and I decided to flee," I began softly. "We were going to take our family and escape. They had a listening device in our home, overheard our plan, and took Jürgen in the middle of the night." Avril covered her mouth with her hand as she gasped in shock. "I don't want you to feel sorry for us, Avril. We made some mistakes, and I wish with all my heart that we had done more. But our situation was far from simple, and at the time, we did the best we could. I just want you to understand that those men controlled every aspect of our lives."

"I'm so sorry, Sofie," she said sadly. "It sounds like you and

Jürgen have been to hell and back." She cleared her throat delicately. "So...there's no truth to the rumors, then?"

An instinct sounded. Why was she pressing this when I was clearly not ready to discuss it? I had only known Avril for a few weeks. She'd been so kind in that time, but we were a long way from the kind of trusted relationship where I could share Jürgen's secrets with her. I decided I'd neither admit to anything, nor would I lie. That only left me with the option to flatter her and try to deflect.

"I'm so grateful for your friendship," I said honestly. "I really don't know what I'd have done without you."

"Don't you even mention it," she said. "You know I just love to chat with you and to hear about your life. I just want you to be happy here."

"I will be happy in time. I'll make this work, one way or another, because this country is our home now. Besides, there's no option to go back to Germany even if things are tricky here at times." She gave me a questioning look, and I laughed uneasily, kicking myself for what I'd almost given away. Jürgen *couldn't* leave, because if he did, he'd likely be arrested. "I just meant Jürgen won't leave, and I won't leave without him." We continued along the aisles, and after a moment, I turned to her and asked carefully, "Did you say Lizzie Miller is telling people these things?"

I was still convinced that visit from the police was her doing. She had no idea what a nighttime visit from a police officer would trigger in me or Jürgen. I might need to build bridges with just about everyone else in town, but I'd be staying well away from *that* woman.

"I'm afraid so," Avril said. "Lizzie is ruthless, absolutely *ruthless*. It's just such a shame that she's so influential with the American wives. I'm sure you noticed she's a lot younger than Calvin."

"I don't pay too much attention to that kind of thing."

"When I first met her, she told me she'd only started dating Calvin because she wanted him to help her brother and she only married him because she was struggling and he was wealthy. She's the kind of woman who doesn't even think twice about using people to get what she wants." Avril shrugged. "I mean, she nearly had a stroke when I mentioned I'd been to your house."

"I do hope I haven't caused you trouble."

"Oh goodness, Sofie, not at all. I'm just worried about *you*. I don't even care how often she asks me not to speak to you anymore—we're friends now," Avril said, beaming. That gave me pause.

"She asked you not to speak to me?"

"I paid no mind at all—don't you worry. Lizzie is just that kind of woman," Avril said dismissively. "The only thing is… Huntsville isn't a very big place, and the rocket program is an even smaller community. I'd hate it if that kind of bad blood spilled over to Jürgen and Calvin."

I thought about Jürgen's concern about his future citizenship application and started to feel uneasy. What would even happen if Jürgen fell out of favor with the rocket program? I could only guess that our fresh start in America would end. And then what would happen to us?

My heart sank. Maybe staying out of Lizzie Miller's way wasn't going to be enough.

"Has Calvin said anything to you about his wife?" I asked Jürgen that night. I was washing the dishes and he was beside me, drying them with a towel. Maybe any ordinary husband and wife wouldn't notice such routine moments in a day, but I tried to be grateful for every single one.

"Not really. He did try to apologize after the party," Jürgen said. He reached past me to put a mug back into a cupboard and explained, "He told me Lizzie's brother served in Europe and has never been the same. But Cal hasn't mentioned you since, which is a little awkward, since he'd been looking forward to meeting you." He paused. "He never said a word about that break-in business. Someone else was behind it for sure—I doubt he even knew the police were called."

"Is he a good man?"

"He's the manager, but I have the greater technical knowledge—there's always a tension in an arrangement like that. But he's kind and generous. I enjoy working with him."

"Lizzie seems a lot younger than Calvin."

"She does." Jürgen shrugged. "So? You're four years younger than me."

"That's hardly the same. I heard she only married him for his money."

"Sofie," Jürgen said, giving a startled laugh. "Since when do you engage in that kind of gossip?"

"I've made one friend since we came here and *she* warned me that Lizzie Miller has been telling the other women that you are a Nazi. That you were in the SS and ran a camp."

Jürgen dropped the dish towel. He bent to pick it up, his movements slow.

"Lizzie Miller has been telling people that?"

"I avoided the question when Avril asked." I hesitated, some instinct niggling at me. "It did seem more of a fishing expedition than an accusation, to be honest."

Jürgen dried the last mug, then hung his towel up on a hook. He exhaled slowly, his expression pinched.

"I know Calvin has only seen the sanitized version of my history—Christopher told me so himself."

"Maybe you should talk to Calvin anyway?" I suggested carefully.

"And what?" he asked bitterly, shaking his head in frustration. "Tell him his wife might be starting rumors that have a hint of truth?"

I understood the self-loathing on his face, even if I hated to see it.

"So what do we do, then?" I asked quietly.

"We have to ignore it. All of it." I opened my mouth to protest, but he interrupted before I could. "Sofie, all of these problems started when you and Lizzie Miller got off on the wrong foot. My work situation is far too important to all of us for me to drag your personal conflict into it."

Jürgen was right. These problems had all started with me and Lizzie at that picnic. One awkward conversation, two women getting off on the wrong foot—Lizzie not seeing our humanity, me getting defensive.

Maybe that was what I needed to fix.

30

Sofie

Berlin, Germany
1938

JÜRGEN MISSED THE BIRTH OF THE BABY. WHAT-ever milestone he was working toward was more important even than the birth of our daughter, at least according to Otto, who wouldn't grant him leave. I left the older children with Adele and went to the hospital alone.

I called him after she arrived. Exhausted but elated, I told him about her delicate features, her barely there eyebrows, her wispy hair. The frustration in his tone was palpable as he promised he'd be home to meet her in a few days.

But the very next morning, Hitler annexed Austria. From my hospital bed I read a newspaper that showed photos of wildly enthusiastic crowds on the streets of Vienna, welcoming Hitler and celebrating the annexation. I stared at those photos for hours, trying to figure out if I could trust the images. Who would welcome Hitler to their nation? Surely this was some artifice invented by the Department of Propaganda.

Jürgen called the hospital to tell me his visit had been delayed again but he was sending a photographer to the hospital as a consolation prize.

"I'll have to name her myself, won't I?" I snapped.

"A good German name. A *strong* German name," he said cautiously. I huffed impatiently. It wasn't as though I was about to name the child Mayim, although I might have entertained that thought under different circumstances.

I stared at the baby. She was sleeping in my arms, innocent and pure, but just like Georg and Laura, this baby would soon be the Reich's hostage, ultimately powerless to choose her own destiny, or even to make her own mind up about the worth of other human beings.

"Sofie? Are you still there?"

Hostage. *Geisel*, in German.

"Gisela," I blurted. Despite its linguistic roots, Gisela was a common name and I knew that no one would even question it. But I'd know. Every time I spoke her name, I'd be committing a quiet rebellion in my heart.

"I love it," Jürgen agreed, sounding relieved.

Eventually, Gisela von Meyer Rhodes would start school, and whatever purity and goodness had existed in her nature would be washed away by hate. Maybe one day I could tell her that from the moment of her birth, I loathed that she was hostage to her country's ideology. There was just nothing I could do about it, other than to leave a clue in her name to prove my regret.

Georg and Laura were now old enough to walk to school alone, and often after I saw them off, Gisela and I would go next door to visit Adele. Something was changing with Jürgen's aunt.

By the summer, she felt faint when she stood in the heat for too long. I feigned a sudden interest in horticulture so I could take over her courtyard garden.

"I'm worried about her," Adele's friend Martha admitted to me one day. Adele was inside making us tea, and Martha and I were picking tomatoes. "She says the new pills the doctor gave her are helping, but she seems frailer."

"What more can we do for her?" I asked Martha. "How can we make her slow down and rest?"

"Adele isn't the kind of woman who slows down with age. She's the kind of fierce warrior who reaches a certain point and realizes she has nothing left to lose. You won't slow her down, Sofie, and even if you did, you'd be taking something away from her, not buying her more time."

"What does that mean?" I said, confused. Martha smiled quietly.

"This money trouble she's having seems to be spiraling, doesn't it? Poor old dear."

Adele was constantly borrowing money now—almost every week she asked for some small amount, and from time to time, she asked for larger sums. Sometimes she'd call to ask over the phone, even though I never let a day pass when I didn't check in on her.

"Why do you ring me to ask me for money?" I asked her one day. She was supervising me as I clumsily deadheaded her small collection of roses. Despite my best efforts, it seemed I was doing a terrible job, because Adele was visibly struggling to bite her tongue.

She came to my side, then whispered, "Even if there are no listening devices in my house, they're almost certainly listening to your phone. I thought it would be prudent for prying ears to hear me spinning a sob story to you, so hopefully they will believe you had no idea I was supporting the Nussbaums if we ever find ourselves in hot water."

"It wouldn't be smart for Jürgen and me to give them money directly, but that's only because of his job. You're not breaking any laws. It's not illegal to support a struggling Jewish family."

"Not yet," she whispered grimly. "And I don't care if they come for me. I'm trying to do two things here, Sofie—I'm trying to help them, and to protect you."

"After the history Jürgen and I have, I'm not sure a few phone calls are going to convince them I had no idea where that money was going."

"People see what they want to see. And you two have done an admirable job of falling into line over these past few years and Jürgen is the star of the rocket program. Hopefully if the time ever comes when I fall under suspicion, you will have earned the benefit of the doubt." She tilted her face toward the sun beneath that wide-brimmed hat and breathed in slowly. Then she looked at me. "Sofie, in these difficult years we've lived through together, you've become very dear to me. I hope you know that."

My eyes prickled. I cleared my throat.

"I do. And likewise."

"It hurts me to say this, but it needs to be said—if I *do* ever find myself in trouble with the Gestapo, you need to do what's best for your family."

I was so startled I almost dropped the clippers.

"What does that mean? You *are* my family."

She shook her head impatiently, waving her hand.

"The only thing I'm doing is slipping as much money as I can get my hands on to the Nussbaums. Things have been so tough for them since Levi's brother was arrested—"

"Uncle Abrahm was arrested?" I gasped. "What for?"

Adele squinted at me, then frowned.

"I'm sorry, treasure. I thought I told you. Abrahm was perceived to be a threat to public order. No further explanation given, and of course the family tried to find him without success. His wife has taken his children to live with her parents in the country. Between the money you've given me and the money my friends and I have scrounged together, we've just been covering the rent."

"How awful," I whispered. I was as distressed at the thought of Adele finding herself in trouble as I was about the Nussbaums' situation. She was so frail—and some days now, so weak. If standing in the sun left her faint, what would a 3:00 a.m. visit from the Gestapo do?

"Can't you feel it in the air, Sofie? It's not just the talk of war, although of course that's part of it. The hatred is escalating. Something is coming…" She paused, her features pinched and drawn. "I can sense it, like when I smell a storm on the breeze."

"I feel it too." The hatred had become almost self-generating now, infecting every corner of our society. It had grown so big and so dark, it threatened to suffocate us.

"The reason I have friends funneling the money to Mayim's family is to try to keep layers between you and them, links in a chain that could disconnect if any part were compromised. But we are clumsy old women—hardly masters of espionage. But if this all blows up, don't you think of it as a problem. Think of it as a chance to assure the Nazis of your loyalty."

"I would never do that," I said stiffly.

"Do you remember what I said to you when Mayim went away? *It's not always the strongest trees that survive the storm. Sometimes it's the trees that bend with the wind.* Remember that advice, Sofie. Especially if at some point, you find that the storm threatens to break you."

In August 1938, Adele called and asked me to help her in the garden. We huddled beneath an umbrella and made a show of hanging frost cloths over her vegetables. Even before I stepped out my back door, I knew why she'd called me.

There were thousands of Poles living in Germany—many of them Jewish. The Polish government had become concerned about a tidal wave of people attempting to return home, so they were making it increasingly difficult to do so. Every Polish citizen who lived abroad for more than five years now had to visit a Polish consulate to have an endorsement stamp added to their passport. It was just announced that those who lacked the stamp after the end of October would lose their Polish citizenship—becoming stateless, just like the German Jews.

"Sidonie is in Krakow," Adele whispered without preamble. "Moshe recently became a father, and she went to help with the new baby a few weeks ago."

"Moshe is married?" I asked, startled.

"Last year, apparently."

"But he's only—" I did the math and winced. "Oh. He's nineteen." Where had those years gone? It had been almost four years since I saw Mayim. I felt a pinch in my chest. "Can Sidonie have her passport endorsed there?"

"Those endorsements are, by design, almost impossible to acquire. She has no choice—she must stay in Krakow."

Adele was so pale that day. I wanted to get her back inside so that she could rest, but I knew she wouldn't be standing in the rain pretending to set up frost cloths if there was an alternative.

"But what about Mayim and Levi?"

"Levi's back has him bedbound these days. He's still here," she sighed, shaking her head sadly. "And of course, Mayim could still go to Krakow, but she will not leave without her father."

"She needs her passport endorsed or she'll be stateless."

"Yes. I need whatever money you can easily access without arousing suspicion. Do you have some on hand?"

"I do. In Jürgen's safe."

"How much?"

"Maybe a few thousand Reichsmark," I admitted. For most workers in Berlin, that was many months' salary. At her look of surprise, I explained, "I started keeping a little extra cash on hand so I didn't have to make extra trips to the bank when you needed it."

"Excellent. Good girl," Adele said, nodding in admiration, and I felt a flush of pleasure. "A thousand will do nicely."

"What will you do with it?"

"Perhaps Mayim can buy some favor with the consulate staff when she goes to request the endorsement."

"She and Levi need to leave, don't they?" I whispered. Adele nodded.

"Mayim will not leave Levi to fend for himself, and I understand that too."

We waited weeks for news. Every now and again, I'd whisper to Adele for an update, but she would whisper back fiercely, "Don't you think I'd have told you if I'd heard anything?"

I went to check on Adele one morning and found her waiting at her kitchen table, sipping a cup of tea. We greeted one another as we always would, and then she pointed to a note she'd scrawled on a piece of paper.

Mayim has tried everything without success. There are rumors that those in her position will be deported soon but Poland will not grant them entry. I don't know what's going to happen. All we can do is pray.

"There's really nothing more we can do?" I mouthed. Adele shook her head sadly and motioned toward her fireplace. I tore up the note and dropped it into the fireplace, watching as the flames curled the strips of paper and turned them into ash.

If you'd asked me before that day, I might have said I was accustomed to hopelessness. But knowing that my friend was in such desperate straits and realizing there was *no* choice I could make to help her, I discovered there were depths of hopelessness I'd never before experienced.

Gisela was especially unsettled that night in early November. I was up and down trying to nurse her back to sleep, becoming more frustrated with every new cry. Eventually, I gave up on sleep and moved with her to the sitting room.

Just as I settled, I was startled by the sound of breaking glass and shouting on the street. I froze in place, telling myself I had nothing to worry about. If there was any sign of trouble, Dietger would have the Gestapo or the SA here in minutes. If I just waited patiently, I'd hear the fuss die down.

But instead came more shouting, many voices now, and then the sound of screaming in the distance—someone pleading for help, the tinkle and crunch of more glass breaking, and then more and more screaming.

I reached for the light switch, my hands shaking so hard by then that I almost knocked the thing over. The light went out, and now the sitting room was almost dark, the dim glow of the streetlights falling in lines across the room through gaps around the drapes. Gisela grizzled and I shushed her, jiggling her in my arms both to expend some of my anxiety and to rock her back to sleep. The sounds of movement were closer— now heavy boots against the sidewalk, many boots, not just a handful of troublemakers as I'd first imagined.

Then came shouts and cheers, and was that a hint of smoke in the air?

I was alone in the house with the children. I'd resented Jürgen's absence more times than I could count, but that night, I almost hated him for it, even though I knew that he loathed the distance every bit as much as I did.

I slipped from the sitting room, back up the stairs to settle Gisela in her bedroom, but then returned to the ground floor. I tried peeking around the drapes but couldn't quite figure out what the activity was—not until my eyes adjusted and I recognized the Brownshirts outside my window. This was government-sanctioned chaos.

I hoped Adele was somehow sleeping through the noise—it was possible; she'd been so exhausted lately. The smoke in the air grew stronger as the crowd expanded and their rowdiness expanded with it. Had our national tinderbox finally been set?

Suddenly I realized that just beyond the low hedge at the front of my house, Dietger was in his coat, talking to an SA officer. I walked briskly to the foyer and pulled a coat over my nightclothes, then quietly opened the front door. Dietger looked up at me in alarm.

"Sofie, tonight is not the night to be out," he said stiffly, glancing along the street, as if he was keeping watch for danger.

"What's happening?" I asked, wrapping the coat tighter around myself. Now that I was outside, I could hear the distant sounds of sirens and gunshots. The chaos seemed to be coming from every direction. It sounded like the end of the world.

"Don't worry," Dietger assured me calmly. "Aryan homes are perfectly safe—the police will ensure it."

"Safe from what?"

"The Jews murdered a German diplomat in Paris. What you are hearing is a necessary retaliation."

Had sleep deprivation driven me insane, or did that make no sense? In the distance, the wail of sirens and the sounds of gunshots and the tinkling of glass crashing to the ground continued.

"Paris," I repeated, fumbling to make sense of it all. "German Jews murdered someone in Paris?"

"That's right."

"But…what's *this* all about, then?" I asked numbly.

Dietger waved his arms, vaguely motioning toward the street. His gaze was hard.

"The Führer has decided that extreme measures must be taken."

Kristallnacht—the night of broken glass—was ostensibly an act of revenge against the Jews by Nazi loyalists. It seemed clear that the death of that young Nazi diplomat in Paris was nothing more than an excuse for the escalation Adele and I sensed coming months earlier. The violence was enacted by the usual suspects, the SS, the Brownshirts, rabidly infused young people who were indoctrinated in school and the Hitler youth program.

The chaos I heard was the sound of the SA smashing every window in the homes of Jewish families. One family was just down the street. They arrested the father and the eldest son and chased the mother and her young children into the street.

Adele had been awake through it all too.

"You should have called me," she said. "We could have kept one another company while the world burned. Did the children sleep through it at least?"

"The older two did. Gisela had a rough night, but it wasn't the noise—that's just how she sleeps these days."

"Perhaps she's teething," Adele said. Then she nodded to herself as she said weakly, "I'll make her some rock cakes to chew on later."

"You look so tired," I said gently. "Have you seen your doctor lately?"

She huffed impatiently.

"He gave me some new pills. Always with the pills. I'm fine, but I'm eighty-six years old. I'm allowed to be tired every now and again."

"I can't believe you finally told me your age."

"That settles it, then. I'm definitely losing my marbles," she said, with a twinkle in her eyes.

As Georg and Laura dressed for school, I told them the bare minimum—there had been some violence the previous night, and they were to go right to school and come straight home. I couldn't bring myself to explain that the violence had been against the Jews. I was terrified of watching them celebrate if I did.

Later, a sense of morbid curiosity drew me outside for a walk, with Gisela settled safely in her stroller. When I reached the house of the Jewish family at the end of my street, I was startled to see people inside. Through a broken window, I watched a woman cheer as she unhooked a painting from the wall. I recognized her. We'd chatted occasionally at the school gate—about this teacher or that, about the weather, about our children and their achievements.

Had she ever really been a cheerful and friendly acquaintance? Through the frame of that broken window, she was a vicious monster, feeding on hate.

"I had it first!" I heard a man shout. My gaze swung to an upstairs window, where I saw two men wrestling.

"I think you'll find *I* did," another man snapped. I felt a jolt of shock to see that they were fighting over a wireless—an item that any family in our affluent neighborhood could have purchased with ease.

Every window in the house had some new horror to display. An elderly woman was sorting through a wardrobe, trying on someone else's coats. A child was using a hammer to smash the glass in a display cabinet while his mother urged him on—a senseless act of destruction, given the door on the cabinet was already broken and neither child nor mother seemed to have any interest in the contents.

Almost in slow motion, I raised my hands to rub my eyes. Surely I was imagining this. Surely no force on earth could make otherwise sensible humans behave with such depravity?

An elderly man approached. He and I exchanged a glance, assessing one another. Maybe he saw something in my gaze, because he suddenly took his hat off and held it against his chest. He stood beside me, staring at the house, and a tear slid from his eye to roll into the lines on his cheek.

"They were my friends," he whispered, his voice thick with tears. "The little girls were terrified. I tried to help them, but there was nothing I could do. Today is the first day in all of my life I have been ashamed to be German."

The depth of emotion in his voice triggered my own. I turned back toward my home, intending to retreat to the privacy of a bathroom so that I could cry, but the day had not finished delivering its horrors. Walking down the street in perfectly neat lines were dozens of children, flanked by their teachers.

Laura's class was at the front of that line, and she saw me first—by the time I noticed her, she was already waving excitedly. I approached her teacher slowly, swamped by a rising sense of dread.

"Out for some exercise?" I tried to keep my tone light, but I was unable to keep the tremor from my voice.

"Oh yes, Mrs. von Meyer Rhodes. Today is such an exciting day for our class."

"Mama, we are going to see the house that has been liberated. A Jewish family had been occupying it," Laura said sweetly, her blue eyes alight with excitement. "Did you know we had a Jewish family so close to our house? It is scary to think, isn't it, Mama? But they are gone now, so it's okay."

"Yes, Laura. It's all okay," I said. A Jewish woman was the second person to hold her when she was born. A Jewish woman was the first person she ever smiled at. Her very first word was *May*. "I'll see you at home a bit later."

I flashed a tight smile at my daughter, then at her teacher, and pushed the stroller forward, walking briskly home. But my footsteps stumbled just a few steps later, when I heard the schoolchildren cheer as they reached the ransacked house.

"The Jews are our misfortune!" they chanted in a singsong, joyous fashion. "They are finally put in their place!"

The violence continued the next night and into the next day. Hundreds of Jews were murdered, still more suicided. Tens of thousands of Jewish men were arrested and imprisoned in concentration camps, the first time arrests were ever openly made on the basis of ethnicity, and the newspapers suggested that all of this had the full support of the German people. But I sensed a different sentiment in the air—that perhaps this time, the Nazi party had gone too far.

But no one said it. No one *could* say it. We had so long been afraid of the consequences of dissent that even as the nation descended into madness, any moral call to rise up against the chaos went unheeded.

The city was finally quiet after two nights of violence. I went to bed early, Gisela beside me in the hopes that we'd get a little more rest, but woke to the shrill burst of the phone ringing just after eleven o'clock. Jürgen often called late like this if he was especially busy and we hadn't spoken in a while, so I was certain he would be at the other end.

"Hello?" I asked breathlessly.

"I hope I didn't wake you, Sofie."

It was Adele, and she sounded weak. The hair on the back of my neck stood up.

"What is it?" I asked urgently. She didn't answer. "Adele—are you sick? I'll come right over—"

"Yes, I am quite unwell, Sofie," she said, slow and labored, as if it were an effort to speak.

"I'm coming—"

"Wait," she interrupted. "Please be sure to bundle up—put your coat on and your warmest winter boots, maybe a nice warm hat too. I really don't want you to catch a chill."

I looked along the hall to the windows above the stairwell. There was ice around the windowpane. Even so, it was unlike Adele to baby me. Something was going on.

I ran back to my bedroom and stared at Gisela on the bed. Georg and Laura were asleep down the hall—but they never woke up when she cried. I couldn't take her with me. I couldn't leave her behind. I groaned and ran to Georg's bedroom.

"Georg? Sweetheart?"

"Hmm?"

He was sleep-rumpled and innocent, and even as I shook his shoulder gently, I felt a tug of love for him in my chest.

"Darling, I have to go next door. Oma needs some help with something. Can you please come and sleep in my bed in case Gisela wakes up?"

He was half-asleep as we walked down the hallway, dragging his feet and squinting his eyes against the light. In my room, he flopped down onto my side of the bed and rested his hand gently on Gisela's back, as if to console her in advance. I propped a pillow beside her to keep her from rolling off the bed. Adele's words were ringing in my ears as I pulled on a felt hat and heavy coat, along with a pair of snow boots.

At the last minute, I stopped at the safe in Jürgen's study

and withdrew every Reichsmark, stuffing them into the pockets of my coat.

I stopped at the bottom of the stairs, just for a heartbeat, thinking of my children asleep upstairs. If love was the antidote to hate, surely the vastness of the love I felt for them could make some difference, even with everything else they were exposed to. The streets were calm, but it felt like the eye of a storm. I was terrified, but I'd heard the urgency in Adele's voice. There was no option to refuse her.

The clouds above were low and heavy, and light snow was falling—just enough to make the path icy. I slipped through the courtyard gate and into Adele's yard, then her apartment. I found her in the kitchen, where she often was. The fire was roaring, and she was slumped at the table, watching the steam rise from a teacup. She looked as weary as I'd ever seen her.

"Oma…" I whispered, rushing to her side.

"Thank you for coming, Sofie… I'm fine. I just… I can't find my medication. Could you look for me? Perhaps in my bedroom…and I'm going to go take a bath while you look. That sometimes helps too." Her voice was uncertain, her breaths coming in pants between words. She was so pale her skin had taken on a blue-gray tone, and when I looked at her hands, they were trembling. But even as she spoke, she was pointing—drawing my attention to a scrap of paper on the table.

I'm fine. Go quietly to the bathroom. Run the water to make some noise. I put the wireless in there too—turn it on and whisper just in case.

She watched to make sure I read the note, and when I nodded, she ripped it up and tossed the pieces into the fire.

I hesitated at her side, but her expression became even more impatient as she waved at me and mouthed, "Hurry, Sofie!"

I went briskly toward the bathroom, my footsteps clumsy because of the heavy boots. The bathroom door was closed, the room dark. I reached inside and pulled the string and gasped.

Mayim was sitting on the closed toilet lid. When the light came on, she jumped, clearly startled, and then she burst into tears and pressed her shaking finger over her lips. I stepped into the bathroom and closed the door. I turned the bath on as if to fill it, then fumbled for the wireless—trying to fill the air with sound.

Mayim and I threw our arms around each other. All I could do was ramble and all she could do was cry, and we were struggling to be quiet as we did so. Mayim was trembling, and so cold her skin felt like ice. I pulled my coat off and slipped it around her shoulders, then buttoned it for her, right up to her chin. She watched me, silent tears still pouring down her face. Her skin was etched with new lines that did not belong on the face of someone so young.

"What's happened?" I whispered.

"Papa is gone."

She was struggling to breathe between her sobs. I pulled her close again, squeezing her tightly, as if I could somehow absorb her pain. But the thing about grief is that even when it's shared, the weight is not relieved.

"It was the first night of the violence. Papa told me to hide under the kitchen sink. They knew my name…about my passport… They said they were going to deport me. Father wouldn't give me up and they shot him. When I came out from under the sink there was blood everywhere. Mrs. Elsas next door said they dragged him down the stairs and threw him into the back of the truck and if he wasn't already dead…"

"Oh, Mayim! I'm so *sorry*."

"I went to Adele's friend's house and she hid me there, but yesterday someone came to warn her that they were coming for me. She sent me to the next woman in the chain, but the same thing happened—that time there was no warning, and I only just made it out the back door before I heard them at the front. I'm sorry to make trouble for you and Adele, but I don't know where Martha lives, and there was no one else."

"Don't be silly," I whispered. "You're my family. You always will be. Is there a plan from here? Can I help?"

"Adele called Martha a little while ago. She asked her to borrow her son's car and come for a visit early tomorrow to help with errands. When she arrives, Adele is going to ask her to drive me to the Polish border…but I don't know what happens after I get there. The border is closed and I have no passport. Adele said she has a little money…"

"There is more in your pocket," I said. She reached into the coat pocket, and I knew her hand had closed over the wad of notes when her eyes welled with relief.

I suddenly realized why Adele had gone to such pains to ensure I wore warm clothing. Mayim was already wearing my coat, but now I took my hat and gently pulled it over her hair, and then I undid my boots. She passed me her shoes—worn flats, desperately in need of a new sole. They reminded me of the shoes I'd worn to the Nazi rally in 1933, and how frustrated I'd been that we had been unable to afford to repair them, or even to replace them. Looking back on that time, I saw myself as a foolish, spoiled stranger.

"Go," she whispered. "Keep the children safe."

"I'm trying," I said, and my voice broke. In that instant, Mayim and I stared at one another—each of us completely unashamed of our distress. *That* was what I'd missed the most. I could always be myself with Mayim. I no longer had that luxury with anyone else, not even with Jürgen, because we could only connect on an insecure phone, and not even with Adele, because of her increasing frailty.

We embraced one last time before I left the bathroom. Mayim closed the door behind me. I heard the bath shut off, and then the wireless, and then finally, the light seeping beneath the bathroom door was gone too. It felt as if she'd disappeared in an instant, or I'd imagined her.

Adele's tea was still steaming by the time I returned to the kitchen. A bottle of her heart medication was on the table next to it, full to the brim with little white tablets.

"Ah, there's your medication," I said lightly, even as I wiped the tears from my face. "Thank you," I mouthed. Adele shook her head, as if to say, *Don't mention it*. She pointed to the notepad in front of her.

If anything happens, there is a letter for you buried in the jar of sweets.

I opened my mouth to protest, but Adele pressed a finger over her lips, then pointed toward the back door, stubbornness in her eyes. "I'm better now and your children are in that house alone."

I bent and, for the first time in all those years I had known her, kissed her cheek. She caught me as I moved to straighten, held me close for just a heartbeat, and then I felt her lips against my cheek. Up close, I could see a purple tinge to her lips and her eyelids seemed heavy, as if she were struggling to keep them open. Her breathing scared me most. It was ragged, as if every breath were an effort, not a relief. I was gripped by a sudden, terrible fear.

"Oma," I whispered. "Why don't you come home with me?"

"I'm needed here. I'll be fine," she whispered dismissively.

Then she straightened and, for the benefit of an audience that may or may not have even been listening, added loudly, "Thank you for coming over to help me."

I had just slipped back beneath the covers of my bed with Georg and Gisela when the roar of an engine sounded. A car door opened, and there was a brief moment of silence before I heard shouting outside my villa.

I sprang out of bed, rushing toward the window to crack it open just a little. The icy air rushed in, and so did the sound of the Gestapo at Adele's front door.

"Open the door, Mrs. Rheinberg!"

How much could she bear?

"Have you got the wrong house, young man?" Adele called from her bedroom window. She sounded stubborn, irritated... and weak. "This is Adele Rheinberg. *Mrs*. Adele Rheinberg. I am eighty-six years old. Do you really have business waking up an eighty-six-year-old woman in the middle of the night?"

"You'll need to let us in, Mrs. Rheinberg!"

There was a long pause.

"No," Adele called back, almost thoughtfully. "No, I don't think I will."

Cursing, I ran down the stairs, pulled on a coat, and stepped outside my front door. I made it to the hedge before Dietger came running toward me.

"Sofie, go back inside," he hissed, pointing to my door. "This isn't about you."

"What's happening with Adele?" I demanded. "She's an old woman, Dietger! They have no business with her. Please go find out what's wrong."

"We need to let this play out, Sofie." He sighed, shaking his head as he glanced toward her house. He dropped his voice, then admitted, "I don't even know why they're here. I didn't call them."

"This is your last warning, Mrs. Rheinberg," someone shouted.

If Adele answered this time, I couldn't hear her. I took a step past Dietger, out onto the sidewalk, just in time to see Adele's front door open. It wasn't her on the other side, but the woman from the studio apartment on the ground floor, looking bewildered and disheveled as the large contingent of Gestapo filed past her. My panic clawed at my throat and left me flushing hot. I took a step toward her house.

"Sofie," Dietger said. He was much closer than I'd realized, and his voice was low. "Go home. Please. Let them handle this."

"But she's a little old lady," I said, and only then did I realize that I was sobbing, and my feet were so cold they were burning. I looked down and realized I was barefoot, standing in the light dusting of snow. I sobbed again and looked at Dietger—the closest thing I could find to a friendly face on that dark street. "She hasn't done anything wrong."

"Perhaps she's suspected of disloyalty to the Reich?" Even he sounded unconvinced. I took another step toward the house. This time, Dietger's hand caught my elbow. He gripped it firmly.

"Sofie, *please*," he said flatly. Then he dropped his voice. "I have to report any suspicious activity and even a hint of suspicious activity from you. Putting yourself right in the middle of a Gestapo operation is the very definition of suspicious activity." He tugged me toward my own house. "Go back inside, Sofie. *Go inside*. Please. You can't help her."

I tugged at his arm but he was gripping me hard, determined to save me from myself.

"Damn you to hell, Dietger," I choked out. He propelled

me toward my house—not with malice, but with determination.

"Surely it would be more comfortable for you in the warm..." It was so cold that when he spoke, his breath escaped as mist. I shook my head, craning my neck toward Adele's building. Would they drag her out? And Mayim too? Would the two of them go kicking and screaming? Would they go silently defiant?

I wanted to go inside to get some shoes...some socks... something to protect my feet, but I didn't dare in case I missed something, and I was too anxious to even sit down, to take the pressure off the burning skin of my ice-cold feet. But minutes began to pass, and the street and the building fell completely silent. Time was elastic. In a city that had been on fire for days, the whole world seemed to have fallen asleep.

"How long has it been?" I asked Dietger eventually. My teeth were chattering so violently it was hard to speak. He looked at his watch, then shifted awkwardly.

"Uh...close to fifteen minutes...?"

Just then, we heard boots on the ground, and I looked up to see the Gestapo filing out of Adele's house—empty-handed. Had she won? For just a moment, I felt a flare of pride and hope—maybe she'd convinced them to leave her be. Maybe she'd even talked them into leaving without searching her house. Maybe...

Dietger held up a hand to me to indicate I should stay on my front porch. Then he jogged quickly over to one of the cars at the curb. He spoke quietly with one of the men. Then his shoulders slumped as if he'd suddenly exhaled. The streetlight above his head brought the shock and the sadness on his face into sharp relief. A feeling of dread hit me so hard, my knees almost buckled.

I ran past Dietger. Past the Gestapo officers, who were sliding back into their black cars. I ran through Adele's lobby and through the smashed interior door into her apartment.

I found her on the floor in her bedroom, lying on her back by the window. Had the Gestapo seen her collapse? Had they even tried to help her?

"Adele," I choked out, dropping to my knees beside her. I took her shoulders in my hands and I shook her limp body. "Adele, please. Please wake up." My breath caught on a sob. "Adele. *Oma*. I can't do this without you."

Should I call an ambulance? A doctor? Should I try to re-suscitate her? I didn't even know how to start, and besides... somewhere deep inside, I knew it was too late. Shaking her body only reminded me how frail she had become in recent times.

I brushed the wispy hair around her face back into place. I touched my shaking fingers to her cheeks and I let my tears rain down over her, anointing her body with my grief and love.

"Sofie?" Dietger was at the door, hovering and uncertain. "Is there someone I can call? Maybe Jürgen? Lydia?"

It took me a few seconds to compose myself enough to speak.

"Did they tell you what happened?"

"They said she'd already collapsed by the time they got inside."

"And was her alleged crime punishable by death?" I said, unable to keep the bitterness from my voice.

"She was suspected of disloyalty to the Reich," Dietger said, his expression hardening. "She would have been taken to a camp anyway." He took a step back from the door, shak-ing his head sadly, then said, so quietly I had to strain to hear the words, "Perhaps this is a blessing." His footsteps retreated.

I looked from Adele's face, relaxed and peaceful in death, to her bed, and the photo of Alfred and her sons that she kept beside it. I started to cry again. I couldn't stay with her body and leave my children alone in the house, but I couldn't bear to leave it.

"Mrs. von Meyer Rhodes?" Two of Adele's tenants were in the doorway. The quiet Bavarian couple who lived in that tiny front room in the front of the ground floor. They kept to themselves mostly, and in the shock of the moment, I couldn't even remember their names. The man walked into the room and extended a hand toward me. I let him help me to my feet.

"Let us take care of her for you tonight," his wife said gently from the doorway. "In the morning, we will call the mortuary."

"She was always so good to us," the husband said gruffly. "When I lost my job, she let us stay anyway, even though it took me months to find work again. It will be an honor for us to sit with her. We will pray over her soul and keep her company until the undertaker comes in the morning."

When I nodded, the man crouched beside Adele's body and whispered, "Let's get you up on the bed, Mrs. Rheinberg."

He cradled her gently in his arms as if she were a child. Then he stretched her out on her bed and even pulled the blanket over her, right up to her chin. I started to cry again at the kindness of his gesture.

People could still be good.

I told the couple I needed to wash my face before I went home and saw my children. I let myself into Adele's bathroom and closed the door before I turned on the light—just in case Mayim was still there. I was relieved to find she wasn't— although I had no idea if she was hiding elsewhere. It was too risky to search for her. All I could do was pray.

There was no answer the first time I called Jürgen's lodgings. The second time, he answered on the third ring, sounding dazed and sleepy. Without preamble, I told him that Adele had passed. I didn't mention the Gestapo or the circumstances of her death. At first, he didn't even react.

"Jürgen, did you hear me?"

"Did she die at home?" he asked stiffly. I was trying to be brave—for him, for Adele, for the children—but that question broke me. In a strange way, Adele had gone to meet her maker on her own terms.

"She did," I said, and then I choked on a sob. "She died at home."

There was another long silence over the phone. Then Jürgen said, "I'm coming home. Right away."

"Will you be allowed to?" I whispered, a sharp edge of bitterness in my voice.

"She was a mother to me," Jürgen said, his voice breaking midsentence. "Of course I'll be allowed to."

He hung up quickly after that. I'd never seen my husband cry, but I understood that he needed to, and I understood his need for privacy.

I was on the sofa later that afternoon, wrapped in Mayim's knit blanket, waiting impatiently for Jürgen to arrive. I had a crumpled, tearstained letter in my hand. I'd fished it out of Adele's sweets jar early that morning before the children woke.

Dearest Jürgen and Sofie,

Jürgen, you were a gift from God to me during the worst period of my life, living proof that no matter how dark the night, the dawn will always come. Raising you and being a part of your life was one of the great privileges of mine. And, Sofie, I have treasured your friendship in these past few years. Do not underestimate yourself. You are stronger than you know.

My loves, these monsters who rule our country are taking us all to uncharted territory, and if you're reading this, it seems I have

*run out of days to be by your side supporting you through it. Be
courageous, but also be smart.*

 *I am grateful for every single minute I spent with you. Please
tell the children their Oma adored them.*
Love always,
Aunt Adele

Ultimately, we would have to burn it. But until Jürgen had
a chance to read it, I could cling to it, as much a comfort ob-
ject as Mayim's blanket had become.

It had been an impossibly hard day. I'd broken the news
to the children on my own, consoled them on my own. I'd
tried to convince Georg to stay home, but he was adamant he
needed to go to school, and although his eyes were red rimmed
as he walked out the door, he hadn't shed a tear. Even after
he left, Gisela and Laura were both so demanding—I felt I'd
been attending to their needs every minute of the day.

The knock at the door was unexpected, and at the same
time, irritating. I just wanted to sit with my grief for a few
minutes. I stuffed Adele's letter into my pocket and dragged
myself to the door, and was startled to find Lydia there.

She was holding a Crock-Pot in her hands, her expression
one of intense sympathy, mixed in with some awkwardness.

"I heard about Adele and I just— Sofie, I'm so sorry. I know
she was important to your family." She extended the Crock-
Pot toward me. "Soup. So you don't have to cook your children dinner tonight."

I took the Crock-Pot and set it on a little table inside the
foyer, and then I turned back to her.

"When did you change your mind about the Jews?" I
blurted. Her eyebrows rose in surprise and alarm. I was a long
way past thinking straight, and that Crock-Pot reminded me
that at her best, Lydia was a great friend—a woman of true

kindness. But something ugly had emerged in her, and I desperately wanted to understand what had changed.

"I always knew," she said quietly. "Don't you remember at finishing school? I was polite to...*that girl*...because that was the way, but I never understood why you couldn't see that she wasn't like us. We had to pretend for a long time, so it was a relief to me and Karl when right-minded Germans came to power in this country."

I never once noticed her reticence toward Mayim. Maybe I saw what I wanted to see. In any case, she'd proved Mayim right. The Nazis didn't make people like Lydia anti-Semitic, not really. They had only uncovered what already existed.

"What about you?" she said gently. "When did you change your mind about the Jews?"

"Deep down, I always knew the truth," I said. "What you say is true. Sometimes you have to do and say certain things for acceptance."

She nodded sadly, misunderstanding me as I knew she would. Adele had been right about so many things—people heard what they wanted to hear. Lydia's expression grew somber.

"And...Adele? Do you know what she was mixed up in?"

I raised my chin, and just as Adele had told me to, I spoke harshly, as if I were handing down a judgment, and not breaking my own heart.

"The Gestapo suspected her of disloyalty to the Reich. I have no idea what the details were."

"I'm so sorry, Sofie," she said again, shaking her head.

"Me too," I said flatly, and then I thanked her and closed the door before I could say something I would regret.

31

Sofie
Huntsville, Alabama
1950

I FOUND LIZZIE'S ADDRESS IN THE TELEPHONE book. She lived just a few blocks away in a very large house by a young but extensive garden. I went there unannounced. It seemed safer to arrive on her doorstep unannounced with a gift, and to look her in the eyes while I apologized.

"Just wait here a moment," I said to Felix, who was sitting in the back seat, playing with his wooden truck. He nodded, distracted by the toy.

I walked up the path to knock on the door, then waited, hovering on the little porch with the cake in my sweaty hands. The door swung open and there stood the man in the brown uniform, the one who walked up and down my street each day. Up close, I could see the embroidery on his shirt. *Henry*, and below that, *Walt's Lumberyard*.

"You," he said. His tone was flat, almost emotionless, but

there was something dark in his eyes that unnerved me. I took a step away from the door.

"Hello," I said nervously. "Is Lizzie home?" The man stared at me, his gaze intense and unblinking. "I'm looking for Lizzie," I said again. "Lizzie Miller? Is this the right house?"

"What do you want with Lizzie?"

"I just wanted to say hello and to drop off a gift," I said uneasily, as I motioned toward the cake with my chin.

"She's not here."

"Could I just leave this here for her?" The man—Henry—ignored the question, staring at me with narrowed eyes. I extended the plate down toward him, but he made no move to take it.

"*You* said segregation is worse than the camps."

He knew about my argument with Lizzie. Worse, he knew exactly who I was. My breath caught.

"No. No, th-that wasn't what I said," I stammered. "I was just trying to explain that anytime you separate a group of people—"

Henry reached for the cake, and for a split second I thought he was going to take it and give it to Lizzie, as I'd asked... But his face was red and his nostrils flared. I only realized I was in trouble when the weight of the plate left my palms.

I cried out, automatically covering my face as he threw the cake, plate and all, into a brick pillar on the front porch, right behind my head. Shards of ceramic and dense cake and sticky lemon frosting rained down the back of my dress. I turned and ran toward my car. If he gave chase, I was done. He was easily twice my size, and *so angry*—

"You don't get to judge us, Nazi!" he called after me, and I was too scared to look back, but weak with relief to hear he was some distance behind me. His voice broke with frustration and anguish as he added, "Stop coming round here. Why do you people keep coming here!"

My hands were too sweaty to grip the key properly when I tried to start the car.

"Come on," I choked out. "Please, start."

"Mama…" Felix said uncertainly. "Mama, is that a bad man?"

The car roared to life. I pulled out onto the street and turned the car toward home.

"Something awful happened today."

As soon as Jürgen came home from work, I pulled him into our bedroom and shut the door. He cupped my face in his palms and stared down at me, concern in his gaze.

"Talk to me. Tell me what's wrong."

"I took a cake to Calvin's house for Lizzie," I whispered. "A peace offering."

"Sofie!" Jürgen groaned as his face fell. "What the hell were you thinking?"

"It was *me* who argued with her at that picnic, but it was *you* the police came for. I thought I could apologize before she stirred up any more trouble." My voice grew more desperate as I tried to explain myself. "I want to build a home here, Jürgen. I don't want some woman whispering to other Americans about me, telling them not to talk to me, telling their kids not to play with ours—gossiping about the worst moments of our lives. We need to build bridges here—not let rifts develop between us and your colleagues' wives. So I tried to reach out to her."

Jürgen dropped his hands from my face and rubbed his eyes. "Christ."

"I don't think she was home, but there was a man there." I swallowed a lump in my throat. "Do you remember the second time the road was graffitied? The man in the brown uniform who was staring at us while you painted?" Jürgen nodded slowly, and I whispered, "He comes past all the time. I just assumed he was walking to work since he's always in the uniform. But sometimes I see him several times in the one day, and not just in the morning and night. He stares at me." I shivered anxiously.

"You haven't mentioned this before."

"Well, it's not just him. Lots of people stare at me," I said, laughing weakly. "You must notice it too."

"Maybe I've grown used to it," he sighed. "So what happened, my love? Did he say something to you about your disagreement with Lizzie Miller?"

"I didn't get a chance to say my name, but he already knew who I was anyway, and he knew about my argument with Lizzie. I asked him to give her the cake and he called me a Nazi, then threw the cake against the pillar right behind me. Plate and all," I blurted. Jürgen's jaw dropped as his nostrils flared, and I hastened to explain, "He didn't hurt me, Jürgen, and he *could* have if he'd thrown the cake a little to the left of where I was standing. I think he just wanted to give me a fright."

Jürgen nodded slowly, his expression dark.

"Calvin did mention Lizzie's brother lives with them."

"His shirt says his name is Henry."

"That rings a bell."

"Lizzie Miller must have told her brother you broke into her house. He told me today we 'need to stop coming round there,'" I said, shivering.

"I have to talk to Calvin, don't I?" Jürgen sighed, running a hand through his hair.

"You said you wanted to stay out of this," I whispered.

"I want to stay out of a disagreement between you and Mrs. Miller." He pursed his lips. "I will not remain quiet when someone threatens my wife."

32

Lizzie
El Paso, Texas
1938

THE NIGHT BEFORE MY WEDDING, HENRY AND I sat on wooden chairs side by side on the porch of my new Federal-style house.

"Are you worried about this business in Europe?" I asked. He shrugged.

"Why would I be worried?"

"Cal seems to think Hitler is spoiling for war."

"Cal is a pretty smart fellow, so he might be right, but even if he is, I can't see us getting involved. It's the other side of the world, for heaven's sakes. All that trouble has nothing to do with America."

Henry was stretched out beside me, his legs propped up on the outdoor coffee table. In one hand, he held a beer, and in the other, a lit cigarette. This was a new habit he'd picked up during his year in the Army, and one I was not fond of. We sat in silence for a moment, and I was worrying about Hitler and Europe and just hoping that Henry was right—but was startled when my brother suddenly burst out laughing.

"What?" I said, alarmed.

"Sorry...sorry. It's just that I'm sitting here on the porch of this fancy house and I can't believe you're really going to *live* here. Mother and Daddy wouldn't believe their eyes if they could see you now. Your new kitchen is as big as our old house."

I couldn't believe I was going to live there either. My new house was every bit as grand as the Hilton, although of course, on a smaller scale. But at four thousand square feet, with four expansive bedrooms and, to my bewilderment, two bathrooms *and* an indoor laundry, it still didn't feel real to me. I knew Calvin was well-off, but we were engaged before I discovered the extent of his wealth. It wasn't just his high-paying job. It turned out his parents were wealthy too.

"Who would have thought you, my roughhousing, horse-breaking, fence-fixing, tractor-driving sister, would become the well-to-do wife of some airplane genius?" Henry chuckled.

"It is a surprising turn," I admitted.

Calvin and I continued to grow close after Henry left until we were unlikely best friends. When he told me he'd fallen in love with me and wanted me to be his wife, I was heart-broken, not pleased. I had no intention of accepting his proposal and figured it would be cruel to stay in our friendship knowing our feelings were imbalanced.

"I know you don't feel the same way about me, and it's perfectly fine," Calvin said quietly. I was relieved, but still confused, especially when he added, "I just can't help but wonder if there's not a solution that would suit both of us."

"A solution?"

"Your whole life is earning minimum wage at a hotel where most of the guests don't even see you, but, Lizzie Davis, you are the kind of woman who deserves to be seen. I hate that you work harder than anyone I know and it's all for so little. And don't tell me you're doing fine, because we both know you're not. You have to work two jobs just to pay your rent on that terrible apartment."

"You've never even been inside my apartment," I replied stiffly.

"I don't need to. That building is one strong wind away from being condemned."

"We didn't even have running water at the farm. This apartment is just fine."

"Why should you settle for *just fine*, Lizzie? Especially when you could be with someone who wants nothing more in this life than to make you happy?" I didn't know what to say. After a while, Calvin took my hand and added softly, "I know from experience that the most important thing in a marriage is a solid foundation of friendship. This is a pragmatic proposal. I've accepted a permanent position at Fort Bliss, so I need to set up a home here, not to mention entertain more, so you could help with all that. And I could help you too. You wouldn't need to struggle for every little thing. You work so hard, Lizzie—when do you even have time to stop and breathe? I could give you the gift of a comfortable life. And maybe, if you let me love you, in time, you'll come to love me too."

I was lonely after Henry left and so damned tired of struggling for every crumb city life had to offer. I'd already reinvented myself once—from farmer's daughter to city battler. I could do it again, especially if it meant making such a good man happy in the process.

"You don't even look the same," Henry chuckled now. That laughter was music to my ears. His appearance had also changed—he looked strong and healthy, and there was a twinkle in his eyes. "You look like some backwater farm girl who found her way to the city, met a rich guy, and now gets to be a trophy wife."

He was teasing and I knew he didn't mean to cause offense, but I gasped as I looked down at my outfit. I'd bought it because the fabric was the color of Texas bluegrass and it reminded me of home. That dress was beautiful, but Henry had a point: it was also something I'd never wear back in Oakden.

But Cal pointed out that most of his colleagues' wives rarely wore trousers and then he gave me a big stack of money, so I bought some dresses.

"And what did you do to your hair?" Henry asked now, chuckling as he reached to touch my head. I slapped his hand away.

"It's called a pompadour, you oaf," I muttered. I'd never really had a clue about how to style my hair—that had never bothered me before, but things were different now. Cal said the best way to learn was to watch professionals, so I'd been booking myself into the salon a few times a week.

"I was surprised when you wrote that you were marrying Calvin," Henry admitted. "You never even liked to date, remember?"

"I know."

"But Calvin is a good guy. Army life has its ups and downs, but I don't think they'd have taken me if he hadn't put in a good word. Things got pretty bad for me for a while there, Lizzie. I wasn't in my right mind. I still have bad days now, but they come and they go, and whether it's a bad day or a good day, I have to get up and out of that bed before God is awake, because that's how the Army works. Your Calvin saved me when he didn't even know me. That's a top kind of man right there. When I couldn't look after you, I was glad to hear he was."

"He really does look after me." And I was trying to do the same for him. I wasn't much of a girlfriend, and our relationship wasn't exactly typical. I was still trying to figure out how to dress and act like the kind of woman a man like Cal deserved to marry.

"This should be the happiest time of your life."

"It is," I said, frowning. "Why would you think otherwise?"

"You're pretty and dolled up, but you're acting like you're not even you." He flicked me a confused glance. "At dinner with Cal and his parents, you hardly said a word." We'd gone to the Hilton's restaurant for old times' sake, and Cal and his mother and father were staying there for the night, since it wasn't appropriate for us to sleep in the same house before the wedding.

"It's a big change." I shrugged. "I'm nervous, that's all."

"I know. I get that. And tomorrow *is* your wedding night. I guess a girl would normally talk to her mother about these things, but with Mother not being here—"

"No! Stop it!" I said, covering my face with my hands. "God, Henry!"

When I peeked out from behind my hands, the relief on Henry's face was palpable. I laughed, despite the heat on my cheeks. But he kept looking at me, that question still in his eyes, and I felt obliged to explain.

"Since even before the drought, everything that came my way meant a struggle. Calvin wants to take care of me. This wedding is the right move for both of us."

"You know I loved Betsy like crazy, but even so, I'm not sure that I'm much of a romantic," Henry said, his voice low. "I'll tell you this much—if I was Calvin and you were Betsy, and Betsy was talking about me like you just talked about Calvin, I don't know that I would want that wedding to happen."

"Henry!"

"You can't marry a man just because he has the money to buy you a big house. That's not how marriage works."

"I'll have a good life with Calvin," I said abruptly. "I'm not using him, if that's what you're trying to imply."

"Maybe you're not exactly using him, but you haven't once told me that you love him either."

"I do love him," I protested weakly. "I just…"

"If you don't want to marry him, it's not too late to stop this," Henry said suddenly. "Calvin *is* a good man, but I know he'd rather you tell him so if you're not sure about this."

I could imagine going inside to my suitcase, still sitting on the dresser, open and still half-full. It wouldn't take me long to repack. Me and Henry could be back at the bus station within an hour. We could take the first bus out of town.

But *then* what?

Henry would have to go back to Kansas on Monday, and I'd be adrift and alone again. And Calvin adored me. He was a wonderful boyfriend—considerate, compassionate, respectful. He'd be a generous provider. There were worse things I could do to support myself than marry a man I held in such high esteem, even if I weren't in love with him. Besides, that might change. I'd never fallen in love with anyone—but maybe I'd just never given a man the chance to win my heart.

"I want to marry him," I said firmly. "Cal and I are going to have a good marriage. You'll see."

33

Lizzie

Huntsville, Alabama
1950

I KNEW SOMETHING WAS UP WHEN CALVIN CAME
home from work one evening and immediately joined me
in the garden. The sun was setting on the horizon, and we
swatted mosquitoes away as we exchanged pleasantries: *How
was your day? Yes, mine too. Pork chops. No, I didn't make dessert.
Sure, I can make an apple pie for tomorrow night.* I picked up my
second watering can and moved to water the broccoli, but
Cal followed me, as if he were trying to gather the courage
to say something hard.

"What is it?" I prompted.

"The police went to Jürgen's house."

I looked at him in surprise.

"They just got around to doing that now?"

"No, they went right away. Jürgen only mentioned it today."

"Oh."

"He's been pretty good about that, considering. I apologized—told him Henry fought in the war and sometimes has vivid dreams."

"Okay," I said stiffly. I knew my brother's problems weren't his fault, but I was also aware that he wouldn't want anyone outside of our circle to know his private business—and that was doubly so for these people.

"It seems there was an incident yesterday."

"An incident?"

"Jürgen's wife came by with a cake for you. A peace offering, apparently," Cal said quietly.

"I was home most of the morning."

"It was early. Maybe when you were out at the grocery store."

"But I didn't see any cake." I frowned. I wasn't sure how I felt about such a gesture. I had no interest in a friendship with Sofie Rhodes, but we weren't exactly at war, either—we'd had one uncomfortable conversation and that was that. Why would she bring a peace offering? Then I thought about the police visiting her home and sighed. Maybe *she* thought we were at war.

"Henry was here," Cal said.

"Henry went to work early yesterday," I said, but then I paused. My days generally looked the same and tended to blend together so quickly. Was it yesterday Henry only had the black coffee for breakfast and refused my offer of eggs, or was that the day before?

"I don't know what to tell you. Sofie asked him to pass it on to you and he…" Calvin paused, then cleared his throat. "Lizzie, she says he threw it at her."

"What?" I said in disbelief, then immediately added, "There's no way that's true."

"Jürgen said it gave her quite the fright. And he said Henry has been walking past the houses where the German families live. Sofie has seen him a number of times."

"Please tell me you aren't buying this. My brother wouldn't hurt a fly. I didn't see any mess from this supposed cake and you know as well as I do it makes perfect sense for him to walk that way to work."

I turned and glanced toward my front porch and a sudden memory flared. Some of the pavers had been wet when I came home from the grocery store. I just figured it was from when I watered the young red buckeye the night before, but what if—

No. I shook my head, frowning. My brother wouldn't throw something at a perfect stranger, even under these conditions. "We don't know these people, Cal. We certainly can't take their word over Henry's."

"Sweetheart. I really need to get to the bottom of what happened," Cal said quietly, but firmly.

"So we'll talk to him," I said impatiently. "He'll tell you she's making the whole thing up."

"I'll have a chat with him tonight and straighten this out."

"We can do it together," I suggested. Calvin shook his head, and as the last of the water poured onto my vegetables, he reached down to take the empty watering can from my hands.

"This is one of those conversations that will be better man-to-man."

"But—"

"Sweetheart," Cal said, and he dropped his voice. "I don't want Henry to feel like we're ganging up on him. Please, let me do this alone."

"How did it go?" I asked, as Calvin came into my bedroom later that night. He quietly closed the door and sat on the end of my bed.

I was sitting up in my nightgown, an untouched magazine

on my lap. Calvin had invited Henry out onto the porch for a beer after dinner and I'd been waiting anxiously ever since.

"He said Sofie Rhodes is lying. There was no cake."

"See?" I said, triumphant. "I told you."

"And he does walk past the German homes, but you were right. It's just on his way to and from work. Sofie Rhodes has only been here for a few weeks and I'm sure it's easy to misread situations when she's navigating a strange country in her second language. I'm still confused about the cake story, but Henry was adamant, and we have to give him the benefit of the doubt."

"So are you comforted?" I asked.

"I'm still concerned about that dream he had," Calvin said hesitantly. He flicked a glance at me. "I'm horrified that the police went to the Rhodes house. I did try to ask Henry how he feels about that dream now, but he seemed so uncomfortable, I dropped it. I suppose he's embarrassed."

"That was weeks ago, anyway," I said. "He's been so much calmer ever since."

"It's just…he does seem different, doesn't he? He's distracted. For all of Henry's challenges over the years, he's never seemed that way to me before."

Distracted. That was the perfect word. Even when Henry was looking right at me, it seemed like his mind was somewhere else.

I had plans to see Becca the next morning. She and Kevin had purchased a new house a few blocks away—a great big two-story place on a huge, empty lot—and they were keen to put in a garden.

"I'll do it for you," I offered when she called. I was excited about a new project—already thinking about how it might come together.

Becca laughed and said, "Don't be silly, Lizzie—I couldn't ask you to do that. Kevin has already found a gardener to do it. I just wanted some advice about what to ask him for."

I'd grown numb to my own boredom for the most part. I had a good life—and it was plenty busy when I wanted it to be, between chores and salon visits and dinners and lunch dates. But every now and again, something triggered a memory of a time when I thought my life would look different.

Even as I prepared to go to Becca's house, I was reliving the disappointment of the moment when she told me someone else would do the gardening. Oh, how I would have loved to pull my boots on that day, to pack my gardening gloves and a notepad to sketch out plans. I'd have thrown myself into a project like that with wild abandon. The yard was a blank canvas, but I'd have turned it into green art.

As I locked the front door, I glanced down at the pavers, thinking about the splash of water I'd seen a few days earlier. Why would Sofie Rhodes make up such an absurd lie? It made no damned sense. I started to walk down the path toward the drive, but at the last second I spun around to stare at the porch, trying to remember exactly which pavers had been wet.

I didn't believe the story about the cake. Of course I didn't.

I set down my handbag and bent to inspect the pavers, feeling disloyal and foolish as I did. I was gratified to find no trace of smeared cake. But as I reached out to use the pillar to steady myself on my heels, I noticed a little chip of white ceramic embedded in the brick, just above my hand. As I brushed it with my fingertip, the ceramic chip fell to the pavers.

I looked around again, seeing my front porch with fresh eyes. If she had been standing at the door and she extended the cake toward him, and Henry took it from her and then lost his temper—

No.

That white chip in the brick was tiny. It could have been anything—even a tiny stone baked into the brick when it was crafted. There were other explanations here and my brother deserved my trust.

I scooped my bag up again and started toward my car, but I skimmed my gaze across the young red buckeye plants in the garden bed along the front of the porch. I felt a pit form in my stomach. He'd missed one jagged shard of ceramic about halfway along the bushes, sitting among leaves. When I bent to retrieve it, I found it sticky with light-colored frosting and a smudge of dark cake, rich with tiny black seeds.

And when I checked through the trash can, I found one unholy mess of cake and plate and dirt, wrapped in newspaper and buried in the bottom.

34

Sofie
Berlin, Germany
1939

JÜRGEN AND KARL CAME HOME FOR A WEEK'S vacation in June that year. I'd seen Jürgen for a few days around Adele's funeral, but we were both so soaked in grief I'd barely looked at him then. This trip was different. In all those months we spent apart, Gisela learned to crawl and be terrified of strangers—she now cried whenever Jürgen tried to pick her up. And over those months apart, Jürgen changed too.

He was quiet, spending long hours alone in his study even though he was supposed to be taking a break. After a few days of this, I stood in front of his desk. He looked up from a blue-print and his gaze was hollow.

"We need to go for a walk and enjoy this beautiful summer day," I said flatly, propping my hand on my hip. "I am going to put Gisela in the stroller. I'll see you outside in a moment."

He didn't even try to argue. He heard in my tone that I

would not be deterred. We began to walk toward the park, and when we reached it, I motioned toward a shaded bench beneath a large linden tree. There we sat side by side, and I turned Gisela around to face us. She eyed Jürgen warily.

"This last year has been very difficult, but the technology is more marvelous than even I dreamed it could be. The next prototype is the A4. This rocket will launch vertically, straight up like this." Slowly, almost dreamily, he raised his hand. "It will ascend at an angle we've calculated with incredible precision—every movement stabilized and guided by a finely tuned gyroscope. After maybe a minute, the propulsion ends. Now this rocket is somewhere in the order of sixty miles straight up. Maybe it even comes near the edge of space. Isn't that remarkable?"

"Sixty miles—"

"But this is just the culmination point," he interrupted, his expression twisting until he looked disgusted. "Because now it starts its descent, and it travels just above the speed of sound. Do you know what that means?" I shook my head, but he didn't seem to notice. He brought his hand down sharply into a fist on the other side of his lap, then snapped it open, exposing his palm. "The accuracy and range will be beyond anything the world has ever seen. And the missile travels faster than the sound it produces, so there is no warning at all—certainly no time for an air raid siren. Say we launch this from the border, as a family in France or Poland or Belgium or Switzerland sits in their kitchen eating their breakfast. That family is gone before they ever knew something was coming for them. The mother has no time to scream to the father that she's going to get the baby. The father has no time to push his son into the cellar to save his life."

Jürgen had always insisted he didn't remember anything

about the morning his family died. He had been lying to me, or at least avoiding a painful truth.

"You were eating breakfast when the bomb hit your house?" I asked gently.

Jürgen suddenly sat up, as if shaking off the memory.

"My point is that scenario I just described to you would seem like a fanciful nightmare to most people, but it's almost within reach."

"We just have to keep playing the game," I said. "Remember? Listen for the music. Ignore the dissonant notes?"

"So I build these bombs and let someone else care about where they land?"

"That's what you have to do."

"When I'm refining the design of a booster or I'm tinkering with the engineers or I'm planning a test launch, I don't think about that theoretical family eating their breakfast. Sometimes I even manage to forget that the sum of all the moving parts is a weapon. But as soon as the work stops, that family is all I can think about."

I looked to Gisela. She was kicking her legs impatiently, craning her neck to look behind her, eager to continue the journey through the park.

"We both know you don't have a choice. The cost of anything but perfect compliance would simply be too high."

He slid his arm around my shoulders and pulled me close, planting a gentle kiss above my ear.

"I'm just following orders. I'm doing what I have to do to stay alive. To keep my family safe," he murmured.

"Exactly," I said.

"That's what I tell myself a hundred times a day, but sometimes I can't help but wonder if that theoretical family eating their breakfast would be satisfied by those excuses. Should we really prioritize the safety of our family over the safety of theirs, Sofie? And does the equation change if, one day in the not-too-distant future, we're prioritizing the safety of our family over hundreds or thousands of families who might find themselves the target of one of my rockets?"

I turned to stare at him. Our faces were so close I could feel his shaky breath against my lips.

"I don't know what to say," I whispered, stricken.

"I don't know what the answers are either," he whispered back. "But we have a moral obligation to ask ourselves these questions."

And it was clear, from the torment in his eyes, he'd been confronting that truth for some time.

Lydia and Karl invited us to join them for dinner the evening before Karl and Jürgen were to return to Peenemünde. While the staff prepared the meal, the nannies supervised the children as they played in a paddling pool in the gardens. Lydia, heavily pregnant with another set of twins, looked exhausted but smiled wearily as she handed us each a glass of champagne.

"I have some excellent news for you both," Karl announced. "I know that Georg is not due to go until his birthday, but I was speaking with Hans's supervising captain and he agreed to admit Georg to the *Jungvolk* early. Congratulations."

The *Jungvolk*—the junior division of the Hitler Youth. I was always going to have to cross this bridge when Georg turned ten—I just thought I had a few more months to come to terms with it.

"The Führer needs young warriors like Georg," Karl said. He looked between the three of us, a glint of determination in his eyes. Just as Jürgen had changed over those past few years, Karl had changed too—he'd become a much harder man, much less inclined to flash his charming smile. "The sooner we get him started, the better—and the early entry reflects just how much the Party values your work, Jürgen."

"Thank you," I heard my husband say. Watching the convincing job he was doing of expressing delight at this development, I understood why he was so tired all of the time.

"On that note," Karl continued, "my friend, there is something I've been meaning to speak to you about..." His charming smile made a brief reappearance. "You're the most senior staff member at Peenemünde who isn't a member of the Party. I know that's just an oversight, but don't you think it's time we rectified it?"

This was a test of loyalty, just like the special *Jungvolk* arrangement, and an explicit threat was no longer required. We all understood exactly what the stakes were.

By the time Jürgen returned to Peenemünde the next day, we were paid-up members of the Nazi party, just waiting for our membership numbers to arrive in the post.

Georg chatted excitedly the morning of his first overnight *Jungvolk* camp, more animated than I'd seen him since Adele's death.

"There's sports and adventure courses and we get to fire guns and we sleep in the tents and they will teach us how to do all kinds of amazing things—even how to serve the Führer better! I'll be in Hans's *Jungenshaft*." This was a unit of ten children, led by a slightly older child. The *Jungvolk* was structured as a paramilitary organization. I was sending my nine-year-old son off to play combat games designed to shape him into a mindless Hitler acolyte.

Georg was already wearing his uniform—shiny black boots and dark shorts, a tie paired with a collared shirt, the *Jungvolk* logo on the sleeve. He'd emerged from his room in the uniform so early that morning, I had a feeling he slipped it on straight out of bed. But he couldn't fix the final part of the uniform without help, and that was why he was standing before me now, chin raised, waiting impatiently for me to put his rolled kerchief around his neck.

"...and we will learn to expel the *Untermensch* and defeat all of the Führer's enemies. It is going to be so much fun!"

It was all a game to Georg—a glorious, fun-filled lark. I slipped the kerchief around his neck, tucked the collar over it, and then reached for the woggle—the loop of woven leather that secured the kerchief in place at his collarbone. I stared down at him until tears filled my eyes.

"What is it?" he asked, suddenly alarmed as he stared back up at me, his blue eyes filled with concern. "Mama?"

I forced myself to smile.

"You're just such a big boy, Georg. I'm so proud of you."

He beamed at me, then straightened his shoulders as he stepped away to pick up the canvas bag containing his overnight things. The bag was almost bigger than he was. He swung it over his shoulder, then stepped toward the door, waving impatiently for me to follow.

At the camp, Laura hovered beside me, taking it all in with big, curious eyes—hundreds of young boys, assembling into perfect lines at the sharp sound of a whistle. I was holding a squirming Gisela on one hip, but Laura took my other hand and tugged it to get my attention.

"Mama, I can't wait until it's my turn." As a young girl, she wouldn't attend the *Jungvolk*—rather, the *Jungmadelbund*, the Young Girls' League, focused on activities deemed suitable for German girls, preparing them for their future roles as mother, wife, and homemaker.

"Soon enough," I replied, my heart sinking as I said it. She would likely start at ten—just a few short years away. I looked back to Georg, who was almost quaking with excitement as the leaders barked instructions at the children to prepare to recite the pledge.

Several hundred boys straightened their spines and echoed in unison the chant my son had already learned by heart.

"In the presence of this blood banner which represents our Führer, I swear to devote all of my energies and my strength to the savior of our country, Adolf Hitler." My son looked right at me and beamed with pride as he chanted, "I am willing and ready to give up my life for him, so help me God."

Adele's apartment was still vacant and I couldn't bring myself to rent it out. We didn't need the money, and the thought of sorting through her belongings was still too much. Every morning, I went into her courtyard to tend to the animals and the plants that remained. On Wednesdays, I packed a basket of whatever was in season, and Gisela and I took a trip to drop it off to Martha.

There were still so many unknowns from the night Adele died. We never figured out how the Gestapo caught wind of the chain of women helping Mayim's family for all of those years, nor did we know why some of those women, including Martha, escaped suspicion. But Martha could explain some things.

"Adele called and asked me to come by in the morning with my son's car. She was trying to stay calm, but I heard her panic." Martha arrived at sunrise—only to find Adele had passed. "I convinced the Bavarians to go to their room and freshen up, and while they were gone, I checked the apartment. I found Mayim hiding beneath the kitchen sink. She'd been there all night." I swallowed a lump in my throat at the thought of that. The same hiding place she'd endured while her father was killed. What a torture it must have been to see history repeat itself twice in just a few days. "I snuck her out the back door and over the courtyard wall. By the time the couple came back downstairs, Mayim was hiding in my son's car and I was sitting with Adele on the bed, calmly saying goodbye."

"I see why you and Adele were friends." I smiled tearfully.

"It was nothing," Martha said dismissively. Then her face fell. "I wish I could have done more for her, Sofie. There were thousands of Poles camping out in the open at the border because the Reich wouldn't let them stay but Poland wouldn't let them in. I don't know what happened after she left my car, but I think of her all the time."

After that, Martha mentioned that her son knew of several other Jews in hiding. I could no longer help Mayim, but that didn't mean I was powerless.

Not even Jürgen knew that every Wednesday I dropped some of Adele's produce off to Martha—caring for an elderly Aryan German, just as the Reich wanted me to do. But in a layer of folded newspaper at the bottom of the basket of produce, there was always a stack of Reichsmark—as much as I could skim without arousing suspicion from Jürgen. I knew he wouldn't protest if he knew what I was doing, but I wanted to protect him, just as Adele had tried to protect me.

I never met Martha's son, but I knew he always visited her on Wednesday afternoons. While he was there, he'd collect the cash and pass it to Jewish friends who needed it most.

I never learned who the recipients were. It didn't really matter. I desperately wanted to help—but I knew, deep down, that my gesture was so small as to be laughably insignificant.

Besides, the gesture was intended to do good, but in a way, it was also selfish. It was the quiet reminder I needed. It didn't matter who I pretended to be. The Nazis could take my best friends and even my children from me—but they would not touch my heart.

"Oh, hello, dear," Martha greeted me that Wednesday. "It's good to see you. And hello, sweet Gisela." Just as Adele might have done if she were alive, Martha bent into the stroller and gave my excited daughter some candy.

I set the basket on Martha's kitchen table. She bustled around the kitchen, chatting about this and that as she made me tea.

"The strangest thing happened," she said. "I got this letter and I don't know what to do with it. I think it might have been incorrectly addressed. Could you take a look and tell me what I should do?"

I accepted the letter as she handed it to me—but almost dropped it when I saw the familiar handwriting.

Dear Frieda,

Do you remember me from those days as childhood neighbors in Potsdam, all of those years ago? You probably do not, so I will try to jog your memory.

There was that time when I fell and broke a bone in my wrist, and as I lay on the ground in such pain, you were so distressed that we forgot our roles somehow, and I wound up comforting you. And then one summer we wanted to swim in the creek but my brother was unwell, so my mother told him he couldn't join us. He set fire to a cloth in her kitchen to distract her and followed us to the creek! Such a rascal back then, and he's such a rascal today—even now that he is a husband and father.

It was his idea that I write you to let you know that I still think of you, even after all of these years. I imagine you will wish you could reply to me, but the timing of this letter is unfortunate, as I'm about to go traveling, so I won't leave a return address for now. Life is too short—one never knows what lies around the corner, so I wanted to send you my well-wishes while I could.

If I settle someplace, I will write you again so you know where to find me. For now, just know that I am happy and well, and

my life has worked out just fine. I will never forget you or your
kindness to me.
Very best wishes,
Anna

Mayim! Frieda—my grandmother's name; Anna—hers. So
many references to our past together, not one of them subtle, but clever Mayim had found a way to hide her identity
in such a way that no one in the world could possibly know
who wrote that letter except me.

"What should I do with it?" Martha asked me innocently. I
looked up at her, my vision blurred from tears, and she winked
at me. "Yes, it's clearly not intended for me. Since there's no
return address, I'll throw it into the trash."

But later, Martha followed me to the door, and as we embraced, I whispered in her ear, "She didn't know where you
lived. I remember she said that, the night Adele died. How did
she find you? And how did you know the letter was for me?"

"I gave her my address as I drove her to the border, just in case
there was anything else I could do for her. The envelope was
addressed to me, but when I opened it, I was so confused to see
the letter addressed to someone else. I almost threw it out, until
I remembered her telling me she met you in Potsdam. Now at
least we know she made it to her family. I hope that brings you
some peace."

I was at Adele's apartment one morning in early Septem-
ber. Gisela, now eighteen months old, was stumbling clumsily around the courtyard, one of the young rabbits following
her like a puppy. I had the wireless on for background noise,
but I wasn't really listening until a sudden flare of trumpets
and drums sounded. The Reichstag had been assembled for an
extraordinary session and Hitler was about to address the na-

tion. There came a cacophony of noise—shouting and cheers from parliamentarians as the Führer arrived.

Hitler announced that Germany had invaded Poland but only as an act of self-defense. *From now on, bombs will be met with bombs.* He told the nation to brace itself. *This will be a fight until the resolution of the situation.*

When the children came home from school, they were abuzz with excitement, although it was clear they had little understanding of what had actually happened. Georg was convinced that Poland had dropped a bomb on Berlin. Laura thought Hitler was at the border, wielding a sword in defense of the Reich. When I went to tuck Georg in, I found him on his knees by the side of the bed, whispering what I thought was a prayer. As I waited by the door, surprised but determined to give him space to pray, I heard the words he was murmuring to a rhythm that suggested he'd said them many times before.

"Führer, my Führer, given me by God. Protect and preserve my life for long. You saved Germany in time of need. I thank you for my daily bread. Be with me for a long time, do not leave me, Führer, my Führer, my faith, my light, Hail to my Führer!"

"Where did you learn that?" I asked, forgetting my plan to give him privacy. Georg climbed up onto his bed and pulled the blankets up to his chin, flashing me a bright grin.

"At the *Jungvolk*," he said easily. I kissed his forehead and turned his light out, and then walked briskly into the study to call Jürgen.

It was too much to bear alone—the "prayer" I'd overheard, the conflict with Poland—what it all meant, and what might happen next. I didn't trust the media anymore, but I had no alternate way to find information. Everything felt completely out of control.

"Hello?" my husband answered gruffly.

The instant I heard his voice, I knew I was going to weep, and I couldn't do that—he'd ask me why I was so upset, and I couldn't tell him because we likely had an audience. I hung up the phone and went to bed, muffling the sound of my sobs by pressing my face into my pillow.

35

Lizzie
El Paso, Texas
1941

"IT'S SO GOOD TO CATCH UP SO I CAN FINALLY get to know you better, Lizzie! We were all so surprised when Calvin told us he was getting married again. Heck, I don't think he'd even mentioned he was dating."

Avril Walters beamed at me as she poured my coffee from the pot. Her husband, Dale, worked with Calvin in the experimental planes division at El Paso, and their baby, Patty, was sitting up at the table next to me, stuffing cake into her mouth.

I met most of Calvin's Fort Bliss friends after we got engaged. They were all involved with his aviation unit—pilots or engineers or specialists of one variety or another. I also met their families. There were Kevin and Becca Llewellyn and their adorable girls, Ava and Brianna; Juanita and Bob and their noisy tribe of sons, who destroyed any room they entered; Trevor and Gail had newborn Toby; and of course, Avril and her husband, Dale, and Patty. I'd attended a few dinner parties with Calvin, but I wasn't quite sure what to make of these women. They seemed so tight-knit already, and Avril wasn't the first one to express surprise that Calvin had remarried.

Most of the time I was fine with our arrangement, but when his friends teased Calvin about our relationship, I felt so self-conscious, I couldn't bear it. I had no idea how I'd react to such a dynamic in a one-on-one conversation, so when Avril invited me for coffee, I always made an excuse. Finally, though, I accepted one of Avril's many invitations to get to know one another better.

"Cal has been so coy about you but I'm dying to know— how did you two meet?" she asked as soon as we settled at her kitchen table.

"I was working at the Hilton," I said. She pushed the cup of coffee in front of me and nodded to encourage me to continue. "He was a guest and we just became friends."

"Tell me everything! Did he sweep you off your feet? Has he told you all about his poor dead wife, God rest her soul?"

"Yes, he swept me off my feet. And we don't talk much about her, to be honest." I sipped my coffee, grateful to have something to do with my hands. It felt like I was being interrogated. "I know her name was Louise."

"So sad," Avril murmured, shaking her head. "How did she die?"

"It was a car accident," I said awkwardly. Poor Louise Miller had been hit by a car on her way to buy groceries.

"Tragic. Thank God he has you now." She poured her own coffee, and then took a seat beside me. "And you grew up on a farm, right?"

And so it went—the kind of awkward small talk I'd never

had much time for. *Yes, I grew up in Dallam County. Yes, I can ride a horse. Only eighth grade. My parents? Dead. Only a brother. In the Army.*

"I'm so glad you came around today," she said at one point. "I know it can be overwhelming meeting a whole new group of friends and those women can be a *lot*." She laughed. "But I have a good feeling about you, Lizzie. I don't care what anyone says—if Cal loves you, that's good enough for me."

She was so friendly and lovely and hospitable, but there were also those little moments where I felt almost like she was warning me—had the other women been gossiping? Had they been cruel behind my back? I told myself I didn't care what they thought, but the truth was, Calvin worked with their husbands and those women were going to be a part of my life for a long time.

I had been bored witless. Cal and I had settled into a routine so sedate, it was almost catatonic. He left for work at Fort Bliss in the morning, and I cleaned the house, and then watched the clock until he got home. I turned my attention to the yard to try to fill my days, tearing up every inch of established garden on that lot and spending a small fortune on young roses and hedges and building a tidy little vegetable garden. That project entertained me for a while, but soon all there was left to do was wait for the plants to grow.

So when Avril called for another coffee date, I agreed. Soon, we were meeting two or three times a week. I couldn't tell if she was just being nice or if maybe she was a little lonely, but I appreciated the company, so I didn't question her enthusiasm too much. Besides, Cal was pleased I was making an effort, and that was good too. I pushed my front door open and waited while Avril walked inside first, holding Patty's hand. As we took our seats in the living room, she smiled.

"I was happy when I heard Calvin bought you this great big house. I'm excited to watch you two fill it with children."

"Oh—" I said, wincing. "No, we won't be doing that." She looked at me in surprise, so I explained. "Calvin is sterile—that's why he and Louise didn't have children."

That was true—Cal suffered a bad bout of mumps as a child. Not that it mattered in our marriage, given we had separate bedrooms.

I had a feeling if I went to Calvin's room, he'd be delighted and that might change, but I had no inclination to do that. From time to time, I wondered if he was disappointed at the way our marriage was panning out. It was too awkward to bring up in conversation, and he *seemed* happy enough, but I knew all too well that when I agreed to marry him, he'd hoped that I'd fall in love with him too.

I realized it was just not going to happen. My feelings had nothing to do with Calvin and everything to do with me. I was more fond of him than ever. I respected him and I admired him. I was grateful to him, and I wanted to please him. I just had no drive toward romantic love, not the way other people around me seemed to.

"Oh gosh, I am so sorry," Avril said. She dropped her hands to her belly, as if to protect it. Her second child was due in a few months. "You know, Becca did say that she thought it was odd that Calvin didn't already have children after being married to his first wife for so long. But you know how those girls gossip and I just thought it was none of my business."

"They gossip?" I prompted lightly. This wasn't the first time she'd made a comment like that. I felt I knew her well enough now that I could gently prod to see what she was getting at.

"It's terrible, and you're such a nice woman. I hate to hear it."

"What do they say about me?" I asked.

"Well, sweetie, there's been a lot of speculation about…" She shrugged, looking around her expansive living room. "Calvin isn't short of a dollar, is he? Gail pointed out that he was just so lonely when he first started coming down from Albuquerque, and with you working at that hotel, they thought maybe you were down on your luck a little and saw him as an opportunity…"

"It was not like that," I gasped.

"And most newlyweds can't keep their hands off each other, but like Becca said, you two aren't like that at all, at least when we're around." My cheeks heated, and I didn't know what to say. I avoided her gaze, my mind racing as I tried to think of a response. Was it really so obvious? How *mortifying*.

"I shouldn't have said anything." Avril winced. "I didn't mean to upset you."

"No, you haven't upset me," I said, frustrated. "I know we're a strange couple. He's older than me and a million times smarter, and—" I waved my hand, indicating the room "—this is normal to him. I grew up in a much humbler home, and I *had* fallen upon hard times when we met. But it was always Calvin offering to help me, never me asking for help. Right from when we met, he was always doing kind things for me—even for my brother. Calvin just loves to look after people."

For a while after that, I kept my socializing with those women to essential engagements with Calvin only. Although Avril *seemed* to be on my side, I felt unsettled around her too. I learned how to dress like them and to style my hair and makeup like they did so I'd fit in, but I knew that, deep down, I had nothing in common with those women.

Besides, bored and lonely in that great big house was vastly preferable to exposed and humiliated out of it. But friendship dramas aside, why wasn't I content? In some ways, I'd felt better about myself back when I was struggling in that apartment, hustling for every cent and working my fingers to the bone.

Henry had transferred to Fort Benning in Georgia and was serving with the 6th Armored Division. We'd established a routine phone call on the first Sunday night of each month.

"Howdy, sis," he always greeted me, and I always exhaled whenever I heard him say those words. The brightness of his tone reassured me that he was okay. My imagination tended to play tricks on me during the weeks between those calls, especially with the situation in Europe deteriorating.

He had a new best friend—a boy from Reno named Bobby— and I got the impression the two of them had become inseparable. Henry was saving money in case he decided to buy a house one day and dating a girl named Flora—at least periodically. She worked in the base's administration office, and it felt a lot like every time Henry called, they'd either broken up again or were back together.

"Would you two make up your minds? Do you want to be together, or not?" I asked him one day, exasperated. Henry just laughed.

"This is a fiery relationship, Lizzie. That's part of the appeal."

I looked at Calvin, who was sitting on the sofa reading, and wondered, not for the first time, what was wrong with me.

"Hey, listen, sis. I have news," Henry said suddenly. My stomach lurched.

"No. Tell me they aren't deploying you," I whispered.

"Where to? To Europe? Of course not. That's a whole mess over there, but it has nothing to do with America," Henry laughed. "No, I was just going to say my unit is coming to

Fort Bliss for training in a few weeks, so I thought I'd take some leave while I'm in town. Can I come stay in your mansion for a few nights?"

Henry arrived on Thursday night, and we spent Friday and Saturday catching up. On Sunday, I made a roast chicken—one of the recipes I'd mastered. Henry and Calvin had never really had much time together, and I was enjoying watching them bond. They were presently in the sitting room, talking about planes.

Everything in the world seemed right that day. I was just about to pull the chicken from the oven. The rich smell was wafting through the house, and I was so happy, I was dancing to the music on the wireless as I served the food.

The breaking news broadcast cut the music off without warning, and I felt a chill run down my spine. I threw my oven mitts onto the floor as I twisted the volume of the radio up.

"Henry!" I cried. "Cal!"

Calvin ran into the kitchen, scanning as if he expected to find the place on fire, but his footsteps came to a halt as the crackling announcement filled the air.

This morning 8:00 a.m. local time in Honolulu...

...severe bombing of Pearl Harbor and the city of Honolulu by Japanese planes...

...fierce fighting in the air and on the sea...

...America is under attack. I repeat, America is under attack...

I was staring at Calvin in horror when Henry appeared behind him. My brother caught the end of the emergency broadcast, and I was staring right into his eyes as the realization dawned on me that the nation was now at war.

36

Sofie
Huntsville, Alabama
1950

WHEN I HEARD THE KNOCK AT THE DOOR, I WAS on my hands and knees scrubbing the oven, my hair in a tangled bun, wearing one of Jürgen's old shirts to protect my cotton dress.

"*Tür*, Mama," Felix called.

"English, please, Felix," I said. Then I corrected him. *"Door."*

"Tür," he muttered again, just loud enough for me to hear. I'd told him no more television that day and he was simultaneously moping and building a tower with some blocks. I scrambled to my feet and dropped my rubber gloves into the sink, then slipped out of Jürgen's shirt and tried to smooth my hair as I walked to the door. I hoped it might be Claudia, coming to thank me for the confectioners' sugar I'd left on her doorstep a few days earlier.

When I swung the door open and saw Lizzie Miller, my

breath caught. She was holding a beige ceramic plate. She was a picture of poise—her vibrant red hair in a pageboy bob, sleek and smooth and curled under at the ends, delicate pearl earrings in her ears, perfectly fashionable makeup and lipstick so pristine I knew she'd freshened up before getting out of her car.

"My brother takes this route through the neighborhood on his way to work, and that's not a crime. If an innocent man walking past your house bothers you, go inside. Don't speak to him. Don't *wave* to him. Don't so much as look at him!"

She was angry—but she was also scared. Of Henry? For Henry? I wasn't sure, but I could see the emotion so clearly on her face, I felt it echo through my body.

"Maybe he needs help," I said flatly. Lizzie Miller's eyes flashed fire and her nostrils flared.

"Don't you *dare* try to tell me what my brother needs," she hissed. "I don't want your cakes and I don't want you to come near us. If you drive past and my house is on fire, do not stop to help. You aren't welcome in this town and you sure as hell are never going to be welcome at my house." She extended the plate toward me. "Here's a plate to replace the one you lost."

"You don't have to—"

"I don't want to owe you a *damned* thing," she interrupted me, thrusting the plate into my hands. She nodded curtly and turned away, her heels clicking against our porch then driveway as she walked toward her car.

"I just wanted to reach out to you," I called after her. "To say sorry for the way I spoke to you at the picnic. I know we got off on the wrong foot—"

She spun back to face me, and this time, the hatred in her eyes was unmistakable.

"What was your husband's rank in the SS? Did he instigate the genocide, or did he just participate in it? And we both know you knew about the camps. If you did nothing to help those people, you're complicit too." Her expression twisted with frustration. "You and your husband do not deserve to be here, living among decent American folk."

"You don't know a thing about me and my husband," I said, forcing myself to keep my tone even, even though I wanted to weep. Lizzie was right—I did not deserve the comfortable life I'd been offered in America. That didn't mean I was about to let her destroy it with her gossip. Maybe Jürgen and I had our share of guilt and shame, but our children were innocent, and for them, we *had* to make Huntsville our home. "What kind of a person would try to undermine a family's new life without even trying to understand their old one? What kind of a person would tell her friends who they were allowed to spend time with, as if she had some claim to their time?" I hated that she might see how much she'd upset me, but I was rapidly losing the battle to stay calm. My voice wobbled miserably as I added, "I feel sorry for you, Mrs. Miller. I really do."

Lizzie Miller stared at me thoughtfully for just a beat. Then she sighed impatiently.

"Here's a tip for you, Mrs. Rhodes," she said, as she slipped her sunglasses back on. "No one wants you here. *No one.* So if an American woman suddenly seems determined to befriend you, you should probably assume she has an ulterior motive."

She revved the engine violently as she drove away, speeding down our street toward her house.

37

Sofie
Berlin, Germany
1941

IT WAS JÜRGEN'S IDEA TO BUY A COUNTRY house, midway between the Peenemünde facility and Berlin. The distance was taking a toll on us all. I agreed we should consider it—but just a few days later, he called to tell me he'd spoken to a Realtor and they'd already found the perfect property: a fully furnished home right on the lake at Tollensesee, ten kilometers from the small city of Neubrandenburg. It would take Jürgen about two hours by car to reach the house—time he felt he could spare as often as twice a month. From Berlin, it would take me just a little longer.

"Could you *really* take a weekend off that often?" I asked him, skeptically.

"Not the whole weekend," he admitted. "But if I worked there during the day, I'm certain I could make this work. And when a whole weekend isn't practical, at the very least, we could have Saturday night together and I could come back here early Sunday morning."

Just a few weeks later, I made the drive for the first time. Laura had turned ten and, after years of anticipation, was now a member of the Young Girls' League. She and Georg were both on camps that weekend, so it was just me and Gisela, alone in the car as we traveled out of the city. I still wasn't convinced by this country-house idea, but we'd gone ahead anyway—purely because Jürgen seemed so desperate to do it.

The house was a simple, half-timbered A-frame. The support beams were left exposed and were painted dark gray, the panels between them a soft cream. The roof was a thick thatching. It was modest but I loved it anyway, and more than that, I loved what the house represented.

Family time. Pure, unburdened family time—something we'd been desperately short on for years.

The house was surrounded by trees, although I'd seen on the drive that there were other homes nearby. There was a small clearing off to one side of the house, but beyond that and the driveway, we could have been in the middle of nowhere. And right in front of the house was a private jetty, stretching out into the water, perfect for fishing or as a platform for launching a boat or even an excited child on a hot summer's day.

"Well?" Jürgen said, as he opened the front door and approached me. The tension I was by then used to in his face had eased, the tight set of his shoulders relaxed. I had a feeling that miracle had only happened in the last few minutes, since he too had arrived at the lake house.

"I love it," I said.

That night, I put Gisela to bed while Jürgen set up a fire in the little clearing beside the house. He dragged chairs out from the dining room table and we sat beside one another, enjoying the bottle of wine the Realtor left for us as a house-warming gift.

The house might one day have listening devices, if it didn't already, and I supposed there was always the possibility of someone in the woods, trying to listen in. But here, by the fire, we were far enough away from the trees and the house that we could be confident no one would hear us.

Despite this, Jürgen remained silent. He sipped his wine, and he sighed, long, contented sighs. And after a while, I started to sigh too—as if we were both breathing out years of tension. I began to enjoy the sounds of owls in the woods and the crackling fire, to breathe it all in, to feel that peace unwinding tension I'd forgotten could be unwound. Beside me, Jürgen's gaze was focused higher. After a while, I followed it, and found him staring up at the white-blue glow of the full moon.

"What are you thinking about?" I asked.

"Many things," he said, his voice husky.

"Such as?"

He glanced at me and smiled.

"You. The children. Work. The moon."

"Always the moon," I said softly.

"When I was a little boy and I went to live with Adele, I promised myself I'd never forget my family," he said quietly. "I remember sitting in that car with her, utterly terrified, deciding that I'd hold their memories so close that I'd never lose them. Then time began to pass, and one by one, the memories slipped away. Now I only remember a handful of things... How ordinary it was as we ate breakfast together. The air raid siren and the panic as my mother went to get the baby and my father shoved me into the cellar—then nothing, until I woke up in the hospital. I do remember the night before. I stayed up late with my father, staring at the moon with this terrible telescope he'd constructed himself. He was an amateur astronomer, obsessed with the moon. He told me that night that he hoped man would reach it in my lifetime."

"You've never told me any of that," I said, stunned. "You always said you didn't remember anything."

"You've always been so much more outgoing than me, Sofie. I've had to share parts of myself with you over the years that were hard to expose—but those memories of my family were just too precious, and part of what made them so was that they were only mine."

"Why tell me now?"

"I've been thinking about those memories a lot lately. It brings me comfort that I don't remember much about my parents. After all, no real sense of who they were means no way to know how they'd have felt about the work I'm doing now."

He said this casually but I heard the pain behind his words, and it left me stricken.

"Jürgen…"

"Name a European city you love and German rockets may one day wipe it off the face of the earth."

I gasped. "Are you close to that?"

"The *components* are all there. In theory—the rest is just a matter of persistence and experimentation to make those components work consistently." He didn't sound optimistic or proud. His tone was heavier than ever.

"The Reich is ever expanding. Even if we landed a man on the moon, Hitler would just want to occupy that too. And Otto says that as soon as we can prove the new prototype works, we'll be asked to produce thousands of them." Jürgen downed the rest of his wine in one gulp, then threw the glass into the fire. I flinched when it shattered. He kept his voice low, but he did nothing to curtail the fury it contained.

"Thousands of them? It's *insanity*. Do you know how we're going to resource that production? It won't be with paid laborers, that's for damned sure."

"How, then?" I asked hesitantly.

"Prisoners," he said, and his voice broke. It was thick with tears as he whispered, "We are already using them to a lesser extent—we hire them from the SS. They bring busloads from the camps every few weeks."

"German prisoners?"

"From all over Europe. Mostly Jews." Jürgen slumped. He lifted a shaking hand to rub his forehead. "If Hitler orders us to go to full-scale production, it will be innocent Jewish men who pay the price."

I'd seen my husband up and down over the years—but I'd never seen him like this. He was broken and angry and hard and almost oozing shame and guilt. A shiver of fear ran through me.

"We tell ourselves that we're only protecting our family, but the family is damaged by our decision to protect it," I blurted. "Georg and Laura are awash in propaganda and we can't correct them. You're a part of something you hate, and I can *see* that it's killing you."

Life in Berlin was close to normal, aside from some rationing and, at one point, a series of air raids. The papers painted the Reich as the victim of European aggression, always pushing forward to do good, never to harm. But the war machine was powered by German men, and when they were released on periods of furlough, they brought reality home with them. I'd heard enough rumors of systemic imprisonment of Jews across the expanded Reich to know there was hideous truth there. These whispers circled around me, each one a tiny piece of a puzzle I knew in my heart was dark, even if I couldn't see the whole picture, and even if, day-to-day, it all seemed so very far away. "Every morning, I wake up and carry on as if this is all acceptable, so I'm complicit too, aren't I?" I whispered.

We sat in silence for a long time, and I sought that sense of peace again, trying to focus on the sights and sounds and the scents of the lake. But I couldn't relax—not after hearing the torment in my husband's voice, and especially not after he turned to me and said quietly, "I would do anything for you and the children. Anything."

"I know." He had more than proved that over these years.

"Every day, when it feels like it's all too much, when I want to scream with the insanity of it all, I think of you and the children and that is all I can do to keep going."

"But the madness is spiraling all over Europe, and we're just sitting here drinking wine?" I cried bitterly.

"That's exactly why I wanted this place. Why we need it. The day might come when we decide that keeping the family safe can't be our highest priority in the context of what's happening." He drew in a shuddering breath. "I realized that if the point comes when we need to draw a line in the sand and say *this far and no further*...well, so long as we're meeting here, we can find a way to speak freely. We can work together to make a plan."

After that weekend, I vowed to make trips to the lake house my highest priority.

Georg had been asking if Hans could join us for a weekend at the lake house from his very first visit, and I'd always discouraged this—wanting to reserve that place for our family. But over the summer of 1942, I finally gave in, and Hans joined us for a week. He was about to turn thirteen, and I sensed he was relieved to have a break from the bustle of his own home. Lydia and Karl achieved their goal of eight children for the Reich, but despite their small team of nannies, it seemed they expected Hans to parent himself. I knew from my own childhood exactly how lonely that could feel.

Despite everything, I liked Hans. He was a lot like my Georg—a good kid, albeit one bent out of shape by Nazi influence. Cut adrift from all of that, I saw the kindness of his heart set free again. If Georg didn't clear his plate after dinner, Hans would remind him. If Laura felt left out, Hans would encourage Georg to include her.

I barely saw the children during the day—they'd disappear out the front door as soon as they were awake and they'd return only when they were hungry or too sunburned to continue adventuring. At night, they tumbled into bed early, resting up to prepare for the next day.

But when the week was over, Lydia arrived to collect Hans. I was expecting her driver to arrive alone, so I was surprised and a little dismayed when she slipped from the back seat of her silver BMW. She'd left her other children behind with the nannies.

"You've been spending so much time down here," she said, as we sat around the kitchen table. "I wanted to see what the place was like."

I set a cup of chicory "coffee" in front of her, then took the chair opposite her to drink my own. I scanned the kitchen, trying to see it through her eyes. I'd given her only scant details about the lake house, knowing she'd picture something grander if left to her own imagination.

"It's been a godsend for us to be able to reconnect while Jürgen is busy with work."

"And he's coming today?"

"That's the plan. He was due last weekend, but something held him up."

"Did he not tell you? That's the main reason I wanted to come by. I wanted to congratulate you." She seemed conflicted, her gaze darting around the room as she gnawed on her lip. "I assumed Jürgen would have told you himself."

"What happened?" I asked her, bewildered.

"He's humble, that's all. That's why he doesn't tell you these things. Or maybe he wanted to tell you in person…"

"If last week is anything to go by, he might just cancel the trip at the last minute anyway. Don't keep me in suspense."

"They are never really sure until they process the results and it seems to take them such a long time. *So* much math." When I nodded, impatient for her to continue, she drew in a deep breath and nearly knocked me off my chair in surprise when she blurted, "But Karl says that from what they know so far, it looks like the test launch last week made it all the way to space."

If this was true, it was remarkable—a world-changing achievement. I was immediately stung that Jürgen hadn't so much as called to let me know, but hot on the heels of that hurt came concern, and realization.

Jürgen always sheltered me from the worst of his work. That he didn't call to let me know about the success of his launch likely indicated there was a dark side to it—something he couldn't talk about over the phone, or maybe something he wasn't yet ready to talk about at all.

Jürgen arrived later that afternoon and was immediately co-opted by the children.

"Watch us swim, Papa!" they cried, and he laughed and promised he would as soon as he set his briefcase inside. I was on the jetty, where I'd been watching Georg, Laura, and Gisela run along the wooden platform and strike dramatic poses as they launched themselves into the water. Gisela, now five, was not yet a strong swimmer, so the older two were helping her make her way back to the shore after each dive.

Jürgen walked down the jetty to sit behind me, leaving room on the narrow dock for the children to run alongside us. He wrapped his arms around my waist, and I leaned against him. It was golden hour; the perfect red-tinged rays of the sun over the lake left me lazy and dreamy. All the world looked like a postcard, but especially with Jürgen's strong torso against my back, and his arms around my waist. We watched the children play in silence for a while, sharing only a chuckle here or there as they performed for us. But Lydia's news this morning hovered at the edges of my consciousness, demanding attention.

"Is it true? Your rocket made it to space?"

"Maybe. Probably." Jürgen paused. "No one can be sure yet."

I twisted awkwardly to stare at him in disbelief.

"Isn't this what you've dreamed of your entire life?"

"Not like this."

He'd been laughing at the children just a moment before, but his gaze grew troubled. I shifted so that I was facing him, intending to give him my full attention.

"Mama! Watch me!" Gisela protested.

"In a minute," I sighed. "I'm talking with Papa."

"I'm still watching, treasure," Jürgen said, glancing at her over my shoulder. I watched the joy on his face as he watched her run the last few steps toward the end of the dock, and saw the amusement in his eyes when she inevitably froze at the last minute and stopped right at the edge to peer down into the water anxiously. I'd been watching her for hours that day, and each launch went the same way, so I knew what came next. Gisela would turn back to make doubly sure she was being supervised, pinch her nose with her fingers, puff her cheeks out with air, and then squeeze her eyes shut before she turned around and jumped blindly from the peer. I saw Jürgen strug-

gling to suppress a chuckle at this ritual—then heard the squeal
as Gisela finally jumped and felt the spatter of water on my
back as she hit the water. But once Gisela was paddling back
to shore with the other children, the smile on Jürgen's face
faded. He gazed into my eyes, growing serious again.

"Otto has requested a meeting with Hitler. He is desperate—
clutching at straws trying to save the program."

"Save the program?" I repeated, alarmed. "Save it from
what?"

"I know the papers say the war is going well, but we are struggling against the Soviets," Jürgen admitted. I'd heard whispers of
the same in Berlin. "The way my program has made such rapid
progress has been through constant experimentation—that's an
incredibly expensive approach. We used to have an unlimited
budget. Then we had a generous budget… Now we've had a
series of budget cuts. Otto has become worried that the program
might shut down if we don't deliver something war-ready soon."

"But…if a rocket reached space—" I said, trying to cheer him
up, but he shook his head.

"That's only part of the picture, my love. We fired several
rockets over these past few weeks. Most failed. One succeeded.
We don't actually know how to produce these things reliably
yet—let alone to mass-produce them, and on a shoestring budget."

"What are you going to do?" I whispered.

"I fantasize about finding ways to undermine our progress,
but I am surrounded by brilliant men. If I attempt sabotage, it
will quickly become obvious to them." His gaze drifted over
my shoulder again, to land on the children. "I'm trapped on
this path where my work is building to something heinous."

Otto and Helene threw a party that Christmas at their lav-
ish home in Dresden. He had climbed the ranks of the Nazi

party and been invited to join the SS—awarded the prestigious role of *Hauptsturmführer*.

When we arrived at the party, Otto greeted us in his full SS uniform—the high leather boots, gray jacket and pants, patches on his collar and shoulders that bore his rank. Helene was pregnant yet again. I'd met her a number of times over the years, and every single time I'd seen her, she'd either been pregnant or holding a newborn. That night, she looked exhausted. Her eyes kept drifting to the ceiling, as if she'd rather be upstairs in bed, or anywhere but that bustling holiday party.

"Congratulations," I said politely, motioning toward her stomach.

"Number eight," she said, and although this was clearly intended as a boast, her exhausted tone, coupled with the way she sighed as she said it, suggested eight was perhaps a few more children than she'd have preferred.

"Still only the three children?" Otto asked me pointedly. At Lydia's suggestion, I'd left Georg, Laura, and Gisela back in Berlin with her children and staff of nannies. "No chance of Mother's Cross for you, then. That must be very disappointing for you both." The Mother's Cross was a medal given to encourage fecundity. The gold rank was the most prestigious, reserved for women with more than seven children. Both Helene and Lydia were awarded theirs the previous August. Otto's gaze slid to Jürgen. "Perhaps we are keeping you away from your bride too much?"

My cheeks heated, and I glanced anxiously at Jürgen, but was surprised to find him nonchalant.

"We have been trying to ensure we have more time together. Given I can't spare the time to come home much, we have purchased a country house at Tollensesee. The work is important, but obviously, so is Sofie's duty to the Reich."

Otto nodded, pleased with this response. I, on the other

hand, was startled by it. Jürgen had said everything he should have said in response to this challenge, but there was a superiority to his tone, not toward Otto—toward *me*. Women in the Reich were expected to be submissive to their husbands, but my marriage had never operated that way. I forced myself to smile politely.

"Are you prepared for our trip in the New Year?" Otto asked Jürgen. He motioned toward the bar, and Jürgen shot me a quietly apologetic glance, then fell into step beside Otto as he made a beeline for the bar on the other side of the room, staffed by men in crisp uniforms.

"If I can manage to give my husband eight children with all of the travel we do now, you can surely manage at least a few more," Helene remarked.

"You travel with Otto?" I asked, surprised. She pursed her lips.

"If you want to climb the ranks of the Party, Sofie, you need to find a way to support the work. I won't be joining him and Jürgen for this trip in the New Year because the baby will come soon, but I've been with him to the camps plenty of times before."

"To the camps?" I repeated, startled. She gave me a confused look.

"We need many more prisoners for the factory." I was so bewildered, I was struggling to keep my expression neutral. "While Otto and Jürgen find new workers, I've been inspecting each facility. There's groundbreaking research happening at Auschwitz, Dachau has a delightful herb garden—oh, and of course, there's the zoological gardens at Buchenwald. You should come along for a trip. It's so important for wives to support their husbands in this work."

"I'll talk to Jürgen about it," I managed.

Later that night when we were alone in our hotel room, I

motioned toward the covers as Jürgen went to turn out the lights, indicating we should pull them over our heads and whisper, but he yawned and shook his head. I shot him a forceful look and he sighed and complied.

"You've been to some of the camps?"

"I'm tired. I don't want to talk about this," he said.

"Helene said she goes with you."

"She's tagged along with Otto a few times."

"She said—"

"I don't want you to come with me, Sofie," he whispered sharply. "Not now. Not ever."

"But—"

"Otto did the deal with the SS—we rent the prisoners off them at a discount. We had the first shipment of workers from the camps a few weeks ago, but they were..." He trailed off, then stopped. I was startled by his choice of words—*shipment*, as if the prisoners were a resource one could send around the country in boxes. The silence stretched, and all I could hear was my pulse in my ears.

"What?" I prompted him urgently.

"I don't want to talk about this with you," Jürgen whispered.

"Tell me," I pressed. "Tell me what was wrong with them."

All of those rumors I'd heard on the streets of Berlin were flying through my mind. I'd suspected all along that the Jews in those places were in terrible danger. Did Jürgen know for sure?

"The prisoners are not being well cared for and that's all you need to know."

The point of pulling the blankets over our heads was to muffle our conversation, but we didn't need to bother that night. Jürgen's voice was so faint that even right beside him, I had to strain to make out each word. It was clear that he was deeply troubled by this development but wanted to protect me from the worst of what he knew and what he'd seen, as he always did.

I couldn't bury my head in the sand. Whatever he was involved in, I was a part of too.

"Just men?" I asked. I shifted closer to him, suddenly feeling very cold, despite the suffocating blanket over our faces.

"No."

I closed my eyes and an image of Mayim flashed before me, her face vivid, as if I'd only seen her that morning.

"You haven't seen Mayim, though?" I had to know.

"The camps are huge, Sofie. Tens of thousands of prisoners in some."

"Do you think she's in one of those camps?"

"I don't know," he whispered. Jürgen folded the blanket back down, exposing our faces to the cool air in the hotel room. I turned toward him.

"Tell me the truth," I whispered.

"I would only be guessing."

"I don't care."

I pulled the blanket up again, and Jürgen whispered, "Most of the Jews are imprisoned in ghettos now."

"That's better than a camp, I suppose. She would be okay there?"

"Of course, my love."

38

Lizzie

Huntsville, Alabama
1950

IT WAS HOT THAT NIGHT AND I COULDN'T SLEEP.
I kept reliving the hurt on Sofie Rhodes's face when I clued
her in to what a raging gossip Avril Walters was.

I felt better having visited her. I knew I'd been rude—
obnoxious, even. I'd intended to be. It seemed that until I figured out what was going on with my brother, the best way
for everything to settle back down was for Sofie Rhodes to
stay the hell away from us.

I gave up tossing and turning and poured myself a cold glass
of water, then went onto the front porch, where the air was at
least moving a little. I rested my head against the back of the
porch swing and closed my eyes.

"Can't sleep either?" Henry said. He walked along the edge
of the porch and took a seat beside me.

"It's hot in there," I sighed.

"I'll wager it's worse upstairs."

"Sorry."

"Don't be," he chuckled, but quickly sobered. "You left the back door unlocked."

"Did I?" I said, wincing. "Oops." He'd been checking every night before he went to sleep, and this was the second time I'd forgotten.

"You're not taking this seriously, Lizzie."

"I am," I protested. "It's force of habit, that's all. We've been here for a year and I've never locked that door. And besides…"

"You haven't seen him," Henry surmised. "So you're not as scared as you should be."

"Haven't seen him?" I said hesitantly. I shot Henry a concerned look, concerned at his use of present tense. Henry sighed impatiently, then lit a cigarette. He stretched his legs out, settling into the seat, and then drew in a deep breath.

"I checked myself into a VA neuropsychiatric hospital in January after I was here for Christmas. I lied when I said I was working at a fair in Nashville. Christmas was the lowest I'd been for a while."

"What? Why didn't you tell me?" I asked, startled. My heart ached at the thought of him going through that alone.

"Do you know that in all the time you've been married, even after all the shit I've put you through in the last five years, I'd never seen you and Cal argue until the last time I visited? I figured if your marriage was in trouble and you were stuck here in backwater Alabama with a bunch of Nazis, you'd need me to have my head right if it all hit the fan."

"Huntsville isn't so bad. And me and Cal are fine." I hadn't realized he noticed us bickering. Henry was always more perceptive than people gave him credit for.

"I love Cal. I really do. But your husband is a part of all of this. He's working with them."

"He's just doing his job."

"Isn't that exactly what half of those bastards at Nuremberg said?" Henry asked. I winced. "Anyway, it doesn't even matter right now. That's not what we need to talk about. We need to talk about Bobby."

"We do?" I asked, surprised. I remembered the friend Henry made in his unit in Europe, even though he'd never told me much about him.

"Yeah," he said. He stared down at the glow of the cigarette in his hand for a moment, drew on it, then exhaled. "I need you to understand something."

"Okay," I said, anxiously.

"That camp we liberated. There was a sign over the gate. One of the guys in the tanks knew a bit of German—he told me it said *every man gets what he deserves*. They called that camp Buchenwald."

"Was this in April of '45?" I asked. Henry wrote me regularly when he was in Europe, but just before the war ended, his letters abruptly stopped. He finished his cigarette and flicked the end onto my grass.

"I knew right away that this was something different from the other awful shit we'd seen already. There were cartloads of bodies stacked outside of the crematorium near the entrance and there was nothing left of those people—just skin and bones."

"That's awful, Henry. I'm so sorry."

"The captain sent us to clear buildings. I was with Bobby and we're just walking through these buildings looking for Nazis and all we're finding is dead people and half-dead people. Sometimes their eyes were dead, even if they were still breathing. Bobby opened a storage room and it all happened so fast. In just a few seconds, the Nazi in that little room shot Bobby and I shot the Nazi and they were both dead and I was just standing over my dead best friend and this dead stranger wondering…who won just now? You know what I realized?" His voice cracked, and the anguish on his face nearly broke me. "We all lost, Lizzie. Every single man and woman and child touched by that war *lost*."

This was a bad idea. For five years, Henry had been unable to speak about this. Talking about it now—stirring up all this pain—could only lead to more chaos.

"Honey, maybe you should just go to bed—"

"*Every man gets what he deserves.* Sometimes I see that camp like I'm still there and it makes no damned sense, except maybe if I left some part of myself behind there."

"Is it getting better as the years pass?" I whispered.

"The first time I went to a hospital was in 1946, not long after I left your place in El Paso. I couldn't hold down a job. Couldn't get out of bed. Couldn't sleep or eat or stay calm in a thunderstorm. Something had to give, so I rang the VA. They said I've got combat fatigue and I just needed to rest. They put me in a hospital and gave me medication to make me sleep all day. I was calm while I was taking it, but coming off it—God, that was the pits. It was clear by then that they were just guessing how to help men like me. Hell, at one point they prescribed a course of 'flower-picking therapy.' And I was desperate, so I went with the nurse, and we picked flowers all day."

"I can't believe you never told me any of this." I wasn't just shocked. I was deeply hurt. Didn't Henry trust me? Didn't he understand how much I loved him—how I'd do anything to support him?

"I was ashamed, Lizzie. I still am," he admitted, sighing heavily as he shook his head. "I just want to be normal again, but it's like my brain is broken and nothing works to make it the way it was. In January I went up to that VA hospital in

Nashville and I told them to do whatever they could to fix me. They said they were having good results from this new therapy. Insulin shock therapy, it's called."

"I've heard of electric shock therapy but…"

"It's the same idea," he muttered. "They use insulin to treat the diabetes too, but for veterans with combat fatigue, they give a huge dose of that medicine every day. Six days a week. Two months." He glanced at me. "My only day off the treatment was Monday. That's why, when I called or wrote you, it was a Monday."

"What does it do?"

"It makes you feel real weird. Sweaty and sleepy and confused and so *hungry*, and sometimes really restless, like I couldn't move my legs and arms enough to burn up the energy in my body. That would get worse and worse until—boom—I'd be so relieved when I knew I was about to go unconscious. I'd stay in that coma until they brought me out of it. They said it would jolt my brain back to the way it was."

"And…has it? Was it worth it?"

"The psychiatrist who discharged me told me it was normal that I'd put on so much weight. Sixty pounds in eight weeks," he said, his voice low. "He said it was normal that my brain would be damaged from the shock but that would get better. But some days now, I'm so confused, I can't even follow basic instructions. I can't remember anything new. I have to write everything down. I can't even add two and two. So no, sis. I don't think it was worth it."

"Why are you telling me this now?"

"The hatred that drove those Germans wasn't some tidy thing you can put a period after and move on from. I saw the inside of *one* camp. Just one out of nearly a thousand of those hellholes, and even five years later my mind is so scarred there's some moments I don't even know what continent I'm on. I let those doctors give me *brain damage*, Lizzie—just in the hopes that I'd feel myself again. And those hospitals are full of veterans just like me, all of us so—" he pointed to his head, shaking his fists beside his head with palpable, painful frustration "—so shaken by what we saw that we might never be the same."

Henry slid off his chair and stretched to his full height, cracking his neck in the process. He glanced down at me, his expression dark.

"You need to understand that these men on Sauerkraut Hill aren't harmless. No one is safe while they're in this country. Not you, not Calvin, not anyone else in this town."

"There's nothing we can do about it, though," I whispered. "The government wants them here."

"I can't control that and neither can you. But those people are the kind of evil you can't even begin to comprehend. You can't take stupid risks like leave the back door open. The devil himself is living two blocks away."

He stared at me until I nodded. Then he forced a smile and took a step toward the house.

"I guess I'm finally tired enough for bed. Good night, sis."

"Good night, Henry," I said, and as he started to walk away, I blurted, "I love you."

He threw a glance over his shoulder as he muttered, "Love you too."

I'd held back my tears while Henry told me his story, but now that I was alone, I let myself cry. It wasn't just the details Henry shared about the camps; it was the thought of him in those hospitals all alone with his pain, too ashamed to even admit how much he was hurting.

For the first time in a long time, I thought of my mother. I remembered her telling me that the women in our family were strong…that we were survivors. But there was a burden in being the strong one. You propped people up, tried to fix their problems for them…and sometimes you got it wrong and made everything worse. Then you had to live with the guilt of that.

I turned my head slightly and looked at the place on the brick pillar where I found that dish shard, and then thought about everything Henry told me that night—his curious use of the phrase *"haven't* seen him" to describe Jürgen Rhodes, as if the threat were both real and ongoing. Henry was hurting all over again, and it was worse this time. Should I leave him be? Or should I try to help again?

I slid off the porch chair and let myself into the house. It was late, but I walked straight down the hall to Calvin's room. I knocked on the door, but he was predictably snoring, so when he didn't stir, I went in anyway.

"Cal?" I whispered, as I sat on the mattress beside him. I reached and shook his shoulder gently, then leaned closer to him and whispered, "Calvin?" He came to slowly, staring up at me with heavy eyelids.

"Lizzie?" he said, his voice rough with sleep and an emotion I couldn't decipher at first. I sat up and he sat up too, then tentatively reached to touch the bare skin between my shoulder and neck as he whispered, "Sweetheart, are you really here, or am I dreaming?"

I had come into his bedroom in the middle of the night for the first time ever. He wasn't wearing his glasses—he wouldn't have been able to see much of me, let alone the distress in my body language. Calvin, half-asleep and apparently living in perpetual hope, had misread the reason for my late-night visit.

I panicked and fumbled for his glasses on the bedside table, handing them to him clumsily as I stammered, "Sorry—sorry I woke you. I just— I wanted to— I was hoping we could talk about Henry. That's all. Just Henry."

Calvin donned his glasses. I shifted a little farther down the bed, away from him, then dared to meet his gaze. My cheeks were hot with shame, but Calvin didn't seem embarrassed—only disappointed.

"I talked to him tonight," I said, the words tumbling out in a flustered rush. "I just… I'm just worried about him, that's all. I know you thought us speaking to him together wasn't the best idea in case he felt cornered, but I think we need to do it. Maybe over the weekend when we all have time."

"Of course," Calvin said quietly. "Anything you need. Are you okay?"

I realized with dismay that *this* was why I woke Calvin up. I was upset, and Calvin always knew how to fix things. Even in that moment, when the uneven emotions between us had never been more evident, Calvin did not miss a beat in his care and attention.

"I'm fine," I said, and I slid off his bed, suddenly desperate to get out of the room. "I'm sorry for— I didn't mean to wake you. I just wasn't thinking straight."

That night, I realized for the very first time that I was torturing Calvin. Yes, he had me living in his house and in his life, and yes, we were the best of friends—but I was ever so slightly out of reach anyway, and even after all of those years, he continued to hope for what could never be.

39

Sofie
Wewelsburg, Germany
December 1944

IT WAS SUPPOSED TO BE THE MOST IMPORTANT evening in Jürgen's career, but the work never stopped. Lydia and I spent a leisurely afternoon pampering ourselves, while Karl and Jürgen threw their tuxedos on and disappeared for meetings in some corner of the vast Castle Varlar. I hadn't seen him since, but I wasn't anxious. This event couldn't start without Jürgen, the guest of honor.

Lydia was by my side as I paused in the doorway to the dining hall, taking in the opulent scene. Most of those in the room were men in SS uniforms or tuxedos. Only a handful of women were permitted to attend.

Lydia was wearing yet another dirndl-style dress—a more formal version with puffed sleeves and elaborate embroidery on the skirt. I was wearing the finest outfit I'd ever owned—finer than my wedding dress. A designer at the *Deutsches Modeamt* fashioned the suit in cream silk, elevated by thousands of tiny pearls and crystal beads.

I was pretending to be excited, but I felt nothing more than a sense of simmering anxiety. I was always anxious around senior Nazis.

I'd been particularly concerned for Jürgen since the rocket program moved to the site they called Mittelwerk in the wake of a British bombing raid on Peenemünde, in the summer of 1943. The move had been unimaginably complex—the entire rocketry operation shifted more than six hundred kilometers across Germany into the tunnels of a supposedly air raid–proof gypsum mine, beneath a huge hill called the Kohnstein. Jürgen and Karl and their staff were tasked with reconstructing the research program *and* establishing a factory to mass-produce the rockets in those mines, and they were given just a few short months to do it.

I tried to call him most days, but his phone usually went unanswered. I'd taken the children to see him several times, only to spend the entire weekend at Jürgen's villa in the nearby town of Nordhausen, waiting for a break in his work schedule that never came. At some point, I'd started to learn more about my husband's life through Karl, via Lydia, than from him directly.

He was busy, but that wasn't why he avoided my calls. He was stressed, but that wasn't why he didn't make time to see me and the children. Jürgen was withdrawing from us, and it was time to force a confrontation.

Lydia and I approached the host at the door, and he greeted us warmly as we introduced ourselves. After checking a seating chart, he led the way to our tables.

"You're here, Mrs. zu Schiller," he said politely, holding out a chair for Lydia at a table near the back of the room.

"Hello, Mrs. zu Schiller," Aldo Radtke said, smiling warmly

at her from his own seat, a few chairs down from Lydia. "And Mrs. von Meyer Rhodes. Congratulations." A decade after that dinner party at Lydia's house, Aldo was no longer fresh-faced and anxious, but he still seemed sweet. He was a key member of Jürgen's team, one of only a handful of colleagues who was invited to join us that evening.

"Hello, Aldo." I smiled, nodding at him. "Thank you."

But Lydia seemed confused. She looked from Aldo to her seat, her expression darkening when the waiter indicated I should follow him to another table.

"You are a guest of honor, Mrs. von Meyer Rhodes. You have a reserved seat at the front."

Lydia was not a woman accustomed to sharing the spot-light, and that night, she was watching someone else bask in it. I gave her an apologetic shrug, and she forced a smile and nodded, as if permitting me to go to my own seat.

The head table was set just in front of a heavy red velvet curtain, facing the rest of the room like a bridal table. Trails of ivy hung along the front, and bright arrangements of win-ter flowers were set between pairs of seats—lily of the valley and pansies and coral bells. The sweet scent rising from the arrangements reminded me of Adele's garden.

I took my seat alone, feeling awkward and on display, and finished a glass of champagne before Jürgen joined me. There were strands of silver along his hairline now, new lines around his eyes, and his tuxedo hung on his gaunt frame. Every time I'd seen him that year, he looked more beaten down. Now, as he sat and shuffled his chair closer to the table, there was barely disguised distress in his gaze.

"What is it?" I whispered.

He turned toward me and whispered heavily, "I've been in-vited to join the SS." I pulled away and stared at him, forcing a smile. *Invited* seemed the wrong word for that sentence, because it suggested there was an option to decline. "Karl too."

But Otto took the seat beside me then, and Helene soon took the seat on his other side. We exchanged pleasantries as my heart raced, and my stomach churned so much I couldn't tolerate more than a bite or two of the elaborate meal.

Was this just a ceremonial appointment—a uniform and title, and that was it? Or would Jürgen be forced to participate in still more activities that went against his values? He obviously knew enough to be worried, but he was so much better at playing the game than I was. He laughed and he joked and sipped champagne and ate his food as if he hadn't a care in the world. But I saw the strain in the lines around his lips and the tense set of his shoulders. I heard the brittleness beneath his chuckles.

I felt the sweat on his palm when I reached to take his hand. Jürgen was scared, and that was more than enough to make me scared too.

The proceedings began in earnest after the dessert plates were cleared. Otto was honored first—called to a podium in the corner of the room by another senior SS official, who gushed praise at his commitment to the Nazi cause and his "genius" oversight of the rocket program, then slipped a red, blue, and white ribbon over his head. The *Ritterkreuz des Eisernen Kreuzes* sat heavy and bold at his collarbone. The Knight's Cross was the highest award in all of Nazi Germany—rarely offered, highly revered. As Otto returned to his seat, the lights dimmed. The heavy velvet curtain behind us drew back. Those of us at the head table awkwardly shuffled around to face a large window overlooking a moonlit lawn.

A crackling anticipation filled the air and a hush swept over the room. A flare burst to life on the lawn, and then came a

roar so loud it made my ears ache. Red and blue fire spilled
from beneath an enormous rocket, and after some seconds,
the missile rose, smooth and steady. There were gasps of delight and cheers, then riotous applause as the rocket disappeared from view.

It might have been going anywhere—into orbit, into space,
to the moon. It might have been taking man to new heights,
expanding our understanding of the universe and the galaxy—
extending our knowledge about our world and ourselves. But
that rocket wasn't a space exploration device—it was a warhead,
destined for some unsuspecting village or city…some innocent
family in their home, just as Jürgen had once feared. His rockets,
now public knowledge, were renamed *Vergeltungswaffe 2*, Retri-
bution Weapon 2, part of the set of Nazi "vengeance weapons"
that were supposed to turn the tide of the war. Since Septem-
ber, over three thousand V-2 rockets had been launched, mostly
against Belgium and London. Each was almost fifty feet high
and weighed thirty thousand pounds. My head ached if I thought
about the scale and size of the operation.

Jürgen was the next to receive his medal, and when he was
invited to the podium, I watched him closely. He had been
quiet and pensive by my side until they called his name. He
played the role so well, he momentarily looked like a different
man as he stood—a stony, cruel version of the man I'd loved
for my entire adult life.

He barked the victory salute back at the official, his gaze
firm and his muscles tense. But once he'd returned to his seat
beside me, and when the lights in that room went down and
the curtain again opened, the burst of flame from another
rocket lit up over the lawn. I dragged my eyes from the rocket
so that I could watch Jürgen's reaction to it.

The colors of the flames were reflected in the sheen of tears in his eyes as he watched the rocket's flare. Jürgen's expression suggested he might have been staring into hell itself.

An instinct sounded. Was he going to refuse to join the SS? Surely not. It would be an act of suicide—

A chill ran down my spine.

What if that was the point?

We were both more than a little tipsy by the time we tumbled into bed, and for the first time in months, we held one another. After a while, Jürgen lifted the blanket over our heads. It had been so long since we'd seen each other, longer since we'd been through this routine, but the act of hiding beneath the blankets was so ingrained in our relationship— as intimate as making love. I took no solace in the action, not that night. We were about to have the conversation I'd been dreading all evening.

"You have to do it," I said. Jürgen remained silent. "Why would *this* be the line you refuse to cross? After everything we've done?" I drew in a breath. "Is it true that the war is almost over anyway? Hitler is losing?"

The papers suggested the opposite, of course. Victory was within reach, and if our troops were pulling back, this was simply for "strategic reasons." But I learned to make the ordinary folk of Berlin my bellwether, and whispers on the streets were that the war was all but lost.

"It is only a matter of time," Jürgen admitted. "And when Germany capitulates, the world will see what we've done across the Reich. The SS has been the driver for so much of the cruelty. I've made more than my share of mistakes in this war, but aligning myself with those bastards cannot be one of them."

I pondered this, my heart sinking. Of course the SS would

be targets—they'd been the architects of the concentration camps.

"So you think if you decline the invitation to join the SS, you'll fare better when the Allies arrive," I surmised.

"Can you really be so naive?" he whispered fiercely. "One way or another, I'm as good as dead. I am the technical manager of a program built on forced labor, Sofie. The rockets are nightmarish enough—they've almost certainly resulted in the deaths of thousands of innocent people. But the Mittelwerk operation is an abomination. I'll hang." His voice broke as he added weakly, "I *should* hang."

"But you were only following orders," I whispered. "You aren't responsible for whatever has gone wrong at Mittelwerk. Are you?"

He sighed then, a miserable, resigned sound that almost broke my heart.

"This isn't a conversation you have under a blanket," I whispered, tearing up suddenly. "Can we talk about this tomorrow?"

I pulled the blanket back down and sat up. Jürgen sat up too, and we stared at each other in the dim light. He pinched the bridge of his nose, squinting as if he were in physical pain.

"Where else can we have the conversation, Sofie?" he mouthed. I started to cry, and he reached to cup my cheek. "We have to talk about this."

I pressed my mouth against his ear and whispered tearfully, "But maybe not when we're so tired and emotional. Maybe not when we're both half-drunk."

He sighed as he nodded, and we stretched out side by side, staring up at the roof. Neither one of us slept much.

At breakfast the next morning, Jürgen and I sat with Lydia and Karl. I saw the tight smile she pinned to her face when she glanced at the medal, already fixed around Jürgen's neck. Her gaze immediately skimmed to Karl's bare neck, and she pursed her lips. Otto and Helene soon joined us. Otto was wearing his Knight's Cross around his neck, a matching pair with Helene's Mother's Cross.

The chefs had prepared a celebratory breakfast for us all— thick slices of salty wild boar bacon, heavy rye bread spread thick with cultured butter. Best of all was the coffee—real coffee, the first I'd had in years, as it had been impossible to find in Berlin during the war. I drank the first cup so fast, I scalded the roof of my mouth.

"Yesterday was an especially successful day with the rockets," Otto announced, beaming as he devoured his meal. "One of the V-2s we launched from Zeeland landed on a cinema in Antwerp. It was completely full at the time! Our early intelligence suggests five hundred enemies may have been destroyed."

A resounding cheer went up from the breakfast diners, but I was doing the calculation in my mind—*an ordinary Thursday afternoon. A cinema, for God's sakes. A cinema couldn't possibly have been full of soldiers. Why are we celebrating the death of hundreds of civilians?* I clapped even though I felt sick.

I looked at Jürgen. He cheered with the rest of them, but his eyes were hollow, as if part of him had already died.

"We need to stop here for the night," Jürgen said abruptly. At breakfast, he asked Lydia if our children could stay at her home for a few extra nights so he and I could share some extra time together. Now we were midway through the five-hour drive from Castle Varlar to his villa in Nordhausen and I was startled at the sudden change in plans.

"Why? Are you unwell?"

He ignored me, turning the car into the parking lot of an

historic, stone-walled hotel in Kassel. Something about his steely silence warned me to leave the question hanging, so I didn't ask again.

Soon, we were alone, with black-washed wooden floor-boards beneath our feet and exposed beams across the sloped ceiling above us. A large bed sat in the center of the room, with soft white pillows and layers of thick blankets. Huge, wood-framed windows washed the room in silver-blue light, reflected off the snow on a nearby rooftop. On any other day, at any other stage of my life, I'd have been delighted by the scene.

"They will bring dinner for us later," Jürgen said, as he sat on the bed and stretched his legs out. He patted the mattress beside him and added gently, "Come here, my love."

"Why did you do this?" I asked, as I crawled up onto the bed next to him. He immediately pulled me close, and I reclined, my ear to his chest.

"A random room in a random hotel that even *I* didn't know I was going to book seemed our best chance at privacy."

"What if the room has a listening device?"

"They can't have one in every room in the country, and even if they do, I checked in under a false name."

We sat for a while as I pondered the risk calculation, too accustomed by then to assuming no space was safe for me to speak freely. I listened to the slow breaths of my husband and the beating of his heart beneath my ear. After a while, he whispered, "There is a sign above the gate at the Buchenwald camp. *Jedem das Seine.*" Roughly, To Each What He Deserves.

"I think about that every day. The people inside those gates have done nothing to deserve their fate. I always thought that hell was a myth. It made good sense that the church would come up with a lie like that—eternal damnation is a strong motivation to convince people to comply. But now I understand that hell is not an abstract concept. It's real, but it's not about pitchforks or rivers of lava. Hell is simply the place where hope is lost." He sighed heavily. "Sofie, even my villa is haunted."

"Haunted?"

"Otto said the villa was a reward. Somewhere big enough for you and the children to come and stay. I was pleased at first—it's a lovely home." His villa was outfitted with expensive furnishings, new appliances, and ample space. "I learned from the neighbors that the villa belonged to a Jewish businessman. They took it from him, and they took his business too. I bought a new mattress, but it is *his* bed I sleep in. When I come home after work, I *feel* him there. We have taken everything from the victims of the Reich. Their homes. Families. Communities. Clothes. Assets. And now we work the prisoners day and night for us at Mittelwerk, and all we give them in return is the chance to take one more breath—there is never any guarantee of more than that. There is no hope of rescue or reprieve. This is what I have done to them."

"Well, *you* haven't—" I started to argue, but behind me, I felt him shake his head fiercely.

"I have been to the camps. I've seen the conditions these people are trapped in. I've stood idly by while Otto and Karl worked them to death at Mittelwerk. Those men build rockets according to *my* instructions. When the story of the war is written, the pages will be full of men saying *I was only following orders* and the world will know that is fiction. Every single time I opted not to take a stand, I *was* taking a stand—for the wrong side."

I sat up, turning to face him. He was shaking with rage and guilt, and when I touched his shoulder, he shook me away.

"None of this is your fault, Jürgen."

He turned to stare out the window. It was freezing outside

and fat flakes of snow began to fall. Without turning back to
me, he murmured, "The only thing that's kept me going the
last few years is that you get to live a reasonably ordinary life
in Berlin with the children. But from time to time, I realize
that it's my fault that you have no idea what it has cost for you
to have that nice life."

"Jürgen…" I whispered, stunned.

"I wanted to shelter you from the horrors of what I was seeing. What I was a part of. But I can't keep doing that, Sofie.
Sooner or later, you have to know the truth."

"The truth?" I repeated hesitantly.

"A while back, I mentioned to Otto that it made no sense
to make the prisoners at Mittelwerk live and work as they are.
I know he hates the Jews. Even at a practical level it seemed
to make sense to be smarter about our work practices. And do
you know what he said?" He didn't wait for my response before he carried on. "He said that whether the workers fall off
a scaffold or die from starvation or disease or go back to the
camps, the outcome is the same. Some of the camps have tran-
sitioned. They are now extermination camps." Jürgen's voice
broke. He cleared his throat, then whispered, "Otto knows
the war is lost—we all do. The Reich will aim to wipe the
Jews from the face of the earth right up until Germany falls."

"But—there must be hundreds of thousands of people in
those camps…"

"Millions," he corrected, and then to my horror, he choked
on a sob. "And they plan to murder them all."

"The logistics of that would be impossible," I said urgently.
"You must be mistaken, Jürgen. This simply cannot be."

"They have developed a gas that suffocates in minutes. Men,
women, children—it doesn't matter to the SS. Thousands of
people die at one time, and some camps are executing them
around the clock."

"You can't be sure. This can't be real. Not millions of people—"

"Sofie. I'm *sure*."

I had been turned inside out—my nerves left raw and my breath shallow. I started to cry, big heaving sobs of shame and confusion and grief. War was always ugly. What Jürgen spoke of was different—a scale of cruelty and violence that was impossible to fathom.

Maybe I had assumed that Germany would fall and the normal rules would apply again—that Mayim would come home or that I'd meet up with her in Poland, and Jürgen might be a prisoner of war, maybe he'd even go to jail, but that eventually, there would be an *after*.

But we were playing by a different rule book—the scale and depth of the Reich's depravity changed everything, and the impact on us was the very least of it. The world would never be the same.

"I've known for months and I did nothing. How many people have died in that time? How many lives could I have saved if I just made different decisions along the way?" he whispered, almost to himself.

My limbs had turned to jelly. I sank onto the bed, my head fell onto the pillow, and I curled my legs up as my sobs came harder. For a long time, we lay like that. Me on my side, facing Jürgen, him on his back, crying silently as he stared at the roof. The light outside shifted as the sun moved overhead, until shadows were falling over the snow, and the room began to grow dark.

"Given everything that's behind and before us," Jürgen said, after a while, "I know you will understand why I cannot join the SS."

My throat was raw from crying, and my eyes swollen from the tears.

"When will the war end?" I whispered, reaching up to touch his cheek. His hand lifted, and for one startling moment, I feared he would push mine away. But instead, he caught it in his, resting his palm over my hand as I touched his face.

"We are losing ground, slowly but surely. I've visited some test sites around the Reich in the last few months and there are signs our troops are deserting already—even our equipment is crumbling. But there's still a long way to fall back before the Allies reach Germany. It may be some months."

I nodded slowly.

"Only a matter of months," I said hesitantly. "And you think…"

"I told you. They will hang me."

"But surely—"

"Sofie," he interrupted me, his voice raw. "If you saw the conditions at Mittelwerk, you would understand why I will hang."

"And if you decline the SS invitation—"

"Whether I wait and surrender to the Allies or refuse to join the SS now, the outcome will be the same. This final line is one I can refuse to cross. It is too late to make one shred of difference to the people we have failed, but at least I will have the dignity of knowing I made *one* right decision."

"Have you thought about what happens to the children if you refuse to join the SS? They will be pariahs," I whispered hesitantly.

"I've thought of nothing but that since last night," Jürgen said abruptly. "Things will be difficult for them until the war ends, but they will recover eventually."

Stricken, Jürgen pulled me close, and I pressed my face into his neck and I wept.

"Hold on," I pleaded, between my sobs. "Just play the game

until the war ends, Jürgen. Just buy us a little more time for a miracle."

"We are the last people on earth who deserve a miracle."

"We've made mistakes, but we aren't bad people."

"You have no idea the things I've seen. The things I've watched happen, without ever once speaking up. You have no idea if I'm a bad person."

He started to cry then in a way I'd never imagined my strong, brave husband ever would.

"I miss Aunt Adele," he choked out, his voice hoarse.

"Me too," I whispered.

"She would know what to do."

It's not always the strongest trees that survive the storm. Sometimes it's the trees that bend with the wind.

I knew exactly what Adele would tell us to do, but I was no longer sure it was the choice we should make.

We checked out of the hotel the next morning. My eyes were puffy and my throat sore from crying, and Jürgen seemed every bit as tender as I felt. We made the final leg of the journey back to Nordhausen without a word. The privacy of the hotel was gone, and neither one of us seemed in the mood to playact. That night we stayed in at the villa, in the home that I now knew once belonged to a Jewish businessman. And just like Jürgen, I felt that man everywhere. By the time the sun went down, I couldn't bear another minute of it.

"I need to go to bed," I told Jürgen, my voice hoarse. Through all of this, he was doing what he'd been doing all afternoon—sitting at the dining room table, marking up diagrams with notes in pencil. He glanced at me, as if he'd forgotten I was there. "Can you come too?"

I wanted him to hold me. I wanted him to lie to me—to

tell me that it was all going to be okay. Instead, he looked
back to the blueprints, his gaze hollow.

"I need this for tomorrow. I'll be in soon."

Jürgen was already out of bed when I woke the next morning. I could hear him moving around in the living room. As
I roused slowly from a fitful night's sleep, he appeared in the
doorway, fully dressed.

"I'm sorry I can't stay to have breakfast with you," he said.
"I have an early meeting and I slept in—I'm already a little
late."

I pushed myself into a sitting position and stared at him.
He was freshly shaven and wearing a suit. He looked at his
watch, clearly anxious about the time.

"What...have you decided...?" I started to whisper, but I
stopped, unsure how to ask him if he'd made a final decision
without giving away his doubts to a potential audience.

He shook his head, then took two steps to the bedside. He
bent to kiss my cheek, then whispered in my ear, "I won't do
anything drastic without talking to you. But if I call and ask
you to come, find a way to get here to say goodbye?"

We'd cleared the air but resolved nothing. I caught his
elbow just as he moved to straighten, and then I scrambled to
my knees and threw my arms around his neck.

"I love you," he said softly.

"I love you too," I whispered.

I dragged myself out of bed after a while, deciding I would
tidy his villa before I started the long drive back to Berlin.
But as soon as I stepped into the living space, I saw the blueprints on the table—the ones he'd been working on the previous night. I hovered over them, trying to make sense of his
scrawl and the diagrams, unable to even decipher what the
component represented.

Then I remembered Jürgen telling me he was staying up to finish the review because he needed the blueprints that morning.

The entrance to Mittelwerk was a large opening at ground level on the side of a hill, guarded by dozens of men in Wehrmacht and SS uniforms. I found the site easily enough. Several officers approached my car the minute I neared their station.

"Are you lost, miss?" a young soldier asked. I fumbled for Jürgen's blueprints, my heart racing as I eyed the gun in his hand and the unwelcoming expression on his face.

But just then, I saw Aldo, a few dozen feet away, supervising a crane lifting some sheets of metal onto the back of a small train carriage. He happened to glance over at me just as I noticed him, and set his clipboard down on a pile of boxes, then jogged toward me.

"Mrs. von Meyer Rhodes," he greeted me. "What on earth are you doing here?"

I looked past him to the entrance. The mouth of the tunnel was maybe two stories high. Two sets of railway tracks disappeared into the darkness, and even from the guard station, I could see people milling about inside. Some were wearing striped uniforms.

If you saw the conditions at Mittelwerk, you would understand why I will hang.

I wanted to understand. I'd allowed Jürgen to shelter me for all of those years, and in doing so, I'd allowed him to bear the burden of a guilt we both deserved to share. I couldn't fix a single thing—but I could face the truth.

"Jürgen forgot some important paperwork," I said. My tongue stuck to the dry roof of my mouth.

"I'll take it," Aldo offered. I shook my head and picked the blueprints up.

"It's very important that I see him myself," I said, my voice growing stronger. "Please, take me to him."

I parked my car off to the side according to the guard's instructions and walked through the gates. Aldo was waiting for me beside a small khaki truck. He looked unsure, glancing between me and the entrance to the tunnel.

"He's quite a way in…"

"That's okay," I said, forcing a confident smile. "I'm not in any hurry."

I took the front passenger's seat and Aldo started the car. As the engine ignited, he glanced at me one last time.

"It's not pleasant in there, Sofie," he said, his voice low. "Are you sure you want to do this? I know Helene Schönerer is well familiar with the camps, but even she found it to be… too much."

"I'm just here to see Jürgen," I said firmly. "Let's get this over and done with."

He sighed and nodded, then steered the car beneath the crane's frame.

"Wind up that window, please." I did as I was instructed, and Aldo did the same on his side, as the car moved into the mouth of the tunnel.

Inside, the light was much dimmer, and at first, it was hard for me to see. As my eyes adjusted, I saw dozens of men working at tables and on components on flatbed train trolleys. Aldo drove slowly, driving around some of these stations, crossing each of the train tracks at different times to avoid carriages left in place. As we moved farther along, the air in the car became so pungent, my stomach rolled with every breath.

"What is that smell?" I asked Aldo. I covered my nose with my hand and tried to breathe through my mouth, but even inside the sealed car, I could taste the filth.

"We had to move quickly after the Peenemünde site was

bombed, and we've had high quotas to meet for the V-2s. There was no time to install sanitation or ventilation…"

Now a few hundred feet into the tunnel, I saw a rough-hewn cross tunnel that seemed to have been cut by hand, the texture of the walls and ceilings coarse and uneven. I was startled to see rows of wooden bunks in the tunnel, most without even a mattress on them, and beside these, drums lined up, one after the other. A man sat on the last drum. His striped trousers were down around his ankles, but he seemed unconscious, leaning back against the wall behind him, his mouth wide and his eyes vacant as he stared at the ceiling. I gasped involuntarily and squeezed my eyes shut.

"They…the prisoners *live* in here?"

I looked out the window again, and now noticed the slumped shoulders of the men as they worked.

"Some live at the Dora camp now, not far from here. But other men still live in the cross tunnels. It's about efficiency, you see. If they are here, we don't waste time transporting them back and forth."

I heard what he was really saying: the rocket program had been deemed more important than anything else—a higher priority than hygiene or dignity or comfort or even the sanctity of human life.

I turned back to face the tunnel in front of the car, but my eyes had finally adjusted to the light and now I saw striped uniforms hanging on skeletal frames everywhere. There were hundreds of men in this section, maybe even more. They were bent over tables, fixing fine parts to small components. They were on scaffolds, working on the lights that illuminated the passage. They were collapsed on the floor, as if they'd died standing and simply folded over themselves. They were pushing train carriages by hand, dozens of men grunting and grimacing as they tried to push components along.

Not one of them looked at the car as we passed, and I wanted nothing more than to look away from them too. Each seemed more drawn than the last, their hair matted, their bodies often showing signs of trauma—a bloodied hand, a severe limp, a bruised face. Every single man was emaciated. I had no idea how they were sustaining the intense manual labor—sometimes I saw four or five men working together to lift one small piece of metal, or two men struggling to push a tiny component into place.

"How do you bear this every day?" I whispered to Aldo.

"I tried to warn you," he said weakly. "This is no place for a lady."

"Is it always like this?"

"It was much worse in the beginning," he said. "This is more orderly…less distressing than it used to be."

My stomach lurched at the thought. I pressed my fist into my mouth. I wanted to pray for strength, but I had the sense that what was happening in those tunnels was beyond the reach even of God.

The tunnel kept rolling on and on. It felt like we'd been driving for hours, although a glance at my watch confirmed it had only been minutes. I was desperate to see Jürgen. I was desperate to get out of there. How did these prisoners endure it?

"How much farther?"

"A few hundred feet more."

"How long is this facility?"

"The entire loop through both is about two miles long."

"Is it *all* like this?" I asked, my voice small.

"Yes."

We drove on in silence. But for the evolution of the rockets on the line, I might have been caught in an endless loop of the same fifty feet of tunnel, a repeated, sickening montage of the absolute depths of human misery.

But then I finally saw Jürgen, his suit protected by a lab coat, clipboard in hand as he stood next to a rocket that seemed to be fully assembled. Aldo parked the car, as he gnawed at his lip.

Just then, Jürgen noticed me. He passed the clipboard to a man beside him, slapping it against his chest in a move that was close to aggression, and, without a word, strode toward me.

"What the *hell* are you doing here?" he hissed.

"I—I came to bring you these," I stammered, extending the blueprints toward him. Jürgen's nostrils flared. He grabbed me firmly by the elbow and dragged me to the cross tunnel nearby. Several workers in striped uniforms scurried from the space as we approached, dismissed without a word. When we were alone, Jürgen dropped the blueprints to the ground and he cupped my face in his shaking hands.

"You shouldn't be here," he choked out, staring desperately into my eyes. "Sofie, I never wanted you to see this."

"I didn't mean to come inside, I promise. But when I got here with the blueprints, I realized this was my chance to understand..." His throat was working as if he wanted to speak, but he didn't say a word—he just stared into my eyes. "Remember? You said I didn't understand. You said I didn't know what it had cost for me and the children to live our lives in Berlin. I wanted to—"

"This isn't a game," he snapped, stepping away from me, pinching the bridge of his nose. He drew in a series of sharp breaths, then dropped his voice as he hissed, "Get out of here, Sofie. *Please.*"

I held myself together until I made it back to my car, out the gates, back onto the main road—but then I swerved to a shoulder and opened the car door just in time to be violently ill.

★ ★ ★

I spent the afternoon in a daze, trying to process what I'd seen at Mittelwerk—but the scale of the suffering was too great to "make sense of."

I wanted to make amends.

There was no way to make amends.

Even if I could have personally freed every man in that tunnel, it still wouldn't be enough. They'd endured conditions and pain and torture that were beyond anything that could be forgiven. Even if they were liberated right that minute, they'd be scarred for the rest of their lives.

Jürgen and I had an odd kind of argument that night—scribbling furiously on paper as we tried to negotiate a safe way to discuss what I'd seen. I wanted to go to another hotel so we could speak freely. He refused—saying it would arouse suspicion. He wanted to "talk about it another time," which I suspected meant he didn't want to talk about it at all. Eventually, I all but dragged him to the bathroom and slammed the door behind us, then turned the faucet on.

"We have to talk about this," I hissed.

"The V-2s have caused significant damage to London...to a few other cities too. That in itself is a tragedy that keeps me up at night. Our intelligence suggests maybe a few thousand people have died," he whispered thickly. "It's horrific. But..."

"But...?" I repeated, scanning his face.

"The guilt of that makes me sick to my stomach, but it doesn't even end there," he croaked. "We are losing that many prisoners every *week* manufacturing rockets. Maybe more. Between accidents, beatings, disease...they take train carriages full of bodies out every day. We produce two things in those tunnels—rockets and death. Mittelwerk is an extermination site, without even the pathetically small mercy of a fast death for its victims."

I thought about how quickly word would spread if Jürgen took a stand and refused to join the SS. Whispers would race like wildfire from Nordhausen to Berlin—through party lines both official and unofficial. Maybe Berlin would fall within just a few months anyway, but it was likely I would be interrogated by the Gestapo too, and I couldn't even be certain I would survive. The children would potentially be left without either of us.

But one day, the war would end. The endless bombardment of Nazi propaganda would stop. And my children could learn that their parents had *tried* to do the right thing. Too little, too late—yes. But they would at least know that there had been a line we refused to cross.

"Follow your conscience wherever it leads you, Jürgen," I blurted. "Do whatever you have to do."

After eleven years of ups and downs and varying degrees of distance between us, Jürgen and I were exactly together, on the same page.

The next morning, Jürgen and I faced one another as I stood beside my car. His eyes were red and so were mine. The sun was low on the horizon and the wind was icy—but the sky above us was blue. I wanted to feel every aspect of the moment. I wanted to remember every detail of those moments with Jürgen, as fraught and terrifying as they were.

We agreed we wouldn't make a fuss that morning, but he and I both knew this would likely be our last goodbye. We discussed trying to bring the children for a final visit—but to arrange that would take time we didn't have. I couldn't bear to lose him, but I knew what the cost would be to keep him. He wasn't willing to pay that price, and now that I'd seen Mittelwerk with my own eyes, nor was I.

To fail a test of loyalty like Otto's invitation for Jürgen to join the SS was suicide. Jürgen was just determined that his death would come on his terms. He didn't have a clear plan for the specifics—he was just going to go to Mittelwerk and look for an opportunity to make one first and last act of defiance, maybe to free a prisoner or two, or to sabotage the line itself somehow.

"I love you more than I knew I could love another person," I said. My whole body was shaking with the effort it was taking to hold back my tears.

His expression softened, and Jürgen reached to cup my cheek in his hand.

"You have made my life, Sofie von Meyer Rhodes. My last thoughts will be of how grateful I have been to share it with you."

And then we kissed, one last time, and I slipped into my car and drove away. Just a few miles out of Nordhausen, I had to pull over to the side of the road because I was sobbing too hard.

Sometimes, I thought I had, by necessity, grown used to living apart from Jürgen. Only now that our connection was likely about to be severed permanently did I understand that it was all that had kept me going through these years.

On that long drive back to Berlin, I wondered how quickly they would come for me. If Jürgen made some dramatic move, it was likely I'd be taken in quickly. I went straight to Lydia's house to see the children, but a black car was already waiting in her drive. I parked near it, not blocking it in. I knew it would soon be driving me away.

40

Sofie

Huntsville, Alabama
1950

IT WAS FRIDAY MORNING AND GISELA HAD BEEN dawdling since she got out of bed. Now we were at the school gate and she didn't want to get out of the car.

"What's wrong now?" I asked her, looking at the school-yard, where a handful of other tardy children were walking into their buildings.

"I just want to go home," she said miserably.

"We can talk about this tonight," I said firmly. "You need to get to class."

She sighed impatiently and slipped out of the car, pausing just long enough to slam the door behind her.

"Mama?" Felix said hesitantly.

"Yes?"

"I need to go to the potty."

"I told you to go before we left."

"I forgot," he said, his voice small.

I sighed impatiently. I usually did the grocery shop on Friday mornings, but instead, I turned the car toward home.

The whole way home, Felix asked about the television—until I came to suspect that there was no urgency for the potty at all. By the time we reached the house, I was well and truly irritable—especially when he made a quick show of using the potty, then ran down the hall toward the living room.

"Felix Rhodes," I said sharply, "you are not watching that television—"

But farther along the hall, past my son at the other end of the house, I saw a blur of movement as someone disappeared into the laundry room.

Someone was in my house.

Should I chase them? Run to the phone? Get Felix out of the house?

The back door slammed. I finally unfroze and ran to the laundry room—making it to the door just in time to catch the barest glimpse of movement as someone disappeared over the low back fence, into the yard of the house behind us.

I quickly dialed Jürgen at work and told him what had happened, my heart still in my throat. Remembering the hostility we'd experienced from Detective Johnson, I didn't bother calling the police.

When Jürgen got home, he went right to the neighbors behind us to ask if they'd seen anyone, but there was no one home, and the intruder was long gone. He then set about making me a cup of tea.

"And you think it was Calvin's brother-in-law?" he asked as he set the tea in front of me. I raised the cup to my lips to find it was far too milky and sweet for my taste. It reminded me of Adele's tea. That both helped and hurt.

"I didn't see his face," I said. My hands were still shaking. "I'm just assuming."

"And did he take anything else or just…?"

"Just the photos," I said, my voice breaking. At first, I couldn't find anything missing. For a moment or two, I almost convinced myself I'd imagined the person in our house. Then I realized the photos were gone from beside our bed. "I need them back."

Jürgen gave me an anguished look and sat opposite me to take my hands.

"I know, my love," he soothed, then paused. "Should we call the police?"

"Is there any point?"

"I suppose not," he sighed. "I should call Calvin, though."

"No," I blurted. Jürgen looked at me, surprised. "Lizzie is just so hateful, Jürgen. You have no idea." I struggled to explain just how distressing her visit the previous day was. It had been such a short encounter—just a few minutes—but her hatred for us was evident, and I still couldn't figure out how to take her odd comment that I'd assumed was about Avril. "I don't want to inflame things with her."

"But the photos, my love," Jürgen protested. "Telling Calvin what happened might be your only chance to get them back."

I covered my face with my hands. Jürgen moved to sit beside me, his arm gently resting over my shoulders.

"I promise I won't make this worse. I just know how much those photos mean to you, and we can't go on like this. Calvin was in a meeting when I left, but I'll go back in to work and—"

"No!" I shivered, shaking my head. "Please. Can you take the day off? I don't want to be alone." His arm around my shoulders tensed, and I turned to press my face against his neck. "I've dealt with plenty of anxious moments on my own over the years. I want things to be different now. I want things to be better here. I want you and me to ride out the hard things together."

"Okay," Jürgen murmured, without hesitation. "I'll call in and let the team know I'm needed at home."

That night, we went out and picked up hamburgers for dinner, and then all four of us cuddled up on the sofa to watch television—Felix at one end, then me, then Gisela, then Jürgen at the opposite end of the sofa, which was as close as Felix could allow him.

"Progress?" Jürgen mouthed, nodding toward Felix over Gisela's head. He flashed me a lopsided smile.

"You're clutching at straws if you think *this* is a win," I whispered back, but I was teasing him. The last few days had been awful, but even in the midst of that, I found myself feeling grateful. It *was* some progress that Felix was finally sitting on the sofa with Jürgen.

Once the children were in bed, Jürgen checked every latch on every window, and then he checked the doors—making sure everything was locked, even though we'd already been through this exercise before we went to pick up dinner. I followed him around, *double*-double-checking, just for my own peace of mind. At the front windows, I scanned the street for signs of trouble.

"Come to bed, my love," Jürgen said, taking my hand. "I'll hold you until you fall asleep."

As we climbed into bed, I turned automatically to the table beside me to look for the photos. When I remembered they were gone, my heart ached.

It was bad enough that our house had been violated—but

the objects taken were so personal, and those images had no value to anyone other than me.

I wondered if whoever took them—be it Lizzie Miller's brother or a stranger—had any idea what they'd really stolen in taking the simple stack of paper that represented my last mementos of Adele and Georg and even Laura, and of course, Mayim.

Jürgen and I destroyed every trace of her from our lives, just as the Gestapo told us to—but that one photo came back to me at the time I needed it most. Was it some kind of penance that even my photo of her kept slipping from my grasp?

41

Lizzie
El Paso, Texas
1943

"THAT'S IT, AVA. JUST TIE THE STALK TO THE stake there—good girl. And, Brianna—take just a little bit of that mulch and put it around the base of the plant."

I knew my whole life that I was not cut out to be a mother, but I'd made a startling discovery—I was a fantastic "aunt" to Becca's two girls, and quite a good gardening teacher. I'd ripped up the roses and the hedges from our yard and converted every square inch of our lot into a Victory Garden, just as the government was encouraging us all to do. Advertisements in magazines gave instructions for growing and preserving our own food to make rations go further, and for the first time in years, my fingernails were black with soil, and I was contributing something.

My garden was the pride of the street and I was coordinating the neighborhood home garden co-op too. The women

I'd been so wary of in the early years of my marriage to Calvin were keen to heed the call to do the same, but not one of them had ever even dug out a weed. This moment called for hands-on participation and, suddenly, everyone wanted some of my time.

Calvin was supportive of my new projects—but I knew he didn't like when they cut into my housekeeping time, and I'd long since come to terms with the fact that I needed to spend more time on my appearance than I preferred. But all that was fine. It turned out I was a woman who was happiest when she crammed a lot into each day.

"You're a godsend, Lizzie," Becca said, as she slid a tray of lemonade onto a table near the garden. "Truly. This garden has been just the distraction we needed. Girls, go wash up and come have a snack."

I slipped my gloves off and took a seat opposite Becca, expressing my thanks as she passed me an icy glass of lemonade.

"Any news on your brother?" she asked, and the pleasure I'd been feeling dimmed.

"They're staged somewhere east—that's all I know. I just don't know…" I sighed heavily and sipped the lemonade. "Henry hasn't called in a long time, and he's been sending me letters that don't say much." Henry's division had been all over for training exercises—Arkansas and Louisiana and California and then New York State. I told myself that Henry was seeing the country, and that with his division training so extensively, he was going to be truly ready to serve if and when they were sent to Europe or the Pacific.

I kept myself busy with the gardens. I made sure of that. Every time I found myself bored, my panic about Henry and the war began to spiral.

"He's going to be okay," Becca said gently. I opened my mouth to point out that she had no way of knowing that—but

I couldn't, because Becca's husband, Kevin, was flying planes somewhere over the Pacific.

If there was one game I'd learned to play well over the years of the war, it was the pretending game. Every woman knew how to play. Whenever we were talking to anyone who had a loved one in the military, we shifted into a mode of forced optimism. The way we spoke to one another sometimes, a casual observer might have thought war wasn't a dangerous scenario at all.

"And Kevin will be just fine too," I said firmly.

Christmas loomed, and I was trying to force some cheer. I invited Becca to bring Brianna and Ava around to spend Christmas lunch with me and Cal. They were understandably worried about Kevin, and I knew Becca was worried about getting through Christmas without him.

I needed a project to distract me too. It had been weeks since I'd heard from Henry, and the war seemed to be spiraling out of control.

I'd just hung a string of popcorn around the tree when I heard Cal come home from work. Christmas carols were playing on the wireless, and the scent of pine wafted through the air. Beside me, a little pile of gifts was waiting for our guests—a junior gardener's set for Ava and Brianna, and some perfume for Becca.

"Sweetheart," Cal said. I looked up at his grave tone, and my stomach dropped. He was holding a postcard in his hand. He looked ill as he extended it toward me. I scampered to my feet and snatched it from his hand.

Dear Cal and Lizzie,
We are shipping out tomorrow, destined for I-don't-know-where.
Sis, I know you are going to fret but please don't. I am serving

with some of the finest men alive, and wherever this war takes us and whatever becomes of us, I know that we will represent this country with pride and honor. I'll write you when I can.

Cal, please take care of my sister, always.

Love,

Henry

42

Sofie
Berlin, Germany
December 1944

THEY TOOK ME TO THE BASEMENT OF THE GE-
stapo headquarters on Prinz-Albrecht-Strasse. My cell was
only a few feet wide in each direction. As the officer escort-
ing me pushed me inside, he barked an order that I wasn't to
speak to any of the other prisoners. Once the door closed, the
cell was completely dark, other than a razor-thin line of yellow light along the top of the door.

There was no bed or toilet, and the walls were lined with
bricks. The tiny space seemed impossibly dark and damp and
cold, and there was no relief to be found, because all I could
do was stand, or sit on that freezing concrete floor and let the
moisture seep through my skirt. The space wasn't even large
enough for me to lie down.

Around me, I could hear the sounds of regret and suffering—
weeping from a cell nearby, shouting in the far distance. Periodi-

cally someone would scream in pain. I thought I heard someone trying to whisper to me from an adjacent cell, but I didn't dare reply.

I had no sense of time, only the growing awareness that while other cell doors were opening and closing, no one came for me. The sensory deprivation was torture in itself—sometimes I wondered if it had only been a few minutes, other times it felt like days. Eventually, I became so desperate to use the facilities I was crying in pain. I thumped on the door and called for help, but no one answered.

I was trying to figure out the logistics of relieving myself on the floor when the door clicked, and then a sudden flash of light appeared as it swung inward. I squinted, and a burst of pain shot through my skull at the sudden brightness.

"Toilet break," a guard said. "No speaking."

As he walked me back to my cell afterward, I gingerly asked for some water. His only answer was the slam of the door as he locked me back inside.

Soon I thought the thirst would kill me, maybe even before the cold. At one point I dozed off, but I woke with a start when a door closed somewhere else in the basement—the echoing vibration of the slam, then the sickening click-click-click of a lock snapping into place. After hours—days?—of darkness, my hearing seemed keener. When my stomach rumbled with hunger, it sounded so loud to me, I wondered if the people in the cells around me could hear it.

Then the door opened again. When my eyes adjusted to the light, I saw that it was the same guard.

"Toilet break," he said. "No speaking."

I wasn't sure how long I'd been in that cell. My body odor was so strong that when I moved, a wave of it washed over me, and sometimes it left me feeling nauseous. With no access to sunlight, not even during toilet breaks, all I could do to judge time was count the interruptions to darkness—the delivery of a bowl of cold oatmeal and a glass of water, periodic toilet breaks. If those things were happening twice a day, I'd been in the cell for ten days—but it felt so much longer. My hips and shoulders were bruised from sleeping curled up on the hard floor. I'd been so cold for so long that my mind felt foggy—like my body was shutting down in slow motion.

This trip out of my cell was different. I found myself sitting in a stark room while a Gestapo officer shouted at me.

"You and your husband are traitors to the Reich! Do you have anything to say for yourself?"

Are my children okay?

Why did you arrest me so quickly?

Did Jürgen manage to do any damage before you arrested him?

Is he gone?

Why are you keeping me alive?

Am I ever going home?

And then—a thought struck me, clearer than all the others.

He had spoken about Jürgen in the present tense. Was that an accident?

I raised my eyes from the table to look at the man opposite me. The disgust in his eyes was hard to stomach. I wondered how he'd feel if he knew he'd just given me an unexpected gift. There was at least a chance that Jürgen was alive.

That was enough to make me strong again, even though my body was weak. I met his gaze as he shouted at me, insults and threats and accusations, but I didn't say a word.

Two men took me again, dragging me with rough hands beneath my arms, along the same corridor—but this time, instead of taking me to my cell, they dragged me up a set of stairs. My eyes watered from the sunlight, but I could make out a car waiting outside. They pushed me toward it and into the back seat.

"Where are you taking me?" I asked. No one answered, but to my surprise, the streetscape around us soon told the story.

When the car came to a stop outside my house, the man in the passenger's seat threw my handbag at me. I fumbled to catch it.

"We'll be watching you," he said flatly. His gaze drifted across to Dietger and Anne's house. There was a figure in the front window.

"That's...that's it?" I croaked. "I can go?"

"We'll be *watching* you," he said again. "Every move you make, we'll know about it."

The house was empty when I let myself inside. The clock on the wall in my dining room said it was two fifteen, but I had no clue what day it was. I knew I'd have to call Lydia sooner or later to ask where the children were, but I couldn't bring myself to do so—not yet. I took a quick shower and changed into blessedly fresh clothes. They hung on my frame—however long I'd been in that cell, I'd lost an immense amount of weight. My stomach still didn't feel right, but I made myself a cup of ersatz coffee and nibbled on some old ginger cookies I'd made before the ceremony at Castle Varlar.

Then came a knock at the front door. I scrambled to my feet and ran along the hallway to open it. Lydia was there, alone. She looked every bit as disappointed as she did angry. She took a step forward until her face was close to mine.

"I'm going to give you the benefit of the doubt and assume you had no idea what your husband was going to do," she whispered fiercely.

Behind her, a car door opened, and I was momentarily distracted by the sight of Gisela running along the path, crying and calling, "Mama! Mama, you're home!"

Lydia took a step back. I crouched to envelop Gisela in my arms as she threw herself toward me, crying into my shoulder. A wave of love and relief washed over me at the weight of her limp body in my arms. Behind her, Laura and Georg were walking along the path too, both looking confused and unsure.

"I missed you so much. I was scared you'd never come back," Gisela wept.

"I'm sorry, my love," I choked out, pressing kisses against her hair. "I'm so sorry I had to go away."

"Welcome home, Sofie," Lydia said flatly. "I have explained to your children that there was a little misunderstanding and you've been away on business sorting it out."

I looked up at her in shock. Was it a kindness that she'd lied to the children for me, or yet another game?

"Thank you," I said. She nodded curtly and spun on her heel and walked away.

Laura remarked that I looked tired, and Georg's frown had never been so deep, but after a few awkward moments, I found myself in the sitting room, surrounded by the children as they filled me in on their "exciting weeks" at Lydia's house.

"...I finished that assessment at school and Mrs. Bruan said it was some of my best work," Laura told me.

"Mama, I climbed the biggest tree at the park..." Gisela said, beaming.

"What business were you attending to?" Georg frowned. "Why do you look so sick?"

"Just some private business," I said firmly. "And I've been a little unwell."

The phone rang, the shrill sound jarring my frayed nerves, and I ran so fast to the study to answer it that I almost tripped over my feet.

"Hello?" I blurted into the handset.

"Hello, my love," he said. He sounded exhausted, but more than that, he sounded defeated.

"Hello," I whispered, tears filling my eyes. There were so many things I wanted to say to him that weren't safe to say, and I knew he wouldn't be able to explain to me what he'd been through either. "Are you well?"

"I'm fine," he said. He didn't sound fine at all—his words were thick and a little slurred, as if his mouth were injured. His tone was heavy with dread too. "I have great news to share."

"You do?"

"I've been invited to join the SS," he said. There was no mistaking that he was crying now, and I gave up trying to contain my tears. Who cared if they heard us now? "I've been awarded the rank of *SS-Sturmbannführer*. It is a great honor." This was a high rank—the equivalent of major in the Wehrmacht. I wondered why our plan failed, but now wasn't the time to discuss it.

"Can we visit you this weekend?"

"I don't want the children to see me like this," he whispered brokenly.

"Okay," I agreed. "We'll wait a few weeks."

When I took the children to visit Jürgen at Nordhausen a few weekends later, there was still a green shadow on his jaw and a purple haze around both of his eyes. He'd warned me he still wasn't himself, but he'd grown impatient to see us.

"Papa," Georg said stiffly. "What happened to you?"

"Ah, silly old thing I am," Jürgen said dismissively, as he reached a hand to touch his face. "I fell down the stairs working late one night."

The girls accepted the lie easily. They each hugged Jürgen, then ran ahead to take their bags into the villa. Georg remained standing by my car, staring at us.

"I know you were in trouble," he said. "I could tell from the way Mrs. zu Schiller was acting while Mama was away. And then you both come home looking like *this*." Even after some weeks, Jürgen and I were both rail thin. I was still struggling to eat normally. Even my stomach was traumatized by the experience. "Papa, I'm not a fool. It's obvious you were beaten. You were both arrested, weren't you?"

"I am a clumsy fool and your mother was away attending to family business," Jürgen said dismissively.

"But—"

Jürgen raised his chin and adopted a tone that left no room for argument. "You've been raised to respect your elders," he barked. "Collect your things and go into the house, and I don't want to hear this nonsense in front of your sisters."

I hated to hear Jürgen take that tone, but I understood why he did. The last thing we needed was the girls becoming suspicious too.

Georg's nostrils flared, but he scooped up his overnight bag from the ground and stomped toward the villa.

"He can accuse us all he wants, but until the war ends and we can explain, we can never confirm his suspicions," Jürgen said heavily. "His whole identity is wrapped up in the Nazi cause. I fear he'd lash out if he knew."

I looped my arms around his neck and stared up at him.

"I love you," I whispered.

The tension in his face eased a little as he stared down at me and whispered back, "I love you too."

Under the blankets that night, with the children all asleep in their beds down the hall, Jürgen's voice shook as he told me how it had all gone wrong.

"Otto was waiting for me on-site when I arrived that morning. It all happened so quickly, before I even had a chance to help anyone. He told me that someone saw us stop at Kassel and asked me why we'd checked in under a false name. I told Otto that I wanted out. They arrested me immediately."

"They must have been following us the whole time," I said. Jürgen nodded.

"I thought they'd just execute me, but there was a beating…" His tone was curt—an unmistakable message that he wasn't yet ready to discuss the assault. My heart broke for him.

"Oh, Jürgen…"

"I thought it would continue until they killed me. But over the days, I realized they were toying with me—beating me unconscious, patching me up again…just trying to get me to break and beg for mercy. But I refused to speak, mostly because I knew you were being held too, and I didn't want to incriminate you. It nearly killed me knowing you were in a cell somewhere, Sofie, but we'd prepared for that."

"We had."

"After… Hell, I don't know how many days, something changed. They sent a doctor in to patch me up again, then took me to the interrogation room and told me a car was on its way to the zu Schiller house to collect the children."

My breath caught in my throat.

"The *children*?"

"God forgive me, as soon as they started talking about the ways they'd torture our children to death, I lost my nerve. I should have expected it," he whispered miserably. "They think nothing of imprisoning and murdering Jewish children. Of course they wouldn't hesitate to interrogate the children of a traitor."

It was one thing to take a stand when Jürgen and I were going to pay the price for it. It was another thing to threaten the children's lives.

Jürgen was freed after he expressed his remorse and begged for another chance, just as the Gestapo hoped. He was again invited to accept an SS rank, and this time he relented.

"You said the rocket program will be forced to wind down soon. Why go to such lengths to force you to join the SS?" I whispered, frustrated and bewildered.

"I think this may be Karl's fault," Jürgen whispered back. "A few weeks before Castle Varlar, Otto suggested we might need to make preliminary plans so we can quickly ensure the destruction of the Mittelwerk site. He suggested we plan to cover our tracks as protection against accusations of war crimes once the Allies take the district."

"Even Otto knows that what has gone on is not right."

"He does. Karl agreed we should be ready, because if we can hide the truth about Mittelwerk, he and I may have a chance at refuge with one of the Allies because of our experience with rocketry."

"Karl isn't a scientist."

"No, but he's a manager with a unique insight into what it takes to mass-produce rockets. Or so he tells me."

"That's absurd."

"It's a fantasy," Jürgen said dismissively. "Even if we could destroy the Mittelwerk site, there would still be witnesses. The truth will prevail. But the thing is—Karl didn't mention Otto 'escaping' with us."

"Because even if you could somehow suppress the truth about Mittelwerk, none of the Allies would ever pardon an SS officer," I surmised heavily.

"Exactly. Otto is a man who delights in cruelty, my love. It wouldn't surprise me if he put us through all of this just to make doubly sure Karl and I were trapped along with him."

We had made one crucial mistake in our attempt to take a stand. We forgot that, in the Reich, control was absolute. There were no measures too extreme when it came to ensuring perfect compliance.

43

Sofie

Huntsville, Alabama
1950

IT WAS STILL DARK WHEN FELIX TUGGED AT MY hand. I cracked my bleary eyes and found him standing against the bed, his face pressed right against mine as I slept.

"Mama," he whispered, then hopefully, "Television?"

"You're surely joking…" I groaned, and I looked at the alarm clock. It was just past 5:30 a.m.—the worst possible time for him to wake me. It was too damned early, but I also knew it was late enough that he'd never go back to sleep. I pushed myself into a sitting position, groaning.

"What's wrong?" Jürgen mumbled beside me.

"Felix wants to watch television—" I started to say, but my words turned into a scream.

We'd left the drapes open a little the night before, and now, in the gap between the drapes, a face stared back at me. Someone was looking through the window.

I grabbed my startled son, instinct forcing me away from the window and out of the room. Jürgen was shouting behind me—*what is it? Sofie?* And then he must have seen for himself. I heard him shout, "Oh my God!"

"Mama?" Felix called out.

"It's okay, baby," I said, my voice shaking as much as my knees. I took him into Gisela's room and all but threw him onto the bed.

"Mama?" she mumbled, even as she opened her arms to her brother.

"Stay here," I said fiercely. "Stay here and stay *away* from the windows."

I ran toward the back of the house—I could tell from the cool breeze coming down the hall that the laundry room door was open. I surmised that Jürgen had gone out that way into the backyard. Had it been Lizzie Miller's brother staring through my window? I thought so, but couldn't be sure. It all happened so fast in the predawn light.

I'd just stepped out of the laundry room into the yard when I heard an explosion—so sudden and so loud that dogs began to bark, and the birds in the trees squawked as they scattered into the silvery sky. My instincts told me to run away from it, but I wasn't sure where Jürgen was, so instead I ran toward the sound. As I rounded the corner of the house, my footsteps stalled. Jürgen was on the ground, in a heap against the wall.

A dozen or so feet away from him in the middle of our small yard, Lizzie Miller's brother was standing with a handgun dangling limply from his hand, an expression of shock and disbelief on his face. He released a low whimper when he saw me. Then he dropped the gun and leaped over the low fence in the back of our yard.

The instant Henry was away from the gun, I ran to Jürgen. He was alive—his eyes wild as he stared at me. His hands were clutching his abdomen. The bloodstain on his nightshirt was spreading fast, and he was sucking in deep, desperate breaths.

After everything we'd survived, I couldn't lose him like this.

"Jürgen—" I whispered. I pressed my hands over his, trying to stem the bleeding. "You're going to be okay. It's going to be fine."

"Sofie," he gasped.

"Gisela!" I shouted. "Gisela, call for help!" Could she even hear me from her bedroom? She certainly would have heard the gunshot, but my daughter was smart. That sound probably drove her to hide. "Someone help us!" I called, and then I went weak with relief when Klaus appeared at the fence next door.

"Sofie? My God! What's happened?"

"Please help us," I said. "Jürgen's been shot." I was dry-eyed and my voice sounded stiff, almost emotionless. My hands, over Jürgen's at his abdomen, were quickly becoming numb. I could hear my pulse in my ears—*thud, thud, thud*. It felt surreal, like I was watching a film.

Jürgen was still panting, but color was rapidly draining from his face. He was losing too much blood. My thoughts were muddled, but one suddenly seemed clear.

I had to keep him calm. I had to reassure him.

"You are going to be fine," I said quietly, staring into his eyes.

"Love...you. The children," he panted.

"Save your breath now and tell me later," I said.

It felt like the ambulance took hours to arrive. I was vaguely aware of Klaus in the yard with us, but it sounded as though he was speaking from a distance as he told me that Claudia took our children to their house to keep them safe. Other neighbors were peering over the fences at us, but when I tried to look at them, my vision swam. I stopped trying after a while, and simply focused on Jürgen.

"You're okay, my love," I told him. Maybe I was dreaming. Maybe that was why it was so hard to speak and to concentrate. "Everything is going to be fine."

The sun was on the horizon when I finally heard sirens in the distance.

Jürgen fell unconscious then, his eyes panicked as his lids fluttered closed, his hands growing limp beneath mine.

That was when the panic my shock had held at bay came rushing in at me.

44

Lizzie
Huntsville, Alabama
1950

JUST ABOUT EVERYTHING SEEMED A LITTLE BRO-
ken when I woke up that Saturday morning.

Cal was trying to carry on as if nothing were wrong, but
he seemed tender almost, as if I'd bruised him badly. I still
had no idea what to do about it. And Henry had been so late
home the previous night I started to suspect he wasn't really
"working late," as he'd claimed all week. Calvin and I agreed
to sit him down for a discussion over dinner, and I still wasn't
sure what we were going to say to him.

I had a lot to worry about with the two men in my life, and
whenever I was worried, I was drawn to my garden. That was
why I was up with the sun that Saturday morning, hoping to
clear out the unwanted plants from a few of my garden beds
before the sun grew too hot.

I was pulling on my boots when I heard the explosion in

the distance—not so close that I felt I needed to run for cover, but close enough that it startled me. It was probably just a car backfiring—some laborer, leaving for an early shift to beat the heat. Nothing to be concerned about.

I started to work on the garden bed just off the laundry room, near the stairs to Henry's apartment. If he was working that day, he'd be down those stairs soon. But just a few minutes later, Henry burst into the backyard through the gate that came from the street. He was wearing nightclothes, and there were sweat marks around his armpits.

"Lizzie!" he whispered frantically. "He was chasing me!"

"What on earth are you talking about?" I gasped. I scrambled to my feet and took my brother's shoulders in my hands. "Are you dreaming again?"

"He came again last night, so I got the gun." My breath caught in my throat. That sound I'd heard wasn't a car backfiring. It was a *gunshot*? "He was coming every night! I had enough, that's all. I told him if he came near you once more, I'd take care of him. I was going to fix it for you, Lizzie, but—" Henry suddenly seemed confused. "But when I got there, they were in bed together, and the little boy came in and…"

I brushed a lock of sweat-soaked hair back from my brother's forehead, forcing myself to smile reassuringly, even though ice was running through my veins. I needed to calm him down. I needed to know exactly what had happened so I could figure out how to fix it.

"Let's go upstairs," I said gently. "You can tell me the whole story, Henry. I'm going to help you figure this out."

I'd never seen my brother cry before, not even in the very worst moments of our lives. He was sobbing now. He shook from head to toe as if he were freezing. Even his teeth were chattering.

"I still don't know what he's trying to do to us," he said. He was seated on the edge of his unmade bed, rocking back and forth like a child. "But he kept coming around here all the time. And then she came too, with the cake! They are up to something. I *know* they are."

Henry was generally tidy, but that was always the first thing to go when his mood was low. I was kicking myself for not checking his room. I had been trying to respect his privacy, but if I'd just come up to his room and seen the filthy way he'd been living, I'd have been able to stop all of this.

There was a tin of red paint sitting on spread newspaper on the floor, with brushes drying on the windowsill. I was confused about that, until I remembered Avril saying someone had been graffitiing the road outside of the Rhodes house. Plates of half-eaten food sat on the table, and scrawled notes were taped to the wall—a dozen or so slips of paper just like the one he'd dropped in my kitchen that day, each one covered with dates and times and seemingly random words. An open box of bullets sat on the little table I'd picked out for him when I was setting up the room.

"She went grocery shopping the last *three* Fridays, but she came home early yesterday. That's when I knew for sure. How did she know I was in the house?" He stood, his footsteps heavy and frustrated as he walked to the table. He pushed the box of ammunition to the side and scooped up some black-and-white photographs, quickly bringing them to show me. "See?" he said, his tone triumphant and accusatory. "This proves it, Lizzie. They're up to something."

I accepted the photographs as he handed them to me. I looked down into the faces of three young children in one. The next was of an elderly woman. And then my stomach dropped as I stared down at what was unmistakably Sofie and Jürgen Rhodes's wedding photo. They were young and innocent and both beaming as if they couldn't contain their joy. Cal's words ran through my mind. *He adores her.* In that photo, Jürgen Rhodes looked like the happiest man in the world.

I flipped to the next photo, and as I stared down at the final one, I felt a pinch in my chest. An even younger Sofie Rhodes, this time with another young woman beaming at the camera, a Star of David pendant hanging from her necklace. They had suitcases at their feet. They looked like their lives were spread out before them, begging to be explored.

"These are just photos," I said to Henry. Intensely personal photos. He'd been in their house—riffling through their things. My head spun.

"But don't you see?" Henry whispered, balling his hands into fists and pressing them to his forehead. "It means something. I just can't decipher it. They're going to hurt you—people like that don't change."

"When have you had time for all of—" I waved around the mess in the room—the notes on the wall, the photos in my hand "—this? You've been working—" I broke off, feeling stupid. I spun toward the nearest notes and my heart sank. These were not Henry's work time sheets. Some were marked with an *S* at the top, some were marked with a *J*. He'd been following them for weeks. "Oh. Oh, Henry…"

"I knew you'd be upset, so I didn't tell you I'd quit, but some things are more important than a job in a lumberyard, Lizzie," Henry told me, stricken.

I should have seen this. I should have known Henry was in trouble—deluded or confused or just plain broken. My gaze went back to the bullets on the table and my heart sank all over again.

"When did you buy the gun?"

"I bought it just before Christmas when I was in a bad way. I was going to—" He broke off, squeezing his eyes shut. "I didn't buy it for Rhodes."

"Henry," I choked out on a sob. *No.* "I want to hear about that. I want to talk to you about that and tell you how much I need you *here*. But right now, I need to know about this morning. Where is the gun now?"

"I dropped it." He squeezed his eyes closed, frustration on his face. "In the yard. You saw him the first time he came here, didn't you? That was the only time he let you see him."

"He wasn't *here* that night, Henry." It was a dream or, I finally acknowledged, a hallucination. Whatever had been happening in Henry's brain, I had no doubt it felt very real to him.

"But he *chased* me this morning!" Henry choked out. "He was going to follow me here to hurt you! I had to stop him!"

"And is he…?"

"I think he's dead," Henry wailed, and the rocking started again. I drew in a deep breath.

Murder was a capital offense in Alabama. Henry was clearly not in his right mind, but I didn't know if that would be enough to save him. He had done this trying to protect me, and now he needed my protection.

I flew off the bed and rushed to his closet. I pulled his suitcase down from the top shelf and started to throw his clothes into it. "Do you remember where that hospital was? The place where you had the insulin therapy?"

"I don't want to go back there," Henry said. "No, Lizzie. *Please.*"

"Honey, you just have to. You need help, and the VA is the best place for you to get it."

"Did I shoot him? Did I dream that?" Henry said, after a pause.

"I don't know, honey," I said, although the sirens in the

distance seemed to be multiplying by the second, so I had a fair idea that he had. Once the suitcase was full, I clipped it closed, then thrust it at my brother. "Take this. Go to your car *right now*. Do you have gas? Money for gas?"

He nodded mutely, staring at me through cloudy eyes.

"Henry, you have to drive yourself back to that hospital in Nashville," I said slowly. I still wasn't sure he understood. And right in that moment Henry's mind was obviously elsewhere—with Jürgen Rhodes, or back in Europe, or already on the road. I took him by the shoulders and gently pulled at him, encouraging him to stand. "Can you do that? Can you get yourself back to the hospital?"

"I— Yes. I think so." The hospital was almost two hours away, but I couldn't think of any other way to get him out of town than to send him under his own steam.

"You can't breathe a word of this to anyone. When you get to the hospital, you just tell the nurse you're confused. You tell her you're seeing and hearing things that aren't there."

"But I'm not—"

"Honey," I whispered brokenly, "I think you are."

"Like…like shooting Rhodes? Did I imagine that?" He sounded so hopeful.

"Yes," I said slowly. "All of this. You've imagined all of it." But then I imagined him checking himself into the clinic and immediately confessing to a potential murder, so I added hastily, "But you mustn't tell them *what* you've been imagining. Okay? Just tell them you're seeing and hearing things that aren't really there and you need them to help you again."

"Why is this happening, sis?"

"I think your mind is tired, and maybe that insulin therapy made it a little bit broken too," I said sadly, reaching to squeeze his hand. "That's not your fault. You need to take some care and rest, and you'll feel better soon. So can you go to the hospital?"

"I can do that." Henry nodded miserably. "Yeah. I can do that."

"I'll take care of everything else, but you have to go, and you have to go now before Calvin wakes up."

45

Sofie
Huntsville, Alabama
1950

THE PARAMEDICS SAID THAT JÜRGEN PROBABLY needed surgery, and that it was serious. Very serious. Klaus retrieved one of Claudia's housecoats for me and I threw it over my nightclothes, intending to go with Jürgen in the ambulance—but then I noticed the blue flashing lights on the street outside my house.

"Take care of him, please," I begged the paramedic, as he shut the door to close Jürgen inside. He nodded at me, his eyes brimming with sympathy. "If he wakes up, tell him I won't be far away." At this, the sympathy intensified. It was clear this man did not expect Jürgen to wake up anytime soon, if at all.

A great wave of emotion was looming over me; I just couldn't allow it to crash—not yet. I had to stay calm until I talked to the police, and in that regard, my state of shock was almost helpful.

"Mrs. Rhodes?" The first officer to approach me was Detective Johnson. He looked sleep-rumpled and irritated. Another man was right behind him—a younger man with light blond hair, and an equally disheveled suit.

"I'm Detective Tucker," the blond man said. "Can you tell us what happened?"

I slowly, carefully explained about waking up to see the face in the window and running from the room to get Felix to safety. But from there, my memory was a little hazy.

"Jürgen must have run out into the backyard—the next thing I knew, there was the gunshot, and by the time I came into the yard, Jürgen was on the ground. Henry was there—"

"Henry?" Johnson interrupted me curtly. "Who is this 'Henry'?"

"He lives a few blocks away, with his sister and her husband. Lizzie and Calvin Miller—"

"Oh," Johnson said, eyes widening. He reached into his pocket and withdrew a notebook. Flicking back a few pages, he raised his gaze to mine. His nostrils were flared. "So you're telling me that Henry Davis—American war hero Henry Davis—was watching you and your husband sleep? And then, unprovoked, he shot your husband?"

"Yes."

"Where are your children now, Mrs. Rhodes?" Tucker asked, not unkindly. I pointed to Claudia's house. Klaus was just a few feet away, watching silently. "Sir. Can you corroborate any of this?"

Klaus looked at me helplessly. I barely knew the man—even less than I knew his wife. He'd been a godsend that morning, but he wouldn't lie for me.

"We heard shouting," he said awkwardly. "Then the gunshot. Then a minute or so later, as I was pulling on my clothes, I heard Sofie calling for help. I didn't see anything."

"Why did you wait before you called for help?" Johnson asked.

"Henry was standing there with the gun," I said. It felt like I was speaking too slowly, but I had an awful case of cotton mouth and I couldn't release my words any faster. "It wasn't until he dropped it that I could finally go to Jürgen. That's when I called out for Klaus."

"And where did Henry Davis go after he dropped the gun?" Tucker asked steadily.

"I bet he disappeared into thin air, Detective Tucker," Johnson said wryly. Tucker shot him an impatient look, then turned back to me.

"Mrs. Rhodes?"

"He ran to the back fence and through that yard—" I pointed in the vague direction.

"Did you see any of that, sir?" Johnson asked Klaus, who silently shook his head. "But you did hear shouting. Before the shot was fired."

"A few minutes before, yes."

"Male voices? Female?"

"Both, I think?"

"Did it sound like an argument, sir?" Johnson said grimly.

"I was asleep, Officers," Klaus said helplessly. "Claudia and I both woke to raised voices but I didn't hear what was said."

All eyes turned to me.

"You're awfully calm for someone who just found her husband shot, Mrs. Rhodes," Johnson said quietly.

"I've had a terrible shock," I protested weakly.

"Women who have terrible shocks become hysterical," he said dismissively.

"We should interview the neighbors behind," Tucker said quietly to Johnson. "They might have seen something."

"Yes," I said, turning to look at their yard. Henry *had* gone that way, I was suddenly sure of it—and then he'd be only a minute or two away from his own house. "But you should go now, in case he tries to escape."

"Mrs. Rhodes. I would think someone in your position would know better than to tell an investigating detective how to do his job," Johnson said abruptly, then turned his gaze to Klaus. "Can the children stay with you and your wife, sir?"

Klaus hesitated, his gaze darting to the house. I knew he was wondering if Claudia would approve of this request.

"Don't worry, Klaus. I'll call Avril Walters," I suggested uncomfortably. I was a little wary of her now, but she was still the only friend I had in Huntsville. "I'm sure she will watch them while I sort this out and while…" My throat tightened. "Just until I make sure Jürgen is okay."

Avril was at the house minutes after I hung up. She had a scarf tied over her rollers and her face was bare, but she'd pulled on a pretty floral sundress. Two uniformed police officers arrived and were watching me as I paced the dining room, and when I heard her car in the drive, they followed me as I went to meet her at my front door. She immediately pulled me into a tight hug.

"What on earth is going on?"

"I don't know how to explain," I said numbly. "Could you just take the children for today? Jürgen is in the hospital, and I think the police want to…" I sucked in a breath, thinking about cold concrete cells and days of no sunlight. "To question me."

"Oh, honey. Of course."

"You're Mrs. Walters?" Johnson said, approaching us.

"I am, sir," she said calmly.

"I'll speak to you alone before you go. Just need to confirm a few details."

She gave me a wide-eyed look as she turned to follow Johnson into Jürgen's study.

"Ma'am," one of the uniformed officers said. "We're ready to take you to the station now."

They left me sitting in the interrogation room at the station alone for over an hour. I was desperate for news about Jürgen—more concerned with his health than my present situation, and that was saying something. The shock had worn off, and now it was a mammoth task to keep myself from spiraling into a panic over memories of the *last* time I was in an interrogation room.

But finally, the door opened, and Tucker and Johnson were there. Both looked grim.

"Is he—" I blurted, but Tucker's expression softened a little.

"No, Mrs. Rhodes. The last we heard, he was still in surgery."

I slumped with relief as the men took seats opposite me.

"You say that Henry Davis shot your husband this morning in the backyard of your home," Johnson said, his tone firm and formal.

"That's right," I said. "Have you spoken to him?"

"We were planning a visit to his home," Tucker said quietly. "But then we talked to your friend. Mrs. Walters."

"Oh?" I said, eyebrows knitting. A shiver of unease raced through me.

"She told us some very illuminating information about your husband's past, Mrs. Rhodes." Johnson frowned. "She said you refused to deny that you were both Nazi party members back in Germany, and that Jürgen was an SS officer who…" His nostrils flared, and he stared at me with barely disguised hatred as he said, "…who ran some kind of concentration camp?"

"It wasn't… I didn't…" I gritted my teeth and tried to calm

down. It would do me no favors to let them fluster me. "I came halfway around the world to be with Jürgen. Do you really think I'd hurt him? Do you really think I'd *come here* unless I loved him?"

"She also tells us that as late as last week, you told her that life was difficult here but that you couldn't return to Berlin because of your husband."

"I said nothing of the sort!" I exclaimed, but then I paused—because I *did* say that going home wasn't an option. Maybe the detectives had twisted her words.

Or maybe she had twisted mine. My heart sank.

"And your husband broke into the Miller household a few weeks ago—"

"He did not!" I exclaimed. "Lizzie Miller made that up." I squeezed my eyes closed. "Or her brother, maybe. I don't know for sure."

Johnson sighed impatiently.

"So your story is that Lizzie Miller made up a story about your husband breaking into her house and that Henry Davis just appeared at your window this morning and, without provocation, shot Jürgen and then ran away."

"He's been harassing us," I said, eyes filling with tears of frustration. "He broke into our house! He threw a cake at me! He's been walking up and down our street staring at me. For all I know, he's been the one painting *that word* on the road outside of our house."

"I didn't see those reports on file," Johnson remarked, almost smug. "Did I miss them? Should I take another look?"

"Jürgen spoke to you the first time that graffiti was found and you told him to just paint over it," I said flatly. "We didn't bother calling again after that. It was obvious you were not going to help us."

"I hear you," Tucker said, dropping his tone, as if to de-escalate the tension. I drew in a shaky breath, trying to calm myself. "But what I don't understand is why no one we've interviewed so far can confirm a single thing you've just told us. Avril tells me you and she have become quite close, yet she didn't mention a thing about this potential—what, assault by dinner plate? Or a break-in? Or Henry Davis lingering outside your house? If any of that really happened, Mrs. Rhodes, you must have been distressed—why didn't you tell anyone? We even asked Klaus Schmidt and some of your other neighbors if they'd noticed anything unusual at your house. They all told us about the graffiti and that scene *you* caused at the Redstone Arsenal picnic, but had nothing else to report."

"When Jürgen wakes up, he'll tell you," I whispered fiercely.

"If he wakes up," Johnson said flatly. "I got the impression that was far from a sure thing when I spoke to the hospital earlier."

I stared at them helplessly, but then a thought struck me. There *were* other people who knew at least part of what had been going on.

"Talk to Lizzie or Calvin Miller."

After that, they moved me back to the cell.

46

Lizzie
Huntsville, Alabama
1950

"HENRY LEFT LAST NIGHT," I SAID BRIGHTLY. I was carrying a basket of linen, freshly stripped from Henry's bed. Calvin liked to sleep in on Saturdays, then usually went into the office for a few hours to catch up on some paperwork while the place was quiet. By the time he emerged from his room, I'd torn through Henry's apartment and stripped the place down to its bones. I tore Henry's notes up into tiny pieces and flushed them down the toilet. The rest of his bullets and a tin of red paint I found in his closet were in a cardboard box in my laundry, along with Sofie Rhodes's photographs, tucked safely in an envelope I'd already stamped and addressed to her home.

There was nothing I could do about the gun, since Henry wasn't sure where he'd dropped it. I just had to hope that since he'd bought it months ago and likely in another city, the police couldn't trace it back to him.

"He left last *night*?" Calvin repeated, frowning. "He didn't even say goodbye?"

"He had a falling-out with Walt at the lumberyard," I said, lying on the fly and hating every second of it. I'd never lied to Cal before. "But Henry heard about a job up north. He just had to be there to start today. So I encouraged him to go."

"You were so worried about him..." Cal said, bewildered. "We were going to talk to him about seeing a doctor today. You just let him leave instead?"

"I figured it was best if he got out of Huntsville."

"How did he even hear about this job?" Calvin said, peering at me. "I didn't hear the phone ring last night."

"You do sleep so deeply," I pointed out. Then I flushed and avoided his gaze, thinking about that awkward middle-of-the-night encounter we'd had on Thursday. I stared at a knot in the floorboards and laughed nervously as I added, "Anyway, he called an old friend late to catch up and that's when he learned about the job."

I felt so many things, and not all of them made sense. I was ashamed and deeply upset for the Rhodes family—something I thought I'd never feel. I was so anxious I felt ill. I was confused. Henry was in trouble, and my instincts were to protect him. That was earnest—a pure expression of my love. But as my brother drove away, I was already wondering if I'd done the right thing.

"I'm worried about him. And more than a little hurt that he didn't say goodbye this time," Calvin admitted.

"He didn't want to wake you," I said. There was a rough edge to my voice, and I hoped that Calvin heard it as sadness that Henry was gone again. He offered me a sympathetic smile, then downed the last of his coffee.

"Do you want me to stay home today?" he offered. "I could help you in the garden?"

"It's going to be so hot," I said, my throat tight. "I'll probably just wash the linen and maybe read a book. You should go."

I knew he'd be back, probably sooner rather than later because it wouldn't take long for word to reach the base about what had happened. My husband would inevitably come rushing home with questions I wasn't ready to answer.

I hadn't let myself think that far ahead. I had to go to the mailbox to send the photos back to Sofie Rhodes, and then I had to find a safe place far from my house so I could dispose of the bullets and the tin of red paint.

As soon as Cal's car left, I ran to the laundry room and picked up the box of things from Henry's room, intending to rush to my car to dispose of it all. But as I reached my door, I heard an engine on the street. Was Cal returning already?

No. It was worse.

A police car pulled into the driveway and parked behind my car. Panicking, I dropped the box to the floor and shoved it beneath a lamp table in the corner of my living room. The lace table square on the table hung only a few inches over the edges. The box was visible, but surely it wouldn't arouse suspicion even if the officers did notice it.

Then I straightened my shoulders, took a deep breath, and opened the door.

I showed Detective Johnson and his partner, Detective Tucker, inside and invited them to take a seat. I offered them coffee, which they declined. I dropped into my armchair when I realized my nervous hovering was probably making me look guilty. When I caught myself picking at the skin around my fingernails, I jammed my hands under my thighs. I resisted a bizarre urge to keep looking toward the box in the corner of the room.

"I'm sorry to interrupt your morning," Detective Johnson said. I remembered him from his previous visit. He looked uncomfortable this time. Beneath my thighs, my fingers twitched. "I have some terrible news, Mrs. Miller. Jürgen Rhodes was shot this morning."

"Shot?" I gasped, feigning shock. "Is he—"

"He's alive," Tucker said. "Unfortunately, it doesn't look good."

If Rhodes did survive, it might mean all manner of complications for Henry—but I couldn't bring myself to hope for any other outcome. Even if Jürgen Rhodes did have skeletons in his closet, I couldn't wish death on the man.

"We've taken Mrs. Rhodes in for questioning, ma'am," Detective Tucker said. I thought I'd misheard them for a minute. I blinked.

"Did you say Mrs. Rhodes—*Sofie* Rhodes?" My hands began to tingle. I was conscious of the thump of my heartbeat against my chest. I thought things were as bad as they could possibly be, but somehow, this was so much worse. My gaze kept drifting across the room, toward the box. I dragged my eyes back to Detective Tucker.

"We believe there was some kind of domestic altercation that led to the shooting," Tucker told me.

"It's shocking, I know," Johnson said sympathetically. "You said Mr. Miller is at the base?" I nodded mutely. "And your brother?"

"He left for a new job up north," I said. "Yesterday."

"Can you tell us where he is? How might we contact him?"

I shook my head. This answer, at least, I'd planned.

"He tends to drift around—but he'll write me once he finds a place to stay."

I kept thinking about the Sofie Rhodes in those photos. There had been so much hope in her eyes. Then I thought about her children. I was certain she only had two with her at that party, but the photos suggested three.

Children in a strange country—they didn't even speak English. Their father might die. Their mother might go to jail—or worse, if she were convicted of murder. Maybe, if Henry had been arrested, he could have used an insanity defense, but Sofie Rhodes would have no such option. She *was* a woman—maybe that would help? Jürgen Rhodes likely earned an excellent salary. Even if he didn't survive, they might have enough savings to fund her defense and maybe—

I froze. Was I really trying to convince myself to let an innocent woman face the death penalty for something I knew she didn't do?

I glanced at the box beneath the lamp table for a split second, then looked back to Tucker. He leaned forward, staring at me with visible concern.

"Mrs. Miller, we know this has been a terrible shock. Would you like us to give you a moment? We do have a few questions we'd like to ask you."

"Me?"

"Sofie Rhodes told us a fanciful tale about your brother harassing them," Johnson said, his tone suggesting he was embarrassed to even repeat the accusation. "She's adamant that Henry was lying about the night he saw her husband in your home. To be truthful, Mrs. Miller, I don't put much stock in what those Germans do or don't say. But I figured we'd come and have a chat with you anyway, just to do our due diligence."

I closed my eyes and tried to concentrate. There had to be a way to fix this. I couldn't do anything to undo what Henry had already done, but there *had* to be a way to save him from prison, to save Sofie Rhodes for her children...

Maybe I sat there a moment too long, because when I opened my eyes, both officers were staring at me, their gazes narrow.

"Mrs. Miller?" Tucker said slowly. "Is there anything you want to tell us?"

For the first time in years, I thought about my mother and the conversation she and I shared beneath the stars about Henry and Daddy, and strong minds and weaker spirits.

You get the brain you're given, and it seems to me that those of us who are strong have an obligation to care for others when they aren't.

My gaze drifted again to the box of evidence in the corner of the room.

I had to protect Henry. I had to help Sofie Rhodes.

I let my gaze linger on the box—long enough that the silence stretched.

After a moment, Johnson rose and walked across the room to the lamp table. He lifted the box up onto the table, peered inside, then looked at me in disbelief.

"Care to explain all this, Mrs. Miller?" he said.

"No," I whispered hoarsely. "No, I don't think I will."

The interrogation room was small, with stark white walls and a large clock over the door. I guessed I'd need a lawyer but I didn't know what I'd say to him, so I hadn't asked to call one. Johnson and Tucker were throwing rapid-fire questions at me. I knew all of the answers, but I hadn't said a word since we arrived at the station.

I felt Mother's memory so strongly in that room. It was like she was trying to tell me something. I just couldn't catch it with all of the noise and the guilt and the fear and the confusion.

"Lizzie," Tucker said, his tone suddenly softening. "May I call you that?" I nodded silently. "The bullets in that box match the type of bullets in the gun we found in Jürgen Rhodes' backyard. You have the photographs Sofie Rhodes says were stolen from her bedroom. You have a tin of paint that might plausibly have been used to harass those Germans up on Saukeraut Hill. We haven't charged you yet because we thought you might have some explanation for all of this, but you won't even try to help us out here. Surely you can see this looks bad?"

"Calvin is out there in the foyer," Johnson added. "He's real upset, Lizzie. Why don't you tell us what happened this morning with Rhodes, and then we'll let you see him?"

I wanted to make my brother okay but I couldn't. I wanted to make Calvin happy but I couldn't. I just wanted to undo what had happened to Jürgen Rhodes—but I couldn't. I wanted to help Sofie Rhodes, who, in this instance at least, was an innocent mother to innocent children.

I just wanted to make everything better for *everyone* around me.

I could hear my breathing echoing in that little room— shallow pants that betrayed my panic. The only way forward seemed to be for me to confess to Henry's crime, but Calvin would see right through that.

"We might take a break," Tucker sighed, and the two men pushed back their chairs and left me alone.

I stared up at the clock on the wall. It was almost 10:00 a.m., and the second hand kept ticking, even though it felt that time had stopped.

47

Sofie
Berlin, Germany
April 1945

THE END WAS COMING CLOSER AND THE MOOD on the streets of Berlin was tense. Some people were stockpiling food and ammunition, others were collecting timber in piles in their yards—ostensibly for "summer projects." Few were willing to admit they were actually preparing to barricade their windows once the conflict reached our streets.

Lydia hadn't spoken to me since my arrest—not until the phone lines at Nordhausen and Mittelwerk went down, at which point she called and acted as if we were still close.

"Have you heard from Jürgen?" she asked pleasantly.

"I'm sorry," I said. "No, not for weeks."

"The last time I spoke to him, Karl said we have to defend ourselves and our homes at any cost and we must fight to the very last. He and I agreed we would never surrender. But…"

Lydia cleared her throat. "If he was *captured*...well, obviously that would be different."

"I don't know what you mean, Lydia."

"The Soviets and the Americans will want our technology. Our knowledge. And God knows the scientists can't manage their own way from the lunchroom to their desks. They need people like Karl to help them or they'd never achieve anything. And of course they'd take our families too. The men would insist upon it."

"I'm not so sure about any of that," I sighed. I knew from Jürgen that this was Karl's expectation, but to me it seemed laughably optimistic. "If I hear anything, I'll call you."

A few days later, Hans called and asked to speak to Georg, and I didn't think anything of fetching my son. I left him in the study to talk to his friend and went back to the kitchen, where I had been cataloging supplies. The city was likely to fall within weeks. Aerial bombing kept us up several nights in a row and it seemed clear this was only just beginning. I was moving every scrap of potential sustenance into the makeshift bomb shelter we'd set up in the small cellar below Adele's building. I was scared, but I'd been scared for so long by then, I'd learned to push through it. The best thing I could do for my family was to be prepared.

The next thing I knew, Georg was in the doorway in his Hitler Youth uniform, a canvas bag hanging from his shoulder. He was fifteen, and a proud, full-fledged member of the senior ranks. His uniform was just a little too large. He inherited Jürgen's height and needed the next size up, but he didn't yet have the bulk to fill it out.

"I have orders, Mama," he told me. His eyes were alight with excitement, as if he'd been summoned to play a particularly thrilling game. It was the happiest I'd seen him since my arrest. "We are deploying immediately."

"Orders?" I repeated blankly. "Deploying?"

"My Hitler Youth division is being deployed to defend Kassel."

He let his bag fall to the floor and he stepped toward me, a grave expression on his face. I set down the bag of flour I had been holding and turned toward him, more confused than alarmed.

"You're fifteen," I said blankly. "You're a child, not a soldier. Who told you you're being *deployed*?" I dusted off my hands on my apron and took a step toward the door. "You've misunderstood, that's all. I'll call the captain—"

"He's on his way to pick me up."

I hated to call Lydia back, but I couldn't think of another way to straighten out this mess. Georg waited by the door as I dialed and spoke to the zu Schiller housekeeper, who went to fetch Lydia. After just a moment, she answered the phone breathlessly.

"Sofie! Do you have news about Karl?"

"No, I'm sorry—"

"Then now isn't a good time. I'm helping Hans pack his bag."

I turned to look at Georg. He had recently started shaving—probably a little before he needed to. The razor had inflamed the hint of acne along his jawline. He had Jürgen's coloring and my intellect. He was handsome and proud, his boots shiny, his tie knotted perfectly—all on his own.

But his skin was red, flushed with irritation and probably more than a little embarrassment.

He was a boy. *He was just a boy.*

"I've just talked to Georg. They can't be deploying children," I said. I could feel the blood thundering around my body—the pulse sounding in my ears and under my skin.

"The Führer has said that we must defend the Reich to the

last," she said impatiently. "These boys have been training for battle for years."

"You're going to let Hans go?"

"I'm worried, of course, but I'm also proud. Hans and Georg are warriors today! It's not for us to decide if they go. They have orders. They simply must obey them," she said. Then she dropped her voice and scolded me. "Sofie, you should have learned your lesson last time. We are to be loyal to the Reich, above all else."

I hung up then without a farewell. My ears were ringing—with shock, with terror, with disbelief. I turned back to Georg.

"You can't go," I blurted. "You need to stay with me."

"I can't refuse orders, Mama. That's treason!"

"But you *can* ignore them, Georg, and you must. We're losing the war," I said, and I reached for him just as he reached down to scoop up his bag. He shook me off, his expression hardening.

"Losing the war? Don't tell me the enemy has fooled you with their propaganda! The Führer says we just need to stay the course. Fight house-to-house, he said. That's how we will be victorious—"

"You have to think for yourself now," I interrupted him urgently. "It's only a matter of time before the rest of Germany falls, and when that happens we will be liberated. It is almost over."

Georg stilled. His gaze sharpened on my face.

"I knew it."

"Knew what?"

His lip curled in disgust, and he shook his head.

"You're disloyal to the Reich and they arrested you because someone found out. You and Papa are probably only alive because his rockets are turning the tide of the war."

A torrent of words waited, boiling in my gut. The time was coming when I would be able to say them.

You were a puppet in the hands of evil men from your childhood, but there is a good person inside of you, and I'm going to help him grow strong again.

But Georg had just inadvertently reminded me why I couldn't yet say those words. If I were honest with him now, he would walk straight to that car or across the road to Dietger to share the news of my disloyalty. I couldn't even blame him. He had been raised with the doctrine of country before family. As far as I could tell, the Allies were still weeks away from Berlin. Would the Gestapo arrest me again? Take me back to the prison?

If they did, my girls would be all alone in Berlin as the city fell. I couldn't risk it. I had to hold my tongue.

All I could do was let Georg go and pray to God that I would get the opportunity to say what needed to be said later, when all of it was over.

"I'm not disloyal," I said, my tone hollow. "I'm worried for you. You're a man now, but you're still my baby."

At these words or maybe my broken tone, Georg paused. Then he stepped toward me and embraced me.

"Mama," he scolded softly. "Don't worry. I know what I'm doing. It's an honor to serve the Führer. Trust in him and know that I'll be safe and back home before you know it."

I threw my arms around his waist and squeezed him tightly.

There were thunderous footsteps on the stairs above us, and Laura and Gisela were there, both beaming with pride through their tears. Georg hugged them both quickly, told them to be brave and to be strong, and then a horn sounded outside. The girls ran to my side, both crying in earnest. I threw an arm around each of them as Georg crossed the foyer quickly to throw open the front door.

"Wait," I blurted. "Wait…"

But I trailed off because there was nothing more to say, and it was obvious that Georg knew it too. He turned back to face us and he raised his right arm defiantly, in a salute to a man who deserved no such honor, a man who had already lost, even if he and my son were yet to recognize it.

"*Sieg heil!*" Georg said. *Hail victory.*

Still crying, my daughters raised their hands to return the gesture. I raised mine too, just as I knew I had to, but it trembled violently above my head.

Georg's tone spoke of his defiance as he gave that salute, but I did not miss the flash of fear in his eyes.

I had no idea what was happening at Kassel over the weeks that followed. I asked everyone I saw if they had any news—occasionally going out just so I could ask the grocer or people on the street. Although she'd never admit it, Lydia was fretting as much as I was, for both Karl and Hans now. To my frustration, she kept arriving unannounced at my house seeking news.

"I'm sure they'll all be fine," she told me, but her voice was strained and she was picking at the skin of her fingernails. "Karl and Jürgen are prized assets in the Reich—they'll be protected no matter what happens. And our boys are soldiers. I mean, they've trained for years for this in the *Jungvolk* and the *Hitlerjugend.*" She paused suddenly, then looked tearfully into my eyes. "But you will tell me if you hear anything, won't you, Sofie? Anything at all?"

I had plenty else to worry about on the home front, because Berlin was rapidly descending into chaos. The Allies were bombing day and night, and Laura, Gisela, and I were on edge all the time—ready to run down to the basement at the shrill burst of the air raid sirens. The city was soon cut off, and there was madness in the air that reminded me of *Kristallnacht*. Homes and stores were ransacked, people were mugged in broad daylight for the simplest of things.

Against this ugly backdrop, the Reich's delusion of hope continued. Cars drove through the streets with speakers on their roofs, blaring reminders to protect our homes and streets at any cost. New propaganda posters appeared on telegraph poles and in letter boxes. Defiant to the end, Hitler continued to incite us to violence in his name.

Laura held one of these posters in her hand at breakfast one morning.

"What's the plan, Mama? How shall we defend our home from the enemy?"

She was thirteen years old. The Nazis had been in power since she was a toddler. How would I ever explain to Laura and Georg why we allowed them to become immersed in this world of idol worship and hate?

I again did the calculation—*Gestapo. Loyalty. Imprisonment.* This time, the city was in such chaos that I felt sure the Gestapo would be busy elsewhere—probably trying to save their own necks. Comforted, I took my first baby step toward a future where Laura and I could connect on honest terms.

"The war is over," I said gently. "We have lost."

"But, Mama—" Laura held aloft the poster, as if I might have missed seeing it "—we must defend our street and our home to the last. See? We cannot allow them to simply take our city."

"Others will fight. This war has taken enough from this family."

"What on earth do you mean?" She looked around, genuinely bewildered. "We've lost nothing!"

I stood abruptly.

"Everything you think you know is untrue. Just like an

infant, you are going to have to learn how to interpret the things that you have seen and heard."

Six-year-old Gisela was seated beside me. She reached to take my hand.

"Don't fight," she said. "I'm scared already. Please let's don't fight."

"We aren't fighting, baby," I told her softly. "It's okay to be scared. Laura and I are scared, and wherever they are, I bet Papa and Georg are scared too."

"I'm going to tell them at my League meeting," Laura hissed. "They *always* ask if our families are loyal. The Gestapo will come for you. That's what you deserve for saying these hateful things."

"There will be no more League meetings," I snapped. "They are readying us to fight with our bare hands. If they cared about us at all, they would tell us to prepare our white flags and to welcome the Soviets. All there is left to do is accept the reality that we were on the wrong side and we lost."

"Why are you talking like this?" Laura cried, her eyes filling with tears. She pushed her chair back and ran from the room, dropping the poster as she left. It fluttered slowly to the ground and drifted under the table. I heard her furious footsteps on the stairs, and then the sound of her door slamming as she ran into her bedroom.

I was tired and worried about Georg and Jürgen and sick of every moment being a battle. I exhaled slowly, dropping my forehead to the table. Gisela squeezed my hand.

"Mama, is everything going to be okay? Do you really promise it will?"

I reached for Gisela, pulling her onto my lap and wrapping my arms around her waist. She turned to rest her head on my shoulder, winding her arms around my neck.

"It is going to be difficult for a little while longer," I replied. "We just have to be brave until things get better."

I had just slipped into bed that night when I heard a car parking on the road outside. I assumed it was someone arriving for a neighbor, but then I heard a soft knock at the front door. Thinking it might be Georg, I flew out of bed and down the stairs to open it.

Jürgen was on the doorstep. He desperately needed a shave and, as I discovered when I threw my arms around him, a shower.

"I'm so happy to see you," I cried. "Where on earth have you been?"

He offered a weary smile.

"The whole team was sent to a ski resort in Bavaria to await further instructions. In the chaos as they were leaving, I stole this car and started making my way back here."

"Lydia thinks she's going to America."

"Well, I'm afraid Lydia may be in for a shock, because Karl surrendered to the Soviets weeks ago," Jürgen said, as he hung his filthy hat on the coatrack. I gingerly scooped it off and set it near his suitcase on the ground.

"That needs a wash." I waved my hand vaguely over the general direction of his body. "*All* of you needs a wash." But then I paused and gasped. "Did you say Karl surrendered to the Soviets?"

"He tried to convince me to go with him. When I refused, he assembled a group of the other scientists, including Aldo, and fled like a rat on a sinking ship. Karl's an SS officer and war criminal, for God's sake, just as I am. Why would anyone pardon us? He's probably in some miserable Soviet prison right now, just where he belongs." Jürgen sighed and shook his head. "Even if they did offer him refuge for some unfathomable reason, what good is freedom to Karl? He had to abandon his wife and children to get it."

I skimmed my eyes down Jürgen's body and took it all in—the scratch on his arm that looked like he'd had an encounter with a sharp bush; the mud on his cheek; the crumpled, smelly clothes.

"It hasn't been easy to get home," he said, following my gaze. "It won't be long before Berlin falls. I'm glad I came—things will get worse before they get better. I'll stay with you and try to keep you and the children safe until it's over. Then I'll surrender to whomever takes the city."

Jürgen was already starting up the stair toward the bathroom. I cleared my throat, and he looked back at me expectantly.

"Georg was sent to Kassel with his Hitler Youth unit," I blurted. Shock echoed across his features, then an unmistakable terror. "I tried. I promise I tried to convince him to stay. There was no talking sense into him."

That night, as terrified as I was, as uncertain as the future was—I had an unexpected blessing to be grateful for. For all that was wrong in our past and in our world, at least Jürgen and I were together in our anxiety and our despair.

I was folding laundry the next day when the knock at the door came. I dropped Gisela's undershirt back into the basket and started walking briskly to answer it, but Jürgen beat me to it.

"...so I decided to come home," I heard him say, his tone gentle. "But come on inside. We'll make some tea and I'll tell you—"

"Just tell me where he is," Lydia said flatly. After a fraught pause, she asked unevenly, "Is he dead, Jürgen? I'd rather know."

"He surrendered to the Soviets," Jürgen said heavily. I had reached the foyer now, and I held my breath as I stared at the doorway. What was she doing there? Did she have news about the boys?

"He wouldn't," Lydia breathed, shaking her head. Her gaze seemed unfocused. "No."

"I'm sure he tried to call you first. The phone lines—"

"The Soviets must have captured him. That would make more sense."

"No," Jürgen said, his voice again gentle, but firm. "He was among the first to go and he went north. He wanted to meet the Soviets as they advanced."

"But...but he said we'd... We were supposed to defend the Reich to the last," she whispered, brows knitting. Her whole expression twisted, becoming ugly and fierce. "No. Karl would face death before the dishonor of abandoning this country—of abandoning his *family*. You're lying."

Sunlight glinted off a windshield behind Lydia, and I stepped forward, trying to peer around her. Her car was parked behind the Army truck Jürgen stole from Mittelwerk, and Hans was sitting in the back seat.

"Hans is here?" I blurted, running to the doorway. "Where is Georg?"

But closer now, I could see Hans properly, and a sense of dread ran through me when I realized he was rocking gently back and forward. He looked up and met my eyes, and even from a dozen or more feet, I could see that his were red rimmed, his face splotchy. He looked so much younger than his sixteen years. He was a traumatized, terrified child.

I didn't need him to say it and I didn't need to hear the

details. The minute I saw Hans's face, I knew that my son was gone.

Lydia suddenly started to cry, her gaze wild and panicked as she looked from Jürgen and me, back to her son in the car. Jürgen ran from the house, down the cobblestone path. He threw open the car door and grabbed Hans by the shoulders, pulling the boy out onto the sidewalk.

"Where is Georg, Hans? Where is my son?"

"He's gone..." Hans wept.

Jürgen was shouting at Hans. Hans was crying. Lydia was wailing. And across the road, Dietger was holding a paintbrush by his side, white paint dripping down onto the footpath. He'd been painting propaganda slogans onto the wall of his house.

Protect your homes! Every citizen must defend the city from the Red scourge—

I turned to see that, beside us, in the building Adele called home for her whole life, her tenants were hanging out the windows, watching too, and in doorways up and down the street, people were coming out to see what the fuss was. Our dawning grief was a spectacle for the neighborhood.

"He's lying," Lydia said behind me. I turned to her, trying to make sense of the words.

"Hans is lying?" I asked hopefully.

"*Jürgen* is lying!" she shouted desperately, as she tugged at her scalp. "Karl wouldn't abandon me!"

"Karl thought he had a chance to save his own neck and he took it. I know it's not what you want to hear but it's the truth," I said numbly. I couldn't deal with her breakdown—I had my own to attend to. I walked slowly down the path toward the curb, closer to Hans and Jürgen.

"We didn't have enough guns. The SS gave us grenades and told us to climb under the tanks and to hold on to them while they detonated. But me and Georg didn't want to die.

He didn't want to die, Mr. Rhodes..." Hans was babbling now, weeping and talking at a million miles an hour, drawing shuddering breaths only when he had to. Jürgen still held him by the shoulders, but now I could see that if he released him, Hans would collapse to the ground. He looked behind us, toward Lydia, and between heaving sobs he choked out, "Mama, I can't do it. Help me, Mama. Please."

Hans said the words, but it was Georg's voice I heard. I imagined that as he took his last breaths, scared and alone, he had called for me just like that. My knees went weak, and I reached for Jürgen's shoulder to hold myself up. Hans fumbled for the car door and threw himself into the back seat.

"He was shot defending his country," Lydia said numbly. She walked past us, leaned into the car to murmur something to Hans, then turned to face me one last time. "Georg died for the Reich, in service of the Führer. He is a hero and you should be proud."

"A hero?" I blurted. Then I laughed bitterly. "He was a *child*, Lydia! A brainwashed, broken child." Lydia gasped, her hand covering her mouth. "Hitler was never worthy of our loyalty and he sure as hell wasn't worthy of the sacrifice of my son's life."

Lydia stared at me, and then she turned to slip back into the car. Her gaze was sharp as she looked at me one last time and said, "The boys were safe—hiding. Georg tried to run away and the Americans shot him in the back. The truth was, if Georg hadn't been a coward, he would have made it out like Hans did."

With that, Lydia slid into the car and her driver took them away.

As the city crumbled around us, I could think of nothing but Georg. Several days passed and I stayed in bed. Jürgen provided the emotional support the girls needed, boarded up windows, and moved the rest of the food down into the cellar beneath Adele's building.

"Sofie," Jürgen said softly. I was sitting on Georg's bed, wrapped in Mayim's blanket. The corners of it were soaked in tears, and I looked at him through bleary eyes. "Come with me."

I let him lead me to the study. He positioned me, blanket and all, in one of the armchairs in front of his desk. I watched as he crouched awkwardly behind his bookshelf, then pressed his shoulder into the side, trying to push it forward. A letter opener and a pair of tweezers were on the floor beside him.

"What on earth are you doing?" I asked, confused.

Jürgen gave a grunt and an extra shove, and the shelf slid forward just a little. He dropped to his hands and knees, then picked up the letter opener and slid it between two floorboards. He pried one up just a little, then reached for the tweezers.

"Just after we married, I was in this study and I dropped a page out of an early draft of my dissertation. It was such a fluke—it floated down from my hand and then slipped right between these floorboards. I got it out just like this," he muttered, jiggling the letter opener and the tweezers. "I thought if I ever had to *really* hide something, this would be the perfect spot."

He made a sudden sound of triumph, then ever so gently pulled a small envelope from the gap. He blew the dust off, gently wiped it on his shirt, then held it out to me in both hands, as if it were made of glass.

"What is it?"

"Open it, my love," he said softly.

I gently tore open the seal, and my heart started to pound as I saw the black-and-white image inside. It was me and Mayim, arms around one another, suitcases by our ankles, beaming at my nanny the morning we were leaving for finishing school.

"My God," I choked out, looking up at him through my tears. I forgot how bright her eyes were and how wide her smile was that day. We were two hopeful kids with the world at our feet, blissfully oblivious to how cruel the journey ahead would be.

"She was here and she mattered," Jürgen said quietly. "The same with Georg. They are gone, but *you* are still here. The girls are still here. I hope this photo helps you stay strong through whatever the future looks like."

I had always loved Jürgen Rhodes, but I'd never loved him more than in this moment—the darkest of my life—when he knew how to bring back in a sliver of light.

48

Sofie

Huntsville, Alabama
1950

AS I SAT WAITING FOR NEWS, I TRIED TO BE grateful that this cell was large and well lit, that there was a mattress and a blanket on the bed, and even if it was out in the open, there was a toilet right there. Focusing on the differences between this cell and the last one I'd been in helped at first—but not for long. By the time the lock tumbled, I convinced myself I was going to be locked in that cell, starving and thirsty and terrified, for weeks without so much as an update on my husband or children.

But then Detective Tucker appeared in the doorway. He avoided my gaze, staring at the floor. My breath caught in my throat.

"Jürgen…" I whispered frantically.

"No," he said hastily. "No, we haven't had news. But you're

free to go." He motioned for me to join him in the hallway and I shot to my feet and followed him.

As we started to walk toward the exit, I asked hesitantly, "But why are you releasing me?" It felt dangerous to ask, as if the question could lead me back into the cell.

"We have a new suspect."

"Henry Davis," I said grimly. He shook his head.

"No, ma'am. Lizzie Miller." I was so shocked I stumbled, and Tucker caught my arm and gave me a sympathetic look. "I'm sorry for the trouble this morning. I imagine today has been stressful enough without this…unfortunate mix-up."

I glanced at the interview room as we walked past, and through the little pane of glass at the top of the door, I saw Lizzie Miller—although at first, I barely recognized her. She was wearing an old man's shirt that was sizes too big for her— so large she'd rolled the sleeves up to expose her hands. Her hair was in a tight little ponytail at the back of her head, and she wasn't wearing makeup—revealing heavily freckled skin and eyelashes so faint they were almost invisible. Her expression was carefully blank as she stared up at the wall. I paused, trying to ignore the impulse to confront her.

She had no more pulled that trigger than I did. That didn't mean she was innocent.

"Can I talk to her?"

"We really don't need any more trouble," Tucker said hesitantly.

"Please."

He sighed as he nodded, and I pushed the door open. I sat opposite Lizzie as if I were the interrogator.

"What do you want?" she said, defensive as always, but I barely heard her. As I stared at her, I was startled to see something in her eyes I'd never noticed before.

Familiarity.

I had also made the wrong choices in a panic to protect my family, and I'd been forced to learn the hard way that even failure did not leave a person beyond salvation.

49

Lizzie
Huntsville, Alabama
1950

IT WAS BUSY AT THE STATION, AND FOR A WHILE, I thought the detectives might have forgotten I was there. But then the door opened and Sofie Rhodes was standing there. She looked even worse than I felt—her eyes red rimmed, her face pale. When she walked, the robe she was wearing shifted, and I saw the dark, dried blood on her nightshirt.

I looked away, suddenly ashamed. I had only ever seen her as an enemy. Now I couldn't pretend that I didn't know she was once young and hopeful, the world at her feet.

"We are the same, you and me," she said suddenly.

"We are nothing alike."

"We are the kind of women who do whatever needs to be done—" she dropped her voice, and her gaze softened as she added "—especially when it comes to our family."

My shoulders slumped. She immediately saw through my

plan to protect Henry, just as I knew Calvin would. Would it matter? Could the police charge my brother for a crime *I* confessed to?

"I hope your husband is okay," I whispered. She nodded to acknowledge she heard me, but her gaze was distant.

"We told ourselves that we were only protecting our family. In the end, we lost our son and our daughter anyway—and what's almost as hard to live with now is that we lost ourselves in the process. It's too late for us to make things right back home in Germany—that's why it's so important to Jürgen and me to build something good *here*." She gave me a sad, searching look. "You only get one life, Mrs. Miller. If nothing else, you have to live it with integrity—true to yourself and your values, whatever the consequences."

She closed the door behind her, leaving me alone again. The second hand on the clock seemed louder than ever. I stared up at it until my eyes watered.

You only get one life, Mrs. Miller.

But that wasn't true. I'd lived many lives. I'd become someone entirely new, just to survive in El Paso. I'd done it again for Calvin's sake, and I'd honed that new persona, desperate to make *him* happy the only way I seemed able. I'd shape-shifted again for the El Paso wives, just so I'd fit in.

And it seemed I'd been willing to do that all over again for Henry; to pretend I was the kind of woman who would shoot a man in his own backyard, to save my brother from himself.

Why had I thrown myself on the grenade of his mess, without so much as a second thought for my own welfare? I'd even been more concerned for saving Sofie Rhodes, a woman I supposedly despised, than I was for protecting myself.

In all of those years since me and Henry left the farm, I had reshaped and remolded and reinvented myself to please other people so many times, I'd entirely lost touch with the woman

I started out as. I'd been living for other people, every single hour of every single day, for more than half my life.

When it all boiled down, I didn't think twice about blowing up my life because I didn't value it. The only life I'd ever loved was the one I'd lost.

I was unraveling in that interrogation room, my perspective shifting and twisting until it felt as though layers were coming away. I never wanted to be a suburban housewife, bored out of my brain, tolerating petty gossip and begging my friends for a chance to plant their gardens. That life was fine for other people, but I had always known what I wanted for myself, and this was never it.

I wanted to help my brother, but constantly trying to protect him from his own mistakes was only hurting him in the long run. He needed to face the consequences this time. I'd fight for him and I'd advocate for him. I'd do whatever it took to find the right treatment for him.

But I could not let him hide from the truth.

I'd finally seen in my own life how much damage that could cause.

Calvin entered the room a few minutes later. He pulled the chair out and sat opposite me, staring into my eyes.

"Lizzie," he whispered brokenly. "What on earth is going on?"

"Cal," I said quietly, and then I squeezed my eyes closed. "I'm sorry. I've made an awful mess."

Calvin arranged a lawyer for me, and with his help, I told the police what really happened. Then we waited at the station until word came that Henry had been safely arrested in Nashville. They told me he was emotional but went willingly as they took him in. About the same time, Tucker told us that Jürgen Rhodes made it through surgery.

"He's still very unwell," he said quietly. "The doctor told me this could still go either way, but this is a start."

Henry was being taken to a facility in Birmingham for the night, and a hearing would be held in the morning. Calvin and I would get up early and travel over to the courthouse so we could support him. The lawyer expected that, for the short term, Henry would be committed, and in the longer term, he'd face trial. I only hoped Henry would forgive me—not for telling the police the truth, but for not getting him help sooner.

I followed Calvin inside our home, so worn-out I could scarcely lift my feet. He went to make us some coffee, and I curled up in my armchair in the sitting room and looked around the beautiful home we'd built. Cal handed me my cup and sat beside me in his own chair.

"Lizzie," he said uncertainly. "What the hell is going on with you?"

"The other night when I came to your room, you thought I..." I broke off, and he gave me an impatient look.

"I was half-asleep, sweetheart—still dreaming a little too. And that has nothing to do with what happened today—"

"It has nothing to do with what happened with *Henry*," I conceded. "But it has everything to do with my reaction to it. I panicked today, and my first reaction was to sacrifice myself."

"That's because you're bighearted—"

"I'm not noble, Calvin!" I exclaimed. "I'm *miserable*." He sucked in a sharp breath, and I closed my eyes, momentarily unable to face the pain in his expression. But I had to be brave, and I had to be strong. For both our sakes. I forced my eyes open and I said quietly, "I'm unhappy, Cal. And I think you might be unhappy too. I wish things between us could be different, but they aren't, and they won't ever be. It's not fair or healthy for us to live like this."

"But we have a good life together, don't we?" he whispered brokenly.

I drew in a deep breath, and for the first time in fifteen years, I told the truth.

"This is a good life," I said slowly. "But it's not *my* life, and that's what I need to find my way back to."

50

Sofie
Birmingham, Alabama
1951

EIGHT MONTHS AFTER MY HUSBAND WAS SHOT, Henry Davis pleaded not guilty by reason of insanity to a charge of attempted murder.

We stayed in Birmingham for the trial, but left the children at home with Claudia. She had been a godsend since Jürgen's accident, especially after I cut ties with Avril Walters and was in desperate need of help. Despite her misgivings, Claudia was too kind to turn away a neighbor in crisis, and we bonded strongly in those tender early days when the doctors were telling me to brace myself for the worst. By the time I was released from jail, Jürgen was out of surgery and missing his spleen. The first few days were terrifying. The next few weeks frustrating. But after all of that, he came home.

And by then, I'd had a chance to tell Claudia the whole, ugly story of our past in Germany, and that made all the difference. Gisela had a new friend in Mila, and Felix and Luis were best of pals too. It was startling how much of a difference those connections made for my children, particularly Gisela, who decided America might not be such a bad place after all.

Jürgen and I both gave evidence during the trial. I was done in just an afternoon, just long enough to confirm the pattern of Henry Davis's harassment and the theft of my photographs. Jürgen's testimony was much more involved, and he was on the stand for days. I'd heard it all before—Jürgen and I discussed everything that had happened so many times I knew his side of the story by heart. Even so, I wept as he talked about how it felt to lie on the grass outside our home, wondering if he was going to die in my arms.

The doctors who testified were all in agreement. Henry Davis was suffering from combat fatigue—but that wasn't the cause of his delusions. He'd sustained severe organic brain damage during an intensive round of insulin shock therapy, which he'd only undergone in a desperate attempt to get some semblance of normalcy back to his life.

"But how are we to know that this is not who Henry Davis was even before that therapy?" the prosecutor asked. That was when Lizzie Miller took the stand. She was barely recognizable— dressed in trousers and flat shoes, her hair longer and pulled into a rough ponytail, her freckles and light eyelashes on full display. She smiled softly at her brother between her answers, as if encouraging him with her eyes. The polished suburbanite had disappeared, but in her place was a warrior.

She advocated for Henry Davis. She told the court about the conversations she'd had with him about his experiences at Buchenwald, about the loss of his best friend, about his desperation to accept any treatment that might help him feel well again in the aftermath of the war. She spoke about her brother with such warmth and fondness that even Jürgen seemed heart-

broken for him by the time she'd finished. When I looked to
the jury, I saw some of them had tears in their eyes.

I knew what the verdict would be long before the trial was
over. I worried that Henry Davis would get off scot-free for
what he'd done to my family. Now I understood that he was
going to be in a prison of sorts for the rest of his life, regardless of the verdict.

The prosecutor rested Henry's case at close of session on a
Thursday, and by Friday morning, the jury returned and Jürgen
and I were walking up those stone steps to the courtroom for
the last time. The trial made national media, although, blessedly,
not a whisper of Jürgen's real history made the press.

We took our seats at the front of the courthouse behind the
prosecutor. On the opposite side of the aisle, Calvin and Lizzie
sat behind Henry. Calvin offered Jürgen a sad, friendly wave.
He had been apologetic and supportive throughout the entire
ordeal, even when Jürgen had to work part-time for months
until he built up his strength. Beside Calvin, Lizzie met my
gaze and nodded politely. I returned the gesture.

I knew Calvin and Lizzie had separated, but it was evident
throughout the trial that they were still close. I wondered if
she and I would have been friends too, had we met under different circumstances. Despite everything, I grudgingly came
to admire her strength and her loyalty to her brother—even
in her clumsy attempt to protect him from what he'd done. I
had a feeling that if that war never happened, and I had just
met Lizzie Miller in a salon or at a dinner party or at a picnic,
we'd have hit it off right away.

I was at Jürgen's side when the jury foreman told us that
Henry Davis had been found not guilty of one count of attempted murder by reason of insanity. No one cheered—there
was no relief, not even from Henry and Lizzie. She reached

forward and squeezed his shoulder, and she kept her hand there as the judge announced that Henry would be committed to a residential facility for treatment on an indefinite basis for the protection of the community.

"Are you disappointed with the verdict?" I asked Jürgen later.

"No," he admitted. "It's fitting. That man needs help, not prison. This feels like closure. I'm ready to put all of this behind us and to start the next chapter of our lives."

51

Lizzie
Dallam County, Texas
1951

IT WAS A BEAUTIFUL AFTERNOON AND I WAS
traveling across the Texas High Plains. It had rained the previous afternoon—one glorious inch of water drizzling down
over hours. The sun was out and there wasn't a cloud in the
sky, but the earth was still damp. I smelled the moisture in
the soil as nature's finest perfume.

The last time I drove down those roads, fences were buried
in dust and every plant in sight was dead and withered. But
today, mature wheat waved in the wind and newly planted
windbreak trees stretched toward the sky around the fields.
Life had returned, and it was glorious.

I turned my car off the main road onto the drive, taking a
route I hadn't traveled for so many years—but it was a journey my heart had made a million times. My breath caught in
my throat when the farm came into view. The gate had been

replaced with a newer style, and beyond it in the distance, I saw a new windmill and that Texas live oak tree, sprawling with new life and thickened branches.

After the trial, I had Henry transferred to a facility in Amarillo. The doctors there weren't nearly ready to recommend release just yet, but I was hopeful that it would happen one day. That new hospital had a gentler approach anyway, treating Henry with psychotherapy and low doses of sedatives only when he couldn't sleep. My brother wasn't the same man he once was—the brain damage wasn't likely to heal, and combat fatigue was going to be a part of his life for a long time. His short-term memory was terrible, and he still got that glazed, confused look on his face sometimes—often when I talked too fast or dumped too much information on him all at once. The delusions and paranoia were gone, but maybe those problems would return one day too.

I'd take him however he came, and we'd navigate all that together.

And like Calvin once told me, every man needed a reason to get out of bed in the morning. That was why, after the trial finished, I picked up my pen and wrote Betsy Nagle a letter. Henry had been writing her too, so she already knew about his struggles and the trial. I just wanted to see if she knew what had happened to my parents' old farm.

Way back in 1935, Judge Nagle sold that patch of land for a song to a man who let the place go to ruin for a while. But the desperate times eventually passed, and the judge's conscience would not let up. In the forties, his finances stabilized again, and he bought the farm back and put some suitcase farmers on it.

Ever since then, a roster of strangers had done a stint on my land, making money for the Nagle family by growing them crops. But the Nagles just so happened to be looking for new tenants, Betsy told me, and her father said I should come right on up to sign a lease.

I had torn Calvin Miller's heart to shreds, but just as I'd always known, he was a good man—the best man. He wasn't obligated to give me a single cent of his money when I walked out on our marriage, but he generously gave me enough money to support myself for a few years while I "found my feet."

I drove all the way up to meet Judge Nagle in Oakden the day I got that letter, only for him to tell me he'd decided not to lease me the farm after all.

"I'm going to sell it to you instead," he announced.

"That's very generous, Judge," I said reluctantly. "But I couldn't afford it."

"You haven't asked me how much I want for it yet."

I had to assume the way we lost our farm to him had haunted Judge Nagle over the years too, because all he wanted to hand it right back to me was for me to repay the money Henry had originally borrowed in 1933. I had plenty to cover the cost of that farm, plus enough to keep myself going until it was productive again.

Even as I drove through the gate, I could see that my farm needed a lot of love and care, but that was okay—I had never been afraid of hard work. The vegetable beds would need to be rebuilt, but the chicken house was where it had always been, ready to receive new tenants. I was relieved to see electric wires running to the house, and a new lean-to bathroom added at the back too. There would be no more midnight outhouse runs in winter, and no more racing around to light the lanterns, because that house would have electric lighting at last, just as Mother had dreamed.

I parked the car and stepped out to turn my attention to the Texas live oak and the little wooden crosses that jutted out of the ground beneath it, marking the space my parents were laid to rest. Beside it, the park bench I had always feared so much had collapsed. Elsie's chair needed some love and I wasn't great at woodwork. That would have to wait until Henry came home.

I started to walk toward that tree, a million images flickering through my mind of the way the farm once was and the way it would be again, now that it was finally ours—mine, and Henry's too, because he would always have a home with me. I pictured him there in that new barn, tinkering with the engine of a tractor. I pictured row after row of vegetables and chickens roaming the garden, and cows back in the field where that big old pond was, the rest of the farm planted with wheat, tended and sowed and lovingly grown by me and my brother.

This, my soul cried. *This was the life you were meant to live.*

By the time I reached that oak tree, I was exhausted and I was overjoyed and I was so damned relieved to be home, I could barely take another step. I dropped to my knees and pressed a shaking hand to the dirt above my parents' resting place.

"I'm home, Mother and Daddy," I whispered, flattening my palm against the cool, damp dirt. "I'm finally home. And I'm going to bring Henry home too."

This felt like the end of a very long journey.

This felt like the beginning of the life I was meant to live all along.

52

Sofie

Huntsville, Alabama
1951

A FEW WEEKS HAD PASSED SINCE THE TRIAL ended and life was returning to our new normal. Felix's reticence toward Jürgen was a thing of the past, and he'd insisted on his papa driving him to his new kindergarten that day. Gisela and Mila liked to walk to school together now, and that meant I was at home when the mailman passed.

I ran through the house to the mailbox—just as I did every day. I'd written Laura so many times over the ten months since we'd arrived in America, but I never heard from her—not even when I wrote to let her know that Jürgen had been shot, or when I let her know he'd finally recovered. I still hoped and prayed to get a reply, but the ritual of checking that mailbox was starting to feel like I was picking a scab, preventing myself from healing.

And once again, the mailbox was empty. My heart sank, and

I turned back to the front door—but to my surprise, Jürgen's car pulled into the driveway beside me.

"What's wrong?" I called, alarmed. He fumbled with the handle on his door, cursed, then threw it open and stumbled from the car.

"Sofie," he said, clearly stunned. He was holding an envelope in his hand, and as he extended it toward me, I saw that he was shaking.

"Is it from Laura?" I whispered, but Jürgen shook his head. Before I could even register my disappointment, he waved the letter and laughed through tears. He ran around the car and came to my side, pressing the envelope into my hands.

"My love. *Read* it."

The letter was addressed to Jürgen at Redstone Arsenal, but that wasn't why my knees went weak.

I knew that handwriting. I'd seen it at school, when we passed notes in class. I'd seen it when she taught Georg to write his name. I'd seen it on a letter I read in Martha's kitchen while the world went to hell around us.

I turned the envelope over slowly and there were those same scripted letters.

From Mayim Elsas (nee Nussbaum)

I had grieved her, and hope can be a dangerous thing. If I believed for a second that this letter really was from my Mayim and then I found out it was not, I'd have to grieve her all over again.

"It's impossible," I gasped, looking at Jürgen with frantic eyes. "It must be a trick."

"Sofie, read it," Jürgen said, gently taking my elbow to ease me down to sit on the step of our porch. I was grateful he did—my knees had gone completely weak.

Dearest Jürgen and Sofie,
I thought you were both dead, and I imagine you might have
assumed the same about me. But you are alive! And I am alive
and well and living in Washington, DC. Please call me as soon
as you get this!
Love always,
Mayim

"How far is Washington, DC?" I blurted. The corners of
Jürgen's eyes crinkled as he smiled and pointed to the phone
number beneath her signature.

"It's a long way by car. No distance at all by phone."

She answered on the first ring, and I imagined her sitting
by the phone waiting, ever since she posted the letter.

"Hello?"

Her soft voice, hopeful and anxious and *beautiful*. I croaked
out her name in response.

"Mayim…"

"Sofie…"

"How?"

She was laughing and crying—something about my snow
boots and money and a *husband and children* and a newspaper.
Over the sound of her sobs and mine, I couldn't make out half
of the words. But who cared about specifics? I was speaking
with a real-life *miracle*. It was some time before we calmed
down enough to swap stories through our sobs.

"I had two precious years with my family after I escaped
Germany, and then two years in the Krakow Ghetto with
them too," she said, but the smile in her voice faded as she
went on. "I survived two years in Auschwitz, although I cannot tell you how. They all died—Grandfather and Mama and
Moshe's wife and son on the first day at the selection, then

Moshe a few weeks later. It was hell on earth, Sofie—things I cannot even allow myself to think of now—but later, when we meet in person, I will tell you…"

"You don't have to," I replied. "But if you want to, I'll listen."

"And *finally*, it seemed to be ending and Soviets were coming and those Nazi monsters sent us on the death march. For all of that time, I'd held on to those snow boots of yours. Some nights I would be sleeping on the ground, so cold and scared and tired, but at least my feet were warm, and I always thought of you. Every night, I thought of you. We were liberated and I was taken to a Red Cross camp, and then I met Ben and I wrote to you."

At this, I gasped.

"I didn't get a letter from you!" I was so sure she'd write to me if she'd survived, so when years went by without word from her, I forced myself to come to terms with her death.

"Laura replied," she said heavily. "She told me you and Jürgen had both been killed for disloyalty. She told me not to contact her again. So I thought you were gone. I mourned you."

"Georg died toward the end of the war. He was shot fighting with his Hitler Youth unit. With Hans." Jürgen had been holding my hand and passing me handkerchiefs throughout the call. At the mention of our first son's name, he squeezed my hand. I stared at him through my tears as I admitted the truth about my daughter. "After the war ended, Laura struggled. She was grieving Georg and unable to let the Nazi ideology go. She and Hans turned to one another for support. At first I thought it was a good thing, because I knew Hans was heartbroken too. But while I was trying to drag Laura back into the real world, Lydia and Hans were determined to keep her in the old one. It breaks my heart that she would find your letter and lie to you, but it doesn't surprise me."

"I'm so sorry, Sofie. I'm just so sorry. Where is she now? Is she with you in Alabama?"

"In time, her relationship with Hans changed—and when I told her I was coming to America to be with Jürgen, she ran away to Lydia's house. I tried to bring her home, but the housekeeper wouldn't even let me see her. Just before we left, Lydia pushed a note through the mail slot to let me know Laura and Hans were married and didn't want to hear from me again." As I explained this to Mayim, I finally realized that the letters I'd been sending Laura since I left Germany would never *truly* reach her, even if Lydia did pass them on, even if Laura did read them. "The end of the war came too late for her," I said, finally accepting the truth myself.

Mayim told me about meeting her husband, Benjamin, at the Red Cross camp where he was working for the United Nations, and how they fell quickly in love and married only a few months later. They settled in Washington, DC, and had their daughters, Sidonie and Celina.

"I have everything I dreamed of," she told me. "A beautiful home. A wonderful, handsome husband and my two beautiful girls. My life is a miracle, Sofie, and every single day I wake up and thank God for it. But then one day last week, Ben came home from work, just about jumping out of his skin because he recognized Jürgen's name in the newspaper in an article about what happened in Huntsville." She laughed weakly. "Ben knows all about you—I swear I've told him every story at least twice. And here we are."

"And here we are," I whispered, laughing through my tears.

There has to be an after, I told Jürgen the previous year when I first arrived in Huntsville. Hearing Mayim speak with such immense gratitude and hope as she told me about the blessings of her new life, I finally accepted a truth that had been gradually dawning on me since Jürgen was shot.

After wasn't going to be a single moment when all of the trauma and the guilt disappeared and everything was okay. There would still be regrets and shame and nightmares and midnight anxieties, but *after* meant waking up every morning and facing each day as it came. It meant extending grace to those who feared me and my family and giving our new community time to learn that we were more than just the mistakes of our past. *After* would be truly mourning Georg and Laura, but it would also mean long car rides to see Mayim and to meet Ben and her children. It would mean never losing the wonder I felt that she had survived.

After would mean living the second chance Jürgen and I stumbled into with constant gratitude, raising our children in love, to counter the immense hate we had seen.

That was how we moved on. And I was finally ready to begin.

★ ★ ★ ★ ★

A NOTE FROM KELLY

STORY IDEAS OFTEN COME WHEN I LEAST EX-
pect them, and this book was no exception. In July 2019, my
friend Teresa invited my family to join hers for a Saturday afternoon outing to Parkes, a small town about ninety minutes'
drive from our homes in Central New South Wales.

Parkes is famous for many things: a fierce rivalry with the
nearby town of Forbes; an annual Elvis festival; and the two-
hundred-foot telescope that juts out of the flat, sparse land-
scape to the north. The CSIRO Parkes radio telescope, known
to Aussies as "the Dish," helped broadcast the 1969 Apollo 11
moon landing. The Parkes Observatory was hosting a festival
for the fiftieth anniversary of that event. As I wandered the
exhibits with Teresa and our respective children, I saw a display about the history of the US space program. It mentioned
beginning in 1950, German scientists worked with American
scientists to develop the rockets that would ultimately see hu-
mankind reach the moon.

I was immediately struck by how unlikely that arrangement was. Just a few years earlier, those men had been on op-
posing sides of a horrific war—but they worked together and
achieved one of humanity's most astounding technological
accomplishments. I started researching as soon as I got home

that night and fell down something of an Operation Paperclip rabbit hole.

I learned that Operation Paperclip was a program to bring the most valuable German scientists across the Atlantic to work for the US government. It was an immense undertaking, involving more than 1,600 German scientists and engineers across many disciplines, from chemistry and physics to architecture and medicine and, of course, rocketry. Most of those German scientists ultimately lived out their lives in freedom and comfort in America, their pasts rewritten so they could be of service to the US government. Many were complicit in war crimes. Others were complicit through their silence.

Just like Jürgen and Sofie, many of these German men would argue that they had only done what they felt they had to in order to keep their families safe. Does that rationale hold out in the face of unfathomable suffering and death? Is there a point where we are morally obliged to take a stand, whatever the cost?

In writing this book, I wanted to show Jürgen and Sofie caught in an unimaginably difficult situation through the Nazi years, as so many German citizens were. But given the choices they make along the way, I'm still not sure my characters deserve the happy ending they find. It's historically accurate that Jürgen's past would be "erased" once he arrives in America, but is it just? I only hope readers will ponder this too.

Nothing about Operation Paperclip was simple—not the politics, the mechanics, or even the ethics. It has been fascinating, frustrating, and heartbreaking to explore some of these issues in writing this book. Thank you so much for taking that journey with me.

History buffs may recognize that Jürgen's career loosely follows Wernher von Braun's career path, although the character of Jürgen, his family, and his reaction to those career events are products of my imagination. And aspects of Mayim's survival and escape were inspired by Gerda Weissmann Klein's experiences, including the ski boots that saved her life—in Mrs. Klein's case, her father insisted she wear them when she was captured. More information about Gerda Weissmann Klein and her incredible life and advocacy work can be found at citizenshipcounts.org/our-founder.

Finally, the character of Aunt Adele was inspired by my husband's late grandmother, Vera Harabajic, who we all knew and loved as "Baba." Baba was one of the fiercest women I have ever met—a matriarch of brutal honesty and boundless love. I hope to have honored her memory by sharing something of her spirit in this book.

Kelly

ACKNOWLEDGMENTS

THANKS TO MY AGENT, AMY TANNENBAUM. Your guidance and advice are always invaluable, but this time around, I truly could not have finished this book without your help and support. Thanks also to the entire team at the Jane Rotrosen Agency.

To Susan Swinwood and the dream team at Graydon House and HarperCollins—I love working with you and I am so grateful for the opportunity to place my stories in such capable and skilled hands.

Thanks also to my Australian publisher, Rebecca Saunders, and to everyone at Hachette Australia. Because of your hard work, my books are available on shelves here in my home country, and that means more than I can explain.

Thanks to the booksellers and librarians who put my books in the hands of readers. And to the bloggers, bookstagrammers, reviewers, and to anyone else who has recommended my books to someone else over the years—thank you for believing in my work and spreading the word.

Thanks to my husband and my children. If we can get through remote schooling while I worked on this book, we can do anything. And thanks to my sister Mindy, especially for dealing with dodgy tradespeople for me so I could write.

And finally—thank you for inviting us to Parkes that day, Teresa and Scott. I bet you didn't realize you'd be inspiring a two-year obsession!

Although all errors remain my own, I'm grateful to the following authors for their works that were useful in the research for this book.

- David Baddiel's *Jew Don't Count* was an excellent resource for understanding the absurd contradictions that underpin anti-Semitism both in the present day and throughout history. Some of these inspired Sofie's thoughts on the rising acceptance of Nazi party ideology in Germany through the 1930s, particularly in the dinner party scene in Chapter 17. Thanks to my friend Kim Kelly for the recommendation.

- In Chapter 12, Lizzie reflects on books she has borrowed from a library, trying to understand Henry's combat fatigue. She mentions she has learned that his trauma returns not as memory but as reaction. This is inspired by *The Body Keeps the Score: Brain, Mind, and Body in the Healing of Trauma* by Bessel van der Kolk, which was published in 2014. This concept gives such valuable insight into Henry's behavior that I have Lizzie reflect on it to help readers better understand his actions.

- *Operation Paperclip: The Secret Intelligence Program That Brought Nazi Scientists to America* by Annie Jacobsen.

- *Our Germans: Project Paperclip and the National Security State* by Brian E. Crim.

- *Von Braun: Dreamer of Space, Engineer of War* by Michael J. Neufeld.

- *German Rocketeers in the Heart of Dixie: Making Sense of the Nazi Past during the Civil Rights Era* by Monique Laney.

- *Huntsville Air and Space* by T. Gary Wicks.

- *Remembering Huntsville* by Jacquelyn Procter Reeves.

- *Soldiers from the War Returning: The Greatest Generation's Troubled Homecoming from World War II* by Thomas Childers.

- *The Great Depression: America in the 1930s* by T. H. Watkins.

- *Crash: The Great Depression and the Fall and Rise of America* by Marc Favreau.

- *The Hungry Years: A Narrative History of the Great Depression in America* by T. H. Watkins.

- *The Fireside Conversations: America Responds to FDR during the Great Depression* by Lawrence Levine and Cornelia Levine.

- *The Farmer's Wife 1930s Sampler Quilt: Inspiring Letters from Farm Women of the Great Depression and 99 Quilt Blocks That Honor Them* by Laurie Aaron Hird.

- *Between Dignity and Despair: Jewish Life in Nazi Germany* by Marion A. Kaplan.

- *Hitler's True Believers: How Ordinary People Became Nazis* by Robert Gellately.

- *The SS: Hitler's Instrument of Terror* by Gordon Williamson.

- *The Nazi Voter: The Social Foundations of Fascism in Germany, 1919–1933* by Thomas Childers.

- *The Gestapo: A History of Hitler's Secret Police, 1933–45* by Rupert Butler.

- *Hitler Youth: The Hitlerjugend in War and Peace 1933–45* by Brenda Ralph Lewis.

- *The Death of Democracy: Hitler's Rise to Power and the Downfall of the Weimar Republic* by Benjamin Carter Hett.

- *Inside the Third Reich* by Albert Speer.

I also found Luke Holland's documentary *Final Account* to be invaluable.

THE GERMAN WIFE

KELLY RIMMER

Reader's Guide

GRAYDON
HOUSE

1. Were you already familiar with the historical events in this story—for example, the rise of Nazi ideology in Germany before the war, the Mittelwerk rocket operation, the Dust Bowl in America and the Black Sunday dust storm, or Operation Paperclip? Are there any aspects of the history referenced in this book that you're curious about looking into further?

2. Sofie and Jürgen make decisions to protect their family, but this traps them on a path they bitterly regret. Was there a point where they could have avoided this fate? If there was a right time to take a stand, when was that moment?

3. Georg and Laura become indoctrinated with Nazi ideology via their school and Hitler Youth activities. Did you know this happened in Nazi Germany? What do you think you would do if this was happening to your children?

4. In Chapter 4, Lydia casually references an anti-Semitic trope. Have you ever heard a friend or relative make such a statement? Did you speak up about it? Why or why not?

5. Lizzie's relationship with Henry shifts over time. What was responsible for that change? Do you think Lizzie makes mistakes trying to care for Henry over the years?

6. Which characters in this book did you like best? Which did you like least? Why?

7. Which scene in *The German Wife* affected you the most and why? What emotions did that scene elicit?

8. Did any lines or paragraphs from the book seem especially memorable to you?

9. Were you satisfied with the ending? What would have been a "just" ending for Jürgen and Sofie? For Lizzie and Cal? For Henry?

10. What will you remember most about *The German Wife*?

11. Who would you recommend this book to?

12. Was this your first Kelly Rimmer book? If you've read any of her other titles, which did you like best?